the girls next door

the girls next door

a novel

cheri crane

Covenant Communications, Inc.

Cover photograph by Maren E. Ogden

Cover design copyrighted 2002 by Covenant Communications, Inc.

Published by Covenant Communications, Inc.
American Fork, Utah

Printed in the United States of America
First Printing: August 2002

08 07 06 05 04 03 02   10 9 8 7 6 5 4 3 2 1

ISBN 1-59156-072-1

This book is dedicated to the original D-6ers: Jan, Verlene, Wende, Marge, Diana, Eileen, and all those we adopted along the way.

To borrow a short poem I learned while at Ricks College:

Our friendship is an island I visit in my heart,
Where we can be together even though we're far apart.

"The 'Spirit of Ricks' is not found in a building, it is not found in a place, it is found in the people . . ."
BYU-Idaho President David A. Bednar

Acknowledgments

There are several people who made this book possible. First and foremost would be my family. Thanks again to Kennon, Kris, Derek, and Devin, the men in my life. I would also like to thank Celinda and Tina Winters, who took me on a marvelous tour of BYU-Idaho to show me the changes that have been taking place on campus. Special thanks to Joy Rowland, an awesome young woman who is a nursing student at what I now call BYI. She answered numerous questions that helped with the development of this story.

I would also like to thank two special cousins of mine, Michelle Humpherys and RaNae Roberts, who spent hours proofreading this manuscript.

A debt of gratitude goes to David G. Woolley for telling me about the Center for Change.

Deep appreciation is also extended to the inspired staff at the Center for Change for the incredible work they do as they help others heal. Special thanks to Dr. Julie Clark, who spent valuable time answering questions as she helped me gain a needed insight into the world of eating disorders. Her philosophy of hope has touched countless lives. Thanks also to Pam Kidd, who works in public relations for the Center for Change. The information you shared was invaluable, as was the tour of the clinic you graciously conducted. I would also like to express admiration and gratitude to Kathleen Slade Hofer, recreation therapist for the Center for Change. Thank you for granting me permission to share the healing art programs you have developed. And to all of the loving, hardworking staff at this much-needed facility: kudos for the great work you do. This world is a better place because of people like you.

I would also like to thank everyone at Covenant for their continued help. Special thanks to Shauna Nelson, who offered encouraging support from the beginning of this project.

Chapter 1

"Uh-oh!" Nineteen-year-old Treena Graham gripped the steering wheel and decreased her speed, but the vibrations grew stronger.

Kassidy Martin turned from the window on her side of the aging blue Chevy Cavalier to glare at Treena. "What's wrong with your car now?"

"Hey, it brought us all the way from San Diego to Utah without too much trouble."

"Except for overheating in Vegas, running out of gas outside of Cedar City . . ."

"So the gas gauge isn't accurate. We needed to stretch our legs anyway, and we only had to walk a couple of miles to find the nearest gas station."

"This car of yours has seen better days," Kassidy pronounced. The defiant look in her blue eyes challenged Treena to argue with her.

Treena shut off the radio and carefully listened. "I'm pulling off the freeway. I think we have a flat."

"Great!"

Ignoring the pained expression on Kassidy's face, Treena slowed the car as she steered it onto the side of the busy Utah freeway. She shifted into park, then reached down and flipped on the emergency flashers. "Maybe we picked up a nail at Uncle Jake's farm."

"But that was clear back in Payson. We've come all the way past Salt Lake this morning."

"Maybe it's a slow leak," Treena suggested.

"Anything from Payson would be slow," Kassidy muttered.

"Stifle the attitude, okay?" Treena retorted. "Uncle Jake and Aunt Carol were good enough to let us spend the night."

"We could've stayed in a motel. Salt Lake has plenty of those. It wasn't that far from Payson to Salt Lake. But no, we had to stay at your relatives' house in Payson where we could bond with all of those smelly farm animals. I especially liked that rooster with the big lungs, the one who woke us up at five this morning."

Treena tried very hard to control her temper; the last thing her friend needed was a heated argument. Forcing a smile at the beautiful blonde, Treena reminded herself how fond she was of Kassidy. "Kass, I know money isn't an issue for you, but I have to be careful about what I spend. This semester of college will be tight for me. Paying for a motel room isn't part of my budget right now."

"What's it going to cost for a new tire?" Kassidy shot back.

"I have a spare in the trunk," Treena replied. Reaching down, she flipped a lever that popped the trunk open. "Now, are you going to help or are you going to sit here and whine?"

"Are those my only options?"

Treena nodded before slipping out of the car. She shut the door and ran quickly to the back of the car before an oncoming semi-truck sped past. Wincing at the gust of dusty air the semi triggered as it hurried by, she offered a quick prayer for safety. Two girls alone on the busy interstate wasn't exactly safe, but they had little choice in the matter. She eyed the flat back tire on the driver's side and scowled. Why did this have to happen now? They were supposed to be in Rexburg, Idaho, by this afternoon.

As Treena opened the trunk, she shook her head at the amount of luggage that had been stuffed inside. Most of it belonged to Kassidy, and it would all have to be removed before she could get to the doughnut tire that was stored inside a special compartment. Sighing, she began unloading the heavy suitcases from the trunk.

"So, how bad is it?" Kassidy asked as she walked back to Treena.

Treena gazed up at the tall blonde. Only Kassidy would wear white khakis and an expensive white sweater on a road trip. Glancing down at her own apparel, a comfortable grey sweatshirt and a favorite pair of jeans, she shook her head. Shorter and a little overweight, Treena was the opposite of Kassidy in many ways. A major difference became apparent as Treena studied her friend's face. Food was how Kassidy dealt with stress. A small chocolate splotch on the corner of

Kassidy's mouth revealed what she had been doing. "Uh, Kass," she said, pointing to the side of her own face.

Kassidy flushed with embarrassment. "Oh, thanks," she mumbled.

Treena averted her eyes as Kassie reached into her pants pocket for a tissue and wiped away the traces of the candy bar or bars that she must have devoured since they had stopped. Shaking her head, Treena wondered what it would take to keep Kassie from doing this to herself.

"I'm hungry too. We'll grab a bite of lunch after we get this stupid tire changed," she said, trying to alleviate the sudden tension between them.

"It is flat then," Kassidy murmured, changing the subject.

"Yeah, it couldn't get much flatter. Let's unload the trunk—that's where the spare is stashed."

Nodding, Kassidy grabbed one of her suitcases from the trunk and set it down by the others on the roadside.

***

Treena applied as much pressure as she could to the stubborn lug nut, but it refused to budge. Muttering under her breath, she stood and kicked at the tire.

"Hey, get out of there, another semi is coming," Kassidy warned.

Hurrying back around by the trunk where Kassidy stood guarding her luggage, Treena wiped the sweat from her face with the back of her hand. As the semi rushed by, a welcome breeze ruffled her medium-length brown hair.

"Is it loosening at all?"

"No."

"Maybe I should try," Kassidy suggested.

Despite the irritation she felt over the entire situation, Treena laughed.

"It's not funny! I'm not as delicate as you think I am."

"Sorry," Treena said, still grinning. "I can't picture you with grease on your hands, especially not in that outfit."

"I can do more than lose beauty pageants," Kassidy sniffed.

"Kassidy . . ."

"Just watch!" Kassidy informed her.

"You don't have to do this."

"Yes, I do!" Kassidy said as she waited for a break in the traffic. "I can't believe no one has stopped to help us."

"Welcome to the times we live in. People are too caught up in their own lives to help anyone else. Besides, it's dangerous trying to stop on the freeway. There's too much traffic. That's how accidents happen."

"I get the point. I just thought some macho guy would take pity on two helpless females."

"I'm not helpless," Treena exclaimed, "and neither are you!"

Kassidy smiled, revealing her perfect white teeth. "True. Here I go," she said, bravely taking the tire iron from Treena. Before she could make her way to the flattened tire, a white sedan with flashing lights pulled in behind them. "This doesn't look good."

"Maybe he'll help us," Treena said hopefully as the highway patrol officer stepped out of his car. She noted the yellow beehive on the door and smiled. The symbol of deseret—a pioneer icon from an era she could hardly fathom. She understood what the symbol represented: the busy bee. Industry, and hard work: the only way she would get through college.

"What seems to be the trouble, ladies?" the middle-aged man asked as he shut the sedan door.

Treena smiled. "Flat tire," she explained.

"I see. Need some help?" he offered.

"Sure," Kassidy bubbled. "We can't get the tire off."

"One lug nut is refusing to cooperate," Treena added.

"Well, let me have a try at it," the officer said, reaching for the tire iron. He waited until a string of cars passed, then tugged at the tire. "You're right, this one is on there to stay," he grunted.

"Now what do we do?" Treena asked.

"The problem is, most garages use an air-powered impact wrench to tighten these things," the officer explained as he continued to struggle. "Then they expect people to untighten them on their own." Rising, he stepped back to where the two girls were standing. "Which is why I always carry a handy geared lug wrench myself." He handed the tire iron back to Kassidy, then walked back to his car.

"I don't feel so bad now," Treena grinned. "I got 'em all but one and not even a grown man could remove it."

"I'm just glad I didn't break a nail trying to do it myself," Kassidy joked as she held up her perfectly manicured hands. Her nails were painted mauve to match her soft, leather shoes.

"That would've been tragic," Treena retorted, pleased that Kassidy was lightening up. Kass could be a lot of fun when she wanted to be.

Both girls stepped out of the way as the officer returned to the tire with a black zippered bag. He unzipped it and took out a shiny silver metal piece that was round on one end and tapered on the other. He fastened a handle on the center of the round piece and attached a socket on the thinner end. "Watch this," he said proudly. "We'll have you girls up and running in no time," he promised as he attacked the tire. Within seconds the lug nut began to move. Thrilled, the girls watched as the kind officer then replaced the flat tire with the small doughnut tire from the trunk.

* * *

Frowning, Kassidy stepped out of the germ-infested bathroom. She reached into the small mauve-colored purse she had slipped over one shoulder and searched for a piece of gum to replace the sour taste in her mouth. Shuddering, she reminded herself that at least she had expelled the chocolate bars from her system. She found a stick of gum, unwrapped it, and set it inside her mouth. An explosion of mint flavoring eased the bitterness. Feeling a little better, she gazed around at the dirty auto garage. This was not her idea of a fun time. Her white khaki pants were no longer spotless. She was hot and tired, but the officer who had helped them earlier had promised that the mechanic who ran this tire-repair shop was fair and honest. The police officer had also stressed that it would be in their best interest to get the flat tire fixed before continuing with their trip to Rexburg.

"That doughnut tire will get you to a garage, but I wouldn't push your luck with it on the freeway. It wasn't meant for long-term driving," he had explained.

Certain the officer was right, Kassidy wished things would hurry along. Avoiding an unidentifiable dark puddle on the floor in front of her, she walked to the car where Treena was waiting. "That bathroom was disgusting," she commented.

"I warned you. But any place in a storm, right?" Treena said, giving Kassidy a pointed look.

Ignoring the insinuation, Kassidy changed the subject. "How long will it take to fix your tire?"

"About an hour. They're working on another car right now, but they didn't think it would take too much longer to finish with it."

"Let's go shopping then," Kassidy suggested. "I'm sure Ogden has a mall somewhere."

"Right. I have a couple of problems with that."

Kassidy rolled her eyes. "Like what?"

"Like we have to walk wherever we're going, and the way our luck's going today, the closest stores are probably on the other side of town."

"Why do they have to keep the car? It's the tire that needs to be repaired."

"Think about it, Kass. They have to patch the hole in the tire, then put it back on my car."

Kassidy wondered why Treena was in such a bad mood. She knew her friend had been relieved to learn that the damaged tire could be fixed. It would be a lot cheaper than paying for a new one. "What's the other problem?"

"I can't afford to go on a shopping spree. Especially after this adventure. I know it could be worse, but it's an extra ten to fifteen bucks I don't have right now. Besides that, I'm starved. If I have to buy anything right now, it's going to be food. We ate breakfast hours ago in Payson," Treena said, following Kassidy out of the garage.

"Your aunt cooked way too much food this morning," Kassidy murmured, remembering the huge meal the woman had prepared: waffles, eggs and bacon, hash browns, toast, and fresh-squeezed orange juice.

"You should be starved too." Treena glanced at her watch. "It's almost 1:30, and all you had for breakfast was a small glass of orange juice."

"I wasn't hungry this morning. I'm still not, but if you need to eat, let's find somewhere close." She glowered at Treena, hoping her friend wouldn't bring up the candy bars, or her trip to the bathroom a few minutes ago.

"Hey, there's a burger joint across the road about a block away." Treena pointed to a drive-in down the road.

"Fine," Kassidy responded. "I wonder if they have green salads."

"Let's find out," Treena said, leading the way.

Chapter 2

Bev Henderson stepped into the recently remodeled apartment, her vivid blue eyes sparkling with excitement as she toted in a heavy suitcase. Her shoulder-length black hair had been twisted out of the way with a black hair clip. A few loose strands had escaped to frame her oval-shaped face. Whistling, she carried the final piece of luggage into the bedroom she would be sharing with her best friend, Karen Randall. Bev set the suitcase down on the bed on the left side of the room, then stretched to relieve a kink in her back.

Bev and Karen were the first to arrive in their three-bedroom apartment. As such, the two friends had decided that meant they could have their pick of the bedrooms. They had selected one at the back of the off-campus apartment, figuring it would grant them more privacy. "This is so great! We have the whole place to ourselves!" Bev sang out.

"That won't last long." Karen brushed a stray piece of blonde hair out of her eyes—brown eyes that reflected worry and a touch of sorrow. Turning, she placed a clothes bag on the bed she would be using.

"Look at that view, at the fine quality bricks that were used in that other building," Bev remarked to Karen, hoping to lighten the mood. They had already voiced their disappointment that the view from both of the back bedrooms was the same—a metal fence below and the side of the brick building on the other side of the fence.

Karen nodded in agreement. "Which drawers do you want?"

"I don't care. I picked the bed. You pick which drawers." Grabbing one of her suitcases, Bev opened it to begin arranging her clothes in the closet they would share.

"You're taller than I am . . . I'll take the bottom drawers."

"Thanks, Karen! That's mighty neighborly of you. Like I told you all summer, we'll make the perfect roommates! We'll be the greatest duo to ever hit BYI!"

"BYI?"

"It's what I've decided to call this place. You know, Brigham Young Idaho . . . BYI!"

Karen managed a weak smile. "What time will our roommates get here?"

"I don't know."

"I wonder what they'll be like."

Bev shrugged. "I just hope we can tolerate each other." She frowned. "Truth?"

Karen nodded.

"I'm a little scared about this."

"Me too," Karen said. "Which is why I'm not going to sit around here and stew about it. I'm heading up on campus to buy my books. Want to come?"

"Nah, I'll stay here and get things unpacked. Then maybe we can go grab a bite of lunch." Bev was bothered by the distant look on Karen's face. "Do you want to take my Jeep?"

"No, campus is only about a block away. I think I can handle the walk. It might do me some good." Karen grabbed her empty backpack, stuffed her wallet inside, and left the room.

"Be careful," Bev murmured, concerned. They had both shed several tears after leaving home that morning. Singing outlandish campfire songs as they had left Blaketown had helped, but Bev knew they were both still struggling. What a strange feeling, excitement mixed with heartache. "We've only been gone from home for a few hours," she said, remembering the sad look on her stepmother's face that morning. It had matched the look on Karen's mother's face. Forcing the images from her mind, she ignored the heaviness in her heart and continued to organize her clothes.

* * *

Karen gazed with interest around the busy campus of BYU–Idaho. She had just come from the Manwaring Center, where she had stood in line for several minutes to purchase the books she needed for her classes that fall. Majoring in journalism, she was excited for this new phase of her life. She had originally planned to attend ISU, but Bev had become enthralled with the idea of attending an LDS Church-owned college. A recent convert, Bev was determined to immerse herself in LDS culture. It had taken quite an effort to get their applications in on time, but eventually, both girls had been accepted for the fall and winter semesters at BYU–Idaho.

As Karen continued to walk around the beautifully landscaped campus, she took a deep breath of crisp fall air. She loved fall, the way nature painted trees with bursts of bright colors.

A sudden breeze blew several strands of her medium-length blonde hair into her face. Smiling, her brown eyes twinkling with delight, she swept the hair out of her eyes in time to run into a tall, gangly young man.

"Sorry," she said, her back smarting from the way her newly filled backpack had pounded against it. She was certain this encounter had left a bruise. "I've been warned about this Rexburg wind. I couldn't even see where I was going for a minute."

"No problem." Leaning down, he began picking up the papers he had dropped. "Is that the Manwaring Center?" He stood and pointed at the large, tan brick building behind Karen.

"It is," Karen replied.

"Cool. I've been walking around, trying to figure out where everything is."

"You've never been here before?" she guessed, smiling up at the slender young man. She liked his soft, southern accent.

"No, I registered on-line back home. I flew into Idaho Falls yesterday. My sister and her husband live there. She drove me up last night."

"Really? Where are you from originally?"

"Tulsa, Oklahoma," he replied.

"Wow! You did travel a bit to get here."

He nodded, flushing slightly. "Where are you from?"

"Blaketown, Idaho."

Grinning, he nodded. "One of my roommates is from Idaho . . . Boise. There's quite a group of you Idahoans here."

"True, but I also know there's a bunch from other states too. Even from other countries."

He glanced down at her. "Kind of neat, huh? The gospel is true, no matter where you live. That's why I can hardly wait to head out on my mission."

Intrigued, Karen returned his smile, surprised that she didn't feel as uneasy around him as she usually did around guys her age. "When will you leave?"

"I'm not sure. I won't be nineteen until January, so I'll go one semester here, then head home to work until I get my call. I'll put my papers in about October."

"That's exciting."

"It is," he agreed, glancing at his watch. "Speaking of excitement, I'd better keep going. I need to pick up my books and pay off my tuition."

"You do know that you'll have to pay your tuition in the Spencer W. Kimball Building?"she inquired. "The bookstore is in the Manwaring Center, but the financial offices are in the Kimball Building."

"Oh, that's right. I keep thinking everything is in the student center. It seems like my sister said something about the Kimball Building last night. Where's it located?"

Karen considered the best route to send him. "Probably the easiest way from here is to cut through the Manwaring Center. Go up to the second floor and exit out the other side of the building. The Kimball Building is on the left, and the Taylor Building is the big white building that will be right in front of you."

"Taylor Building?"

"It's where a lot of the religion classes are taught. It's beautiful. You'll have to explore it sometime. The chapel is really nice."

"I'll check it out," he promised. "Thanks for setting me straight."

"Anytime."

"Hey, I just realized I didn't get your name."

"Karen . . . Karen Randall," she added, stressing her new last name. Her mother had remarried four months ago. That same day,

Karen had been sealed to Edie and Brett Randall in a beautiful temple ceremony. Because of that, and a reason she didn't care to think about, Karen had dropped her biological father's name.

"Well, hi, Karen Randall. I'm John Daniels," he said, reaching to shake her hand. "You have the distinction of being the first girl I've met at Ricks College."

"You mean BYU–Idaho?" she teased, reminding him of the recent name change. Smiling, she considered that she had undergone the same process. Same person, different name. Different family. Different feeling, but a change for the better. Would it be like that for the college?

"Oh, yeah. Sorry. I'm the last Daniels to come here. There were five kids ahead of me. I guess old habits die hard. Everyone else attended Ricks College. I'll be the only one to attend BYU–Idaho."

"That's neat. Something to brag about someday."

"Exactly!" he exclaimed. "So, Karen Randall, where are you staying, in case I get lost again?"

Now it was Karen's turn to blush. Her first day at college and already she was being hit on. Her stepfather had warned her about that.

"Don't worry about it, you don't have to tell me," John said quickly.

"No, it's okay; I think we freshmen have to stick together."

He nodded. "I'll be living at Cottonwood Apartments."

"Where's that?"

"You know where the football stadium is?"

"It's down below the Hart Building, right?" Karen asked, referring to the building that housed several gyms, a swimming pool, and other athletic arenas.

"Yeah. My apartment complex is about a block and a half from the stadium. Down by that laundromat."

"That'll come in handy," Karen observed.

"It will. I doubt our complex laundry room will be able to handle all of my dirty clothes. I plan to dirty them all before I force myself to do my own laundry. My mama kind of spoiled me at home. I don't suppose I could talk you into taking over?" he joked.

"Not hardly," Karen laughed. "I'll be doing well to keep up with my own laundry."

"Can't blame a person for trying," he said, this time grinning broad enough to reveal a dimple in the middle of his left cheek. "So, where are you staying?" he tried again.

"Baronnessa."

"Is it far from campus?"

"Nope. Just down that way, on the other side of the Bunkhouse Apartments," she said, gesturing with her hand.

"Just over there, right?" he asked, pointing west.

"Yeah."

"Cool! I might come see you sometime, if you don't mind." He smiled shyly. "Could I ask which apartment?"

"D-6."

"Got it. I'm in seventeen—if you ever need me."

"That's good to know."

John shuffled the papers in his hand. "Well, this has been fun, but I'd better go get this all taken care of so I can stay here this semester. See y'all later," he said, walking toward the Manwaring Center.

"Count on it," Karen said, feeling lighter inside. Maybe her mother was right. Maybe she would meet some nice guys here at college. Humming, she continued forward, in no hurry to return to her apartment.

* * *

"Bev?" Karen called out as she entered the apartment. She closed the door that had been left open. Had someone else arrived? "Bev?"

"Back here," a muffled voice called out.

Karen swung the heavy backpack off her shoulders and set it on the kitchen table before walking back to the bedroom. "Are you the only one here?"

"Yeah."

"Why was the front door open?" Karen asked as she stepped inside their bedroom.

"Sorry about that. I ran down to my Jeep to grab a box I left in the back. I guess I forgot to shut the door. I'll do better, I promise."

Karen smiled as she glanced around the room. Bev's clothes were neatly put away, her bed was made, and her tall friend was now hanging posters on the white wall above her bed, Mormonads she had recently purchased at an LDS distribution center. The four large posters depicted significant aspects about LDS standards. One indicated the importance of staying morally clean. Another encouraged adherence to the Word of Wisdom, extolling the advantages of avoiding items that could harm the body like alcohol and tobacco. Another served as a reminder to study the scriptures on a regular basis. The final poster stressed how crucial it was to remember that no matter how dark life seemed, the Savior was always there with unconditional love. "Wow! You've been busy!"

"Yep!" Bev pulled a piece of white putty loose from the square in her hand. She worked it with her fingers to make it more pliable. "I hope this stuff works as good as it says it does. I'd hate to have these posters assault me in the middle of the night."

"I can't believe they won't let us make any holes in the walls."

Bev turned to grin at Karen. "Think about it though . . . six girls . . . hanging pictures randomly, it would be a mess. Holes all over the place."

"We could fill them with putty later on."

"Now you sound like me. Your mother would be proud—I'm finally rubbing off on you."

"You must be," Karen laughed. "I even talked to a guy today."

"You?" Bev said with mock horror. "Miss Shyer-Than-Most?" She pressed the final poster in place, then jumped down off the bed and gazed at the wall. "Not bad. A little off-centered, like me." She turned to Karen. "So, tell me about this guy you met, you little flirt," she teased.

Karen stuck her tongue out at Bev.

"Oh, come on, you at least got his name, right?"

"His name is John Daniels, and he's from Tulsa, Oklahoma. He has blonde hair, bright blue eyes, and is very tall. He's a freshman like us, he's the youngest in his family, and he has a sister who lives in Idaho Falls."

Bev offered a low whistle. "You do move fast."

Karen rolled her eyes. "We bumped into each other in front of the Manwaring Center. The wind kicked up and blew my hair into my eyes."

"Very romantic. I'll have to try that."

"You're already spoken for, remember?" Karen pointed out, referring to Tyler Erickson, a recently returned missionary and older brother of their friend Sabrina.

"Hardly," Bev countered. "Tyler hasn't even asked me out yet."

"The key word here is 'yet.' Why do you think he transferred to Ricks?"

"You mean BYI?" Bev stressed.

"BYU–Idaho," Karen replied as her stomach growled. She glanced at her watch. "Are you ready for lunch yet? I'm starved."

"So I heard," Bev quipped. "Sure, I think I've done all the damage I can for one day." She pushed the leftover putty inside its cardboard container. "There's plenty of putty for you to use later," she offered, "if you ever decide to unpack your stuff."

"I'll get to it. Maybe I'll do it after lunch or later tonight. There's so much to see; I hate to sit in this apartment."

Bev smiled warmly at Karen. "It'll get better. This is a big change for both of us. Eventually this place will seem like home, but for now, it's natural that we miss our families. That's why I've been trying to stay busy. When I think about how Mom looked this morning—"

"Let's go," Karen said, refusing to discuss what was going on inside of her. Reflecting on the changes in her life was the last thing she wanted to do. "Hamburgers or pizza?"

"Your call." Bev grabbed her purse before following Karen out of the apartment.

* * *

"Okay, now what do you think?" Bev asked as she paraded in front of the floor-length mirror. Grinning, she admired the colorful straw hat she had placed on her head. A large red carnation dangled from a red polka-dotted scarf tied around the center of the hat.

Karen laughed. "I dare you to wear that to your first class."

"You would, wouldn't you," Bev replied, moving across the aisle to the assortment of hats they had discovered at the Rexburg Deseret Industries, a popular secondhand thrift store. "Here, let's find one for you." She rummaged through the pile, then pulled out a bright pink cap and smiled at the layers of rounded pink petals that decorated the top.

"I'm not wearing that," Karen protested as Bev firmly placed it on top of her head.

"Look in the mirror," Bev managed to say before she burst out laughing.

"Oh, it's lovely," Karen said, pulling a face in the mirror at Bev.

"I think so too," Bev replied. "Now, let's find the perfect outfits to match our hats." She grinned. "Then let's head back to our apartment before the rest of our roommates arrive."

"No! I can tell what you're thinking. We don't want to make a bad first impression."

"Oh, lighten up. We'll tell them we're from Blaketown, Idaho—they'll understand."

Karen shared a disgruntled look with Bev.

"Come on, it'll be fun."

Karen stared at her reflection. "This hat is hot pink."

"And there are some bright green polyester bell-bottoms with your name on them," Bev said, moving across the room. "They'll go perfectly with your blonde hair!"

"Absolutely not! This is crazy."

Bev grinned. "That's why we *have* to do it. Please?" It had taken hamburgers and chocolate milkshakes at McDonald's, a romp through a local park, and this shopping adventure at D.I. to get Karen to smile again. If dressing up in ridiculous outfits would keep her from sinking back into an emotional pit, it was worth it.

"Okay," Karen reluctantly agreed. "But I get to pick out what you're wearing. Deal?"

"Deal!" Bev agreed, leading the way through the crowded aisles.

Chapter 3

"Here we are," nineteen-year-old Meg Denton announced before shutting off the engine of her white Geo Metro. Glancing in the rearview mirror, she adjusted the wire-rimmed glasses she wore to downplay her brilliant green eyes. Her long red hair was woven into a tight braid and pinned against the back of her head. Today the braid was so tight it had given her a headache, but it was the price she often paid to escape notice.

"Finally," eighteen-year-old Jesse Waterman complained.

Meg watched as her younger cousin climbed out of the Geo, sensing Jesse was only too glad to unfold her long legs. Tall and slender, Jesse seemed to tower over the small car.

Jesse ran a hand through her short auburn hair as her laughing brown eyes explored the parking lot of Baronnessa Apartments. "I feel like we've lived in that car for two days."

"We have," Meg replied, stepping out of the car to stretch. Four inches shorter than Jesse, she had inherited a curvaceous build from her mother, something she detested but endured. She had learned that a harsh glare usually discouraged unwanted attention from passing males.

"How many hours have we traveled to get here?" Jesse asked.

"We left St. George yesterday. It took us about nine hours to reach Salt Lake." She glanced at Jesse. "If we hadn't made so many stops along the way . . ."

"So I drank a lot of pop! It was hot."

"We left my aunt's house around noon today, because *somebody* had to sleep in." Meg gave Jesse a pained look, then consulted her watch. "It's now 3:00 P.M.—you do the math."

Jesse shook her head. "Come on, Meg. You love me, and you know it."

"Our mothers are first cousins. We are related, but that doesn't mean I have to love you."

"Ouch. Spoken like a true friend," Jesse replied. "Well, should we start hauling our stuff upstairs?"

"That would be the most logical thing to do," Meg replied. She moved around to the back of the car, missing the disgruntled expression on Jesse's face. Unlocking the back of the small car, she began handing items to her younger cousin.

"Whoa, slow down! I'm not a packhorse," Jesse complained, staggering under the weight of the two heavy suitcases Meg had handed her.

"I drove, you slept. Now it's your turn. You tote, I'll direct," Meg said, grabbing a light bag before leading the way across the parking lot.

"I think you got the better end of this deal," Jesse grumbled as she followed Meg across the parking lot.

* * *

Certain she looked like an idiot, Karen forced herself to sit down on the couch in the apartment living room. Why had she given in to Bev's latest brainstorm? Bev's ideas usually led to trouble or humiliation, depending on the situation. Silently groaning, Karen wondered which one it would be that afternoon.

"Someone's coming up the stairs," Bev said as she replaced the straw hat and tied the red polka-dotted scarf in a large bow under her chin.

"Are you sure they're our roommates?" Karen asked, hating the outfit Bev had picked out for her. Not only was she wearing the bright pink hat, but she had given in to the green bell-bottoms and was wearing the ugliest purple turtleneck she had ever seen in her life. Silver high heels, sparkling with layers of glitter, complemented her fashion disaster.

"I don't know, but we want to be ready if they are," Bev replied, adjusting the wide, gold belt Karen had found for her.

Despite her mood, Karen smiled; Bev looked hilarious. She was wearing black-and-green-striped capri pants topped by a red and green plaid maternity top. The taller girl had managed to fit into the burnt-orange leather boots with a wedge heel that were too tight, an item Karen had taken great pride in selecting. Both girls were wearing the makeup Bev had brought up for Halloween, adding the final touch to their garish appearance.

"They're coming this way," Bev exclaimed, racing to sit on the couch beside Karen. "Try to look dignified," she instructed as two girls walked by the living room window. One girl stopped and stared, dropping the suitcases she was carrying to hold her sides while she laughed. The other girl continued to the door, missing the sight on the couch.

* * *

"This key isn't working," Meg complained, giving it another try. When the door finally opened, she gazed with dismay at Jesse. "What is your problem? What's so funny?"

Unable to speak, Jesse pointed at the window, grabbed her stomach, and howled.

Disgusted by her cousin's strange behavior, Meg entered the living room, her eyes growing huge at the sight of Bev and Karen. "Oh my," she muttered.

Jesse stumbled inside the apartment, pointed to Bev and Karen, and burst into renewed laughter. Meg stood in shock, her mouth open as she stared at the girls on the couch.

"Why Darcy Ann, how rude," Bev exclaimed, using a dramatic hillbilly accent. "Can you believe the manners of some people?"

"Unforgivable," Karen replied, sounding like a tragic southern belle. "*Never* have I been so insulted." She pulled out a small fan and began to wave it in front of her face. "Mama told us there'd be people like y'all in the big city."

"Are you guys for real?" Jesse asked, wiping the tears from her face.

"Emmy Sue, did you hear what that person said?" Karen asked, pointing at Jesse.

"I did, Darcy Ann. It makes me feel as if to faint," Bev said, falling back onto Karen.

"Uh, Emmy Sue, what ever did you have for lunch?"

"Why ever do you ask, Darcy Ann?"

"Does the term *heavyweight* hold any special meaning for you?" Karen ducked as Bev reached back to smack her.

"You guys are a riot," Jesse exclaimed, a wide grin on her face. "I was afraid I'd been sent to the land of Molly Mormondom, but I sense I'm in the presence of greatness." She held out her hand to Bev. "Jesse Waterman."

Bev stood up, giving Karen an indignant look. "Darcy Ann Fettuccini," she said, shaking Jesse's hand.

"Wait a minute, I thought she was Darcy Ann," Jesse retorted, glancing at Karen, then back to Bev.

"She's got you there, brilliance," Karen said, laughing at Bev. "Busted!"

"I knew you guys were pulling a fast one," Jesse hooted, reaching to shake Karen's hand. "No one could possibly look that bad without going to a lot of effort."

"We do look beautiful, don't we?" Bev said with a grin.

"You look . . . interesting," Meg replied, unamused by what she was seeing. What kind of silliness was this?

"I need my camera," Jesse exclaimed, rushing out the door. "Hang on a second. It's still down in Meg's car."

"You'll need the keys," Meg said, hurrying after Jesse. She quickly caught up with her younger cousin near the stairwell. "Jesse, we need to talk to the manager."

"Why?"

Meg pointed back at the apartment. "Those two aren't normal."

"That's what makes this so cool. We'll have a blast living with them!"

"Jesse, we're here to learn. Remember what your mother said?"

"She never said we couldn't have fun while we learn," Jesse countered. "*You* can go talk to the manager if you want. *I'm* staying in that apartment!"

"We have to stay in the same apartment. I promised my mother and yours."

Jesse shrugged. "Then I fail to see the problem. I'm staying in D-6. That means you will, too." She grabbed the keys from Meg's hand and hurried down the stairs to the parking lot.

* * *

Karen closed her eyes. This was worse than she had imagined. She could still feel the redhead's harsh glare. Shuddering, she wished again she had vetoed Bev's idea.

"I told you we'd be a hit," Bev said, grinning at Karen.

"With one of them," Karen replied, opening her eyes to glower at Bev. "I don't think the other girl—the redhead wearing glasses—"

"What about her?" Bev prompted.

"She didn't look too thrilled when she saw us."

"To know us is to love us," Bev insisted.

"I'm not sure we'll ever see that happen with—we didn't even learn her name."

"Here's our chance," Bev whispered as the redhead reentered the apartment. "Hi there. We didn't get properly acquainted before. I'm Bev Henderson and this is Karen Bey—"

"Randall," Karen corrected, giving Bev a livid look. She had stressed to Bev earlier that she never wanted to hear the name *Beyer* again.

"Are those your real names?" Meg asked suspiciously.

"Cross our hearts and hope to die," Bev replied, reverting to the southern drawl.

"They're our real names," Karen stressed.

"And you are?" Bev invited.

"Too mature for this kind of thing," Meg said, glancing from Bev to Karen. "I don't want to hurt your feelings, but you need to know that I'm a sophomore. This is my second year at Ricks—I mean BYU–Idaho. Sorry, I'm still getting used to the new name. Anyway . . . Jesse is my younger cousin. Her mother begged me to take her under my wing. It's my job to see that she doesn't get into any trouble while she's here. Jesse's had a rough time. In a nutshell, her parents are divorced and she's a little bitter right now."

"Then a good laugh is what she needs," Bev said, bristling over the lecture. "If you can't take a joke—"

"What my friend means, " Karen interjected, "is that we didn't intend to upset you. We were homesick and spent the afternoon trying to cheer ourselves up. We thought it would be funny if—"

"Oh, good! You're still decked out," Jesse exclaimed as she burst through the door. "When Mom bought this camera, I never thought I'd use it." She smiled at Bev and Karen as she aimed the camera in their direction. "This is definitely a Kodak moment!" A bright flash temporarily blinded both girls. "I'm taking another one—I want to make sure this turns out."

"I have an idea: let's get your cousin to take one of all three of us," Bev encouraged, still blinking from the flash.

"That would be great," Jesse said. "Meg, would you do the honors?" she asked, holding the camera out to her cousin.

Karen made a mental note. The redhead's first name was Meg. She watched as Meg sullenly took the camera from Jesse.

"Thanks, Meg. You're such a sport." Bev batted her eyes. "Isn't she a sport, Karen?"

Karen jabbed Bev in the ribs. She didn't want to do anything to further alienate Meg.

"Why don't I stand in the middle of you two?" Jesse suggested.

"Good idea, Jesse," Bev said, rubbing her side as she moved away from Karen. "What's your last name, Meg?"

"Denton." Meg pointed the camera at the three girls. As she snapped their picture, a loud voice startled her from behind.

"Now here are some real babes," a young man hooted from their open front door. "You girls are fly!"

"Don't you know it!" Bev said, blowing a kiss his way.

Hamming it up, he pretended to catch the kiss, then sent one to Bev. "You're the girl of my dreams, a real woman." His friends chuckled behind him as he held his hands over his heart. Kneeling down in dramatic fashion, he motioned for Bev to come sit on his knee.

"But you're a stranger," Bev countered. "Darcy Ann, you remember what Mama said about the danger of strange men," she said to Karen.

"Danger-stranger, that's me," the young man enticed. "Come here, you beautiful woman!"

"Hey, she's spoken for, dude," another male voice asserted.

Bev screamed when a tall young man with brown hair and magnetic green eyes pushed his way inside of the apartment to get a closer look. "Tyler!"

Now it was Karen's turn to grin. Tyler Erickson had recently returned from serving a mission in California. They had met him last December. Since that time, Bev and Tyler had developed strong feelings for each other. Laughing now at the expression on her friend's face, she could hardly wait to see how Bev handled this one.

* * *

"Hey there, foxy women," Tyler teased, grinning at the way Bev and Karen looked. He had an advantage over the other young men who had gathered outside their apartment door: he knew what these two girls really looked like. Both were exceptionally attractive, and to his way of thinking, Bev was the most beautiful girl he had ever met.

"Tyler, what are you doing here?" Bev asked as her face turned a deeper shade of scarlet.

"I'm a poor college student—like you," Tyler said. "Thought I'd come see if you were all settled in."

"I didn't think you were coming up until tomorrow," Bev stammered, reaching back to hit Karen as her friend pushed her toward the handsome returned missionary.

"Is that a camera I see?" Tyler asked, glancing at the camera in Meg's hand.

"Yes," Meg stammered.

"Would you mind taking a picture of me and my girl?" Tyler asked, enjoying the outraged expression on Bev's face.

"I'll do it," Jesse volunteered, grabbing the camera away from Meg. "This is my camera, I'll do the honors."

Tyler pulled Bev close to his side and tried to keep her there as Jesse snapped the picture.

Sputtering, Bev pulled away. "Ooooh, you . . . you . . ."

"Ah, ah, ah," Tyler responded, patting Bev on top of her straw hat, "it's not nice to call people names." He turned to Jesse. "Can I have a copy of that picture if it turns out? I think the people back home would enjoy seeing it in the local newspaper."

"Sure," Jesse replied.

"You send that to Blaketown and so help me—"

"Go for it, Tyler," Karen encouraged. "I happen to have a few connections with the newspaper staff—I only worked there all summer. I'm sure they'll run that picture for me."

"That would be great," Tyler exclaimed, moving out of Bev's reach.

"I gather you've seen this gorgeous babe somewhere before," Jesse guessed.

"Oh, yes. We're from the same podunky town," Tyler responded.

Bev slapped Tyler lightly on the arm. "You, sir, are a cad," she declared, reverting to the hillbilly accent.

"If you've claimed that one, can I have the other one? Or maybe that gorgeous redhead," the young man at the door said, gesturing with his hands in appreciation of Meg's figure.

"Oh, you mean Meg," Bev said, pointing to the older girl.

Tyler caught the outraged look on Meg's face and glanced at Bev. "I sense a bit of frostbite heading your way," he whispered. He smiled at the young man who had first flirted with Bev. "Try Karen. She's friendly and, as far as I know, she's unattached."

"Thanks, Tyler," Karen said snidely.

"Karen. I like the sound of that. Yee-ha!" the young man exclaimed as he rushed into the apartment to chase Karen around the kitchen.

"This has all been very entertaining, but we have a lot of unpacking to do," Meg insisted, her cheeks flushed with embarrassed rage.

"Mom has spoken," Bev proclaimed as she followed Tyler out of the apartment. "As for you, I will get even!"

"Promise?" Tyler goaded.

"You can count on it. When you least expect it, WHAM! You'll wonder what hit you."

"I'm already wondering that," he murmured. Since meeting Bev, he had found it difficult to think of anything else. During the summer, Bev had come over frequently to visit with Sabrina, his youngest sister. They had spent hours playing board games, talking, and laughing. Together the three of them had seen a couple of movies in the local theatre. They had also gone on pizza and hamburger runs, which had often included Karen. Then, just when he had decided to ask Bev out on an official date, she had made it clear that she was heading off to college. She was going to be a doctor. How could he compete with that?

Ignoring his family's teasing jibes, he had transferred to BYU–Idaho. He didn't want anyone else snatching Bev before he had a chance to make up his mind about her. But now, here he was, wondering what to do about this beautiful young woman in the ridiculous hillbilly outfit. "I must be crazy," he mumbled.

"What?"

"Nothing," he said, embarrassed that he had spoken his thoughts out loud. A sudden scream interrupted. "It sounds like your room-mate needs rescuing." He slipped back inside the apartment with Bev and laughed. The young man who had been chasing Karen had managed to pull off the tight, pink hat. Everyone stared in amazement at the tangle of blonde hair sticking out in a ridiculous fashion.

"Bev, you are so dead!" Karen promised as she ran to hide in the back bedroom.

Bev sank onto the carpeted floor as she laughed over her friend's humiliation. "Jesse, I dare you to run back and take her picture now," she managed to say.

Chuckling, Jesse shook her head. "I may be a lowly college freshman, but I'm not stupid."

"Jesse's right. This has gone far enough," Meg snapped. She snatched the pink hat out of the young man's hand, then herded everyone out of the apartment except for Bev and Jesse.

"I'll be back," Tyler said, doing his best imitation of Arnold Schwarzenegger before the door closed. He grinned when Bev blew him a kiss through the living room window. Wiggling his eyebrows in response, he wasn't amused when the curtains were immediately closed, blocking his view of Bev. "That's a real piece of work you're living with," he mumbled, guessing Meg had shut the drapes. Turning, he headed down the apartment stairs.

Chapter 4

Later that night, Karen dragged Bev from their bedroom and forced her down the hall. Meg had summoned them all to meet in the living room, stressing that they needed to start things off right if they wanted to draw closer together as an apartment.

"I'm a big girl, I can walk by myself," Bev protested, pulling loose from Karen's tight grip. "What does boss woman want now anyway? She ruined my romantic moment with Tyler."

"Romantic moment? As I recall, you were dying because Tyler saw you dressed like a hillbilly freak. Come to think of it, I was dressed the same way because you insisted that we look like social misfits this afternoon. I was also chased all over the apartment by a jerk and publicly humiliated. The way I see it, you owe me. Now march!"

Leaning against the wall, Bev refused to budge.

Sighing, Karen tried a different tactic. She knew Bev was more stubborn than she could ever hope to be. "Bev, please? This is our first night together . . . let's try to make it work."

"Yeah, whatever," Bev grumbled.

"We got off to a bad start earlier. Maybe this will help," Karen smiled, hoping to make amends. She wasn't encouraged when Bev rolled her eyes at the sound of Meg's voice.

"Karen? Bev?" Meg called from the living room. "We're waiting."

"You might wait a long time," Bev growled.

"Let's go," Karen whispered. "It probably won't be as bad as you think."

"No, it'll be worse," Bev grumbled as she followed Karen into the living room.

"Meg's already making up house rules," Jesse informed the two friends as they walked around the couch to where the other girls were waiting.

"Oh, really?" Bev replied.

"Nothing's etched in stone," Meg began, "but I am suggesting that we have family prayer as an apartment. If some of you would rather not participate, that's your choice. I learned last year that the best way for roommates to get along is to continue doing those things we've been asked to do as a family back home," she explained.

"Family prayer?" Jesse whined.

"It's a good idea," Karen said. "What could it hurt?"

"My knees," Bev answered as she exchanged a conspiring look with Jesse.

"Use a pillow," Karen replied. She wished Bev would quit antagonizing Meg. In the few hours they had spent together, it became clear that Bev and Meg were destined to drive each other crazy. Bev disliked Meg's air of self-importance; Meg had zero tolerance for Bev's warped sense of humor. Sighing, Karen suspected it would be an interesting semester. She glanced at their other roommates, Treena Graham and Kassidy Martin, college sophomores who had arrived from San Diego, California, two hours earlier. Kassidy had long blonde hair. Tall and slender, she looked like she had walked out of a glamour magazine. Since her arrival, Kassidy had kept to herself, claiming she wanted to unpack her clothes before they wrinkled. Treena was an outgoing, slightly overweight brunette whose sense of humor rivaled Bev's—much to Meg's dismay.

"Let's get this over with," Kassidy sighed, kneeling down on the carpeted floor of their small living room.

"Spoken like a trooper," Treena said, kneeling down beside her friend. "I'll bet Kassidy would even be happy to offer the prayer. She's been practicing all day to keep my car going."

Kassidy gave Treena a pained look.

"I'll say it," Meg volunteered, kneeling next to Treena.

"Oh yeah?" Bev retorted. "Well, I say if Kassidy wants the honor—"

"I don't want the honor." Kassidy glared at Bev.

"I'm getting a warm, fuzzy feeling here," Treena joked.

"Ditto," Karen echoed, forcing Bev to her knees.

"Ow! Hey, do that again and I'll . . ."

Karen's brown eyes showed little fear. She knew Bev wouldn't hurt her. "You'll what?"

"Do this," Bev said as she pushed Karen.

Caught off balance, Karen fell onto her side. "You are in such trouble," she promised, sitting up.

"Girls, that's enough! If you want to rough each other up, save it for later," Meg scolded. "Let's just say the prayer and go to bed. Church starts at 9:00 in the morning."

"Church?" Jesse complained, kneeling down beside Bev.

"Church. And don't give me that look. I promised Mom—"

"I don't care *what* you promised your mother, I'm not—"

Bev leaned over to Jesse. "I'll give you a ride in my Jeep," she enticed.

"You have a Jeep?" Jesse asked.

Bev nodded.

"Awesome. Dibs on shotgun," Jesse said.

"We can all fit in Bev's Jeep," Karen offered, smiling at her roommates. Maybe this would be a way to soften things between them.

"Lovely," Meg muttered under her breath.

"What do you say, Meg? I'll go to church if we all ride in Bev's Jeep," Jesse challenged.

Kassidy's blue eyes glittered. "If anyone wakes me before noon, they'll regret it."

"Now, Kassidy," Treena began.

"I mean it, Treena," Kassidy warned.

Shrugging, Treena smiled apologetically around the room.

"Okay, those of us who *are* going to church will need to be up by 8:00 A.M. at least. Our church meetings will be held on the third floor of the Manwaring Center on campus. It will take at least fifteen minutes to get there, even in Bev's Jeep," Meg informed them.

"Not if I'm driving," Bev said, giving Meg an indulgent smile.

"You wanted to say the prayer," Karen stressed, hinting for Meg to keep things moving.

Meg folded her arms and waited until everyone had knelt in place. Lowering her head, she began to pray.

* * *

"*'You wanted to say the prayer!'*" Bev mimicked a few minutes later in the privacy of their bedroom. Still annoyed over the family prayer disaster, she glared at Karen.

"Things were getting heated. I figured it was time to move on."

"I'll say. I'm looking for a new apartment."

"Bev!"

"I can't take living with a psycho like Meg."

"She's not a psycho," Karen replied. "If anyone's a psycho, it's Kassidy."

"I'm with you there," Bev agreed. "She's like an overgrown Barbie doll with a major attitude."

"Treena seems neat, though."

"Yeah, I can handle Treena . . . and Jesse."

"Because Jesse has you up on a pedestal," Karen teased as she changed into her nightshirt.

"Maybe I belong on a pedestal!"

"Now you sound like Meg," Karen blurted.

Bev grinned at her best friend. "I knew it! I knew she was getting to you, too. You're just a better actress than I am." Ignoring the surly look on Karen's face, Bev changed into the nightshirt Tyler's sister, Sabrina, had given her. It was identical to Karen's, with one exception, the color. Karen's nightshirt was red and grey, Bev's was blue and grey. "We're twins . . . in more than one respect," Bev exclaimed, parading around the bedroom.

"No one would ever mistake us for twins," Karen refuted.

"And we have the same standards, which means Meg is getting under your skin too."

"She's a little difficult to like, but—"

"A little? Try a lot!"

"We have to make the best of it," Karen insisted as she placed her jeans on a hanger and set them in the closet she shared with Bev.

"Says who?"

"We're just starting out here. We don't know Meg. Maybe this is how she acts when she's nervous."

"Right," Bev snorted with disbelief. She picked up her clothes and threw them into the plastic lavender laundry basket she had placed on the floor on her side of the closet.

"Let's give her a chance . . . and Kassidy."

"Kassidy too?" Bev groaned as she sank down on top of her bed. Stretching out, she rested her head on the plump new pillow she had brought.

"Kassidy, too," Karen repeated. "I have a feeling there's more to Kassidy than what we're seeing. Why else would Treena agree to room with her again this year?"

Laying her arm over her head, Bev considered that possibility. Then she pulled herself up into a sitting position and grinned at Karen. "This is why you're majoring in journalism."

"What?"

"You notice things most people miss."

"You're the compassionate one, future doctor," Karen said, bowing in mock deference to her friend.

"Get used to that," Bev replied, still grinning. "Most people will bow to me before I'm through."

"Oh, yeah?" Karen challenged, giving Bev a push that toppled her from the bed. She laughed as Bev crashed onto the carpeted floor between their beds.

"What was that for?" Bev sputtered, glaring up at Karen.

"Now we're even," Karen replied. "You tipped me over during our family prayer fiasco."

"I was keeping a Blaketown tradition alive," Bev said, rising to her feet.

"What tradition?"

"Cow tipping," Bev chuckled.

"Not funny," Karen replied. Before she could say anything further, their bedroom door flew open.

"What's going on in here?" Meg demanded, her green eyes flashing. Her long red hair had been loosed from its punishing braid and hung down the back of her shoulders.

"And this would concern you because . . ." Bev disputed.

"Because I'm trying to study my scriptures before I go to sleep, and my bedroom *happens* to be across the hall from this room!"

"Sounds like a personal problem," Bev retorted.

"What?" Meg said, her face now matching the color of her hair.

"Meg, we're sorry," Karen apologized. "We didn't mean to disturb anybody, right Bev?"

Bev ignored the pleading look on Karen's face and continued to glower at Meg.

"These walls are paper-thin," Meg continued.

"Which I think is a plus," Jesse interrupted, poking her head inside the room. "That way I won't miss out on the excitement. Which is good 'cuz I have to use the facilities right quick. Turn up the volume so I won't miss anything," she instructed before heading toward the bathrooms down the hall.

"It's already past eleven o'clock," Meg said, pointing to her watch.

"The woman can tell time," Bev said, feigning shock, doing her best to annoy Meg.

Meg's eyes narrowed. "This woman has had all she can take from—"

"Oh, gross! What happened in here?" Jessie cried out.

Angrily adjusting her glasses, Meg went to check on her cousin.

"Bev," Karen chided, when Meg left.

"*Karen*," Bev returned. "C'mon, let's see what's wrong with Jesse," she said, leaving the bedroom, certain Karen would follow. She paused as she approached the bathroom counter. A large mirror filled the space above the long counter that held two white sinks. Across from the counter were two small rooms, each containing a toilet and a shower. Jesse was standing outside one of the small bathrooms holding her nose.

"Man, that is disgusting!" Jesse complained.

"Let me see," Meg insisted, pushing Jesse aside. "Okay, who's sick?"

"What?" Bev asked.

"Take a look," Meg said, moving out of the way.

Bev poked her head inside the door and flinched. It was obvious that someone had lost the contents of their stomach and hadn't bothered to clean up after themselves. Wrinkling her nose, she stepped out to where the others were waiting. "Karen, don't go in there. It's pretty bad."

"Who's sick?" Meg persisted. "This is just great! I'm a nursing student. I can't afford to miss any classes, and now someone has the flu!"

"It's Kass," Treena said, slipping from the bedroom she would be sharing with Kassidy. "She doesn't feel well tonight."

"What's wrong?" Karen asked.

"I'm not sure," Treena replied. "She'll be all right. It's probably nothing. You guys go to bed. I'll take care of Kassidy . . . and her mess."

"That's all I need, to be exposed to the flu," Meg huffed as she stomped down the hall to her bedroom.

Amused, Bev watched as Karen followed behind Meg, obviously trying to get on the older girl's good side. Karen, the peacemaker, hard at work again.

"Well, I hope this other side is clean, 'cuz I've really got to go now," Jesse said before disappearing inside the other bathroom.

"I know I saw some paper towels around here somewhere," Treena mumbled.

"They're in the kitchen by the sink," Bev replied. "Do you need some help?"

Treena shook her head. "No, I'll get it. And Kassidy will be fine . . . but don't plan on us going to church tomorrow."

"Okay," Bev said. "I'm just down the hall if you need me," she added before stepping way from the bathroom. "You might try some Sprite over ice," she suggested over her shoulder.

"Good idea," Treena replied. "I saw a pop machine down by the lounge."

Bev pictured the brick building that contained several pieces of old furniture, a large TV, and a piano. "I'll go get a bottle for you," she offered.

"I'll wait and see if she wants to try it first," Treena answered. "Thanks anyway."

"Okay, good luck."

"I'll need it," Treena muttered before heading into the kitchen for the paper towels.

Chapter 5

Karen glanced around at the large campus theater that would serve as the chapel for their student ward. Located on the third floor of the Manwaring Center, the auditorium-style room was filled with interlocking, padded, folding chairs, something she decided was a plus. Leaning back in her chair, she continued to watch as members of the ward trickled in. Meg had seen to it that they were fifteen minutes early, giving them time to adjust to their new surroundings. "I wish Kassidy and Treena would've come," she said to Bev who was sitting on her left side.

"Treena said Kassidy still wasn't feeling good this morning," Bev replied. "We'll tell them all about church later. You're the writer, take a few notes. Start with how cool our bishopric seems to be."

"Our bishop is young," Karen commented. "I'd guess he's in his late twenties."

"I'm sure he'll age before the year's over."

"Especially if *you* have anything to do with it," Karen teased, laughing when Bev turned her head away, pretending to be hurt. "You'll break him in right."

"Do you mind? I'm trying to have a spiritual moment here," Bev said, doing her utmost to imitate Meg.

"Me too," Jesse whispered.

"You guys are terrible," Karen rebuffed, glancing across the room at Meg. The older girl was visiting with two young men dressed in dark suits. "Who's Meg talking to?"

Jesse shrugged. "Knowing Meg, they're probably future General Authorities. They would be the only ones considered worthy of her attention."

"She's not that bad," Karen countered.

"She is, too. Why do you keep sticking up for her?" Bev asked.

"I don't know. I guess I feel sorry for her."

Bev scowled. "I feel sorry for us. Maybe that's why Kassidy is sick. She knows what we're in for with Meg."

"Maybe Meg can't help the way she is," Karen said, ignoring Bev. "Jesse, you've known her longer than us—"

"Unfortunately," Jesse answered, accepting a quiet high five from Bev.

"Tell us about her. What's her family like?"

Jesse frowned. "My mom and her mom are first cousins."

"I am so sorry," Bev interjected.

"Thanks," Jesse said, grinning. "It's been a hardship."

"Jesse, I'm serious! If we're going to survive as an apartment, we need to understand each other. Help us understand Meg," Karen pleaded.

"Got a few weeks?" Jesse quipped.

Annoyed by Jesse's reply, Karen shook her head.

"I understand Meg," Bev offered. "The woman's on a power trip: *'I'm a sophomore. I know everything there is to know about college life. I will share the wonderment of my knowledge with you lowlife freshmen. You may thank me later.'*"

"You sound just like her," Jesse marveled. "What a gift!"

"Please . . . Jesse?" Karen tried again.

"Okay, you asked, here goes. Meg's wound too tight. She takes herself and life much too seriously. She's always grumpy, which I don't understand. What does she have to complain about? She comes from a good family. Her dad's the bishop in her ward at home. He's been the bishop for five years."

"Five years? Wow, that's dedication," Bev marveled.

Jesse smiled at Bev. "Yep. That's her family—dedicated Mormons. They eat, sleep, and drink the gospel . . . all eight of them."

"Eight?" Karen gasped. She was the only child in her family. There were times when she had wished for brothers and sisters, when she had wondered what it would be like to live in a crowded house filled with love. Bev was the closest thing she had to a sibling.

"Meg is the oldest of six children," Jesse replied.

Bev grinned. "That explains the bossy attitude."

Jesse nodded her agreement. "And to Meg's family, the LDS Church is everything!"

"Is that a bad thing?" Karen countered.

Jesse shrugged again. "I think it is when that's all that matters. It's like Mom's relationship with Meg's mother. My parents got divorced when I was a freshman in high school. Mom has had a rough time since then."

Karen saw Jesse wince, an indication that Jesse's mother wasn't the only one who was struggling.

"The night after everything was final, Meg's mom brought over a casserole," Jesse continued. "A casserole—can you believe it!"

"It sounds like she was trying to show that she cared," Karen said sympathetically.

"It would've meant a whole lot more if she had come over to spend some time with my mom, if she had visited with her over how she was feeling. Instead, it was like, 'Here's a casserole. Now everything will be fine. Oh, gee, look at the time! I need to hurry home and read my scriptures.'"

Surprised by the bitter edge in Jesse's voice, Karen raised an eyebrow.

"Oh, it gets better. Since the divorce, Meg's family has made us feel like charity cases. Things have been tight financially, but we get by. Mom has a good job—she works at a bank. And there are only three of us."

Karen gave Jesse an inquiring look.

"I have a younger brother, Mitch. He's twelve now."

"That's cool," Bev replied. "I have two younger brothers. They're twins—five year olds. They keep our mom hopping."

"I'll bet," Jesse said, smiling. "Especially if they're anything like you."

"Good one, Jesse," Karen approved.

"Thank you," Jesse drawled.

"You were telling us about *your* family," Bev prompted, changing the subject.

"Oh, yeah. Where was I?"

"Something about how your mom works at a bank."

"She's a loan officer; she even has her own office. We'll never be rich, but we manage. Dad sends us money once in a while, whenever he can. But he's not . . . well . . . I'd rather not talk about Dad, okay?"

Silently aching for Jessie, Karen understood. She felt the same way about her own father, Roger Beyer, a man who was currently serving time in prison for an assortment of charges that ranged from theft to kidnapping. She had been the intended victim of the kidnapping, a ploy to hurt Edie, Roger's ex-wife and Karen's mother. As far as Karen was concerned, Roger Beyer could rot in prison.

"Anyway," Jesse continued, "about six months after the divorce, every time Meg outgrew anything, her mother brought it over for me to wear." She gripped the armrests of the chair. "As soon as the woman left, I stuffed everything into a bag and hid it in my closet. When the bag was full, I threw it into the trash. Mom dug it out and donated it to D.I. She said if I was going to be ungrateful, she'd send that bag of clothes to a place where it could help people. Like I'm sure I would be caught dead wearing anything Meg wore! We don't have the same style, and not to be rude or anything, but—"

"You're hardly the same size," Bev offered.

"Exactly! She's a bit more endowed than I am."

"A bit?" Bev teased. "Meg's built like Marilyn Monroe!"

"Marilyn Monroe?" Jesse asked.

"My dad's a big fan. He has several of her old movies on video," Bev explained.

"I've seen pictures of her. Well, if Meg's a Marilyn Monroe, what am I?"

"Oh, I don't know, maybe a cross between Gumby and Goofy?" Bev teased.

"That's enough, Bev," Karen said, sensing this might be a sensitive issue for Jesse. "How did you and Meg end up rooming together?"

Jesse gave Bev a look of disgust, then focused on Karen. "When Meg's mom found out that I was thinking about coming here, she forced Meg to take me on as a roommate. My mom thought it was a wonderful plan. I guess she assumed Meg would keep me out of trouble—like I'm sure Meg could stop me if I decided to do something she thought was out of line."

"Meg makes you feel like you're indebted to her," Bev guessed.

Jesse tightened her grip on the arms of her chair. "You've got it! That's all I've heard since we left St. George—how lucky I was that she had a car and could drive me to Rexburg, and how neat it was that she could show me the ropes at college, and how I should be more grateful for this opportunity. The main reason I came to Ricks—I mean BYU–Idaho is that my mom attended this college when she was my age. It meant a lot to her that I come here . . . that and I was granted a full-ride scholarship."

Karen's eyes widened, surprised by this news.

"I may not act like it, but I have a decent set of brain cells. I scored 33 on my ACT."

"Wow!" Karen exclaimed, impressed. "That's great! I received a partial scholarship—nothing like yours, but it will pay for most of my tuition," she revealed. She reflected on the money she had made during the summer. It would help pay for her books, rent, food, and other expenses. Things would be tight, but she felt she could do it without working part-time while she was trying to go to school. "I'll bet you had all kinds of colleges after you," Karen mused.

"I had a few offers. I almost went with the University of Utah. They have a computer science program I'm interested in. That's what I'm going into, computer science."

"We have a genius to help us with any computer glitches we may run into," Bev chuckled. "I brought up my dad's old computer. It may need a few overhauls this year."

"What's Meg going into?" Karen asked.

"Nursing," Jesse snorted. "She's getting her RN; then she wants to become a physician's assistant. I heard all about it on the way here." She frowned. "I can't imagine anyone going into something like that. Who would want to take care of sick people? Yuck!"

Bev scowled. "I guess you didn't know I'm a premed major."

"You too?" Jesse groaned.

"It's a dirty job, but somebody has to do it," Karen chuckled.

"At least you know how to have fun," Jesse replied.

"True," Bev agreed. "Laughter is the best medicine."

Jesse sighed. "I wish Meg felt that way. She's so uptight, she squeaks when she walks."

"You've noticed that too?" Bev glanced across the auditorium at Meg. "Maybe we need to find her a man. That might improve her disposition."

"Good luck! She acts like men are a plague on society."

Bev gaped at Jesse.

"It's true! Any time a guy seems interested, she sends him packing."

"What a big surprise," Bev commented.

"Meg didn't date much in high school," Jesse shared. "Mom said she got involved with a guy up here last year, but it didn't turn out very well. As soon as he started getting serious, she dumped him."

"I wonder why," Karen pondered, focusing on Meg.

Bev smiled. "She's a social butterfly today. Do you see any potential sparks of romance over there?"

Jesse glanced at the two young men who were visiting with Meg. "I'll bet they were her family home evening brothers last year. They have to be nice to her."

Bev turned to Karen. "I'm having one of my incredible ideas."

"The kind that always gets us into trouble?"

"No, the kind that will help us keep our sanity this year. We'll transform Meg into dating material."

Karen studied her friend's face. "You're serious about this, aren't you?"

"Look at it this way; we're helping our fellow kind, we're be smoothing the way of her progression, we're—"

"Not interfering with Meg's life."

"I'll be nice to her," Bev dangled in front of Karen.

"Not sincerely," Karen argued.

"I can be very sincere . . . when I want to be."

"You guys want to help Meg find a boyfriend?" Jesse asked.

Bev turned to smile at Jesse. "Something like that, yeah. Even if it doesn't turn into anything serious, it has to help put her in a better mood."

"Count me in," Jesse said, grinning.

"Count silently, here she comes," Karen warned.

"Can we count on you?" Bev asked.

Karen studied Bev's face before replying. "Only if this doesn't hurt her in any way."

"You've got it!" Bev promised.

"All right, I'll help," Karen whispered as Meg sat down next to Jesse.

"The meeting will start any minute," Meg announced, pointing to the front of the auditorium where the bishopric was gathering.

"Good," Bev replied. "Say, Meg, who were those young men you were talking to?"

"Why?" Meg asked suspiciously.

"Just curious. They looked like friends of yours."

"They were my family home evening brothers from last year," Meg said, missing the jubilant look Jesse gave Bev.

Bev forced a smile at Meg. "They seem like nice guys. Returned missionaries?"

"Yes, and they both have girlfriends, so forget flirting with them," Meg snapped.

Karen did her best to stifle a snicker as Bev looked insulted.

"I'm not interested in them."

"She already has a boyfriend," Karen volunteered.

"I do not!" Bev sputtered, blushing.

"That guy who asked me to take your picture yesterday?" Jesse speculated.

"That's the one," Karen replied. "His name is Tyler."

"We're just friends," Bev countered.

"Which explains why your face now matches Meg's hair," Karen whispered in Bev's ear. She moaned when Bev reached down and pinched her arm.

"Let that be a lesson to you," Bev said. "I always get even."

"So do I," Karen promised, jabbing Bev in the ribs.

"Can't you two behave?" Meg asked, annoyed.

"I'm behaving," Jesse said innocently.

"For once," Meg retorted, "all of you sit there and be good. These meetings are so reverent, the Spirit fills the room."

At that moment, Bev's stomach rumbled. Embarrassed, she pressed her hands against her abdomen. "Nice! Here we go, an organ recital!"

"It's fast Sunday, don't worry about it," Karen soothed. "We're all in the same boat."

"Shhh!" Meg directed at Bev and Karen.

"You heard the woman, 'Shhh,'" Jesse repeated. As she leaned forward to retrieve the miniature hymn book from her large scripture bag, Bev gave her a small push, causing Jesse to land on the floor on top of her scripture bag.

"Jesse, quit clowning around," Meg said sharply.

Bev kept a straight face. "Yeah, Jesse! That's improper behavior, especially in a dress."

"Watch your back," Jesse mouthed at Bev.

The amused glimmer in Bev's blue eyes challenged Jesse's threat.

"You weren't going to provoke Meg anymore, remember," Karen whispered.

"I will be *so* good," Bev replied, her expression indicating the opposite.

* * *

"Try some Sprite," Treena encouraged, holding the green-tinted plastic bottle toward Kassidy. Since last night she had tried to get Kassidy to eat or drink something, but the beautiful young woman stubbornly refused to cooperate.

"No," Kassidy moaned. "I ate so much junk food yesterday that I'm paying for it now."

"You didn't eat that much," Treena replied, thinking of the small salad Kassidy had partially eaten yesterday afternoon at the cafeteria. The only other thing she had seen Kassidy eat after that was a handful of cherry Nibs. But there was no telling what her friend had downed in secret. Sighing, Treena sat on the edge of Kassidy's bed and set the pop bottle on the desk that separated the twin beds in their bedroom.

"You should've gone to church with the others."

"I'm not leaving you here alone when you're this sick."

"Why do you care so much?"

Treena gazed down at her hands. They had had this conversation a hundred times, but for some reason Kassidy found it reassuring. Sighing, Treena recited the words Kassidy needed to hear. "We've been friends since junior high, right?"

Kassidy nodded.

"You've always been there for me, and I will always be there for you—no matter what."

"Serious?"

"Count on it! You're an awesome friend, Kassidy. You're beautiful, talented— "

"Even if I didn't win the pageant this summer?"

Controlling the tremor in her voice, Treena forced a smile. "Kassidy, you were the first runner-up. You did great!"

"But I didn't win."

"You beat out fifty other girls to place in the top ten."

"But I wasn't good enough to win."

Treena frowned. "Forget what your mother said. She didn't mean it."

"You didn't see the look on her face."

Deciding to try a different route, Treena played with the silver class ring on her right ring finger. "Your mother was disappointed because she knew how much you wanted to win."

"You didn't hear what she said. She claimed I messed up, that I wasn't perky enough, that I didn't give a good enough answer to the question they asked me."

"You're beautiful, inside and out. It doesn't matter what anyone else thinks!"

Bursting into tears, Kassidy sobbed against her pillow.

"Kassidy . . ."

"Leave me alone!"

"I'm not leaving," Treena said stubbornly. "Haven't you learned that by now? I'm not going anywhere," she soothed, trying to comfort her friend.

Chapter 6

Using two thick hot pads, Karen lifted the small black roasting pan from the oven and set it on top of the stove. She then used one of the pot holders to lift the lid from the roaster. The smell of roast beef and onion steamed from the pan.

"That smells great! Man, am I starved!" Jesse sang out as she set the table for dinner.

Karen turned from the stove, smiling. "Good, this roast is cooked to perfection. The baked potatoes are done too. We'll be feasting soon."

"I can't wait." Jesse placed the final piece of silverware on the table, then approached Karen. "How long have you known Bev?"

"I feel like I've always known her," Karen replied. "We've been friends since first grade."

"Wow! That's a long time."

"It is, depending on the day."

Jesse frowned at the carpeted kitchen floor.

"I was kidding."

"I know. It's just . . . I was so blown away by her testimony this morning during Fast and Comedy Hour."

"Fast and Comedy Hour?"

"That's what I call fast Sunday at home," Jesse explained. "Our ward is very entertaining."

"I see," Karen laughed.

"Bev had me fooled," Jesse continued.

"What do you mean?"

"I thought she was a rebel—like me. But she's a rock, like Meg."

Karen grinned. "Don't ever let Bev hear you say that," she advised.

"Okay, but from what I saw last night—and even this morning when we were getting ready for church—I never would've guessed that Bev had a testimony like that. She had nearly half of the ward in tears."

"Including me," Karen said, remembering how touched she had been by Bev's testimony. She knew how much the LDS Church meant to her friend; it had become an anchor in her life. "Jesse, Bev's been through a lot," she tried to explain. "The Church has given Bev a solid foundation. It's helped her change in so many ways."

Jesse gazed steadily at Karen. "Oh?"

"I won't say any more than that. What Bev chooses to tell you is up to her. I will say this, she was baptized just a few months ago."

"Bev's a convert?"

"Yep. I think in some ways, we all are, but for Bev, it's been a long journey. She may joke around a lot, that's her personality, but inside her heart the gospel of Jesus Christ means everything to her."

"I could tell. In fact, don't say anything to anybody," Jesse stressed, "but it's the first time I've ever felt anything from someone else's testimony. It was weird. It kind of burned right here," she said, gesturing to her heart.

"That's how it starts," Karen answered, thrilled by Jesse's unexpected candor.

"Don't tell *anybody*—not even Bev!"

"I won't. But someday you should tell Bev what you told me," Karen encouraged.

Shrugging, Jesse grabbed a plastic pitcher and began filling it with cold water from the kitchen faucet.

"You should tell Bev what?" Bev asked, stepping into the kitchen.

Karen shook her head at Bev. "That you're supposed to wear a dress all day on Sunday."

Grinning, Bev strutted around in her jeans and loose sweatshirt. "I'm comfy! I can only stand wearing a dress for so long; then it has to come off."

"Meg won't like it, which is why I'm going to change right now," Jesse said, setting the pitcher of water on the table before she disappeared down the hall.

"You're such a good example," Karen said with a warm smile.

"That's enough out of you."

"I mean it, Bev. What you shared today in church was awesome."

"Oh, that," Bev said, blushing. "I don't know what came over me."

"I do," Karen said, continuing to smile. "It's called the influence of the Holy Ghost. A lot of us needed to hear what you had to say, including Jesse."

"I think Meg about swallowed her teeth. Good thing she doesn't wear dentures."

"I'm glad she was there to hear you. Maybe now she'll start to realize who you really are."

"And who am I, really?" Bev probed.

"You're one of a kind—you defy description," Karen said before she started to carve the roast.

"I hope that was a compliment."

"It was," Karen assured her.

"Thanks . . . I think." Bev leaned over the roast and inhaled deeply. "That smells wonderful."

"Thanks."

"How did you get stuck with kitchen duty?"

Karen dished up the slices of beef she had carved from the roast. "I volunteered last night. I had brought up a roast and some potatoes. I thought it would be a nice way to start things off."

"It is. Let's eat! I'm famished."

Before Karen could reply, the apartment door swung open and Meg walked through.

"It's about time! Dinner's ready," Jesse chided as she stepped into view. Dressed in an old pair of jeans and a T-shirt, she plopped down in a kitchen chair.

"Okay," Meg murmured as she walked past Jesse and turned to head down the hall.

"Is she all right?" Karen asked, concerned. "She looked a little pale."

"She must be sick, she didn't even notice my charming outfit," Jesse said, sounding disappointed.

"Maybe Meg's caught what Kassidy has," Bev suggested.

"I don't think so, not that quick. But I do wonder why Meg stayed after church today," Karen said. "She wouldn't tell me what was going on, but I saw her disappear into a room with the bishopric after Relief Society."

Bev shook her head. "Karen, you're missing your true calling. You should become a detective, not a journalist."

"Same thing," Jesse said as she snatched a small piece of meat from the plate Karen had carried to the table.

"Maybe Meg's been nabbed for a calling," Karen guessed aloud, reaching playfully to slap Jesse's hand as it wandered near the meat plate again.

"Ow," Jesse grumbled, drawing her hand away. "That first piece tasted so good, I wanted a second opinion."

"Get everyone in here, and we'll all eat," Karen said, watching as Jesse hurried out of the kitchen to round up the rest of their roommates. "She must be hungry." Turning, Karen stepped to the fridge for the green salad she had thrown together earlier that morning.

"Did we bring any sour cream?" Bev asked, scanning the fridge.

"Nope. I forgot. But we have real butter! I got into Mom's stash before we left home," Karen replied, reaching into the fridge to draw out the glass butter dish she had brought from home. She handed it to Bev, then grabbed the salad and shut the fridge door.

Bev set the butter on the table. "This will do. At this point, ketchup on my sandals sounds appealing. I'm starved!"

Jesse reappeared with Treena. "This is it, folks."

"Kassidy doesn't want anything?" Bev asked.

Treena shook her head. "She's asleep. I'll make some toast for her later."

Karen focused on Jesse. "Where's Meg?"

"She doesn't want to break her fast yet," Jesse replied. "She said she'll eat tonight."

"The woman has her agency," Bev said, gesturing to the table.

Karen slipped into a chair behind the kitchen table. Rectangular in shape, the table came with a brown Formica finish and six brown vinyl chairs.

"This looks wonderful, Karen," Bev complimented as she sat down next to Karen.

"Thanks. Remember that as you're cleaning things up," Karen replied with a smirk.

Bev feigned a scowl. "KP duty?"

"I'll help," Treena volunteered.

"Yes, you will," Bev assured her.

"Tonight we should figure out a schedule—assign duties, figure out a menu for the week . . . if we want to go in together on food," Karen suggested.

"It's a good idea," Treena said. "We can pool our resources. I think it will work better than each of us trying to buy our own food."

"Sounds good to me," Jesse assented as she sat down across from Bev.

"Ditto," Bev agreed.

Karen focused on Treena. "Do you think Kassidy will be okay with this?"

"Sure, just give her a day or two to bounce back. She'll get into the swing of things."

"Jesse, do you think Meg will be all right with this arrangement?" Karen pressed.

"No, because she wasn't the one who suggested it," Jesse replied. "Can we eat now? I'm wasting away and the food is getting cold."

"All right," Karen nodded.

Treena sat next to Jesse, leaving the two end places for Meg and Kassidy.

"Who wants to do the honors?" Karen asked.

"If it means we get to eat, I will," Bev volunteered, folding her arms.

Secretly enjoying Bev's offer, Karen folded her arms.

* * *

Treena wiped the table a final time with a moist dish rag. She set the dish rag in the sink, grabbed a dish towel, and dried the table. When she finished, she walked to the fridge and draped the dish towel over the metal handle. She gazed at Bev who was rinsing dishes in the kitchen sink. "Where did Karen learn to cook like that?" she asked, moving to help with the dishes.

"It's a long story," Bev said as she rinsed off another plate to place in the dishwasher that had come with the apartment.

"I'm not going anywhere for a while," Treena said, glancing at the pile of dirty dishes still on the counter. "It doesn't look like you will be either."

"True," Bev agreed. "Okay, here goes. Karen was raised mostly by her grandmother, Adele Hadley. Everything Grandma Hadley cooked was out of this world."

Treena set a handful of rinsed silverware inside the dishwasher. "Where were Karen's parents?"

"I'm not sure that I'm the one who should be telling you any of this, but it's not easy for Karen to talk about," Bev replied.

"Where is Karen?"

"Back in our room writing in her journal. She'd kill me if she knew I was out here sharing all her secrets."

"I don't want to cause any problems," Treena murmured.

"No, it's okay. Sometimes Karen has bad days. She's pretty sensitive, so things hit her hard. I think it would be a good idea if at least one of our roommates had a clue about what is going on with her . . . in case there's a problem when I'm not here."

"I understand," Treena replied, thinking of Kassidy. She reached down into the sink for the forks Bev had rinsed.

"This is quite a story, but I'll tell you if you won't tell any of the others. I don't know any of you very well yet, but I sense I can trust you to keep things quiet."

Treena nodded. "I promise not to breathe a word," she said as she placed the forks into the dishwasher.

"You'll probably meet Karen's mom in the near future. I know she and my mom were planning to visit before the weather turns nasty. They're pretty good friends—which hasn't always worked to our advantage. Especially when they combine efforts to control me and Karen."

"I doubt you two need much controlling," Treena replied.

"Oh, you'd be surprised. Jesse will have to show you the pictures of what you and Kassidy missed Saturday afternoon. Karen and I sort of dressed for the occasion."

"Dang that rotten car of mine!" Treena exclaimed. "I knew we were missing out on all the fun while my tire was being fixed."

"Don't worry about it. I'm sure we'll supply plenty of future entertainment."

"I hope so. Now, what were you going to tell me about Karen and her mother?" she asked, steering Bev back to the original topic.

"Oh yeah. Karen's mom—Edie. I don't want you to think any less of Edie Randall because of what I'm about to tell you. Edie is an awesome lady."

"I don't judge people by what others say. I like to make my own decisions."

"Same here," Bev replied. "Well, bottom line, Edie was an alcoholic. Edie's father was killed in a bad accident when she was a teenager. She got mixed up with a bad crowd . . . you know the drill."

"It can happen. It must've been tough on her," Treena observed.

"It was. Then Edie married a royal jerk named Roger Beyer. That was Karen's father."

Remaining silent, Treena reached for the cups Bev had rinsed.

"Roger had a drinking problem too, only he got mean when he drank. He usually took it out on Edie—something she put up with for a few years. One night he went too far and tried to hurt Karen. That's when Edie left him. They were divorced not long after that."

"I'm glad," Treena asserted.

"Me too. Edie took Karen to live in Blaketown, the place where Karen and I are from. They stayed with Edie's mother for a while, but the alcohol got in the way again. Edie dated a lot of losers. One guy landed her in prison."

"You're kidding?" Treena asked, her dark eyes reflecting concern.

"Unfortunately, no," Bev said in a hushed voice. "Her boyfriend robbed a convenience store. Edie didn't know anything about it, but she was the one driving the car after he tried to get away. She was drunk, which didn't help matters. Edie was arrested and sentenced to prison for being an accessory to an armed robbery."

"That's terrible."

"It was. I'll never forget how hurt Karen was. She was only thirteen."

"You were friends back then?" Treena asked, reaching for the rinsed plates that were now sitting in the sink.

Bev nodded. "We've been friends since grade school."

Treena began setting the stack of plates inside the dishwasher. "Like Kassidy and me."

"You've known each other that long?" Bev asked, surprised.

"Since junior high."

"It sounds like we have a lot in common," Bev observed.

"Yeah, I guess we do." Treena frowned. "How long was Karen's mother in prison?"

"Three years."

"Wow. I can't imagine how hard that must've been."

"It was a nightmare, and when Edie was released, Karen all but hated her."

"I can understand why," Treena sympathized.

"Yeah, but you'd never guess that now. They are *so* close."

"How did that happen?"

"Edie quit drinking in prison. When she got out, she promised Karen she would never touch the stuff again—and she hasn't. Edie went to work at the local hospital. She earned her LPN a few months ago. She's an awesome nurse, one of the best. She even got active in the LDS Church. When Karen saw that Edie was sincere about changing her life, she softened toward her. Things were going well. Then, Adele, Edie's mother, died last year. Edie and Adele were just starting this great relationship; then Adele was killed in an earthquake last fall."

Treena's eyes widened in wonder. "Are you sure you guys are from Idaho?"

"I know. Earthquakes are more up your alley—the California thing to do—but once in a while we get hit with one. Last year's was awful."

"It sounds like it. I've experienced a few minor ones, but nothing serious. And I've never known anyone who died in an earthquake."

Bev began attacking the roaster with a scouring pad. "I hope you never go through that. It was tough, especially for Karen. Adele was more of a mother than a grandmother."

"Karen must've been devastated," Treena mused.

"She was. There are still times when it hurts her, but now she has Edie back in her life. Edie married a great guy named Brett Randall a few months ago. That's why Karen's last name is Randall now. She doesn't want anything to do with her father, and I can't blame her; I've met the guy. Karen's so much better off with her mother and Brett."

Treena looked lost in thought. "A mother's love is important."

"I know. I've been blessed with two wonderful mothers."

"Two?"

Bev continued to scrub the pan before answering. "I've pretty much told you everything about Karen. Again, please don't say anything to anyone, or I'll be in trouble."

"My lips are sealed."

"It's only right that you hear about me, too. Karen would never breathe a word of this, so it will have to come from me."

Setting another plate in the dishwasher, Treena waited for Bev to continue.

"My mother had cancer and died when I was six years old," Bev said quietly. "A few years later, my dad remarried a woman named Gina."

Treena shook her head. "Is there anything you and Karen haven't been through?"

Bev chuckled. "I'm sure there is. It's just the fun of the latter days. Look around. Everyone's going through stuff."

"I know, but I'm not sure I would call it 'fun'," Treena responded. "How do you get along with your stepmother?"

"At first I made Gina's life miserable. I love her so much now, but when I was younger, I didn't want her to replace Mom. I hated Dad for remarrying. I was a real brat!"

Treena dried her hands on a dish towel, then smiled kindly at Bev. "I'm sure you weren't that bad."

"Ask Karen sometime—I was! And like Karen's mother, I thought I'd found the solution to what I was feeling in alcohol . . . I'm a reformed alcoholic." Bev glanced down at the shorter girl. "Shocking, eh?"

"There's not much you could say that would shock me," she declared.

"I wasn't born and raised in the LDS Church like all of you. I'm a convert. I was baptized last year. In fact, my dad and Gina were baptized the same day I was."

"That is so neat," Treena said, amazed. "I assumed you were always a member."

"I am now, thanks to Karen's example. She had a lot to do with me joining the Church. She also helped me kick my drinking habit."

"A good example is important," Treena agreed, her mind drifting to Kassidy. "I'm glad you've had someone like Karen in your life."

"We've shared a few adventures. I think the way Karen handled losing her grandmother did more to influence me than anything else. It broke Karen's heart to lose Adele, but her testimony kept her going. When I saw how much comfort she drew from that, I knew this Church was what I wanted in my life."

"It does offer a lot of strength and answers. I wish everyone could see that."

Bev caught the sad look in Treena's eyes. "Well, I've certainly spilled my guts. Now it's your turn. Tell me about you and Kassidy," she invited.

Before Treena could reply, a plaintive cry came from the front bedroom.

"Treena!" Kassidy repeated.

Treena set the dish towel down on the counter. "I'd better go see if she's all right."

"We'll talk later, okay?" Bev stressed.

Nodding, Treena moved from the kitchen into her bedroom and shut the door.

Chapter 7

Edie Randall took a deep breath before following her husband up the cement stairs. How would Karen respond to the news they had come to share? She was still stunned herself. Even though she had suspected it was true for nearly a month, today she had asked the doctor to double-check the test results. He had assured there was no mistake and had instructed her to set up another appointment for next month.

"Careful," Brett Randall said as he led Edie up the stairs of the apartment building.

"I'm fine, Brett," Edie replied. "I just hope Karen's here."

"We could've called from Idaho Falls and warned her we were coming."

Edie shook her head. "No, she would've asked why we were in Idaho Falls, and knowing her as I do, she would've dragged it out of me over the phone. I want to tell her in person—I'm not sure how she's going to react to this."

"She'll handle it okay," Brett said as he stepped onto the landing of the middle section of the large apartment complex. "What number is her apartment?"

"Six," Edie said, following him as they searched for the right apartment. "There it is," she said, pointing to a white-painted metal door.

Brett squinted. "It says D-6."

"That's the one. She's in building D."

"I hope that's not a reflection of her current grade status," Brett said, grinning.

"It had better not be," Edie responded. "She's only been in school for two weeks. I doubt she's had time to let her grades slide." She stole a quick peek through the opened curtains in the front window and was impressed with how clean the living room and kitchen areas looked.

"I don't see anyone in there," Brett said. "I told you we should've called."

"Try knocking. Maybe she's studying in her bedroom."

"You wish," Brett teased. "She's a college coed, remember?"

Looking extremely annoyed, Edie glared at her husband.

"You look cute when you're angry."

"I'm not angry."

"But you are cute," he insisted.

"You're pushing your luck, dear," Edie announced. "Knock!"

"Aye, aye, cap'n," he clowned, saluting her. As he reached to knock on the door, a loud squeal startled them both.

"Mom!"

Edie leaned over the black metal railing and spotted Karen and Bev on the sidewalk below. "Hi there," she squeaked out as her throat tightened. The tightness reached into her stomach and twisted into knots. How would Karen feel about this drastic change in all of their lives?

"What are you doing here?" Karen asked, handing her backpack to Bev. Turning, she ran toward the stairs.

"Hey, what do you think I am . . . your servant?" Bev complained.

"Something like that," Karen called over her shoulder. "Thanks."

Bev shook her head. "You owe me big time."

"We'll make it up to you," Brett promised, gripping the rail as he smiled down at Bev. "How about dinner tonight—our treat."

"Deal!" Bev replied, making her way to the stairs with both backpacks.

"I can't believe you're here," Karen exclaimed as she bounded onto the landing. Hurrying forward, she threw herself into her mother's arms.

Closing her eyes, Edie hugged Karen tight, this younger version of herself. The resemblance between them was apparent, even to those who didn't know them well. "I've missed you," she whispered, fighting tears.

"Same here." Karen pulled back to smile at her mother. "Mom, is something wrong?"

"No," Edie said as tears streamed down her face. "But I do have something to tell you."

"*We* have something to tell you," Brett said, reminding them both of his presence.

"Sorry, Brett," Karen said, giving him an intense hug. "Better?"

"Much," he exclaimed.

"I hate to complain here, but this is heavy," Bev said, moving into sight.

"Here, I'll help you." Brett hurried forward to collect Karen's backpack. "Good heavens. What do you keep in here, an anvil?"

"Something like that." Karen refocused on her mother. "Mom, why are you crying?"

"Because I'm so happy," Edie insisted.

"Hey," Brett admonished, "no hints until we step inside the apartment."

"You're pregnant!" Karen guessed, reading the answer in her mother's face.

"You take all the fun out of everything," Brett protested. "How did you know?"

"Is that it?" Karen excitedly asked. "You had every sign before I left home. I didn't say anything, but I wondered."

Thrilled by Karen's response, Edie reached for another hug. "You're finally going to be a big sister!"

* * *

Edie glanced around the busy restaurant, Frontier Pies. Decorated with a myriad of antiques, it emitted a homey atmosphere, the perfect setting to celebrate their good news. She was relieved over Karen's positive reaction. She still couldn't believe that Karen had already figured things out. Some signs had been obvious, like the morning sickness, but she hadn't thought her daughter had been around enough to notice. This was something Edie had wanted for so long, a second chance, a distant dream she hadn't allowed herself to hope for until today.

"This is great! I'm glad you guys are here," Karen bubbled.

"I'm glad we are too," Edie agreed. "Tell us about your roommates," she invited.

Bev looked up from her bowl of clam chowder to grin at Karen's mother. "Please, we're eating," she joked.

"They're not that bad," Karen countered as she selected another bite of salad.

"We could've brought them with us for dinner," Brett reminded them of his earlier offer.

Bev shook her head. "Trust me, it never would've worked. Kassidy would've refused because she doesn't believe in eating. Meg would've turned you down because she's Meg. If Treena and Jesse had been around they would've come. They're cool. But Jesse has a late class, and Treena works part-time at Albertson's as a checker. She doesn't get off until about eight tonight."

"But if Kassidy refused to come, Treena wouldn't have come either," Karen pointed out.

"She does tend to stick pretty close to Kassidy," Bev agreed, stirring her soup.

"This sounds interesting," Edie commented. She glanced at Karen for an explanation.

"It is. We're still not sure what the deal is there, but I think Kassidy has some major problems. Treena's tight-lipped about it. All she says is that Kassidy isn't feeling well."

Bev looked up from her soup. "She spends a lot of time praying to the great white porcelain."

"This sounds familiar," Brett said before trying more of his clam chowder.

"Quiet, you," Edie replied.

"You've been sick?" Karen asked, concerned.

"A little."

Brett looked astounded. "Every morning I wake to the sound of a roaring ocean. Then I realize we're nowhere near a beach—it's your mother losing the contents of her stomach."

"Mom?"

"Don't worry, I did the same thing with you," Edie informed her daughter. "It's a normal thing for me. Even the doctor said it was nothing to worry about."

"Unless it goes past the first three months," Brett imparted.

Bev snapped her fingers. "I'll bet that's it!"

"That's what?" Karen asked, confused.

"Kassidy's problem! Think about it. The way she keeps to herself; she won't eat; she's sick all the time; she's moodier than Meg. I should've thought about this one before."

Karen lifted an eyebrow at her friend. "I seriously doubt—"

"What else could it be?"

Edie's eyes widened with alarm. "Am I following you two on this one? You think your roommate . . . uh . . ."

"Kassidy," Bev supplied.

"Kassidy . . . is pregnant?" Edie asked, alarmed.

Bev shrugged. "It would explain a lot."

"I don't think so," Karen disagreed.

"What do you think is wrong with her?" Bev responded.

Karen chewed her bottom lip for a few seconds.

"Well?"

"I have my own suspicions—from what I've seen the past few days."

"Care to enlighten us?" Bev pressed.

"I'm guessing here, but it adds up. Remember the editorial I did for our high school newspaper last year, the one on eating disorders?"

Bev stared at Karen.

"Don't look at me like that! It's a possibility. She has classic signs."

"She's a toothpick with eyes, gorgeous, and from what Treena tries to tell us, she's very talented. Guys are already falling all over her. Why would Kassidy have an eating disorder?"

Edie gave Bev a sad look. "It would surprise you how many girls are dealing with this problem. A high school student is in the Blaketown hospital right now, hooked up to IVs because of severe dehydration. She's anorexic. She's lost so much weight, it's scary."

"Who?" Bev demanded to know.

"I'm sure it's someone you know, but I can't say—hospital confidentiality," Edie stressed.

"Not Terri or Sabrina?" Karen asked, concerned.

Edie smiled warmly at her daughter. "No, your friends are doing very well. They miss you two, but other than that they seem fine. That reminds me, they said to tell you both 'Hi!' and to give you a big hug."

"I think we already did the big hug thing," Bev teased. Before Edie could reply, their waitress appeared with a large tray and four steaming plates of food. "This looks *so* good."

"What did you order?" Karen asked as Bev received her plate.

"Stir-fry chicken," Bev replied, inhaling deeply. "What's yours?"

"Malibu chicken," Karen answered.

"Same here," Edie said, her mouth watering. "It sounded so good."

"Most food sounds good to you after twelve o'clock each day," Brett teased as he cut into his country-fried steak.

"Not funny," Edie protested.

"How could anyone hate food?" Bev marveled after sampling a bite of her dinner.

"It happens," Karen replied. "When I did research for that article last year, I learned that most of the time there's an emotional issue behind an eating disorder."

Bev reached for her glass of Sprite and took a sip. "Like what?"

"Didn't you read my editorial?"

"Probably, but you've written so many wonderful articles, I can't keep everything straight," Bev stated.

"Good answer," Karen returned. She frowned at her plate of food. "Most girls with this problem have very low self-esteem; some have been abused. They transfer their inner pain to a hatred of their body. They think they're fat, ugly, and undesirable. Instead of expressing what they're really feeling in a normal way—"

"Like yelling? That always works for me," Bev commented.

"Me too," Brett agreed, grinning at Edie.

"No comment," Edie said as she sliced off another small bite of chicken. She knew Brett rarely raised his voice in anger. During the few minor disagreements they had had since their wedding, he had proved to be very patient and calm. She was the one who expressed her emotions in a more vocal fashion.

"Instead of finding a healthy outlet for their pain," Karen continued, "they bottle up what they're feeling, and it comes out in other ways."

"You mean they get mad, so they starve themselves or throw up?" Bev questioned.

"It's more complicated than that," Karen stressed, reaching for her root beer. "It's like a release for them."

"Karen's right," Edie agreed. "I learned the same thing when I was working on my nursing degree last year. Sometimes these girls think it's a way to regain control over their lives."

"What?" Bev asked. "How does throwing up give you control?"

"They make themselves vomit. It's something they can control. And in an abusive situation, whether it's sexual, physical, or verbal, it becomes a way for these girls to cope with whatever it is they're facing in their lives. It's not a good way to handle stress, but they cling to it," Edie explained.

Karen nodded. "From my research I learned that these girls usually hate themselves. They're perfectionists, and if they don't measure up to who they think they should be, they punish themselves. Unfortunately, purging or food denial can destroy them if they don't get the help they need to recover. It becomes a slow form of suicide."

"Wow! This is pretty dark stuff," Bev said, frowning.

"Yes, it is," Edie agreed, "and the problem is getting worse. Even in our little town of Blaketown, it's on the increase. It breaks my heart. These girls are talented, beautiful, daughters of God, but through Satan's misdirection, they're being bombarded by negative messages that tear them down."

"Negative messages?" Bev asked.

Edie nodded. "From home, school, and friends. And have you ever noticed how skinny most models or celebrities are? On TV, in magazines, in movies—it's like our entire culture is being defined by what the media considers to be the perfect body."

"Your body is perfect," Brett complimented.

Edie blushed. "Maybe you think so now. How about in five or six months when I'm so huge it'll take a forklift to get me into the car?"

Brett laughed. "I'll learn the song, 'She Ain't Heavy, She's My Wife.'"

"Good one," Bev agreed, humming the tune to "He Ain't Heavy, He's My Brother."

"Okay, comedians, this is serious!" Karen scolded. "What Mom said is true. Some girls look at what the world considers to be the perfect body and then starve themselves to fit that mold. And all of the advertisements about instant weight loss don't help. Pay this amount and be beautiful! What a racket! Most of those products are so unsafe it's scary. People don't realize that most magazine and book covers are computer enhanced. They take an average body and transform it into an unreachable version of perfection."

"Exactly my point about Kassidy," Bev replied. "She already has a perfect body. Why would she starve herself?"

Karen shrugged. "Maybe she's skinny because she diets; her metabolism may not handle food like yours does. Jesse is another example of that. She eats like a horse!"

"Another reason not to invite her to dinner," Bev quipped to Brett. "You saved a bundle not bringing her along tonight."

"And she never gains a pound," Karen finished.

"You think Kassidy has a messed-up metabolism?" Bev questioned.

"Maybe. She also may have some emotional issues going on that we know nothing about."

Bev frowned. "I have a hard time feeling sorry for her. You've seen how ritzy her clothes are. That girl comes from a wealthy family. And again, guys practically drool over her."

"We don't know much about her background. Who knows what secrets lurk in her past?"

"True," Bev conceded. "We all have a few of those," she murmured, looking down at her plate.

Edie set her glass of Sprite down on the polished wooden table. The last thing she wanted was to dampen the spirits of these two girls. Deciding enough had been said about Kassidy, she moved on to something she hoped would be lighter. "Tell us about the rest of your roommates."

"Oooh, let me share about Meg," Bev said, a delightfully wicked gleam in her eye.

"Bev . . ." Karen cautioned.

"They're going to meet her, they might as well know what they're in for."

"She sounds entertaining," Brett commented.

"Oh, she is," Bev assured him.

"She's okay. Maybe a little uptight," Karen countered.

"That's an understatement," Bev interrupted.

Edie smiled at Bev. "Not your version of an ideal friend?"

"Hardly," Bev snorted. "It's like living with a drill sergeant."

"Meg has been pretty mellow lately," Karen pointed out.

"Except when I'm around."

Karen gave her an annoyed look. "Maybe if you stopped provoking her."

"All I have to do is enter the same room she's in."

"'*Meg, have you ever thought about styling your hair?*'" Karen mimicked.

"I was being helpful," Bev said in her defense. "We're trying to get this woman married off, remember?"

Edie glanced at Brett. "Sounds like these two are having fun at college."

"We are," Bev protested. "We like our other two roommates. Treena is a hoot . . . when she's not worried sick about Kassidy. And Jesse . . . well, Jesse is hard to describe."

"I call her Bev Junior."

Bev gave Karen a defiant look. "I beg to differ."

"You two are so alike it's sickening," Karen insisted.

"That must be why you get along so well," Brett said, grinning.

"Will they all be home when we take you back?" Edie asked.

"I don't know. Tonight our student ward is having an activity night," Karen explained. "Something about relay races on the football field. I'm not sure when they'll return."

Bev shook her head in disgust. "Yeah, get this: they put Meg in as one of our ward activity leaders. She's like a glorified Laurel class president."

"She helps plan activities for our ward," Karen disclosed.

"The best part is she has to work side by side with a guy she can't stand," Bev chortled.

"Who?" Edie asked.

Karen set her glass of root beer down on the table. "A returned missionary named Ryan."

Edie looked thoughtfully at Karen. "Why doesn't Meg get along with him?"

"Because Meg's a prude and Ryan's a ton of fun." Laughing, Bev avoided the reproving look on Karen's face.

"I've got to meet this Meg and see if she matches the image in my head," Brett said before finishing off the last of his steak.

"She won't match up," Bev told him.

"Why is that?"

"From the back, she's a knockout. Even from the front, she's not too bad. But one look at that caustic expression on her face and you'll want to run screaming in the opposite direction."

"I see," Brett said, hiding his smile behind the glass in his hand.

"Where's Treena from?" Edie asked.

"San Diego," Karen replied.

"Treena and Kassidy have known each other since they were in junior high," Bev added.

Edie set her fork on her plate. "They've been friends for a long time, like you and Karen."

"Yep," Bev answered.

"And Jesse's hometown is?" Edie inquired.

Karen looked up from her meal. "St. George, same for Meg—they're cousins."

"They are?"

Bev nodded in agreement. "Don't hold that against Jesse."

Edie studied Bev's face. "I gather you and Meg will never be bosom buddies."

"You gather correctly," Bev assured Karen's mother.

Brett glanced at his watch. "Well, ladies, should we go buy a few groceries, then take you back to your apartment?"

"Sounds good," Karen said gratefully. "We've been pooling our resources, but we could use a few extras."

"Yeah, somebody forgot to add toilet paper to our shopping list last Saturday," added Bev.

Brett grinned at Bev. "This sounds like an emergency situation."

"It is! We've been getting by with a box of Kleenex in one bathroom and a roll of paper towels in the other . . . guess which room is the most popular?" Bev queried.

"That's a tough call," Brett replied. He smiled at Edie. "Should we help them out?"

"We'd better. I'm sure I'll need a potty run before we leave their apartment tonight."

"You guys aren't driving back to Blaketown tonight?" Karen worriedly asked.

"Nope. We already made reservations next door at the Cottontree Inn," Brett replied. "Don't stress, I plan to take good care of your mama. The good doctor said she shouldn't sit with her legs bent for an extended period of time."

A concerned look crossed Karen's face.

"Karen, it's nothing to worry about." Edie flinched under her daughter's probing stare. "I've noticed that my ankles are a little swollen by the end of each day. It's just fluid."

"Is that normal?"

"For a pregnant woman about my age, yes."

"This early in the pregnancy?"

"I'm two months along," Edie revealed. "My body's schedule has always been irregular, so I didn't think anything was going on, until about a month ago, when I started with the morning sickness." She frowned over the look on her daughter's face. "Karen, quit worrying. It'll be all right. Brett and one of our home teachers gave me a priesthood blessing last week."

"Why?"

"Like Brett said, I've been a little sick," Edie explained. "The blessing helped. I was promised that the baby and I will come through this just fine."

Karen pushed her chair away from the table. "I'm glad you're staying in Rexburg tonight."

Edie nodded. "We checked in before we drove over to your apartment complex."

Karen turned to her stepfather. "Brett, would it be all right if we took Mom back to your room? She should probably lie down for a bit. I'll stay with her if you want to take Bev to get a few groceries."

Edie exchanged a look with Brett. They both knew what Karen was trying to do: Karen wanted some private time with her mother.

"Are you okay with that plan?" Brett asked Edie.

Rising from the table, Edie nodded. "Maybe a short rest would do me some good before I meet these interesting roommates we've heard so much about. Let's go," she said, leading the way as Karen, Bev, and Brett followed close behind.

Chapter 8

Edie unlocked the motel room and gestured for Karen to step inside. She walked in behind her daughter, shut the door, and began unzipping her blue Columbia coat. She shook her head when Karen moved to help her. "Karen, I'm pregnant, not an invalid, okay?"

"Sorry," Karen muttered as she removed her own jacket.

"The baby and I are both going to be fine," Edie stressed. She hung up her coat and Karen's maroon jacket, then moved to the king-sized bed and sat down. "Have a seat," she invited, troubled by the anxiety that filled her daughter's dark eyes. "I'm glad you came up with this idea. I am tired, and I think we need to have a chat."

"Shouldn't you elevate your feet?" Karen asked as she sat beside her mother.

Refusing to answer, Edie smoothed her daughter's blonde hair away from her face. "You're a bundle of nerves tonight. What's wrong?"

Close to tears, Karen shrugged.

"Is it just my pregnancy?"

"I couldn't handle it if anything happened to you," Karen said in a hoarse whisper.

At a loss for words, Edie pulled her daughter into a hug. She gently caressed Karen's back as the young woman began to sob. After several minutes, Edie voiced her concern. "Hon, I know one of your biggest fears is losing someone else. And next month will be tough on both of us," she said, referring to the anniversary of her mother's death. "Don't make yourself sick worrying over me."

"I can't help it," Karen murmured.

"Maybe we should've waited on the priesthood blessing. I wish you could have felt the Spirit in that room. The baby and I will be fine." Edie tightened her hold on Karen. "Why don't we have Brett give you a blessing when he and Bev get back?" she suggested.

"I don't want Bev to know I've been upset," Karen protested, pulling away from her mother.

"And how are you going to hide the fact that you've been crying?"

"You've got your makeup bag here, right?"

Remaining silent, Edie gazed at her daughter.

"I don't want Bev to think I'm a total boob."

"Karen, we're talking about Bev, your closest friend," Edie tried to reason with her.

"I know," Karen sniffed.

Edie studied Karen's face.

"What?"

"Are you and Bev getting along okay?"

Karen looked away from her mother's penetrating gaze.

"You're getting on each other's nerves, aren't you?" Edie waited for a reply, then sighed. "I was afraid this would happen." Rising, she went into the bathroom to retrieve a handful of tissue for Karen.

"I can get that," Karen objected.

Returning to the bed, Edie handed the tissue to her daughter. "Tell me what's wrong," she said, sitting down. "What's going on with you and Bev?"

"It's nothing," Karen stammered as she wiped at her eyes and nose. "But it's not like I thought it would be."

"What's not like you thought it would be?"

"I don't know. I'm trying so hard to keep peace in our apartment—"

"And Bev isn't exactly going out of her way to help you with this," Edie guessed.

Nodding, Karen wiped away a fresh tear as it ran down her face. "She acts like I'm siding with the enemy if I ask her to tone it down. She's so critical of Meg and Kassidy—you heard her during dinner. She won't even give those two girls a chance."

Edie chose her words carefully. "You've always loved Bev's sense of humor. You know she doesn't always mean what she says when she's trying to be funny."

"She's still funny—at least she tries to be—but I hate being caught in the middle."

"Karen, you can't change or control anyone but yourself."

"I know."

Edie brushed Karen's cheek with the back of one hand. "Then stop trying to be the mediator. If Bev and Meg have a problem with each other, they're the ones who will have to work it out. Don't make it your responsibility. You can't control Bev, Meg, or Kassidy. All you can control is how you react to the situation."

Karen gazed down at her hands.

"Sweetheart, you're very mature for your age—you always have been. Until now, you've been an only child. You've lived in a world of adults . . . and I'm sorry about that."

"Mom—"

"Let me finish. Bev has been good for you. She's a blithe spirit," Edie said with a smile. "Sometimes she's too quick to speak her mind, but that is a young lady who knows how to have fun. She's passionate about life and a friend you can count on when things get tough."

Karen nodded.

"Enjoy this time with her. Be happy."

"That's not always easy."

"But it is possible, especially when you're comfortable with who *you* are. That's something I've had to learn the hard way." Edie gazed intently at her daughter. "Who are you, Karen?"

Karen shrugged.

"You're the only one who can answer that question. But I'll tell you who I think you are. You are a beautiful, talented young woman; you're extremely levelheaded and very sensitive."

"Too sensitive," Karen replied.

"There's nothing wrong with being sensitive, especially about other people and their feelings," Edie assured. "That's a special quality you possess. You're a good balance for Bev. Sometimes she gets too self-involved."

"Sometimes?" Karen said wryly.

Edie smiled. "Bev's mother would be the first one to tell you that. In fact, when I talked to Gina the other day, she told me how worried she was about you two rooming together. Her prayer is that you don't end up hating each other."

"I could never hate Bev, she's my best friend!"

"Then, as the saying goes, 'don't sweat the small stuff'. And when it gets too bad, talk it out with Bev. Level with her. Tell her what you're feeling. Don't let it build up inside of you until you're ready to explode like tonight. Okay?"

Karen nodded. They both jumped, startled when they heard someone fumbling with the lock in the door. "They're back already?"

"Sounds like it," Edie replied.

"I look terrible."

"You look fine," Edie said as Brett and Bev burst into the room.

"Karen, did you see that pool downstairs by the lobby? Let's go grab our swimsuits and make good use of it," Bev suggested. "There's even a hot tub."

"Maybe later," Karen mumbled.

"How's our patient doing?" Brett asked brightly.

"Better than the physician," Edie replied, giving her husband a knowing look as Karen averted her face to hide her red, swollen eyes.

Bev moved to the bed and gazed down at Karen. "I can see that."

"Brett, I think Karen could use a blessing. She's worrying too much over me and the baby. We're also approaching a difficult day," Edie added, experiencing an inner pang as she thought of her mother's tragic death.

"Do you want me to round up someone to help, or will a father's blessing do?" Brett asked, waiting for Karen's response.

"A father's blessing will be fine," Karen said in a hushed voice.

"I should've done this before you headed off to college," Brett said, closing the door to their motel room. "It didn't even occur to me until after you'd left."

"A father's blessing?" Bev asked, curious.

"It's a way for fathers to invoke special priesthood blessings upon their children as needed," Brett explained. "It can provide comfort and guidance, depending on the circumstances." He grabbed a padded chair and set it near the bed. "Would you like one tonight, too?"

Bev considered his offer, then shook her head. "If you don't mind, I'll wait until I come home. I'd like to ask my dad for one of those."

"I'm sure he'd be delighted to give you one," Brett replied. "Karen, have a seat," he said, patting the chair. "We'll have you feeling better in no time."

"I hope so," Karen mumbled, moving to sit on the chair.

* * *

Shivering from a brisk breeze, Edie placed an arm around Karen's shoulders as they walked up the stairs toward the apartment. "Are you cheering up?"

"I'll be all right," Karen said. "We Randalls are tough."

"Yes, we are," Edie agreed, laughing. She was pleased that Karen had chosen to change her last name. It thrilled her to know that since the temple sealing, Karen belonged to her and Brett for all eternity. Still, she couldn't help but wonder if her daughter would ever come to terms with her biological father. Deciding now wasn't the time to bring up that painful topic, she kept things light. "Even Baby Randall's pretty tough."

"You mean my little sister?" Karen replied.

"You think it's a girl?"

"That's my son you're talking about," Brett complained behind them. "Little Brett Junior!"

"We'll see," Edie laughed.

"Are you guys coming?" Bev called back, already at the apartment door. "Hello all, did you miss us?" she chirped as she burst inside the apartment.

Before anyone could reply, Karen walked in with her mother and Brett. Brett followed Bev into the kitchen with three plastic bags of groceries he had purchased for the apartment of girls.

"Thanks, Brett," Bev said, hurrying to put the gallon of milk she had been carrying into the fridge. "We owe you one."

"Can't have you going without the necessities of life," Brett quipped, pulling out a package of toilet paper.

"Yay!" Jesse cheered from the living room.

Meg rose from the kitchen table where she had been studying. "Thank you," she murmured, glancing from the groceries to Brett.

"You're welcome," Brett replied, smiling at the attractive redhead.

"Meg, Jesse, I'd like you to meet my parents," Karen said as she introduced Brett and her mother.

Edie smiled at the two girls. Earlier they had decided that was the best way to handle the introductions. She knew that for now, Karen wanted to avoid the complicated details about the past.

"Nice to meet you," Meg said, offering a small smile.

"Yeah, same here," Jesse said, rising from the couch. "Have a seat," she invited.

Edie glanced around. "Where are the other girls?"

Meg closed her books and walked into the living room. "Treena just came home from work. She's in the bedroom with Kassidy. Jesse, tell those two that Karen's parents are here."

"Right," Jesse replied, saluting her cousin. She exchanged an amused look with Bev before hurrying off to find their other roommates.

"Mom, you can sit here on the couch, maybe stretch out your legs," Karen insisted, guiding her mother to the worn sofa.

Meg gave Bev an inquisitive look.

"Her mother's pregnant," Bev whispered to the older girl.

Meg's eyes widened with surprise. "I see," she murmured as Karen continued to fuss over her mother.

"Karen," Edie warned, "I've rested enough. I'd like to meet your roommates." Sitting on the couch, she motioned for Meg to join them in the small living room. "So you're Meg?"

Nodding, Meg sat on a Herculon chair near the window. Brett sat on the couch beside Edie, while Karen and Bev rested on the arms of the couch.

"Karen says you're from St. George," Edie said, trying to initiate a conversation.

"Yes, I am," Meg replied.

"How do you like coming up to the frozen wastelands of the north?" Brett quizzed.

"It's a change from St. George," Meg answered.

"I'm looking forward to the skiing I've heard about up this way," Jesse added, stepping back into the living room with Treena. "This is Treena," she said, introducing the older girl.

"Hello, Treena," Edie said, smiling at the short brunette. "We're still missing one."

Treena looked uncomfortable. "Kassidy isn't feeling well. She doesn't want you to catch something from her, especially since you're . . . I mean," she paused, glancing at Bev for help.

"I see my fame has preceded me," Edie said, glancing at Bev.

"Uh . . . yeah . . . well, I kind of told Treena earlier before she went to work," Bev admitted.

Edie laughed at the embarrassed look on Bev's face. "Yes, I'm expecting. Karen finally gets to be a big sister."

Meg gazed at Edie. "This is your second child?"

Edie nodded.

"Really?" Meg said, intrigued. "Would you mind if I asked you a question?"

Hesitantly shaking her head, Edie wondered where this was heading.

"Karen told me you're a nurse. I'm going into nursing too. I'm curious, did you delay having children after Karen was born because of your career?"

Edie frowned. "Something like that," she said, glancing first at Brett, then at Karen for support. She missed the concerned look that passed between Treena and Bev.

"Do you regret waiting?"

Still not sure what Meg was getting at, Edie studied the coed's face. Suddenly, it dawned on her why Meg might be concerned about this issue. "Are you thinking of postponing your future family?"

Now it was Meg's turn to look discomfited. "I . . . well . . . maybe we could talk about this later," she said, rising from the chair. "Here, Treena, Jesse, you can share this chair. I need to get back to my studying. I have a test tomorrow." She forced a smile at Karen's parents. "It was nice to meet you."

"It was nice to meet you too," Edie replied, as Meg moved into the kitchen to gather her books. When she disappeared down the hall, Edie turned to Karen. "Is she all right?"

"That's debatable," Bev replied.

Jesse moved to the chair her cousin had vacated, offering to share it with Treena. When both girls had settled into place, Jesse smiled at Edie. "Don't worry about Meg, that's her way."

"I warned you," Bev said, grinning at Brett.

"She seems like a nice girl," Edie replied. Then, deciding to change the subject before Bev could argue, she smiled at Karen's other roommates. "Treena, Karen mentioned you're from San Diego. Why did you come all the way to Ricks?"

"BYI," Jesse and Bev said in unison.

Edie looked confused. "BYI?"

"It's something I came up with," Bev replied. "It's our nickname for Brigham Young University–Idaho."

Edie smiled apologetically. "Sorry, old habits die hard. It'll always seem like Ricks to me."

"Don't worry about it. I slip up all the time," Treena replied.

"Which is why her parents sent her here," Bev teased.

Treena shook her head at Bev. "We won't even go into why your parents sent you here."

"Why did you come here?" Edie restated her original question.

"My parents thought it would be a good place for my first college experience," Treena answered.

"And was it?" Brett asked.

"I love it here," Treena exclaimed. "Most of the teachers put an LDS slant on their teaching. It's an awesome place, especially when you're away from home for the first time."

"That's what we were thinking," Brett replied, casting a grin toward Karen. "These two had almost decided to go to ISU, which is a good college too—but we felt better about them coming here—at least for this first year."

"And now that it's becoming a four-year college, we won't have to deal with transfer issues," Bev pointed out.

"This is where my mom went to college," Jesse offered. "She was hoping I'd follow in her footsteps."

"With an IQ like yours, you could've gone anywhere," Bev stated.

"True, and I'll probably transfer out somewhere else next year. But to keep Mom happy, I'll stick it out this year. It'll be a challenge, enduring Bev and everything," Jesse joked, "but Meg assures me it'll be character building."

"I see," Edie said, smiling. Relaxing against the couch, she continued to ask questions, determined to get acquainted with the girls who would be sharing so much with her daughter.

* * *

Meg reread the same page twice before closing her book and setting it on the desk beside her bed. Why couldn't she concentrate? A dull pain was settling behind her eyes, indicating eyestrain. Deciding to take a break, she leaned back against the wall. It was tempting to stretch out on the bed beneath her and relax for a while. She closed her eyes as a quiet knock sounded at the door. "Come in," she invited, her green eyes blinking open.

"Hi again," Edie said as she slipped inside the spotless room.

"Hi," Meg responded, sitting up. She picked up her glasses from the desk and put them on, an instinct she had developed through the years. Her eyes weren't that bad, but she felt naked without her glasses.

Edie sat down on the end of Jesse's bed. "We thought you girls might enjoy a dip in the pool at the motel where we're staying. Would you like to come?"

Meg shook her head. "I appreciate the offer, but I need to keep studying to be ready for tomorrow."

"Good grades are important to you," Edie guessed.

Nodding, Meg wondered if Karen had any idea how lucky she was to have such a beautiful, intelligent mother. She pictured her own mother and grimaced—there was no comparison. Bringing six kids into the world had permanently altered her mother's figure. The woman rarely bought new clothes for herself and in Meg's opinion, her mother did little to try to better herself.

"And, as I recall, nursing courses are tough."

"They are," Meg agreed. "Are you an RN or an LPN?"

"An LPN," Edie replied. "I'm not sure I'll ever have the time to go for my RN."

"Because of your baby?"

Edie nodded. "I want to do things right this time. In fact, I'm not working after this baby makes his or her appearance."

"My mother felt the same way," Meg sighed. "She wanted to be an architect. She has a gift with art—she can draw anything—but she gave it up to marry Dad and have a family."

"Is that a bad thing?" Edie probed.

"I think it is, especially when you become a nonperson to raise kids."

"I see. And is that how your mother feels?"

Meg shrugged. "I know I don't want to end up like her: married . . . six children . . . nothing to show for your life . . ."

"I'd hardly call having six children an insignificant accomplishment," Edie marveled.

"What's so great about it?"

"I wish Karen could have grown up surrounded by brothers and sisters."

Detecting the emotion in Edie's voice, Meg gazed at Karen's mother. "You regret not having a larger family?"

Edie nodded. "And I missed so much of Karen's life. She grew up without me. My mother spent more time with her than I did."

"But you're a nurse! You help people, you've made a difference in their lives."

"The place where a woman can have the greatest influence is in the home."

"I don't think so," Meg countered.

"I'll admit, being a nurse has its rewards. It gives you a warm feeling inside when you can ease someone's pain."

"That's why I'd like to become a physician's assistant, maybe even a doctor. I want to make a mark in this world. I don't want to waste my time." Meg paused, deciding she had said too much.

Edie smiled warmly at Meg. "I think it's important for girls to develop skills, to gain an education. The economy is so messed up, it nearly takes both parents working full-time to make ends meet, something I'm sure Satan has had a hand in. He knows that if he can keep mothers out of the home, he can have a greater influence over the youth." She paused, as if reflecting on her own childhood. "I'll never forget the warm feeling I always had inside when I came home from school each day. My mother was there to greet me, to hear about my day. Mom never had a degree behind her name, but in my opinion she was one of the greatest women who ever lived."

"Because she sacrificed her life to raise you?"

"No. Because she was comfortable with who she was and because her love for me saved me from ruining my life." Rising from the bed, Edie gazed steadily into Meg's eyes. "I'm sure you'll make a wonderful difference in this world, but remember: The greatest joy comes from family life."

"My mother says the same thing."

"She knows what she's talking about," Edie assured, smiling.

"Mom!" Karen sang out.

"And *that* is the most incredible title anyone can ever earn," Edie added.

"Mom?"

"In here," Edie replied, smiling as Karen poked her head inside Meg's room. She turned to Meg. "Are you sure you won't come with us?"

Nodding, Meg grabbed her book from the desk and pretended to study.

"We'll see you later, then," Edie replied, stepping out into the hall.

When they left, Meg shoved the book away. Rising from her bed, she closed the bedroom door, and stretched out on her bed to take a nap.

Chapter 9

"How did you sleep last night?" Karen asked her mother, gazing across the wooden restaurant table. Brett had offered to treat her and Bev to breakfast and both girls had willingly accepted, joining her parents at Frontier Pies early that morning.

"She sawed down a forest," Brett teased, reaching for his orange juice.

"If anyone was powering up the old chain saw, it was you," Edie countered. She glanced around at the empty restaurant. "Where is everyone else? I know we're not the only ones staying next door."

Bev looked at her watch. "They're probably still asleep. Maybe you two kept them up all night with your combined chain-saw orchestra."

Edie reached into her glass of ice water and flicked a few droplets across the table at Bev. "For the record, I do not snore!"

"Hey, watch it—don't touch the hair! I spend hours getting it to look this good."

Brett grinned at Bev. "I figured you ran your fingers through it after sleeping on it all night to get that effect."

"It takes talent to get this tousled look," Bev countered.

"I see," he said in mock deference.

Bev lifted her water glass in a threatening manner.

"Settle down, you two. Didn't you get wet enough last night?" Edie asked, referring to the huge water fight Bev, Karen, Jesse, Treena, and Brett had engaged in the night before in the motel's indoor swimming pool. "You almost got us kicked out of the motel."

"Now they won't have the expense of having the carpet shampooed," Brett replied.

"No, *now* they'll have to pay to have the chlorine sucked out of it," Edie said.

Karen laughed and shook her head. "Sounds like you two will have a fun trip home."

"Oh, we will," Brett said, wiggling his eyebrows. "The best part is making up."

"I so didn't need to hear that," Bev replied, laughing.

"Likewise," Karen agreed, enjoying the embarrassed look on her mother's face.

"Thanks again for letting us invade the pool last night," Bev said before sampling her apple juice. "It was a much-needed release."

Karen exchanged an amused look with her mother. She had dunked Bev numerous times last night, ridding herself of the anger she had been harboring the past two weeks.

"No problem," Brett replied. "I'll let Edie check us out when we get ready to leave."

"Thanks a lot," Edie retorted. "I say you're the guilty party; you face the music."

"All right," Brett sighed. "I'll take it on the chin. I'll explain that you can't control your daughters."

Edie looked puzzled. "My daughters?"

"There's Karen, Bev's practically family," Brett said, counting on his fingers, "Jesse, and Treena, the two we adopted last night."

"Note he said 'we'," Edie stressed. "That makes you half liable for the mess they made."

"It wasn't that bad, was it?" Karen asked.

Edie smiled. "No, I just like giving Brett a bad time."

"Now I have witnesses," Brett exclaimed. "Karen, your mother freely admitted that she gives me a bad time."

"I think your fun is just starting," Bev said, winking at Brett.

"You can say that again," Edie replied, suddenly looking very pale. "Dang, I thought those crackers I ate earlier this morning would take care of this," she said, rising from the table. She hurried toward the rest room, followed by Karen.

"Good timing," Brett commented as the waitress brought out their order. "Well, Bev, I seem to be in a delicate way."

Bev grinned, waiting for an explanation.

"I'll be eating for two for a while," he sighed, glancing at his wife's plate. "I doubt Edie will feel up to eating any of that—maybe the toast."

"Like I said, your fun is just starting," Bev quipped, eyeing her omelet.

"I think you're right," he agreed before cutting into a sausage patty.

* * *

Edie sank gratefully into the comfortable easy chair. She had come to give Bev's stepmother a full report on their daughters, but wasn't feeling her best.

"So you think the girls will be okay?" Gina Henderson asked as she brought Edie a small mug of caffeine-free herbal tea.

"Thanks," Edie said, taking the tea from the attractive brunette. "And to answer your question, Bev and Karen were getting along fine when we left yesterday morning." She glanced around the large living room, admiring the new furnishings. Gina had redecorated in shades of blue, alternating light and dark hues for contrast. The chair she was sitting on was a beautiful slate-blue color, complemented by pale blue pillows.

Gina sat down in a navy blue recliner across the living room from Edie. "I'm glad. I've worried about those two rooming together."

"That's why I dropped by this morning. I knew you were concerned," Edie said before taking a small sip of the hot liquid. "This tea tastes wonderful."

"Hopefully, it will help you feel better," Gina replied, giving Edie a discerning look.

"You already know my news?"

Gina nodded, her dark eyes twinkling. "Bev told me last night when she called."

"I should've guessed she'd tell you," Edie said, laughing.

"I'm glad somebody did," Gina replied, doing her best to appear hurt.

"I planned to tell you," Edie assured. "I wanted to wait until I knew for sure."

"It sounds like you've been sure for quite a while."

Edie chuckled. "The morning sickness has been a good clue."

"That's why I fixed tea for you. You look pale this morning."

"I forgot how sick I was with Karen," Edie confessed. "This has to be another girl."

"I don't know, I was horribly sick with the twins," Gina countered. "Boys can make you feel just as rotten."

"How are Drake and Jake doing?"

"Fine. They love kindergarten, but they miss Bev terribly—we all do," she added.

"I know. It was hard to leave Karen yesterday, but I had to pretend I was fine when I told her good-bye so that she could handle it." Edie gazed at Gina. "Tell me it gets better."

"I wish. I get so excited whenever Bev calls, then I bawl for an hour when we hang up. I can hardly wait for her to come home next weekend, but I know how hard it will be when she heads back."

Edie smiled. "The joys of motherhood." The two friends sat in contemplative silence for several seconds, reflecting on the changes in their lives.

"Tell me about their roommates," Gina requested.

"Two of the girls seem down to earth. Karen and Bev get along with them very well."

"You're talking about Jesse and Treena?"

"Yes," Edie replied, looking up from her mug of tea. "Jesse and Treena came over to the motel to swim in the pool. Those two are characters."

"No wonder Bev likes them so well," Gina interjected. "She's always saying something about one or the other whenever she calls."

"Does she ever say anything about Meg?"

Gina glanced at Edie. "Tell me Meg's not as bad as Bev makes her out to be."

Edie took another sip of tea before replying. "She's not. I visited with Meg while we were at the apartment. She is serious minded and very goal oriented—"

"And she thinks Bev is too silly," Gina guessed.

"That sums things up. Bev has a sense of humor, and Meg is lacking in that department."

"They'll drive each other crazy," Gina worried.

"Like I told Karen, Meg and Bev will have to come to terms with each other. No one else can do it for them." Edie took another small sip of tea, hoping it would settle her stomach. "The ironic thing is that both girls are going into the medical profession."

"They are?"

Edie nodded. "Meg is in her final year of the two-year RN program."

"And Bev is going into premed."

"Exactly. I think these girls have more in common than they think. They're intelligent, compassionate young women. The problem is, they are both leaders."

"Bev makes a terrible follower," Gina agreed, smiling.

"Bingo. In my opinion, that's the main problem."

Gina breathed out slowly. "May the Force be with Meg."

"And with Karen," Edie added.

"Karen is stuck in the middle trying to play peacemaker?"

"That's my take on the situation."

Gina settled back in the recliner. "The best thing we can do is be supportive, hit our knees on their behalf, and let them resolve the situation."

"Agreed," Edie replied, "although I do think I managed to diffuse Karen while we were there. It could've been an ugly explosion."

"I can't see Karen losing her temper like that."

Edie smiled. "Trust me, I've born the brunt of it before. It's not a pleasant thing. And Karen is one to let things build inside. When something is bothering her, it takes a crowbar to pry it out."

"Bev is just the opposite. You always know exactly where you stand with that young woman," Gina chortled.

"Sometimes I wish Karen was more like that," Edie sighed.

"And I often wish Bev was more like Karen," Gina returned.

"Maybe they'll rub off on each other," Edie said, grinning.

"One can hope." Gina pushed back in the recliner to elevate her legs. "Tell me about the other girl—what's her name?"

"Kassidy," Edie answered.

"Ah, yes, Kassidy . . . the recluse."

"Bev's told you about that?"

"A little," Gina answered. "She said Kassidy spends most of her time lying on her bed or throwing up. Is that true?"

"I'm afraid so," Edie answered. "Karen thinks Kassidy might have an eating disorder."

Gina frowned. "What do you think?"

"I'm not sure. She stayed in her room the entire time we were at the apartment. I poked my head in her bedroom to check on her before we left. She didn't say much. She's a beautiful girl. I don't understand why she would want to starve herself, if that's the problem."

"Bev said that several guys are already chasing Kassidy."

Edie stared down at the mug in her hands. "That isn't necessarily good."

"I know," Gina agreed. She gazed across the living room at Edie. "Does it seem like there are a lot more troubled young people in the world today, or are we old enough now to notice it more?"

"Maybe both."

"I love my new calling with the Young Women," Gina continued, "but most of my Mia Maids come complete with a bundle of troubles."

"I was a bundle of trouble when I was that age."

Gina smiled sadly. "I don't think any of us were perfect."

"Somehow I can't picture you causing anyone grief."

"You didn't know me then," Gina replied. "My past might surprise you."

"Not anymore, nothing surprises me," Edie countered.

"I pushed the boundaries myself a time or two."

Edie took another sip of tea before replying. "I suspect we all do on occasion. That's what worries me about Karen. She never has caused any trouble. We've had our differences, but it was mostly my fault."

"And you're afraid, now that she's away from home, she might make a few mistakes?"

Shrugging, Edie drank the last of the tea and set the mug on one of the coasters that had been placed on the cherry wood coffee table. "The standards taught by our church have always meant so much to Karen. And, compliments of me, she's seen firsthand what can happen when you turn your back to those guidelines."

"So, what are you worried about?"

"The stress load that girl is under."

"Stress load?" Gina repeated, confused.

"It surfaced earlier this year, during the summer. She's still so bitter toward her father. I know it's eating away at her."

Gina smiled sympathetically. "Roger?"

Edie nodded. "It isn't the easiest thing I've ever done, but before Brett and I married, I tried very hard to forgive Roger for everything he did."

"And Karen?"

"She hates him—she's convinced she always will."

Gina tapped the arm of her chair. "You don't think she'll ever forgive him? I never thought Bev would ever forgive me for marrying her father, but things are so much better between us now."

"There's a major difference—you love Bev. Roger has never cared about anyone but himself. Karen's heart wound goes very deep on this one."

"And she won't talk about it?"

"If her reaction the last time I brought it up was any indication, no."

"That bad, eh?"

Edie flinched at the memory. "Remember that temper of hers I was telling you about?"

Gina nodded.

"It was awful. She was so furious she didn't speak to me for almost two days."

"With Bev, whenever she's upset, it's like standing in the middle of a typhoon without an umbrella. But once the storm passes, the sun comes out and all is well."

Laughing, Edie leaned back against her chair. "She *is* very passionate about things."

"I'll say. Which reminds me, did Karen or Bev say anything about Tyler Erickson?"

Edie shook her head. "Now that you mention it, his name never did come up."

Gina played with the arm cover of the recliner. "Maybe I'm wrong, but the last time I saw Tyler with Bev, I could've sworn sparks were flying."

"Karen's certain something's going on, but I don't think they've been on a date yet."

"I guess that's a good thing. Not that I have anything against Tyler, but he's older, ready to settle down, and Bev is so young."

Edie gazed thoughtfully at her friend. "My mom used to tell me that the worries grow right along with your children. I'm afraid she was right."

"That's a cheery thought," Gina groaned. "I can't see Bev married, at least not right now. And she has set so many goals for herself. Someday she'll make an excellent doctor."

"None of us can control the future, for ourselves or our children. We can plan, we can prepare, but this life is meant to be a trial of faith. Sometimes we just have to trust in the Lord."

"Where did that come from?" Gina teased.

"Brett. He told me that the day Karen left for college. I want to protect her from so much, spare her any pain that I've endured."

"I hear you. I feel that way about all three of my children."

"Do you suppose our Father in Heaven ever feels that way about us?"

Gina nodded. "I'm sure He does. He sends us to Earth, knowing we'll each decide who we'll be. He can guide and protect, provide answers to our questions, but we determine the kind of lives we'll lead."

"I know," Edie sighed. "We're told that we need to follow the example He set as a parent, but sometimes, it's so hard. Sometimes you wish you could force your children to do everything the way you think is best."

"But they wouldn't learn." Gina stared at her curtains. "I could lock Bev in a closet until she's thirty, but she wouldn't be happy. She has to be free to make her own choices."

"And if she falls in love with Tyler?" Edie probed.

"I'll have to accept it," Gina conceded. "And if Karen chooses to hate her father the rest of her life?"

"She'll turn into a grumpy old woman."

Gina grinned. "Now, Edie."

"I can't change it," Edie said grudgingly, "but that doesn't mean I have to like it."

"True," Gina said with a smile. "Now, how's that tender stomach of yours?"

"Surprisingly better." Edie smiled.

"Good. After a depressing conversation like that, we need ice cream. Are you up to pralines and cream?"

"Lead on," Edie said as she followed Gina into the kitchen.

Chapter 10

Bev gazed around at the wilting flower beds and wondered why Tyler had brought her here. A series of early frosts had dulled the beauty she knew was usually present in this section of the college campus. Not that she was complaining; at least they were finally starting to spend some time alone.

"What do you think?" Tyler asked. "They call this The Gardens. They say it captures the Spirit of Ricks."

"And what exactly is the Spirit of Ricks?" Bev retorted, wondering what wilted flowers had to do with the college.

"Let's see if I can remember what I heard at the orientation meeting—you should know, you were there: 'This college provides a nurturing, spiritual environment where we students can blossom as the rose,'" he said, extending his arms in a dramatic fashion.

"Now you're being silly," Bev retorted. "These roses are history," she added, taking in what was left of the colorful campus garden. "But I'm sure they were beautiful a couple of weeks ago," she added, laughing at the annoyed look on his face.

"I'll have you know this place is pretty special. They're even changing the name to honor Thomas E. Ricks. And when the flowers aren't dying, they're gorgeous. I came here the first week of school and was very impressed."

"Alone?" Bev asked pointedly. She knew this was a favorite romantic haunt, something Karen had dragged her to see nearly a month ago. She had avoided it since then, hoping Tyler would bring her. True, the flowers were on their last legs, but better late than never.

"Alone?" Tyler teased. "Why would I come here alone?"

"Oh, I see how it is. You're one of those RMs I've been warned about," Bev said, disgruntled. She knew Tyler was too good-looking to escape notice and had seen for herself how other girls gazed longingly at him.

"And what is wrong with being a returned missionary?" he demanded to know.

"Nothing, if you can keep your act together," Bev replied. "Truthfully though, I've never seen so many RMs crowded into one place before. I feel like I'm on display twenty-four-seven," she said, attempting to make him jealous. Two could play at this game. The truth was, she had turned a few heads herself in recent weeks. "BYU–Idaho, the wife-hunting capital of the LDS kingdom, the place where RMs flock by the dozens."

Tyler feigned mock horror. "How disgusting! I guess I hadn't noticed how many RMs there are on campus."

"That's because you're one of them," Bev said, fleeing onto a wooden bridge that crossed a small pond.

"Now you've done it," Tyler panted as he followed behind Bev. He caught her at the middle of the bridge and whirled her around. "You're in major trouble," he threatened.

"I'm scared," Bev retorted, her pulse quickening when Tyler refused to let her go. This was as close as she had ever been to him. Last Tuesday he had held her hand as he had escorted her to the weekly devotional held in the Hart main gym. They had sat together, enthralled by the speaker, a visiting General Authority from the Quorum of the Seventy.

Two nights ago, Tyler had invited her to grab a hamburger and then go bowling on campus at the Manwaring Center. This afternoon, he had positioned himself outside of the Taylor Building, waiting for her as she left her last class of the day, intent on bringing her to see The Gardens. Now, here they were, in the most romantic spot on campus. Did it mean anything?

"I'll have to take drastic measures," Tyler continued.

Bev could tell he was nervous by the way his hands had started to sweat. Content to remain where she was, she wondered if he would finally kiss her.

"Boy, this place is popular." Tyler pointed to two other couples who were walking toward them. He pulled back from Bev, but continued to hold tight to one of her hands. "But no matter, you've insulted the great bastion of manhood," he said, leading her down the bridge toward the pond. "Now you must atone."

Guessing his intent from the mischievous glint in his green eyes, Bev struggled to pull free. "Tyler, let go of me. I swear—"

"Swearing's bad," Tyler said, cutting her off. He grinned as Bev continued to try to pull away. "My mama always said, 'you have to wash those bad words out,'" he said with a drawl, doing a bad imitation of Forrest Gump.

"Tyler! I mean it! You get one hair of my head wet and I'll—"

"You'll what?" Tyler asked, stopping by a large bush inches from the pond.

"I'll kick you!" she promised.

"I already get a kick out of you," he countered, smiling. Pulling her close, he lightly kissed her lips.

Caught off guard, Bev pulled back, too stunned to speak.

"I know I'm a bit rusty, being an RM and everything, but it wasn't that bad, was it?"

Slowly shaking her head, Bev leaned close for another sample. "That was anything but bad," she stammered a few seconds later.

* * *

Bev wandered from the kitchen into the living room of the small apartment and sank onto the couch. It had finally happened—the moment she had dreamed about all summer. Tyler had finally come through. She had looked forward to this for weeks. Why did she feel so strange?

"Bev, why did you set your backpack in the kitchen sink?" Jesse asked from the kitchen.

Flushing, Bev continued to sit in silence on the couch in the living room.

"Bev?" Jesse repeated.

Karen stepped into the living room from the hall and met Jesse's questioning look. "What's up?"

"That's what I'd like to know," Jesse said, pointing to Bev's backpack.

Lifting an eyebrow, Karen walked into the kitchen and lifted Bev's backpack from the sink. "Grab a dish towel," she said to Jesse. "The whole bottom is wet."

"That's because I just finished the dishes," Jesse replied.

"Finally," Karen emphasized.

"I knew as long as I had them done before dinner tonight, I was all right."

Karen wiped off the bottom of the backpack, then set it on the kitchen table. "What is going on with Bev?" she mouthed to Jesse.

Jesse shrugged.

Turning, Karen gazed at her friend. "So, Bev, did anything interesting happen today?"

Bev remained silent, too caught up in her own thoughts to register what Karen had said.

"Bev?" Lifting an eyebrow, Karen walked into the living room and sat down next to Bev on the couch. "What's with you this afternoon?" she asked. "Uh-oh, I detect an interesting fragrance—that aftershave Tyler always wears. Bev, were you with Tyler?"

"What?" Bev responded, snapping out of her dazed reverie.

"I said, how are things with you and Tyler?"

Bev blushed.

"Oh my heck—he kissed you, didn't he?" Karen guessed, laughing.

"Bev owes ice cream?" Jesse said, giving Bev a disgusted look as she moved into the living room. "I thought that would be Kassidy's privilege. But if that's what happened, pay up, Bev! That old Ricks tradition has become a house rule for D-6."

"Look, guys, I don't want to talk about it, okay?" Bev said, rising from the couch.

"Oh, come on," Karen teased, "all this time you've been complaining because he hasn't touched you."

"I'm out of here," Bev said, reaching into the pocket of her jeans for the keys to her Jeep.

Karen looked puzzled. "Bev, what's wrong?"

Bev paused by the front door. "Nothing . . . everything." She ran a hand through her thick, black hair. "I'll be back," she said, opening the door to leave.

"Want some company?" Karen offered.

Bev hesitated. She wanted to talk to Karen but didn't want to make Jesse feel bad by excluding her.

Jesse shoved her hands inside of the pockets of her green khaki pants. "You two go ahead. I need to go up to the computer lab to finish some homework anyway."

"We could drop you off on the way," Bev said, grateful for Jesse's tact. "Where do you need to go?"

"The Romney Building," Jesse replied. "Let me grab my backpack," she said, disappearing down the hall.

"I do want to talk to you, Karen," Bev said quietly, "but not in front of anyone else."

"Okay," Karen responded, moving back into the kitchen to retrieve her purse.

Jesse reappeared with her navy blue backpack. "Let's go."

Nodding, Bev stepped out of the apartment.

* * *

Jesse walked down the hall of the Romney Building, stopping when she reached room 271. She entered the large room and glanced around at the twenty-nine computers that were available to computer science majors. This afternoon, most of the computers were already in use. She spied an open one on the other side of the room and claimed it. Pulling off her backpack, she set it on the floor by the chair, then sat down and focused on the computer screen. Typing in her password, she opened her account on the Linux operating system, ready to tackle the programming assignment she had been given that day.

She began by accessing her e-mail, thrilled to see a message from her mother. They communicated by e-mail at least once a day. Not only did it keep the phone bill down, it was a fun way to keep in touch. They often exchanged humorous e-cards and animated cartoons to brighten the day. Clicking on the message her mother had sent that day, Jesse eagerly scanned through it.

Jesse,

Hope your day is going better than mine. Guess who stopped in to see me? Yep, Penny. I swear that woman is going to drive me crazy. I guess she thinks she needs to keep an eye on me now that you're up in Rexburg. She assumes it's a fair trade-off since Meg is doing such a good job of taking care of you.

Jesse laughed, enjoying her mother's droll sense of humor.

Penny thinks she's found the perfect guy for me—again! This time Mr. Perfect's name is Charlie, another loser who's divorced like me.

Frowning, Jesse wished her mother would quit referring to herself as a loser. She also wished Penny would quit trying to find her mother a boyfriend. A part of her still hoped her parents would get back together.

Don't worry, I'm sure this date will turn out like all the others I've been on. I'll have a horrible time, then I'll promise to never put myself through that ordeal again, until Penny comes up with someone else. Oh, well, she's bound to run out of available bodies soon. How many single LDS men can there be in St. George . . . that are under the age of fifty? I realize we're the retirement capital of the West, but I want to make it perfectly clear that I'm not looking for anyone who thinks denture cream is an ideal topic of conversation.

Chuckling, Jesse read the rest of the message, then began typing a reply.

Dear Mom,

It sounds like you've had an interesting day. Tell Meg's mom to get a life. With five kids still at home, you'd think she'd have more to do than to try to set you up.

Things are interesting here. I think Bev is falling in love. She came home from school and set her backpack in the kitchen sink. When we tried to ask her about her day, she just sat there in this stupor. I can't believe she's sinking so low! She has that same sappy look on her face that we see on Kassidy's from time to time. How disgusting!

Karen's with Bev right now trying to get the latest scoop.

Jesse clenched her fists, doing her best to ignore how left out that made her feel. She felt closer to Bev and Karen than she had ever felt to any of her friends in high school. The fact that there were still things that Bev would only share with Karen hurt.

I guess there's a reason why Karen's going into journalism: she's good at digging for details.

Jesse reread what she had typed and frowned. She erased the last sentence and tried to sound more upbeat with the rest of her message.

* * *

Karen glanced at Bev, concerned. Bev had remained silent on their trip to the local park, her frown deepening with each passing minute. Karen brushed a strand of blonde hair away from her face, relieved when Bev finally pulled the Jeep along the curb and shut off the engine. Karen waited, taking her cues from Bev.

"Let's get some air," Bev suggested, stepping down out of the Jeep.

Karen opened the door on her side and lowered herself to the ground. She followed Bev to a deserted picnic table and sat down next to her friend.

"You were right. Tyler kissed me this afternoon," Bev admitted, her face reddening.

"I'm sorry about the cracks we made earlier," Karen apologized.

"The thing is . . . it was great!"

"Then why—"

"I don't know," Bev said, cutting Karen off. She rested an elbow on the table. "I'm feeling so many things right now. It's stupid! It's not like he's the first guy who's ever kissed me."

"I know," Karen said, smiling. She could remember the details that surrounded Bev's first kiss, something that had happened during their junior year of high school.

"Why is this so different?"

"Tell me what you're feeling."

Bev groaned. "Like I'm floating on clouds—but I'm scared, too."

Karen studied the perplexed expression on Bev's face. "Are you in love with Tyler?"

Rising, Bev walked to a nearby tree and gave it a vicious kick. "Ow!"

"What did you do that for?" Karen asked, stifling a grin as Bev limped back to the table.

"I'm trying to jar myself back to reality. The thing is, I can't fall in love right now."

"Why not?"

Bev gave Karen a pained look. "I'm going to be a surgeon when I grow up, remember?"

"Who says you can't do both?"

"Both?"

Karen gave Bev a gentle nudge. "There are a lot of surgeons who are married."

Bev's face colored again. "Who said anything about marriage?"

"Bev, if you've got it this bad for Tyler, I'd say it's only a matter of time."

Bev glowered at Karen. "He kissed me, okay? He didn't propose."

"Yet," Karen added, her brown eyes glistening as it hit her how much she would miss Bev if she married Tyler. "I've seen that look before."

"No way. I have *never* felt like this before!"

"Not on *your* face . . . on my mother's," Karen explained, "when she started dating Brett."

"Oh," Bev replied, breathing out slowly. "That's not good."

"No, it isn't. It would change all of our plans."

Bev nodded.

"It would be a terrible thing for you to fall in love and get married. That means I'd have to put up with Meg all by myself," Karen teased, doing her best to smile.

"Jesse would help you."

"That's a comfort," Karen said, shaking her head.

Bev sank down on the wooden bench of the table. "I'm not ready for this."

"If it's meant to be . . ." Karen ventured.

"I know! We'll find you a guy right away! We'll have a double wedding, then find apartments in the same complex. After we've all graduated from college, we'll find jobs in the same town—live on the same street. Our kids will play together . . ." Bev said, tearing up. "It's all going to change, isn't it?"

Karen nodded.

"Why does this have to happen now?"

Silently asking the same question, Karen stared at a distant tree as her friend continued to bemoan an uncertain future.

Chapter 11

Gina smiled as Bev began gathering dishes from the dining room table. Her stepdaughter had matured so much the past month. All summer she had begged Bev to help her with the dishes. Now, without a word, the young woman had already started to clean up the mess that had been made during dinner.

"Well, if you two are going to clean up, I think I'll take the twins out back for a quick game of football," James Henderson said, smiling at his two young sons.

"Yay!" Jake said as he bolted from the dining room to retrieve his Nerf football. Drake raced behind him.

"Be careful," Gina insisted, smiling as James pulled her close for a kiss. When James left the room, she turned and caught the troubled look on her stepdaughter's face. Picking up an empty casserole dish, she followed Bev into the kitchen. "So, what's going on with you?"

"What do you mean?" Bev asked as she started rinsing dishes in the sink.

"That look on your face speaks volumes."

Bev set another plate inside the dishwasher, then straightened to face her stepmother. "How did you know you were in love with Dad?"

Gina chewed her bottom lip. It was what she had feared: Bev was falling for Tyler. "The way I felt when we were together was a big clue."

"How did you feel?"

"You ask tough questions," Gina replied, laughing. "There was a physical attraction between us," she said, flushing slightly, "but it was more than that. I felt happy, kind of light inside. It was always comfortable between us. And we were good friends. We could talk about anything." She gazed steadily at Bev. "Sound familiar?"

Bev returned Gina's intense gaze. "Yes."

"I was afraid of that." Gina pointed to the stools near the kitchen counter. "Sit and tell me about it." She sat down and waited until Bev was sitting beside her. "Let's hear it."

For several minutes, Bev shared details of the dates she had been on with Tyler, including how she had felt when he had finally kissed her. "It was everything I thought it would be," she said, turning crimson. "But now I'm scared."

"Why are you scared?"

"Am I ready for this? What if he doesn't feel the same way? What about all of my plans?"

"You sound confused," Gina observed.

Bev nodded miserably.

"Have you talked to Tyler since he kissed you?"

"Briefly. He came by before we left this afternoon. He had decided not to come home with us and stopped to say good-bye."

"And?"

"We kidded around like we always do."

"You didn't talk about what happened between you two the day before?" Gina asked.

"No. I think we were both avoiding that subject."

"Did he kiss you before you left?"

Bev blushed.

"Okay, I think I got my answer."

"It wasn't like before, though. It was quick, over before it started. Of course, Karen was watching . . . and half of Baronnessa."

"And on Thursday you were by yourselves."

Bev nodded.

"In a very romantic setting."

Bev's blush deepened. "You think it was the location that made the difference? I mean, Thursday it was like . . . Well, there aren't words to describe it."

Gina lifted an eyebrow. "That isn't exactly what a mother likes to hear," she teased.

"You know what I mean."

Nodding, Gina laughed, letting her stepdaughter off the hook.

"Today it was like I had been kissed by my cousin. What's going on with me? Why would it feel so different?"

Gina smiled. "I would say it's because you're both nervous. The thing is, Bev, you've crossed that line: you're no longer *just friends*. You've started a physical relationship. My advice would be to take it slow and see what happens."

"How do I know if he's the one?"

"I'm not sure there is only one right person for you. But if you're lucky enough to find someone to love, don't be afraid of it. Don't rush into it either. Give it time to develop into something special."

"Like what you and Dad have?"

"Right."

"Will I know if I'm in love with Tyler?"

"I would hope so. But it's different for everyone. Some people seem to fall head over heels from the beginning. Others start a comfortable friendship that transforms into love with the passage of time."

"Why is this so complicated?" Bev groaned. "How will I ever figure things out?"

"Let me ask you this: how would you feel if Tyler started seeing someone else?"

"I'd kill him!"

"So you do have some strong feelings for him."

Bev frowned. "Quit it. You have the same look in your eye that Karen has had lately."

"What look?"

"That sad, puppy-dog look."

"It's because we both love you, and we sense where this is heading." Gina reached across the counter to squeeze Bev's hand. "We're happy for you, but sad for us."

"I feel the same way."

"You do?"

Bev nodded. "I feel happy for me, but sad for me."

Gina laughed. "Love isn't a bad thing, you know."

"It's not what I had planned right now."

"Life seldom is," Gina replied, slipping down from her stool to give Bev a hug.

* * *

"How was your weekend?" Bev prompted late Sunday afternoon as she drove herself and Karen back to Rexburg.

"Nice, kind of strange, but nice."

"Strange?"

"It's different now," Karen explained. "Mom and Brett treat me more like a guest than family."

"It was like that for me, too, part of the time." Bev smiled as she reflected on the long talks she'd had with Gina. "But I'm glad we came home this weekend."

"Me too," Karen agreed. "Did you tell Gina about Tyler?"

"Is there any doubt?" Bev asked, focusing on the passing landscape. The sun was setting over a distant mountain range, spreading radiant bursts of pink and orange across the darkening sky. Crooked rows of pine trees crowded along the side of the road.

"All she had to do is take one look at your face," Karen teased.

"It's not *that* bad," Bev argued.

"Right," Karen replied. "Did she give you good advice?"

Bev nodded, skillfully maneuvering the Jeep around a large rock that had rolled down onto the road.

"Okay, let's hear it."

"She said that I need to give it time and see where this relationship is heading before I panic. She also believes the same thing you do."

"Oh?" Karen quizzed.

"She thinks wedding bells might be in the near future," Bev said, glancing at Karen. "Don't look so smug! Things can change, you know."

"I know," Karen said, frowning.

"Now what are you looking so somber about?"

"I hate growing up," Karen announced.

"Me, too. It takes all the fun out of life."

"Then let's promise to never allow that to happen."

"Agreed," Bev said, grinning at Karen. "I say we start by eating lunch at McDonald's tomorrow."

"McDonald's?"

"Yeah, we'll order the Happy Meal. Jake and Drake told me they have cool toys this month, characters from some Disney movie they saw last week."

"Good deal," Karen replied, her mood brightening. "Happy Meals here we come. I'll meet you around noon tomorrow in front of the Snow Building."

"You're on!" Bev exclaimed. "We'll celebrate the passage of our childhood with style!"

* * *

Kassidy opened the front door of the apartment and peered inside. Meg wasn't at her usual position studying at the kitchen table, but it was Sunday. Meg had made it clear that studying on Sunday was a cardinal sin. Kassidy wondered what Meg would say about the bag of food she had purchased earlier that evening. Deciding she didn't care, she entered the apartment and shut the door. She walked to the bedroom she shared with Treena and stepped inside, closing the door behind her. Treena was at a Relief Society board meeting; she had been called to serve as a Relief Society teacher. "More power to you, Treena," she muttered under her breath. "Get enough brownie points to save us both." She set the bag on her bed, then locked the bedroom door. *I should have at least an hour before she gets back,* Kassidy thought, sitting on her bed. Picking up the bag, she dumped out two packages of cookies, a small container of chocolate milk, and a bag of miniature Snickers bars. She ignored the familiar feeling of self-loathing and tore open the nearest bag of cookies to begin her frenzied feast.

* * *

As Bev drove up the street that led to the Baronnessa Apartment complex, she spotted a lone figure walking beside the road near a street lamp. "Hey, isn't that Treena?"

Karen followed Bev's gaze. "It looks like her. What's she doing out tromping alone at night?"

"I don't know, but I'm picking her up," Bev said as she drove past Baronnessa to where they had spotted Treena.

"You two have good timing," Treena said when she climbed into the back seat of Bev's Jeep.

"Yeah, well, I'm glad we came along. You're not supposed to be out walking by yourself," Bev chided, shaking her finger at her roommate. "Bad things can happen to girls when they wander around by themselves at night."

"Oh, right! Guys don't even give me a second glance," Treena quipped. "Now, if I looked like Kassidy, I might have something to worry about."

Karen wondered if Treena was as lighthearted about that as she sounded. "Where have you been?"

"I had a Relief Society board meeting."

"Don't they hold those in the Baronnessa lounge?" Karen asked.

"They did last time. The thing is, since they changed the boundaries for the student wards, we're mixed in with that apartment complex up the street. Tonight the meeting was held in their lounge."

"I see," Karen replied.

"Did you miss us?" Bev asked as she pulled into the Baronnessa parking lot. She drove around searching for a place to park, silently cussing the cramped blacktop.

"Is there any doubt? Meg and Jesse were at each other's throats most of the weekend."

Bev shook her head. "I don't suppose Jesse came off the triumphant winner?"

"Not even. Meg tends to get her own way."

"That's for sure. Did she drag you all to church this morning?" Bev asked as she finally spotted a vacant parking place.

Treena smiled. "Yep. She even got Kassidy to go."

"That's great," Karen exclaimed.

"Yeah, I figured Kass would come around eventually. She'll get more involved in things."

Karen glanced over the seat at Treena. "I hope so."

"Boy, am I glad I finally found a place to park!" Bev exclaimed as she shut off the engine. She handed her keys to Karen and climbed out of the Jeep.

"In a hurry?" Karen asked.

"I'm in need of *the facilities,* as Jesse would say," Bev called over her shoulder, sprinting for the apartment stairs. "I'll come back later for my suitcase."

"I'll bring it up for you," Treena offered, following Karen to the back of the Jeep.

"Thanks," Bev hollered as she began to run up the stairs to the middle row of apartments in their building. She held her breath, hoping the door to their apartment was unlocked. Finding that it was, she offered a silent prayer of thanks and hurried inside. As she made her way down the hall, she noticed the water was running in the sink. Puzzled, she glanced around, but could see no one. She turned it off, then understood who had most likely left it running. The noise from the water had masked that someone was throwing up in the second bathroom. Betting it was Kassidy, Bev slipped inside the first bathroom and shut the door.

* * *

Certain she was in for another lecture, Kassidy lay down on her bed and gazed up at the ceiling, at the white swirled patterns that had recently been painted.

"Why do you keep doing this to yourself?" Treena asked, sitting down on Kassidy's bed.

Kassidy's gaze shifted to her quilted bedspread, a gift from her paternal grandmother. A southwestern design, it was done in shades of blue and green.

"You're killing yourself! You know that, don't you? And why? What is so wrong with gaining a little weight?"

"Do you know what I would look like if I ate like you?" Kassidy asked, her blue eyes flashing as she glared at Treena.

"Thanks," Treena mumbled.

"I didn't mean it that way. You're lucky, you can eat things and it doesn't matter. It blends with how you look normally."

"Uh-huh, so it's okay if I look a little chubby but not you?"

Kassidy groaned and closed her eyes.

"Kassidy, you promised to quit doing this. Remember last spring when I almost took you to the ER? You said you would stop making yourself throw up."

"I've tried!"

"Not hard enough. The thing is, Karen and Bev aren't stupid. I'm sure Meg has suspicions. Jesse never says anything about it, but you're not keeping this a secret anymore!"

"I'll quit. Don't say anything. I promise I'll quit."

"I've heard this before," Treena said wearily.

"Give me another chance," Kassidy begged, her eyes filling with fresh tears.

"I don't know, Kass, I think you've got a serious problem."

"I'll quit throwing up—and I'll eat healthy things, I promise!"

Treena hesitated.

"Please, Treena. I know it's wrong and I'll quit. I promise I'll quit." Her face contorted with guilty pain.

"Oh, all right. But I promise, Kassidy, if you start in again, I'll tell everyone what's going on. I will not stand by and watch you kill yourself!"

"Thanks," Kassidy breathed, relieved. "I'll be fine. You'll see. I won't do this anymore."

Looking unconvinced, Treena slowly nodded.

Chapter 12

Kassidy waited as the young man she had met last week came around to her side of the car to open the door for her. She smiled demurely as Jay helped her onto the sidewalk. Tall, with thick blonde hair, Jay was a returned missionary, someone Kassidy had met at the campus library. She had been working on a theme for her English class when Jay had approached her table. Sitting down across from her, he had initiated a conversation, explaining that he had wanted to talk to her for nearly two weeks. He had then invited her to the classical concert that had been held last Thursday, something they had both needed to attend for a humanities class. She had agreed to go, and now here they were, in front of Pizza Hut for their second date.

Jay continued to hold onto Kassidy's hand as he guided her toward the pizza parlor. Annoyed, she wondered why most guys thought the perfect evening included getting something to eat.

"Where do you want to sit?" Jay asked, glancing around the busy restaurant.

"Wherever you'd like," she replied as she began the charade of having a good time.

"How about over there in the corner for a little privacy?"

Kassidy lifted an eyebrow. Jay was attractive, which was why she had agreed to go out with him a second time, but she felt he was coming on a bit strong. At the apartment, when he had stopped to pick her up, he had seemed jealous when she had kidded around with Bev's boyfriend, Tyler. She had enjoyed the look of frustration on her roommate's face and the embarrassed look on Tyler's. What she hadn't liked was the dark look on Jay's face.

Inside Pizza Hut, she allowed Jay to escort her to the secluded corner and sat down across from him. She had already decided this would be her final date with Mr. Jay Michaels. True, he drove a nice car, but she didn't like the possessive traits that were surfacing.

A waitress brought menus and glasses of ice water to their table. Kassidy glanced at the menu and decided to order a small salad.

"What are you majoring in?" Jay asked before reaching for his glass. "I forgot to ask you Thursday night."

"General studies," Kassidy replied dryly. Last week, Jay had been too busy telling her about his mission heroics to let her get a word in.

"General studies," Jay repeated. "That's a good way to get some of those required classes out of the way before you decide what to do."

"I can't decide what to major in," Kassidy said. She sipped at her water to avoid Jay's searching gaze.

"Not me. I've always known what I want to do with my life."

"Oh," Kassidy said, pretending to study her nails. She noticed the nail on her right ring finger was chipped. Sighing, she knew she would have to redo all of her nails tonight. Sometimes she envied Treena, who rarely painted her nails, caring little for how long they were. How would it be to live as though poise and appearance weren't key factors in life?

"I've always wanted to be a lawyer. That's where the money is, you know. Law. Right now I'm saving everything I can to get into a better school, which is why we're eating pizza tonight. But someday that'll change. Lawyers make good money—they live the good life."

"Is that a fact?" she said, stifling a yawn. Her father was a lawyer and was a very wealthy man. In her opinion, that didn't mean he lived the 'good life'.

"Who knows, maybe I'll even get involved in politics."

"You'll run for President?" Kassidy asked, amused.

"No, I wouldn't aim that big—maybe governor," he answered, staring briefly into space.

Kassidy rolled her eyes. This was the kind of guy her mother wanted her to marry. Good-looking, ambitious, someone intent on making money. She smirked, imagining her mother as she bragged to her friends. *Kassidy married a lawyer. He's going to be a governor someday. I always said my daughter would go places.*

" . . . and so, of course, I have to be careful about who I marry. It would have to be someone who would be well liked by the media . . . someone like you," Jay said.

Kassidy snapped out back to reality to stare at Jay. Was this guy for real? "Jay, you can't be serious!"

"I know, I'm getting ahead of myself," Jay interrupted, "but there's a natural chemistry between us. I knew there would be. The first time I saw you, I knew you were the one. I even prayed about it, and I had a very strong impression that I needed to meet you."

"You seem like a nice enough guy," Kassidy began, "but I don't think—"

The waitress reappeared. "Have you decided what you would like?"

"We'll take a medium Chicago Special with everything but onions," Jay responded as he gathered the menus.

"Anything else?" the waitress asked as she took the menus from Jay's outstretched hand.

"I'd like a salad," Kassidy said, her blue eyes flashing.

"Oh, sure, bring us both dinner salads while we wait for the pizza."

"I don't want pizza!" Kassidy exclaimed.

Jay was clearly embarrassed by her response. "Why didn't you say so earlier?"

"You didn't ask," Kassidy tersely replied.

"Maybe I should give you a few more minutes," the waitress suggested.

"No, just bring what he ordered," Kassidy directed.

"That was awkward," Jay said, the dark look returning to his face.

"Sorry, but you didn't ask me what I wanted."

"Everyone likes the Chicago Special."

"I'm not everyone," Kassidy retorted.

Jay forced a smile. "Which is why I want to get to know you better. You are different, a cut above the crowd."

Kassidy cringed. She knew what he really meant: she was pretty. It had been that way her entire life; people had always treated her a certain way because of how she looked. No one cared about who she was, no one except for Treena.

Somehow Kassidy made it through the rest of the date. She let Jay do most of the talking, something he seemed happy to do. She learned that he had grown up in the Boise area. His father had served in the state senate, which was probably why Jay had such an interest in politics. His mother had stayed at home to raise Jay and his three brothers. Of course Jay's mother was a beautiful woman, capable of anything—a potential mother-in-law from Hades, in Kassidy's opinion.

"You've hardly touched your slice of pizza," Jay said, motioning to Kassidy's plate several minutes later.

"I'm not hungry. The salad filled me."

Jay laughed. "If it helps you keep that figure, I won't push."

Kassidy glowered at him, but he didn't notice as he stood and reached into his back pocket for his wallet.

"I'll go pay the bill. I'll be back in a few minutes."

"Don't hurry on my account," she muttered under her breath. She drank the last of the ice water in her glass, then stood, anxious to return home and end this disastrous date.

* * *

"I'm sorry you have such a headache," Jay said as he walked Kassidy up to her apartment. "I thought you'd enjoy seeing a movie tonight."

"The headache started during dinner," Kassidy lied. "I'm not up to a movie tonight."

"Okay, well, maybe next time."

"Maybe," Kassidy said, vowing to herself that there would never be a next time. She could hardly wait to get away from this guy. When they arrived at her apartment, she reached for the doorknob, relieved to escape Jay's egotistical manner.

"Not even a handshake?" Jay asked, sounding hurt.

"Oh, all right," Kassidy grumbled as she turned to shake his hand.

He gripped her hand inside of his own. "Kassidy, you do believe in the power of the priesthood?"

Confused, Kassidy nodded.

"I know things weren't perfect tonight, but you and I are meant to be together. I've had a personal revelation that confirms this."

"You're kidding," she replied, wishing she had followed her first inclination to head inside the apartment and close the door in his face.

"As a priesthood holder, I'm entitled to this kind of direct revelation."

Kassidy stared at Jay. What was he talking about? She flinched when he leaned close to kiss her. "Jay! Stop it! I don't want to kiss you!"

"C'mon, Kassidy. I know you want to."

"No, I don't!" Kassidy insisted as she struggled to escape his tight grip.

"Is this guy bothering you?" a familiar voice asked.

"Gary—thank heavens you're here," Kassidy said, pulling away from Jay to hurry to her family home evening brother's side.

"Who are you?" Jay demanded indignantly.

"Someone who thinks you had better move on," Gary Dawson said, standing protectively between Jay and Kassidy.

Kassidy gave Gary a grateful smile. He was two inches shorter than Jay, but was solidly built, broad through the shoulders, but narrow through the waist. His strong muscles testified of the years he had worked with his father on a ranch near Ashton, Idaho.

Jay's blue eyes smoldered with resentment. "Kassidy, you know what I've told you is true. If you're in tune at all, you'll know," he said, brushing past Gary. "I'll be in touch," he added before disappearing.

"Are you all right?" Gary asked, focusing on Kassidy.

"That guy's wacked out," Kassidy said, trembling. "I just met him last week, and he acts like he owns me."

"Did he hurt you?"

Kassidy shook her head.

"You're shivering. Let's go inside your apartment and see if Treena's around," Gary invited. "It's locked," he added as he tried the door.

"I have my key." Kassidy rummaged through the small black purse she had brought with her until she found it. She then handed the key to Gary and waited as he unlocked the door.

He reached inside the apartment to flip on the living room light. "Hello?" he called out. "I don't think anyone's here," he said, motioning for Kassidy to step inside.

"Treena had to work tonight," Kassidy said, only too glad to enter the sanctuary of her apartment. "Bev's probably with Tyler—he was over earlier tonight. I have no idea where the other three are."

"I'm not leaving you here alone. That weirdo might come back."

"I can lock the door," Kassidy replied.

"I'd still feel better if someone was here with you. I'll stick around, but first I need to make a phone call. I was heading over to Jennifer's apartment to help her study for a Spanish test."

"You speak Spanish?"

He nodded. "I served a mission in South America . . . Argentina."

"I didn't know that," she said, gazing with interest at Gary. He wasn't as handsome as Jay, but she felt safe around him. He was friendlier than their other family home evening brothers. Gary had been willing to lend a hand anytime they had needed him since school had first started.

"Is it okay if I use your phone?"

Kassidy nodded, sitting on the couch. While Gary was preoccupied on the telephone, she studied his profile. He had a rugged look that was attractive. His short brown hair was a little unruly, but it was the warmth that radiated from his brown eyes that really captured her attention. He seemed so sure of himself. She had heard him talk in church last week and had been impressed with his knowledge of the gospel. Why couldn't a nice guy like him show up in her life? Why did it always have to be someone like Jay?

* * *

"I told Jennifer I'd come over later," Gary said, hanging up the phone. Turning he smiled reassuringly at Kassidy. She still seemed shaken by her encounter.

"You didn't tell her what happened with me and Jay?" Kassidy asked, frowning.

Gary walked over to a nearby chair and sat down. "I told her that a friend needed me and I'd be over as soon as I could."

"Is Jennifer your girlfriend?"

Gary grinned. "We've been out a couple of times. We're mostly friends. She's in our student ward, you know. She just lives a couple of apartments down from your apartment."

"I know," she said quietly.

"It looked like this jerk you were out with tonight wanted to be more than friends," Gary said, focusing his brown eyes on her face. Kassidy Martin was easily one of the most beautiful girls he had ever met. It bothered him that she looked so sad.

"If I'd had any idea what he was like, I never would've agreed to go out with him!"

"Like my mother is always warning my sisters, some guys can do quite a song and dance. They hide who they really are." Gary paused as the truthfulness of his mother's advice hit home. At the beginning of the year, he had thought that Kassidy was a rich, spoiled beauty. As time went on, he was beginning to think there was more behind Kassidy's cold facade than what had first appeared. He had seen a sorrowful look in her blue eyes on more than one occasion. During last week's family home evening session, he had picked up on some unspoken tension between Kassidy and Treena. He knew Treena was Kassidy's closest friend but sensed something was wrong. Since school had started, he had also caught the unsubtle hints dropped by Bev and Jesse that Kassidy had some major problems.

"Gary, can I ask you something?"

"Sure."

"It's about the priesthood. Is there some unwritten code that only priesthood holders are entitled to personal revelation?"

Gary breathed out slowly. This was going to be an interesting conversation.

"I always thought that everyone was entitled to that sort of thing."

"They are," Gary agreed, "but only if they're living righteous lives."

Kassidy's frown deepened. "So if a worthy priesthood holder gets a revelation that he's supposed to marry a certain girl, that's how it's supposed to be?"

Perplexed, Gary gazed down at his hands. What was Kassidy getting at?

"Even if the girl doesn't feel the same way?" Kassidy continued.

"Is that the load of bullarky that guy tried to shove at you tonight?" Gary asked, finally guessing what was behind Kassidy's question.

Kassidy nodded.

"I knew I should've thrown his rear down the stairs!"

"But maybe he's right. Maybe I'm the one who's mixed up."

"Kassidy, do you like the guy?"

She shook her head vigorously.

"There's your answer. Follow your heart. You're entitled to as much personal revelation as he is! It makes me furious when I hear about guys who try to use the priesthood to get their own way or to dominate others. It's wrong. That's not what it's for!"

"What is it for?" she asked.

Gary reflected on what he knew about Kassidy. Treena had told him that Kassidy's mother was a member of the LDS Church but had been too caught up in social circles to get involved in service-oriented callings. Her father claimed he had no use for religion—Treena didn't know if he even belonged to a church. As a result, there was probably a lot about the LDS Church that Kassidy didn't understand.

"Is it a secret?" Kassidy prompted.

"No, and you've probably heard this before. The priesthood is the authority to act in God's name. Through that sacred gift we can bless the sick, administer sacred ordinances, and help people relearn that they're beloved children of God."

"Like when you served your mission?"

Gary nodded. "You can serve a mission too, someday, if you want. You don't have to hold the priesthood to do that. In my opinion, women don't need the priesthood to stay close to their Father in Heaven."

"You believe that women are as important as men?"

"More so," Gary grinned. "My dad may run the farm, but it's my mother who keeps us in line."

"Your mother must be a wonderful woman," Kassidy said wistfully.

"She is. She's a character, but what a rock in the Church. She's got a heart of gold. She'd do anything for anybody."

"You must love her a lot."

"I do, and someday I'd like to find a girl just like her."

Kassidy stared down at the carpeted floor, a pained look on her face.

"Greetings all," Bev sang out as she entered the apartment with Tyler. "Gary, what are you doing here?"

Gary glanced at Kassidy, still troubled by the expression on her face. "Kassidy, I think you need to tell your roommates about this guy, in case there's trouble later."

Bev sat down on a kitchen chair. "That guy you went out with tonight? Jay something?"

Kassidy slowly nodded.

"What did he do?" Bev asked.

Gary saw the flush in Kassidy's face and knew she wasn't about to explain what had happened. "He's convinced Kassidy is meant to be his wife."

"Only in his dreams!" Kassidy snapped.

"Really?" Bev responded as a smile tugged at the corners of her mouth.

Gary shook his head at Bev; this was not the time to indulge in lighthearted banter. By now he knew Bev well enough to know that she enjoyed teasing her roommates.

"Are you okay, Kassidy?" Tyler asked.

"Yeah . . . great . . . fine," was the terse reply.

"Are you here for the night?" Gary asked, silently pleading with Bev to show more compassion toward Kassidy.

"Yep," Bev said, still grinning.

"Good. I need to leave, but call me if that jerk comes back," Gary said to Kassidy.

"Yeah, sure," Kassidy murmured before retreating to her bedroom.

"She's really upset, isn't she," Bev said, surprised.

"You might say that. That's why I stayed—I didn't think she should be alone," Gary said as he moved to the front door. "See if you can get her to tell you what happened. And I meant what I said, if that guy shows up again, call me. I'll set him straight in a hurry!" he said as he walked out the door and closed it behind him.

* * *

"That's interesting," Tyler said as he continued to stare at the closed front door.

"What?"

"Did you see the look on Gary's face? I think he likes Kassidy."

"Gary?"

Tyler nodded.

Bev glanced at the door, then at Tyler. "You're way off. Gary's one of our family home evening brothers. He's just being nice. He doesn't have feelings for Kassidy."

"We'll see," Tyler replied.

"He's not her type. She likes them tall, good-looking, and loaded with money!"

"And she can probably hear every word you're saying," Tyler rebuffed.

"So? Maybe she needs a reality check once in a while," Bev said as she closed the door that led to the hall. "There, now she can't hear a word. Happy, sweet cheeks?"

"Now I am," he said, pulling her close for a kiss.

Chapter 13

As the annual homecoming celebration drew close, Jesse began speculating on her roommates' prospects. She pulled herself up to sit on the cluttered bathroom counter of their apartment and began counting on her fingers. "Let's see: Tyler will take Bev to the dance, Kassidy will have to settle on someone from her all-male harem, Meg will spend the night studying up on campus, Kassidy will probably set Treena up with someone. Karen . . . now that's tougher. She's been out with a couple of different guys, but nothing has clicked; I'm sure she'll get asked, though. That leaves me," Jesse said, turning to stare at her reflection in the mirror. "I am *not* going with Meg to study on campus! Maybe that would be a good night to hit a movie. I'll borrow Bev's Jeep and head down to Idaho Falls. Tyler drives her everywhere, so it's not like she needs her car."

"What do I need?" Bev asked as she stepped into the hall.

Startled, Jesse jumped down from the counter. "When did you get home?" she asked, relieved that it was Bev. Meg would have ripped into her for sitting on the counter.

"A few minutes ago. I understand you'd like to borrow my Jeep."

Jesse shrugged, embarrassed that Bev had overheard the conversation she had had with herself.

"What makes you think you won't get asked to the homecoming dance?"

"Maybe the fact that I've never been asked to a dance before."

Bev glanced in the mirror and flipped a stray piece of black hair back into place. "I think we should all get dates and plan a fun evening together."

"Right! Meg'll really go for that!"

"She might. I happen to know someone who wants to take her out."

Jesse stared at Bev. "No way!"

"Yes way!"

"Who?"

Bev smiled. "I can't say, but I know someone is trying to get up enough nerve to ask her to the dance."

"Did you have anything to do with it?"

"Me?" Bev asked, gesturing to herself.

"I knew it! Whose arm did you twist?"

"There was no arm twisting involved . . . maybe some bribery."

"Bribery?"

"You aren't the only one who wants to use my Jeep," Bev replied. "I made a deal."

"Meg will be furious when she finds out!"

"She'll never know, right?"

"These lips are sealed," Jesse promised.

"Besides, this guy likes her. He thinks she's pretty, a bit stand-offish but very pretty. I assured him that she was shy."

"And he fell for that?" Jesse gawked, dumbfounded.

"Maybe it's true."

"And maybe the Pope will join our church."

"It could happen," Bev countered, "*if* he met the right pair of missionaries."

Jesse glanced around to make sure no one else could overhear. "Who is it?"

Bev paused as if debating with herself. "Ryan Smith," she finally whispered.

Jesse's mouth fell open in shock. "Ryan?"

"You know, the guy who helps Meg with the activities in our ward."

"Meg hates him."

Bev laughed it off. "You know that old adage about how opposites attract?"

"Those two are about as different as night and day," Jesse interjected.

"Exactly, which is why I'm thinking there will be a natural attraction between them. Ryan's full of life, has a sense of humor, loves a good time—"

"Meg is crabby, grumpy, likes being alone—"

"Which is why we need to draw her out of her shell!"

Jesse gazed in amazement at Bev. "You just want to get her married off."

"I have your best interests at heart. If I don't come back next semester—"

"Compliments of lover boy," Jesse said, disgusted.

"I won't be here to keep Meg in line," Bev continued.

"True," Jesse sighed.

"Will you help me with this?"

Jesse exhaled deeply.

"Please?"

"Karen already said no, huh?"

Bev nodded.

"I'm in," Jesse said, smiling. "But don't start lining me up."

"I won't," Bev promised, the grin on her face insinuating that someone else might.

* * *

Kassidy shivered as she walked along the campus sidewalk. She wished she had worn a jacket, but earlier that morning it had seemed warm. The Rexburg wind had changed things in a hurry. She blew on her hands then jumped, startled, when someone honked a horn.

"Kassidy, you're freezing. Come on, I'll give you a ride," Jay Michaels offered, pulling his blue sports car beside the sidewalk.

"Jay, I'm not interested, okay? I've already told you that a hundred times!"

"It's just a ride."

"With you it's never *just a ride*. No thanks," Kassidy said as she turned away from Jay and moved down the sidewalk. She shuddered when Jay tore off down the road, his tires squealing his frustration. "I wish he would leave me alone," she muttered as a different kind of cold crept inside her heart.

"I wish he would too."

Kassidy looked up to see Gary standing in front of her. "Where did you come from?"

"Weed Science."

"Weed Science?" she repeated.

"I'm learning how to weed things out. Want some help in that department with Jay?"

Smiling, Kassidy wished it were that easy. Everywhere she went, there was Jay, intent on convincing her that they were a match made in heaven. "Weed Science, huh? That sounds interesting. What are you majoring in?"

"I'm going for a Bachelor's degree in Agronomy."

"Agro what?" she asked, confused.

"It's a fancy way to say that I want to be a farmer when I grow up."

Kassidy laughed, picturing Gary in a pair of old bib overalls, standing with a pitchfork, reminiscent of the famous painting *American Gothic* by Grant Wood.

"What are you majoring in?"

"I'm taking general requirements. I'm not sure what I want to be when I grow up."

"That's a tough decision to make," Gary agreed.

"Have you always known you wanted to be a farmer?"

Gary nodded. "I've always enjoyed helping Dad on our farm. I love animals and watching the crops grow. I even get a kick out of baling hay."

"Baling hay?" she asked, confused.

"We Idaho farmers are good, but we haven't figured out how to produce hay that grows naturally in attractive bundles. We use mechanical contraptions to take care of that for us. It's called baling. Then in the winter months when the animals need something to eat, we feed them bales of hay."

"This is going to sound like a stupid question, but what exactly is hay?"

"Hay . . . dried alfalfa," he explained. "We grow it during the spring and summer, cut it, dry it—"

"And bale it," she said, cutting him off. "I get it now." She grinned. "I've never seen a real farm before."

"If you ever want to, let me know. I happen to know the owners of a farm near Ashton, complete with cows, chickens, horses, and several attractive hay bales," he said, wiggling his dark eyebrows.

Kassidy absorbed the open invitation to visit Gary's home, then asked, "Where are you heading right now?"

"Back to my apartment to grab some lunch."

"Me, too," Kassidy lied. She had actually been on her way home to sleep. Eating was something she only did when Treena was watching.

"How would you like to come over for lunch . . . my treat?" Gary asked.

Kassidy hesitated. She wanted to sleep through what was left of the afternoon. It had been another in a series of rotten days, starting with the wind that always managed to tangle her long blonde hair as she walked to class. All day she had been hit on by various males. She had received a C+ on a paper she had spent quite a bit of time writing. Then this unpleasant encounter with Jay.

"I promise I'm a good cook. My mom made sure of that."

"You can cook?" Kassidy asked, surprised.

"It's not hard, once you learn a few basics, like there's a big difference between tablespoon and teaspoon." Gary grinned. "What do you say? You look like you could use some cheering up."

"What's on the menu?"

"I was thinking about whipping together a nice omelet," Gary said, walking beside her.

"With cheese?" Kassidy loved the taste of cheese but rarely ate it because of the fat content.

"Your choice. If you want, we can fill yours with veggies."

"Mushrooms?" Kassidy asked, as her mouth watered.

"I think so. We used some last night on homemade pizza."

"You made pizza?"

Gary laughed. "It's not that complicated."

"I have a difficult time picturing you in an apron."

"I happen to look very cute in my apron," Gary insisted.

Kassidy shook her head. "You own an apron?"

"It was a gift, one my mother made for me. It has tractors all over it and a big pocket on the front where she embroidered my name."

"She made that for you?"

"She makes a lot of stuff like that. You should see the stocking she knitted for Christmas my first year in the mission field."

"Wow! My mother never does anything like that."

"What does she do?" Gary asked.

"She doesn't work, if that's what you mean. My dad makes enough as a lawyer to buy her anything she wants."

"She's a homemaker?"

"Not even," Kassidy said vehemently. "She's involved in so many different organizations like Save the Whales, the Creative Arts, and the Literary Guild that she doesn't have time to clean the house."

"Who keeps it up?"

"Our maid," Kassidy replied.

"I suppose you have a cook who fixes dinner too?"

Kassidy nodded. "It's the same lady. She takes care of all of that, which is why I never learned how to cook. I guess I could have learned if I'd wanted to. I never was interested."

Gary offered a low whistle. "You've led quite the life."

"I'd trade with anybody . . . well, almost anybody," she said, thinking of Meg. In her opinion, Meg was the orneriest girl she had ever met. All she did was study and gripe at everyone else.

"You're kidding," Gary said as they stopped in front of The Bunkhouse Apartment complex. "It doesn't sound like you've had things that bad," he added, reaching into his pocket for the key to his apartment.

"Maybe not, but when I hear people like you describe what your families are like, it makes me feel like I missed out on something. Your adore your mom, right?"

Gary nodded.

"I hate to be around mine."

"Why?"

"I've never measured up to what she thinks I should be. She started entering me in pageants when I was about four. She figured I would become Miss California, then go on to win the title of Miss America. I couldn't even win the county title this last summer."

"Serious?"

Kassidy nodded. "I'm a big disappointment. My mother wanted me to become an art major. I like to sketch things, but not for other people. Mom spent a fortune on art classes I hated because I always had to draw what the instructors wanted." She followed Gary inside his apartment, setting her backpack down on an old brown couch.

"Did you ever tell your mother that you didn't like those classes?"

"I tried, but then I'd get hit with how ungrateful I was, how I didn't appreciate the sacrifices she and Dad were making so that I could have the best of everything. They never understood that I didn't want the best of everything. I just wanted to be me, to live a normal life." Kassie paused. Why was she telling Gary all of this? She watched as he walked into the kitchen and flipped on the overhead light. Moving to the fridge, he pulled out a dozen eggs.

"So what is a normal life?" he asked as he set the eggs on the counter.

"This," she said, gesturing around the cluttered apartment. "Real life . . . being with friends. Not always worrying over stupid things like hair, makeup, clothes, or being perfect twenty-four hours a day," she said closing her fists, flinching when her sharp nails bit into the flesh of her hands.

"Uh-huh," he said as he selected a medium-sized bowl from the cupboard.

"You should've heard the lecture they gave me last year when I decided to come with Treena to Ricks."

"Let me guess, your parents wanted you to go somewhere else."

"A specialized college for budding artists."

Frowning sympathetically, Gary shook his head.

"I had to come with Treena—she's the only friend I have who understands me."

"How did you two meet?"

"We went to the same private school. Treena's parents couldn't really afford it, but they didn't want her to attend a public school, something about wanting to shelter her from the rough stuff that can happen. Anyway, we were the only two Mormons in the school, so we started hanging out together."

"I wondered how you two had become such close friends."

"Treena is a good friend, better than I deserve."

Breaking a couple of eggs into the bowl, Gary grabbed the milk from the fridge and added some before whipping the eggs together for Kassidy's omelet. "Why do you say that?"

"She's always there for me, even when I'm a jerk. And she tries to help me with . . . stuff."

Gary set the bowl on the counter by the stove and located a small frying pan. He added a dab of butter to the pan and placed it on a burner. "What kind of stuff?"

Kassidy gazed at Gary's back. She felt comfortable talking to him, but wasn't ready to reveal the dark secret that only Treena knew.

"You don't have to answer," Gary said, glancing over his shoulder at her. "I'm a snoop, but a harmless snoop."

"That's good to know," Kassidy replied, moving closer to the stove to watch in fascination as Gary poured the egg mixture into the pan. Grabbing a nearby set of salt and pepper shakers, he sprinkled both condiments over the mixture in the pan. "You're right; this doesn't look that hard."

"It's not, or I couldn't do it," Gary said, laughing. "The best part is it doesn't cost that much to make. Now, what should we fill it with?"

"What do you have?"

Gary moved to the fridge and pulled out a small container of mushrooms. "How about cheese and mushrooms?"

"Sounds good."

"I'll throw these mushrooms in now, then you tell me how much cheese you want."

"Not a lot, just enough to give it some flavor," she instructed.

He added the mushrooms to half of the bubbling egg mixture in the pan, then reached for a small block of cheese. Grabbing a knife, he handed it to Kassidy.

"What's this for?"

"Your first cooking lesson. Cut a piece of cheese from the block, then grate it. Just don't get your fingers in the way." He led her to the counter and pulled out a plastic cutting board. He rummaged through a drawer until he located a metal grater. "There, you're all set."

Kassidy cut a thin piece of cheese and obediently grated it. She then brought the grated cheese to the stove. "I just sprinkle this over the mushrooms?"

"Sprinkle some of it over the mushrooms, then I'll show you how to fold the top over. You can melt the rest of the cheese on top. That's what I usually do."

Nodding, Kassidy sprinkled cheese over the layer of mushrooms, then watched as Gary expertly folded the omelet in place. "This is so cool."

Gary grinned. "Wait till you taste it."

Kassidy added the rest of the cheese on top and watched it melt.

"Grab a plate, and you're in business."

Moving across the room, Kassidy retrieved a plate from the cupboard.

"I'll hurry and throw mine together, and lunch is served."

Kassidy gripped the plate in her hands as she moved back to the stove.

"There's some salsa in the fridge if you want to doctor it up," Gary suggested as he slid the omelet onto her plate.

"I'll pass. This looks great the way it is."

"A lot of things are that way," Gary said. He waited until Kassidy met his lingering gaze, then smiled warmly.

Keeping her thoughts to herself, Kassidy returned his smile, then retreated to the small dining room table to sample their creation.

Chapter 14

"Have you decided who will be your date to the homecoming dance?" Treena asked.

Kassidy glanced up from the book she was trying to read, one Gary had loaned her that was entitled *Born to Win*. He had borrowed it from one of his roommates, a psychology major named Ed.

"Who's the lucky guy?" Treena persisted.

"I don't know," Kassidy mumbled. She had been asked to the dance by five different guys—including Jay—but none of them appealed to her. They were all good-looking; a couple of them had even seemed nice. The problem was, she was beginning to wish that Gary wasn't involved with someone else. She knew he had already asked Jennifer; he had even asked for Kassidy's help in creating an invitation. Giving in, she had helped him compose a cheesy poem that he had attached to some flowers she had recommended, daisies in a multitude of colors, something she was certain Jennifer would receive later that day. Frowning, she decided she hated Jennifer.

"The dance is a week away, next Friday."

"I'm aware of that," Kassidy answered.

"You can't leave those guys hanging on the line forever. Pick one and let the rest off the hook so they can ask someone else."

"I'll deal with it, okay?" Kassidy snapped.

Looking hurt, Treena rose from her bed and left the room.

"Treena, I'm sorry," Kassidy called after her friend, but there was no response. Sighing, she refocused on the book in her hands. She stared at a list of traits, recognizing several in herself. "Afraid of or hurt by others—yes," she said quietly. "Puts up a good front—not usually," she answered. "Feel bad about myself—bingo. Fearful of the future—yes. Waste time—always. Use my talents—not at the moment. Don't understand myself—yes. Feel hemmed in—oh, yeah, especially when I'm home. Usually say the wrong thing—just ask Treena. Don't like myself. Gee, that's a toughie," she murmured, her gaze wandering to the small trash can where she had hidden an empty bag that had contained small Milky Way bars. "This is depressing," she said, turning the page. She read the book's instruction to look at the traits that she thought applied to her personality. *Is there a pattern? Are they winner traits, loser traits, or a mixture? What traits would you like to change?* "I hate you, Gary," she grumbled, turning back to reexamine the list of character traits. Muttering under her breath, she set the book on the nightstand and stretched out on her bed for a nap.

* * *

Meg ignored the pain radiating from her back and continued to read. *Just a few more minutes,* she promised herself. Then she would get up and stretch.

"Are you going to the dance?" Jesse asked, sitting next to Meg at the kitchen table in their apartment.

Choosing to remain silent, Meg began making notes in her binder.

"Meg?"

"I'm trying to study, okay?" She pushed down on her pencil with too much force and broke the lead tip. "Great!"

"You never have any fun," Jesse lamented. "You need to loosen up and enjoy life once in a while—like the homecoming dance next week. I think you ought to go."

Meg showered Jesse with a look of supreme annoyance.

"Ryan's a nice guy."

"Then why don't *you* go to the dance with him?"

"He asked you," Jesse replied.

Meg breathed out slowly. "Ryan and I are too different. It would be a disaster."

"What's the big deal? It's only a dance. He'll take you to dinner and you'll go dance a few numbers. Who knows, you might even enjoy yourself."

"Why are you so concerned about me going to this dance?" Meg asked as Jesse avoided her piercing gaze.

"I don't want you to miss out on all the fun."

"Right!" Then, as an idea surfaced, Meg smiled. She knew Jesse would never go for it and it would stop her from being such a pest. "Tell you what. I'll go to the dance with Ryan *if* you get a date too."

Jesse's brown eyes widened with surprise.

"What do you say, Jesse? Do we have a deal? If you don't get a date, I don't want to hear another word about Ryan."

Before Jesse could reply, the doorbell rang. Rising, she hurried to answer the door. As she swung it open, two young men dressed like clowns pushed their way into the apartment.

"We're looking for someone named Jesse Waterman."

"I'm Jesse."

"We have a singing telegram for you," one clown explained. He pulled out a pitch pipe and blew into it.

"Mi-mi-mi-mi-mi," the two clowns sang out, both missing the pitch.

"Uh, guys," Jesse began, her face turning a deep shade of crimson.

"Jesse Waterman, we bring a message to you, from someone who would like to express their point of view," they sang at the top of their lungs.

Meg winced at their discordant tone. Kassidy walked out of her bedroom to stare at the off-key duo. No one else was in the apartment to enjoy their performance.

"Someone thinks you're very cool, someone you've met here at school.

"He would like to know if you would agree to be his date for the Homecoming Jubilee."

"Jubilee?" Kassidy mouthed to Meg, who shrugged.

"Come on, girl, be a sport! A cool dude longs to be your escort. Give him the answer that will make his day. Please say YES without delay!" The clowns smiled broadly as they sang out the final note.

"Who are you? Who put you up to this? Bev?" Jesse sputtered.

"We are instructed to give you this card and wait for your answer," the taller clown said as he handed a small sealed card to Jesse.

"This is so—"

"Fun! Right, Jesse?" Meg said, enjoying her cousin's humiliation.

Muttering to herself, Jesse ripped open the small envelope and read the card.

"Who's it from?" Kassidy prompted.

"A friend," Jesse said, turning a brilliant shade of red. "Someone you don't know. Patrick Roberts. He's in most of my computer classes."

Meg laughed. "And what is your answer to *Patrick?*"

The tables turned immediately. "The same one you'll be giving," Jesse laughed. "Anybody have a pen?"

"Jesse!"

"A deal's a deal. You said you'd go with Ryan to the dance if I got a date."

Meg rolled her eyes. A date with Ryan was the last thing she wanted.

"You actually agreed to that?" Kassidy asked.

"She did," Jesse gloated. "And the best part is, it was her idea."

Groaning, Meg sank back in her chair. What had she been thinking?

* * *

Gary took a deep breath. The moment he had spent all week preparing for had finally arrived. Unsure of the reaction he would get, he took his time climbing the stairs that led to apartment D-6. He stood in front of the white metal door for several minutes before reaching to knock. He was certain his heart was going to pound out of his chest before someone answered.

"Hey, Gary," Jesse exclaimed as she opened the door. "Come on in!"

"Gary, you're just in time for dinner. What a coincidence," Bev teased their family home evening brother.

"We have plenty," Karen offered. "Grab a plate."

"What's on the menu?" Gary asked, keeping one hand tucked behind his back as he leaned against the doorframe.

"Tacos," Treena answered.

"Who made them?" he challenged.

"We all helped, even Kassidy," Treena responded.

Gary grinned as Kassidy glowered at Treena. "Kassidy helped?"

"Not funny, Gary," Kassidy retorted.

"What did she do?" he asked, curious.

"She washed the lettuce," Jesse informed him. "Now, are you coming in so we can quit letting in moths?" she added, swatting at a large moth that had flown inside.

"Hmmmmmm," he said, wondering if he had made a big mistake doing this in front of the entire apartment of girls.

"Gary, get in here!" Bev ordered.

"Yes, ma'am," Gary replied, jumping inside the apartment. Six pairs of eyes stared at the large bouquet of daisies he had been hiding. He was particularly interested in a set of blue eyes that widened with comprehension.

"Who is that for?" Jesse asked.

"I found these lying in front of your door," Gary answered. "I couldn't see what the attached card said. Can you make it out, Jesse?"

Jesse read the name in silence, then glanced at Kassidy. "What a big surprise. She's been getting stuff like this for over a week."

Kassidy pointed to herself. "Me?"

"Yep," Jesse confirmed. She took the flowers out of Gary's hand and marched across the room to give the bouquet to Kassidy.

Kassidy stood, her cheeks flushed. Stepping away from the table, she removed the envelope from the flowers and set the bouquet on the counter.

"Well, are you going to eat or what?" Bev asked. "We've already said the blessing, and to be honest, we're starving."

"Go ahead. It looks good, but I'm stuffed. We cooked hamburgers about an hour ago," Gary responded, his focus still on Kassidy.

Shrugging, the five girls began assembling their tacos.

Using a sharp knife, Kassidy slit open the envelope.

Gary saw that her hands were trembling as she pulled out a familiar-looking computer card, the same one she had helped him design earlier that week. He could almost see the words as Kassidy began reading the card:

Roses are red, mud is yucky; to have a friend like me, you're pretty darn lucky.

Sunflowers are yellow, grass is green, we'll have the best time you've ever seen.

Grinning at the surprised look on Kassidy's face, Gary longed to ask her how it felt to be reading the card she had thought she was designing for someone else. He had known that jealousy had tainted the composition, as well as the computer graphics she had chosen to "enhance" the card's message—sappy-looking flowers and potatoes with cartoon faces.

Lilacs offer a hint of romance. Be my date for the Hallelujah Homecoming Dance.

Only pansies will say no, please say yes, my little Idaho potato.

The only change Gary had made to Kassidy's card was to draw a line through Idaho. He had written California off to the side.

Kassidy gazed up at Gary. "Are you serious?" she mouthed to him.

Gary wiggled his eyebrows and motioned for Kassidy to follow him out of the apartment.

"What is with you two?" Treena asked.

"I think Gary's in on whoever asked her," Jesse guessed. "What do you think, Meg?"

"Who knows?" Meg said sullenly.

Bev glanced at Karen. "Did you see the way they were looking at each other?"

Karen shook her head.

"And you call yourself a reporter," Bev chortled. "I think Tyler's right, something's brewing here."

"They're just friends," Treena replied. "I would know if it was anything serious. Kassidy tells me everything."

* * *

"You big jerk!" Kassidy exclaimed as she smacked Gary on the arm. "Do you know what you put me through the past two days?" she exclaimed as they stood together out on the balcony. She was still reeling from his surprise invitation. What did it all mean?

Gary laughed. "It was a riot watching you make that card."

"And all this time you planned to ask *me*—not what's-her-name?"

"Jennifer? No. Like I told you a while back, we're just friends. Besides, she'd already been asked by someone else."

"Ooooh, you . . . man!"

"That hurts," he joked. "So, what's your answer?"

"I ought to make you stew over this until next Thursday."

"I deserve it," he admitted. "But you won't, right—'cuz you think too much of me."

Kassidy glared at him.

"Well?"

"I'll go, but mostly because it will help me out of the bind I'm in," she said, determined to hide the excitement she felt.

"You're in a bind?"

"You're not the only one who has asked me."

"I know. But I'm more special than all those other guys."

"What makes you think so?"

"I don't think—I know!"

Kassidy shook her head.

"That was a positive response, right? My roommates were betting I'd come home wearing those flowers I brought you."

"Your roommates are very intelligent."

"Is that a 'yes'?"

"I'm still thinking about it," she replied calmly.

Gary grinned. "How did you like picking out your own flowers? Originally, I was thinking of getting roses."

"You would've brought me roses?" she asked.

"But you insisted on daisies."

"Daisies are nice," she said. "I'm just glad I didn't convince you to pick a bouquet of dandelions."

Gary laughed. "Now that would've been funny!" he chortled as Kassidy continued to glare. "We haven't had a chance to talk for a couple of days," he said, changing the subject. "How are things going?"

"So-so."

"Have you been reading my roommate's book?"

"Some of it," she admitted.

"What do you think?"

"I think you shouldn't push your luck tonight," she replied, poking him in the ribs. "I also think if I spend any more time out here with you, my roommates will grill me for answers. They're dying to know what this is all about."

"What is it all about?"

"Good night, Gary," she said, moving toward the door.

"Your answer was *yes*, right?"

Smiling, Kassidy nodded before slipping inside the apartment.

"Sweet!" Gary said after the door was closed. Whistling to himself, he turned and walked away.

* * *

"I can't believe you and Gary are dating," Treena stated again, a hurt look on her face.

Kassidy sighed. Everyone in the apartment had been shocked by the news; Treena had been stunned. "Why is that so hard to believe?"

"You're so different," Treena said as she wiggled into a nightshirt.

"That's a bad thing?"

Treena shrugged. "I've seen you with a lot of guys, Kassidy. Gary . . . well he—"

"You think he's too nice for me," Kassidy said, finishing the sentence.

"That's not what I meant."

"Then what is your problem?"

"I don't want to see either of you get hurt."

Kassidy glared at Treena. "I'm not out to hurt Gary. We're just good friends, okay?"

"Okay," Treena replied. Brushing past Kassidy, she reached for the door.

"Treena, I didn't mean to leave you out of this. I wasn't sure what to say about Gary. He makes me laugh; he makes me feel better when I'm having a bad day."

"Good for Gary," Treena said a bit sarcastically as she opened the door to leave the room. "I'm glad you found *someone* who can," she added, pulling the door shut behind her.

Groaning, Kassidy fell onto her bed. Why was Treena so upset? As a familiar pain surfaced, so did the desire to consume what she had hidden in her bottom drawer. She fought it for several minutes, then rose from her bed and grabbed her backpack. She emptied the books and binder onto her bed, then hurried to the dresser. Opening the bottom drawer, she lifted up the folded sweaters and pulled out two bags of miniature chocolate bars. Stuffing them inside her backpack, she zipped it shut and flung it onto one shoulder. She turned and grabbed her jacket from her bed, certain she would need it.

As she stepped into the hall, she could hear Treena gargling in the bathroom. She was certain all of her other roommates were in for the night. Slipping into the living room, Kassidy quietly unlocked the front door and walked outside. She checked her jeans pocket for her apartment key, then she shut the door and hurried toward the stairs.

When she returned two hours later, the door was still unlocked. Plagued by guilt, she stepped inside the apartment. Sinking down on the couch, she thrust her backpack away as if it were the culprit. She sat alone in the darkness and longed to cry, aching for the release it would bring, but knew the tears wouldn't come—they never did when she needed them most.

Chapter 15

"Kassidy, you know a lot about hair and makeup. Help us out here," Bev pleaded as she forced Meg to sit down in the kitchen chair they had placed in front of the large bathroom mirror.

"Bev," Meg warned sternly.

"Relax. If you don't like it, you can fix it the way you want." Bev motioned to Kassidy.

Kassidy gazed at Meg's reflection in the mirror. "I don't suppose you have contacts."

Meg shook her head.

"Too bad. You have gorgeous green eyes," Kassidy commented.

Meg squinted at her reflection.

"Not when you pull a face like that," Bev said, handing Meg her glasses.

Giving Bev a dirty look, Meg replaced her glasses and gazed at her reflection.

"You need those to see?" Kassidy pondered.

"Duh!"

Kassidy patted Meg's shoulder. "Sorry, I'm thinking out loud. Okay, the glasses do make you seem more sophisticated, more mature. Let's concentrate on the hair."

"Let's not," Meg countered as she attempted to stand.

"Meg, you promised to behave," Bev reprimanded, pushing her back onto the chair.

"I promised to go to this stupid dance tonight. That's all I promised!"

"Meg, haven't you ever wanted to get all dressed up for the fun of it?" Kassidy tempted.

Meg shook her head.

"Give me one hour. Then if you don't like it, you can redo it yourself," Kassidy coaxed.

"One hour," Meg stated firmly, glancing at her watch.

Giving Bev a jubilant look, Kassidy began undoing the tight bun that held Meg's long red hair captive.

* * *

Jesse gaped at her cousin. "Meg?"

Uncomfortable with the way everyone was staring at her, Meg was tempted to leave the living room.

"You're beautiful!" Karen said, smiling her approval.

"That's *not* what I was going for," Meg stammered. She glanced down at the dark green gown Kassidy had borrowed from someone in their student ward. It fit perfectly, accenting what Mother Nature had blessed her with. Her red hair had been restyled in a becoming fashion, long soft curls replacing the severe braid she usually wore.

"Meg, you look great!" Treena encouraged.

"You think so?"

Treena nodded.

"We tried to tell you that, but you wouldn't listen to us," Bev said, reaching to give Kassidy a high five.

"Karen, you don't think this is too much?" Meg persisted.

Karen shook her head. "That dress was made for you. But there's something missing."

"Besides her smile?" Bev interjected.

"She needs a necklace. I have one that will work. Come back to my bedroom, and I'll dig it out for you," Karen offered.

"You won't need it tonight?" Meg queried.

Karen shook her head. "It doesn't match the dress I'm wearing," she said as the two young women disappeared down the hall.

* * *

"I'm next," Jesse said, eagerly grabbing a kitchen chair.

Kassidy glanced at her watch. "Okay, but remember: perfection takes time, and we're running short of that." She smiled at Treena. "Do you want some help getting ready for tonight?"

Treena shook her head. "Perfection has never been my style," she said, moving past Kassidy to enter their bedroom. She glared at Kassidy before shutting the door.

Bev gave Kassidy a quizzical look.

Shrugging, Kassidy managed a weak smile. Treena had been giving her the cold shoulder for a week. She hated it but didn't know how to fix things between them. She knew she was partially to blame—Treena had been furious with her for disappearing last Friday night. Though she had tried to apologize, Treena had refused to listen. She hoped Treena wouldn't sulk all night. Gary had arranged for his roommate, Ed, to ask Treena to the dance. They would be doubling tonight, but the way things were going, Treena's current mood could ruin the whole evening.

"Make me beautiful," Jesse exclaimed. "Meg and I are cousins, you know. That means we inherited some of the same genes."

"Would that be the Wrangler variety?" Bev teased.

"I said g-e-n-e-s, not j-e-a-n-s," Jesse fired back. "Kassidy, do your stuff."

Kassidy smiled. She hadn't had this much fun in a very long time. It felt good to know that she could use some of what she had learned in varied pageants to help her roommates prepare for the dance. "Come on, Jesse. When we're finished with you, that computer nerd of yours will wonder what hit him."

"Cool," Jesse said as she followed Bev and Kassidy to the bathroom.

* * *

Patrick Roberts stared at Jesse. "Wow," he finally managed to say.

Jesse twirled around in front of him. "Not bad, eh?"

"Not bad at all," he agreed. He handed her the wrist corsage he had brought with him: three small, pink carnations surrounded by bits of green fern and white baby's breath.

Jesse smiled. Earlier in the week she had told him that she would be wearing a long, pastel-pink dress, something she had borrowed from Karen. Her brown eyes brimming with excitement, she turned her back to Patrick and handed the boxed corsage to Bev. "How do you put these things on?" she asked in a hushed voice.

Smiling, Bev took the corsage out of the box and helped Jesse fasten it to her left wrist. "There you go, Princess Jesse. You look great."

"So do you," Jesse replied. "I wish I could be here to watch Tyler's eyes bug out of his head," she said, gazing with admiration at the lavender prom dress Bev had chosen, something Bev had told her she had worn to the Blaketown senior prom last year.

"Uh, Jesse, we need to go," Patrick said, glancing at his watch. "We're supposed to meet my roommates and their dates in about ten minutes."

"Have fun," Bev whispered.

"We will. You behave tonight," Jesse retorted. "Make Tyler keep his hands to himself."

"We'll see," Bev laughed. "Maybe I should say the same thing about Patrick."

"Right," Jessie said dryly. Patrick was a computer science major who wasn't much to look at, but he did possess a fun sense of humor.

"You kids have a good time," Bev called out as Patrick escorted Jesse to the door.

"Bye, Mom," Jesse retorted before leaving the apartment.

Bev picked the empty corsage box off the table and set it on the counter by the fridge so Jesse could use it later to store her corsage.

"Has Jesse left already?" Meg asked, stepping into the kitchen.

"You just missed her."

Meg frowned. "Did this Patrick guy seem all right?"

"I'm sure they'll be fine."

"I should've insisted that Ryan and I go with them."

"Quit worrying," Bev advised. "Enjoy tonight."

"Jesse hasn't dated much. She doesn't know how guys can be sometimes."

"I'm sure Patrick is harmless." She gazed inquisitively at Meg. "Incidentally, how can guys be sometimes?"

Flushing, Meg refused to answer.

"Bev, have you seen my earrings?" Karen asked from the hallway.

"Which pair? You've only got a million of them!"

"That pair my mom gave me for Easter, the silver ones with the touch of blue. They're spiral shaped."

Bev nodded her approval over the blue formal Karen was wearing. "I know which earrings you're talking about. They would look perfect with that dress."

"Help me find them," Karen pleaded. Together, she and Bev hurried down the hall.

Meg wandered near the front room window and peered out. "Please watch over Jesse," she silently prayed. "And help me survive this night," she fervently added.

* * *

Meg had to admit, the evening was going much smoother than she had envisioned. The dinner had been surprisingly wonderful, a meal cooked by Ryan and his roommates for their respective dates. They had served green salad and a fancy lasagna that one of Ryan's roommates claimed was from an old family recipe. That had been followed by generous portions cut from an ice-cream-cake roll.

Throughout the evening Ryan had been attentive and had treated Meg with the utmost respect. He had complimented her appearance generously when he first picked her up, then had steered to safer topics throughout the rest of the evening, sensing her discomfiture.

Later, Meg learned that Ryan was a gifted dancer. Deciding she might have been too hasty in her earlier assessment of this young man, she began enjoying herself. After dancing for nearly an hour, she caught a glimpse of Jesse in the west ballroom of the Manwaring Center and talked Ryan into maneuvering to her cousin's side. "She was nervous about tonight. I want to make sure things are going okay," she explained.

"No problem," Ryan replied as he skillfully guided them toward Jesse and Patrick.

As they drew near, Meg was alarmed by how close Patrick was holding her cousin during the slow song. "Jesse!" she called out, trying to be heard above the loud music.

Turning her head, Jesse's eyes widened with surprise. "Meg, how's it goin'?"

"Good," Meg replied.

"Whew," Ryan joked, wiping his forehead. "I've tried to be impressive."

"I'll bet you have," Jesse said, grinning at the dark-haired young man.

"I've been impressive, too," Patrick quipped. "And the evening's still young."

Jesse laughed, missing the frown on Meg's face.

Ryan saw the look and flinched. Bev had warned him that Meg was the mother of their apartment. "She watches over Jesse like a mother hen," Bev had declared. "If you want to enjoy the evening with her, don't double with Jesse and her date. Meg'll spend the whole night fussing over her cousin."

"Should we go get some punch?" Ryan suggested now, hoping to drag Meg away from Jesse.

"In a minute. I need to . . . uh . . . use the little girl's room," Meg replied. "Jesse, want to come with me?"

"Okay. Patrick, keep Ryan out of trouble until we return."

Nodding, Patrick stepped back as Meg hurried Jesse from the ballroom.

"Want to get some punch?" Ryan asked, feeling defeated. "We may be here awhile."

Patrick sighed. "Sure, why not?"

* * *

"Do you want to tell me the real reason you dragged me in here?" Jesse prodded as she followed Meg inside the crowded rest room.

Meg glanced around, then led Jesse to a vacant corner. "How have things gone tonight?"

"Good, till now. What's wrong? Has Ryan done something to upset you?"

"No," Meg responded. "I'm worried about *you*."

"Me?" Jesse laughed. "Why?"

"This Patrick . . . how well do you know him?"

Jesse rolled her eyes. Earlier, she had figured she had lucked out; Meg hadn't had time to grill Patrick or lecture her before they had left the apartment.

"I noticed he was holding you a little close on that last dance."

"It was a slow dance."

"But you don't need to dance together that close."

Gritting her teeth, Jesse remembered Bev's admonition that they make this an enjoyable evening for Meg. "Okay, I'll keep some distance between us. Happy?"

"And later, after the dance, are you getting together with his roommates and their dates?"

Jesse shrugged. "I'm not sure. Why?"

"It's not a good idea to spend a lot of time alone with a guy, especially one you don't know very well. Maybe you should stick with me and Ryan the rest of the night."

"Meg, I'm eighteen years old. My mother trusts me, why don't you?"

"Because I know things can happen."

Jesse shook her head. "Meg, I don't know what your problem is. Let's go back to the dance. You enjoy your date and I'll enjoy mine. And keep in mind that I was actually blessed with a brain that functions," she said before leaving the rest room.

* * *

"Having fun?" Gary asked as he and Kassidy swayed in time to the slow song.

"This has been a wonderful night," Kassidy confirmed, "except for two things."

"Let me guess: Treena's attitude and the run-in with Jay."

"Yeah. Other than that, it's been a perfect evening."

"What's up with Treena?"

"I'm not sure," Kassidy hedged. She hadn't told Gary about her problem with food, certain he would be repulsed by it. She figured her disappearance last week was the reason for Treena's cold silence. "Treena's been acting this way since last week. She was after me to make up my mind about who was taking me to the dance and I kind of snapped at her. Then you asked me to the dance, and she was upset because I hadn't told her I was interested in you."

"And are you?"

"What?"

Gary grinned broadly. "Interested in me?"

"Of course. After all, you *are* a very impressive agronomy major."

"You even pronounced it right," he chuckled. The song ended, and they drifted to a group of chairs that lined the wall of the ballroom. "Have you tried to talk things out with Treena?"

Kassidy nodded.

Gary gazed at her steadily.

"Okay, maybe I haven't tried hard enough."

"You've told me several times that she's been a wonderful friend to you. That friendship is worth saving. I think you need to find out what's going on with her."

"Something's wrong; she's never been like this." That part was true. Treena had been mad before but had never completely blocked her out. Frowning, she knew she had broken her promise to Treena—she had given in to the temptation to binge and purge. But it was Treena's fault. If Treena hadn't put her on such a guilt trip over Gary, she wouldn't have done it.

"Talk to her—but not tonight. You'll both be too tired. Wait until tomorrow. Go for a walk or something, and clear the air between you."

"Good idea," she agreed.

"As for Mr. Michaels, he'd better keep his distance and learn to keep his mouth shut."

"I'm sure I've been called worse things than what he said tonight, probably at every pageant I've ever participated in."

Gary bristled. "You shouldn't have held me back. I should've escorted his sorry—"

"Gary," she said disapprovingly.

"—carcass outside and taught him a few manners, farmer style."

Kassidy frowned. "Truth?"

Gary nodded.

"I felt sorry for his date tonight. Jay must've dragged her all over the place trying to find me. And the way he was behaving, she won't enjoy herself at all."

"He's a jerk, and that's putting it nicely, but we're not going to let him ruin this night for us. Are you up for some more dancing?"

"What do you think?"she replied, rising from her chair. She reached for his hand and then led him back out onto the dance floor in time for an upbeat number.

* * *

Bev felt like she was gliding on air as she danced around the crowded room in Tyler's strong arms. He looked sharp in his charcoal-colored suit. A light grey tie complemented the suit, a perfect blend for her soft lavender dress.

Earlier, they had gone with his roommates and their dates, which had included Karen, to McDonald's for dinner. They had thoroughly enjoyed eating Happy Meals and playing with the toys that accompanied each meal. The best part had been the confusion evident from the other customers and the McDonald's employees that they would dress up to eat at a fast food restaurant.

When they had finished their hamburger feast, they had piled into three cars to drive across town to Millhollow for generous servings of frozen yogurt. Now they were scattered across the ballrooms of the Manwaring Center with the understanding that they would meet downstairs by the bookstore at 11:30.

"Want some punch?" Tyler asked as the slow song finished.

Bev shook her head. She wanted to stay on the dance floor, content to float around the room in Tyler's arms. Unfortunately, the next song featured a fast, catchy rhythm.

"Are you sure?" Tyler tried again.

"Let's get some punch," Bev said, noting the beads of perspiration on his forehead.

"Good idea," he replied, leading her across the room. "Hey, there's Karen and Wes."

"Where?" Bev asked, glancing around.

"Sitting over by the wall. Why don't you go have a seat, and I'll get us some punch?"

Nodding, Bev walked to the line of chairs. As she approached, she noticed Wes was using the old stretch-and-yawn technique to get his arm around Karen. Amused, she smiled until she saw the look of panic on her friend's face. *Not again*, Bev moaned. She was tempted to stay out of sight, hoping Karen could work through this on her own. *Come on, Karen, relax. Wes is a nice guy. Tyler thinks the world of him. He won't try anything out of line.* Bev shook her head as Karen stood, then bolted across the room. Frowning, Bev moved forward until she was standing in front of Wes. "Where's Karen?"

"She said she needed to use the rest room," Wes explained, looking disgruntled. "Have I done something tonight to upset her? She seems kind of standoffish."

Bev shook her head. "Wes, the problem isn't you," she said sympathetically.

"Let me guess, she's waiting for a missionary?"

"Something like that," Bev said, deciding it was an easy way out.

"I should've known someone as cute as Karen would already have a steady boyfriend," Wes sighed. "Oh well, she's my date tonight, right?"

"Right. I'll go check on her." She smiled warmly at Wes. "Have you had any fun tonight?"

"Yeah, considering she wants to sit out all the slow dances."

"Hang in there," Bev replied. "I'll go find her. Tell Tyler where I went."

"All right," Wes said, leaning back against his chair.

Bev carefully made her way through the mass of dancing bodies as she searched for Karen. She located her friend outside of the ballroom, standing near a window. "Are you okay?"

Karen glanced at Bev. "I needed some air. It was getting claustrophobic in that room."

"I see," Bev said, painfully aware of the problem. Since the attack Karen had suffered during their junior year of high school, Karen didn't trust guys. Thankfully, she had been rescued in time, but she still struggled with some emotional issues. "Was Wes crowding you?"

Karen nodded.

"He's a nice guy, Karen. He'd never do anything to hurt you."

"I know. It's just . . ."

"I know," Bev replied, forcing a sad smile. "Do you think you can go back in?"

"Maybe."

"Would it help if Tyler and I stuck around?"

"Yes," Karen said quietly.

"You've got it. Now let's go have some fun, all right?" Bev said, willing Karen to smile. When she continued to frown, Bev pulled her into an intense hug, then led her back inside the ballroom. *Please help Karen through this night,* she silently pleaded, *and keep her from hating me because I made her come.*

Chapter 16

Bev hated doing laundry on Saturdays; it was the busiest day of the week for the Baronnessa laundry room. That meant she would have to scramble for a washing machine, then for a dryer with each batch. She would spend most of the morning camped out in the laundry room, waiting for empty machines. Because she had neglected her mountain of laundry last weekend, it was crucial to tackle the formidable task that day. Sighing, she asked Karen if she needed anything washed before she headed down.

"I washed my clothes Wednesday afternoon," Karen answered as she sorted through her backpack.

"Want to come with me?"

"I would, but I need to head up on campus and gather some research for an article I'm writing for *The Scroll*," she said, referring to the campus newspaper.

"I see," Bev said, gazing at her friend's back. She had picked up last night that Karen was blaming her for the way things had gone at the dance. True, she had been the one to talk Karen into going to the dance, but it wasn't her fault that Wes had decided to pull out all the stops to impress her. After they had returned to the dance floor, Wes had seemed determined to break down Karen's wall of indifference. Ignoring Karen's protests, he had insisted on dancing through a series of slow songs, certain he could win her away from an imaginary boyfriend. Bev grimaced. Maybe it *was* her fault. "If you change your mind, you know where to find me," Bev said now, lugging her laundry basket out of the room.

Karen offered a feeble wave and continued to rummage through her backpack.

* * *

"You beat me down here," Bev puffed, toting her clothes into the humid laundry room.

Treena glanced up from the book she was reading. "I usually get it done during the week, but between my work schedule and school, it didn't happen this week."

"I hear you," Bev said over the noisy machines. "Is anything open?"

"I think that washer on the end is finished. I'm not sure whose clothes are in there, but maybe they wouldn't mind if you set them on top of a machine somewhere."

"Good idea. They can't expect people to wait until they decide to trundle down here," Bev said as she carried her laundry basket to the far end of the laundry room. After she set her clothes down, she opened the washing machine and glanced inside. A batch of varied darks lined the inside of the washer. She pulled them out and piled them on top of the next machine. When she had retrieved the final piece of clothing, she sorted her clothes and filled the washer with a large batch of whites. "Oh, great!" she exclaimed.

"What's wrong?" Treena asked.

"I forgot my laundry soap. I left it sitting in my closet."

"Use mine."

"You don't mind?"

"Go for it. It's sitting in my laundry basket."

"I'll pay you back," Bev promised, crossing the room to retrieve the small bottle of liquid Tide. "This is what my stepmother uses all the time."

"It was on sale last week," Treena commented. "That's one advantage to working at a grocery store—I know about all the specials."

Nodding in agreement, Bev returned to the washing machine to add the detergent. Then she dug inside of the front pocket of her jeans for the quarters she had been hoarding for two weeks. She had learned that quarters were like gold to a college student. Shoving the coins into the washer she fired it up. She pushed the remaining quarters inside of her pocket, picked up the bottle of Tide, and walked back to Treena. "Thanks," she said, replacing the detergent in Treena's basket.

"Anytime."

"How did things go last night? You were already in bed when I got home."

Treena shrugged, engrossed in her book. "It wasn't the greatest. Ed's a psychology major. I felt like he was analyzing me all night."

"I'm sorry," Bev replied. She spent several seconds studying Treena's face before attempting another conversation. "You've been quiet the past few days. Is everything all right?" she inquired, sitting beside Treena in a plastic chair.

"No."

"Want to talk about it?"

Treena closed her book and set it on the dryer behind her.

"Problems with Kassidy?"

"You might say that."

Bev offered a sincere smile. "I won't pry, but if you need me, I'm here."

"I know," Treena said softly. "I've been tempted to talk to you for quite a while."

"I think you owe me. I spilled my guts to you that first weekend we were here."

Treena focused on the floor.

"You look like you're carrying the world on your shoulders. What's wrong?"

"If I tell you, you have to promise you won't say anything to anybody—not even to Karen."

"No worries there. She's not speaking to me this morning."

"Was her date that bad?"

"In her opinion it was."

"Everyone has an opinion," Treena said sadly. "In the past, my opinion was that secrets should be kept. But when a life is at risk . . ." she paused, looking uncertain.

"This sounds serious."

"It is," Treena assured her. "Let me ask you something. If Karen was involved in something that could be life threatening, what would you do?"

"Whatever it took to save her life," Bev exclaimed.

"That's my initial response too. But if Karen tearfully promised to never do it again, how would you handle it? Would you keep giving her more chances, or would you take action?"

"We're talking about Kassidy, right?"

Treena nodded.

"And you've promised never to tell what's going on with her?"

Again, Treena nodded.

"What if I helped you out and guessed what it is? Then it's not like you actually told me."

"You know?"

"Karen's the one who figured it out. She's convinced Kassidy has an eating disorder."

Treena sank down in her chair.

"How bad is it?"

"Bad."

"Bulimia?"

"Yeah."

Bev released a slow rush of air. Beside her, Treena began to cry. Unsure of what to do, Bev placed an arm around Treena's trembling shoulders.

"She keeps promising to stop, but she never does. I know it's killing her. Other people can't see the differences yet, but I can: the bags under her eyes, the lack of energy, the fits of nausea even when she doesn't binge."

"She needs help."

"She'll never get it," Treena said, wiping at her eyes.

"Do her parents know?"

Treena snorted. "Her parents have pushed her to be what they think is the perfect daughter. Her mom wants her to become a glamour queen; she doesn't care what Kassidy wants."

"What about her dad?"

"He's so busy making his fortune he can't be bothered. Kassidy is like a doll to him, an object he uses whenever he wants to impress people with his solid family life. 'Here's my daughter, Kassidy. Isn't she beautiful?' The thing is, she feels like she'll never measure up to what her parents want. She lost a pageant over the summer—you'd have thought it was the end of the world. And she placed, she was the first runner-up. She has a voice like an angel. You should hear her sing sometime. I remember sitting in the audience, feeling so proud to be her friend. She's beautiful and talented . . . and all her mother did was yell at her because she lost."

"You're kidding," Bev said angrily. "No wonder she's a mess."

"I don't think either parent has ever told her that they love her. And if they have, she probably doesn't believe them because they never show it."

"Does her family belong to the Church?" Bev questioned.

"Her mother does, but she's not very active. And I'm not sure what church her dad belongs to. Kassidy told me that he thinks religion is a farce."

"Does Kassidy have a testimony?"

Lifting an eyebrow, Treena stared at Bev.

"Treena, you know my background—I told you I was an alcoholic."

"Yeah."

"I didn't tell you that for a while I was in a rehab center."

Treena's eyes widened.

"It didn't help me much, but while I was there, I did learn about self-destructive behavior. Drinking, drugs, smoking, eating disorders—they all have something in common."

"What's that?"

Bev took a deep breath. "Most of the time people use those things to block out pain. I mean, yeah, a lot of people get hooked because their friends are doing it, or they think it's the cool thing to do. But in my case, and Karen's mom was the same way, we were hurting so bad that we turned to something we thought made it better. It doesn't make it better; it only adds to the pain."

"How do I get Kassidy to see that?"

"I don't know. I think she needs professional help. And she has to learn to love herself to beat this. That's why I asked if she had a testimony. Mine has been an anchor in my life. It made all the difference in the world. The more I learned about who I am and why I'm here in this crazy world, the better things seemed to be. Knowing I'm a daughter of God, that I have unlimited potential . . . it was like a door opened, and the ache in my heart drained away."

Treena remained silent for several seconds. When she spoke, her voice was strained. "I know what you're trying to say, but there is a difference: you have a loving, supportive family; Kassidy doesn't. You also have Karen. You two are like sisters."

"But there's you. Kassidy has you for a friend," Bev emphasized.

"I'm not sure what I am anymore. I feel like I'm a combination friend, mother, and guardian. Right now, Kassidy resents the heck out of me because I'm trying to keep her alive."

Bev leaned back against her chair. "What about other family members?"

"Kassidy's the only child in her family."

"What about grandparents, aunts, uncles, cousins?"

"It seems like there's an aunt somewhere, her mother's sister. I assumed she'd be like Kassidy's mother. I don't even know where she lives."

"I wonder if there's a way to find out."

Treena straightened in her chair, a look of hope in her eye. "Kassidy's address book."

"Can you check it out?"

"Probably. She's always leaving her purse in our bedroom. The problem is, she's usually in there lying on her bed."

"Does Gary know about any of this?" Bev asked, struck by another train of thought.

"I don't know. She didn't even tell me they were becoming an item. It's almost like she was hiding it from me."

"Why would she do that?"

"I'm not sure." She frowned. "And I did a really stupid thing . . . I snapped at her the night Gary asked her to the homecoming dance."

Bev arched her eyebrows, puzzled. "Why?"

"I'm not sure. Frustration, I guess. I worry about her so much, and when I found out she was keeping things from me, it made me wonder how many other secrets she'd been hiding. She had promised to quit throwing up. I thought maybe she was getting on top of it. Then when I found out about Gary, I wondered if she had been less than truthful about the bulimia. I said some things I shouldn't have said."

"Treena, I think you've done remarkably well. Look what she's put you through."

"But I blew up at her. Then, when I had had a chance to cool down, I went back into our bedroom to apologize, but she was gone. Her jacket and backpack were missing. I knew immediately what she was doing. She had shut a sweater in her bottom drawer. When I opened it, I found where she has been keeping her stash of munchies."

"Munchies?"

"Candy bars, cookies, doughnuts—it's all there under her sweaters."

"She binges, then purges."

"Yeah. She eats till she makes herself sick, then she throws up her toenails."

"Not good."

"Not good at all," Treena agreed.

"Look, I know you promised Kassidy, but I think we need to get her some help."

"Who do we tell?"

Bev thought for a moment, then suggested, "How about our bishop?"

"I've thought about it before, but I feel like I'm betraying Kass."

"Let me be the heavy. I'll go talk to him."

Treena shook her head. "No, I need to be there. Maybe I can help him understand how this started."

"When did she start?"

"I think she toyed with it on and off during high school. She never has eaten much around other people. I suspected then that she was anorexic. It wasn't until we lived in the same apartment last year that I caught on to what she was really doing. She promised me then that she would quit," Treena said as tears made a fresh appearance.

"She will. We have to help her realize that she can beat this thing."

"You think she can?"

Bev nodded. "With our help she will."

Chapter 17

Late that afternoon, Bev drove Treena up to the Manwaring Center where they met with the bishop of their student ward. After enduring a few minutes of light conversation, the two girls shared what was going on with Kassidy.

"I think something needs to be done," Bev stressed, hating what this ordeal was doing to Treena and Kassidy.

"You're right to be concerned," the bishop said. "This can be a potentially life-threatening situation. Unfortunately, Kassidy probably won't cooperate, even if I call her in here. Like Bev pointed out a few minutes ago, she has to want to stop. That's the key." He paused, as if in deep thought. "You girls keep a close eye on things this next week. Don't let Kassidy spend time alone. I know that may not always be possible, but do the best you can. In the meantime, I'll get in touch with LDS Counseling Services and see what I can learn." He focused on Treena. "You mentioned Kassidy might have an aunt?"

Treena nodded.

"See if you can locate her. Feel the water with her. If you think she might be a positive influence with Kassidy, that might be the best way to put together a family support system."

"And if she's just like Kassidy's mom?"

"Then we'll try something else. Regardless, we'll try to keep her from destroying her life."

"She has seemed happier since she started hanging around with Gary," Bev observed, remembering how cheerful Kassidy had seemed at the dance the night before.

"Does he know about Kassidy's problem?" the bishop asked.

Treena shook her head. "At least I don't think so. He knows something isn't quite right, but I doubt Kassidy has told him anything. She's so ashamed of what she's doing, she doesn't like to talk about it, not even with me."

"Understandable. Which is why I'm going to wait before I approach her. I need some time to pray about it—this is a very delicate problem." He smiled at the two young women. "You're to be commended for having the courage and compassion to come forward. I'm sure it wasn't an easy decision for either of you to make."

Remaining silent, Treena clenched her fists.

"Treena, despite what you may think, you are the best kind of friend Kassidy could possibly have," he assured her. Rising from his desk, he shook hands with both girls before escorting them to the door of his office. "Keep in touch, and let me know if things get worse."

"All right," Bev promised.

"Do your other roommates know anything about this?"

"I think they suspect," Bev replied, "especially Karen. The other two have never said anything about it."

"Let's keep it quiet for now. If you two can pull off keeping an eye on her without her catching on, we'll be doing well."

Silently agreeing, Bev and Treena left the office and returned to their apartment.

* * *

"Want to check out my hay bales next weekend?" Gary asked, grinning at Kassidy.

Kassidy glanced up from the kitchen table in her apartment. "You're so subtle."

"I'm asking if you want to see my farm—the place where I grew up—meet my parents, that sort of thing," he said, shifting around in his chair.

"Whoa, Farmer Brown. Aren't you pushing things a bit fast?"

"You said you'd never seen a farm before. I think it's high time you did."

Kassidy smiled. Gary had spent most of the afternoon with her, helping her with an essay assignment for her English class. Although writing wasn't her favorite pastime, Gary had made it bearable. "Sure, why not?"

"All right! I'll let Mom know we're coming." He looked at his watch. "It's way past my supper time. How about we grab a bite downtown somewhere?"

"Go ahead, I'm not hungry."

"Well, I'm starved. Come with me. If you want, you can order a salad or soup or something light, but I need to eat."

"What about your nightly meal with your roommates?"

"We do our own thing on Saturday," he replied. "Mostly because we try to get dates. If you're stuck in the apartment on a Saturday night, that's grounds for being labeled a total loser."

Kassidy smiled. "Really?"

"It's a fate worse than death! Now, are you going to make me suffer humiliation, or will you agree to accompany me to the restaurant of your choice—if it's not too expensive?"

"How can a girl turn down an offer like that?" Kassidy teased.

"You can't. It's not allowed," Gary said, standing up to stretch. "By the way, I was going to ask you earlier but I forgot. Did you get things worked out with Treena?"

"I haven't had a chance to talk to her, but she does seem more like herself today."

"Where is she, at work?"

Kassidy stood to gather her books. "No, she's hanging out with Bev today. They were doing their laundry together this morning. Then they came back here, dumped off their clothes, and headed out somewhere. Treena seemed fine. I'm not sure what her problem has been."

"Maybe it was one of those woman things," he quipped.

Picking up a discarded wad of paper, Kassidy threw it, hitting him on the side of the head.

"What was that for?" he asked, feigning surprise.

"Guess!"

He picked up the wad of paper and threw it up in the air, catching it in his other hand.

Kassidy shook her head. "You may throw that away."

"You don't want me to return your shot?"

"No."

"How about if I throw some water on you instead?"

"Gary!"

"Or maybe grab you like this and show you how an Idaho farmer keeps the womenfolk in line," he said. Rushing forward, he grabbed her and began to tickle her stomach.

Giggling, she collapsed to the floor. "Gary, stop it!"

"Say the magic word," he said, kneeling down as he continued to tickle Kassidy.

"What magic word?" she managed between giggles.

The front door opened as Treena and Bev returned to the apartment.

"This looks interesting," Bev commented.

Gary stood and pulled Kassidy to her feet.

"Treena, I think Kassidy owes us ice cream."

"It looks that way," Treena replied.

"Not even," Kassidy retorted, slapping Gary's arm. "Gary, tell them we didn't kiss."

"Not yet," he said, winking at Bev.

"Can we plan on ice cream for Sunday dinner?" Bev asked. "We need a dessert for tomorrow."

Gary laughed. "Judging by the look on Kassidy's face, I don't think so." He lightly pinched Kassidy's cheek. "Will you still have dinner with me tonight?"

"If you stay here, Kass, you're doing dishes," Treena threatened with mock severity.

"I guess I'm going with you, Gary," Kassidy said as she gathered her books from the kitchen table, "to keep you from becoming the apartment loser."

Gary chortled as Kassidy went into her room to put her books away.

* * *

While Gary was distracted, Bev and Treena exchanged a concerned glance. On the way home from the bishop's office, Treena had confided to Bev that she had never seen Kassidy act like this around a guy before. Her usual pattern was to go out with them a time or two, then drop them. From what Treena had seen last night and today, Kassidy had fallen hard for Gary.

"Bev, what if he doesn't feel the same way?" Treena had asked earlier.

The question haunting both girls, they smiled politely until Gary and Kassidy left, then discussed possible outcomes for the budding relationship.

"If Gary isn't serious about her, she'll go to pieces," Treena predicted as they searched through Kassidy's things for the address book.

"Gary's a nice guy. I don't think he would purposely do anything to hurt her."

"But if he learns she has some problems——let's be realistic, Bev. He's a returned missionary. He's probably looking for wife material."

"And you don't think he'll find that in Kassidy?"

Treena shook her head.

"Where did this come from?" Bev asked, picking a book up from the desk.

"It's something Gary gave her to read a couple of weeks ago."

Bev thumbed through the pages. "He knows," she asserted.

"What?"

"Look through this book and then tell me he doesn't know what's going on."

Taking the book, *Born to Win*, from Bev's outstretched hand, Treena flipped through several pages. She read a few lines here and there, pausing at the following paragraph that had been highlighted with a yellow marker:

Every infant needs touch to grow. Positive stroking encourages infants to grow into the winners they were born to be . . . Your own mental and physical health are likely to be related to the ways you were touched and recognized. If you have negative patterns about touch or recognition and wish to expand your capabilities, it is never too late to learn how.

"I wonder if she highlighted that," Treena mused aloud.

"Highlighted what?"

Treena handed the book back to Bev. She waited until Bev had had a chance to read through the paragraph, then asked, "What do you think?"

"Kassidy is full of surprises—and Gary knows more than we think."

"I hope so," Treena said. "The fact that he's got her reading something like this is a step in the right direction."

"And look what I found sitting here on her side of the desk," Bev said, holding up a yellow highlighting marker.

"Maybe things aren't as bad as we think."

"Maybe not, but I'm still glad we talked to the bishop about it. Like he said, Kassidy needs a support system; she needs help. The thing is, Heavenly Father knows what Kassidy is going through. She's one of His beloved daughters. He'll watch out for her," Bev stated with conviction.

"True, but I still believe in that old Arabic saying."

"What's that?"

"'Trust in God, but tether your camel.'"

"Which means?"

"Have faith that God will help us, but only if we're willing to do our part. So, let's keep looking for that address book and then, while I'm gone baby-sitting for the apartment managers tonight, do what you can to keep Kassidy from being alone."

"You're baby-sitting again?" Bev asked.

"Hey, it's a way to make more money, something I always seem to need," Treena said with a smile. "Now, back to Kassidy. If Gary makes her eat tonight, I'll bet she'll fake being sick. She'll come home to throw it up," she warned. "See if you can keep her from doing that."

"Right," Bev returned. "How long did you say you'll be gone?" she asked, a worried look on her face.

"Probably till midnight. Audry said that she and her husband are counting this as their date night for the week," she said, referring to the apartment managers. "They're heading down to Idaho Falls to a wedding reception, and from there who knows?" She glanced at her watch. "Speaking of which, I need to run down to their place in a few minutes."

"If it gets too complicated with Kass, I'll come fill in for you," Bev offered.

"You can handle this. We're in this together now, remember?"

"I know," Bev replied. "Good luck to us both."

"I gather you've met Audry's kids."

Bev grinned. "They make my twin brothers look like angels."

"I have to think of the money."

"Is it worth it?"

"Probably not," Treena said as she hurried from the bedroom.

Chapter 18

A week went by. During that time, Bev and Treena took turns keeping an eye on Kassidy.

As far as they could tell, she hadn't thrown up in their apartment while they were around. There were those times when they were in class, unable to stop Kassidy if she chose to go home, binge, then purge. Aware that they were doing the best that they could, they still worried.

Their bishop called twice to see how things were going. They hadn't been able to get hold of Kassidy's address book but promised to keep trying. He told them he had found out some exciting news about a counseling center for eating disorders in Orem, Utah, and that as soon as he had talked to someone at the center, he would be in touch.

Brightening at this news, the two girls renewed their efforts to find Kassidy's address book, sensing they might need the support of a family member.

"It's got to be in her purse," Treena said Thursday night after she had returned home from working at the grocery store.

"We've looked everywhere else," Bev agreed. "How can we get it from her?"

"I don't know. We can't be too obvious," Treena replied, following Bev into the kitchen.

"She loves to do hair and makeup. What if I ask her to give me some pointers tonight when she gets back with Gary?"

"I could hurry and look through her purse."

"I think that's our best bet," Bev said, smiling.

"I hate being sneaky."

"She'll thank you for this someday."

"Maybe," Treena said, frowning. "I don't know, Bev. I hope she won't hate us for what we're doing."

"Think of the big picture, Treena. What's the most important thing here?"

"I know . . . but it's hard."

Agreeing, Bev began removing dishes from the kitchen sink. "I'll get these done right quick. I put them off earlier to finish an assignment for my chemistry class."

"I'd offer to help, but I've got a ton of homework to tackle myself."

"Next time," Bev said as she began rinsing plates to load into the dishwasher.

* * *

"Why are you so nervous tonight?" Karen asked, glancing up from her journal.

Bev turned to face Karen. "I'm not nervous."

"You've been pacing around this apartment all night."

As if to prove Karen wrong, Bev flopped down on her bed. "I need to talk to Kassidy. I'm waiting for her to get home."

"What do you need to talk to her about?"

"Hair, makeup, that sort of thing."

Karen smirked. "Yeah, I believe that one. You've never let anyone do your hair or makeup since you were about seven."

Jesse slipped inside their bedroom. "I'm hurt."

"Why?" Bev asked.

"Why didn't you come to me for hair and makeup tips?"

Picking up a pillow, Bev threw it at the slender girl.

Jesse caught it with ease and threw it back, hitting Bev in the head. "There, I like that tousled look much better."

"You'll think tousled look," Bev threatened as she chased after Jesse. Catching her out in the hall, she pushed Jesse to the carpeted floor, then began running her fingers through Jesse's hair.

"Stop it," Jesse laughed.

"What is going on out here?" Meg demanded to know as she walked out of her bedroom. "I should've guessed," she said, glaring down at Bev and Jesse. "This is why I can't study in this apartment," she snapped. "I don't know why I even try!"

"Sorry," Bev said, sharing a grin with Jesse. "We'll settle down."

"Right," Meg snapped. "I'm heading down to Idaho Falls tomorrow for another clinical session at the hospital; I'll be working in the pediatric unit. This is the only time I'll be able to study for a test I have the next day. Thanks for helping me out!" Moving back to her bedroom, she firmly shut the door.

"What's up with her?" Bev asked as she stood. "She's grumpier than normal."

"Ryan," Jesse explained, rising from the floor.

Bev laughed at the way Jesse's short auburn hair was sticking out in every direction. "Ryan?" she managed to ask.

"He was flirting with someone else Tuesday night at that ward activity he and Meg threw together—the chess tournament."

"No wonder she's so moody."

"I don't know what's going on with those two. Last Friday they seemed like the perfect couple, but he's been avoiding her ever since."

"I'll talk to him and see what the problem is," Bev offered.

Grabbing a brush, Jesse nodded. "You sure made a rat's nest out of my hair."

"You deserved it."

"What does Jesse deserve?" Kassidy asked, stepping into the hall.

"When did you get back?" Bev asked.

"A few minutes ago. I was in time for Meg's lecture . . . that's why I kept a low profile."

Bev smiled. "Yeah, I guess we need to keep things quiet tonight." She glanced at Jesse, who was still trying to untangle her hair. "Kassidy, could you answer a few questions that Jesse and I have about hair and makeup?"

"Now wait a minute. This new look of mine is your fault," Jesse pointed out, turning away from the large mirror. "I'm not into doing hair and makeup, okay?!"

"As I recall, not long ago you were complaining about not dating," Bev returned. "We could both benefit from Kassidy's talents.

I'm thinking of going for a new look, and well, you need to start acquiring one."

"Thanks," Jesse said, scowling at Bev.

"Could you help us out tonight, Kass?" Bev pleaded.

"Sure. Let me put my jacket and purse away, and I'll be right with you."

Thrilled she had pulled off her part of the deception, Bev stepped next to Jesse. "You do know I'm kidding about the hair and makeup thing?"

Looking unconvinced, Jesse nodded.

"You don't have to stick around if you don't want to."

"Actually, this might be more fun than watching Meg study."

"Cool," Bev said, glancing up as Kassidy moved back to the bathroom.

"Okay, what did you want to do?" Kassidy asked.

Bev ran a hand through her thick black hair. "Give me some ideas. What hairstyles would look best with my face shape?"

* * *

When Kassidy left the room, Treena rose from her bed, pushed the door partially closed, and hurried to the desk where Kassidy had set her purse. She took out Kassidy's wallet and moved things around until she found what she was looking for. Her hands shaking, she thumbed through the address book. Uncertain of the aunt's last name, she watched for the name Kassidy had mentioned—Janice. Praying Bev could keep Kassidy occupied long enough, she went through page after page, finding what she was looking for toward the back of the small book—Janice Wharton. She grabbed a piece of paper from her side of the desk and scribbled down the telephone number and address, her eyes widening when she saw that Kassidy's aunt lived in Chubbuck, Idaho. *That's not far from here*, Treena thought. *Bev and I could drive down on Saturday while Kassidy is in Ashton.*

"Let me grab a book from my bedroom. It shows several different hairstyles," Kassidy said out in the hall.

Treena jumped. Picking up the address book, she shoved it back inside of Kassidy's purse.

"Kassidy, wait a minute! What do you think about this?" Bev said in a valiant attempt to give Treena more time.

Treena folded the paper she had written the address on and tucked it into the back pocket of her jeans.

"This book will help. Let me grab it," Kassidy insisted.

Sitting on her bed, Treena tried to look natural. Then she saw Kassidy's wallet sitting on the desk.

"Oww!" Bev cried out from the hall.

"What's wrong, Bev?" Kassidy asked.

"Pain, right here," Bev exclaimed.

Breathing out a silent thank-you, Treena picked up Kassidy's wallet and replaced it inside Kassidy's purse. She then stretched out on her bed to read in a children's literature book. Sighing, she hoped the adventures she might experience teaching elementary-age children would pale in comparison to what she had endured with Kassidy.

* * *

Praying she had given Treena enough time, Bev wondered how much longer she needed to keep up the pretense of being sick. She remained doubled over, gripping her side with her hand.

"Jesse, run and get Meg," Kassidy said as she stayed with Bev.

Jesse ran down the hall after her cousin.

"What's wrong with Bev?" Karen asked, walking down to the bathroom.

"Stomachache," Bev said through clenched teeth.

"What's going on?" Meg asked, pushing everyone out of the way to take a look at Bev. "Where do you hurt?"

"Here," Bev said, pointing to her stomach. She glanced up as Treena stepped out of the bedroom. The confident smile on Treena's face gave her the sign she needed.

"I don't think it's your appendix," Meg said.

"I had that out when I was nine," Bev replied, anxious to get this ruse over with. "Whatever it is, it's not as bad now."

"The cramps are letting up?" Meg asked.

Bev nodded. "Maybe I just need to lie down. Karen, could you help me out here?"

Karen slipped an arm around Bev's waist and escorted her toward their bedroom.

"I'll be fine," Bev called back. "We'll talk later, okay, Kass?"

"Yeah, get to feeling better," Kassidy encouraged.

"Kass, tell me about your date tonight," Treena said, leading Kassidy into the living room.

"Karen, let me know if Bev gets worse," Meg instructed as she moved back inside her own bedroom.

"I will," Karen promised. "I'm sure she'll be fine, though."

"I hope so," Jesse said, following behind Karen and Bev.

"Jesse, have you seen my blue highlighting pen?" Meg called out.

"Dang it! I forgot to put it back in her bag," Jesse mumbled, hurrying into her bedroom.

Karen guided Bev into the bedroom they shared. She helped Bev onto her bed, then stood with her arms folded, looking down at her friend.

"What?"

"I know you're faking, so quit with the dying routine. What's going on?"

"Maybe it was dinner tonight. Jesse tried to cook, remember? That stuff she passed off as gravy could work as cement," Bev said, referring to the biscuits with sausage gravy Jesse had prepared that night. Claiming it was one of her favorite meals, Jesse had had a difficult time following her mother's recipe.

"I don't know what you're up to, but I can tell when a scam is going down," Karen insisted.

Bev grinned. "Karen, I have my reasons, okay? Someday I'll tell you all about it, but for now I need you to trust me. Will you help me out?"

Karen remained silent.

"Please? It's for an important cause."

"All right. But this had better be good."

"It is," Bev promised solemnly.

"How's Bev doin'?" Jesse asked, poking her head inside the room.

"I think she needs to get some rest," Karen replied, "but she'll be all right."

"Meg said to tell you that she has some Pepto-Bismol, and Kassidy has some laxatives if that's the problem."

"Laxatives would be a good idea," Karen said, glancing down at Bev. "I think she needs to clean things out, get stuff moving through there."

Jesse obediently hurried from the room.

"I'm not taking a laxative!"

Karen smiled at Bev. "It won't kill you. Besides, you just said that you ate cement for supper. Laxatives will help."

"Karen!"

"Are you feeling set up? Paybacks are bad, huh?"

"This isn't funny!" Bev exclaimed.

"Relax, if she comes in here with it, I'll put it in my purse. Maybe one of us will need it sometime."

Bev glowered at Karen when Jesse reappeared a few minutes later with a glass of water and two small tablets.

"What is that?" Bev asked.

"Take it. Kassidy said it's a natural laxative. Better for you than some. It should help."

"I'm sure it will," Bev muttered, taking the tablets and water from Jesse while Karen tried not to laugh.

* * *

"Feeling better?" Treena asked sympathetically.

Bev glared from the couch.

"You shouldn't have taken that stuff last night."

"I figured it was the only way to throw Jesse, Meg, and Kassidy off the trail. Karen knows something is going on, but she has no idea what."

Treena stifled a giggle, then tried to pass it off as a coughing fit. "Karen seems to be enjoying your discomfort this morning," she choked out.

"Yeah, well, lucky me, that stuff they gave me last night was the extra strength version. Evidently, I'm a bit sensitive to it."

"Are you going to be okay here by yourself?" Treena asked, sobering.

"Yeah, go to class. I haven't missed any days yet this term. It won't kill me to miss today. I don't dare get away from *the facilities,* if you know what I mean." Bev grabbed her stomach.

"Are you all right?"

"Never been better," Bev said as she fled to the bathroom.

* * *

That afternoon as Bev lay dozing on the couch, Kassidy cautiously crept into the apartment. She tiptoed past the living room, walked into her bedroom, and shut the door. For almost a week she hadn't felt the *urge to purge,* as Treena called it. But today, as she fretted over meeting Gary's parents, she struggled with an increasing inner pressure that demanded release. "I can't do this. I can't," she murmured, lying down on her bed. She tried to push from her mind the thought of how wonderful the chocolate cake on the kitchen counter would taste. "No! I am not going to do this," she lectured herself as her body screamed for food. Several minutes went by as her resolve faded. Giving in, she tiptoed into the kitchen and took the cake Karen had made the night before. She tensed when she heard a sound from the living room, then relaxed when she realized it was Bev's soft snore. Quietly selecting a fork from the silverware drawer, she escaped into her bedroom and shut the door.

* * *

"I don't know what happened to your cake." Bev slowly sat up to face Karen. She had retreated to her bed earlier that afternoon to sleep through the worst of her self-induced illness.

Karen glared fiercely at Bev. "I baked that cake for the guy I met the first week we were here—John Daniels. He's in my religion class. He has been feeling down lately and I thought a homemade chocolate cake would cheer him up."

"Karen, look at me. Do I even appear to be interested in food right now? I don't think so!" White-faced, Bev knew she looked as bad as she felt. The mirror in the bathroom had confirmed that for her hours ago.

"No, but my guess is you didn't eat it. You probably threw it away to get even with me!" Karen's dark eyes blazed with fury.

"Right! I couldn't even punch my way out of a paper bag right now, but I supposedly destroyed an entire chocolate cake! And why would I be trying to get even with you, anyway?"

Karen pointed at Bev. "Because you're blaming me for this when you were the one stupid enough to take those laxatives last night. I just can't believe you would be this immature! I made that cake from scratch!"

Bev sat in stunned amazement. How could Karen think she would do such a thing? On the contrary, if she had known Karen was making a cake for a guy, she would've done anything in her power to help, not hinder, this progressive step.

"Thanks a lot," Karen said as she stormed out of their bedroom.

Too weak to follow, Bev collapsed back on her bed and groaned.

Chapter 19

"And this is my favorite hay bale. I call him Belvadere."

Kassidy groaned. "Are we quite through with this lovely tour of your haystack?"

"You're not enjoying it?" Gary feigned surprise.

"I've seen about all of the hay bales I can handle—for now," she said, her breath visible as the sun began to sink from sight. Kassidy watched as it started to slip behind violet-colored mountains, spraying the sky with streaks of pink and orange. Gary was right, the Ashton area was gorgeous. Earlier he had taken her to see one of his favorite places, Mesa Falls, a beautiful landmark located north of Ashton. She had loved the way the crystal water had cascaded over jagged rocks to crash noisily below. Across from the falls, a moss-covered rock wall had added a dash of color, a vivid green, lending a sense of enchantment to this magical place. She had understood immediately why he loved it.

"Hey, if you look over there, toward the east, you can see the Idaho side of the Teton Peaks," he said now, pointing toward a distant mountain range.

Turning to look east, she could barely make out the famous mountains.

"Cool, huh?"

"It's great! You know, I've never been to Jackson—that's where the Tetons are, right?"

Gary nodded. "We'll have to remedy that. I'll take you over there sometime, okay?"

Kassidy nodded.

"For the moment, how would you like to check out a horse or two? I think we have time before dinner. Besides, it's warmer in the barn."

"I love horses."

"Ever been on one?"

Kassidy shook her head. "No. But I've always thought horses are majestic animals."

"Oh, they are. Especially when they're trying to throw you off in the mud." As he led her away from the open-end shelter where the hay was stored, Gary reached for Kassidy's hand as they walked toward a medium-sized barn.

"How many horses do you have?"

"Four," was the reply. "We used to have five, but Dad sold one last year to finish paying for my mission."

"I'm sorry."

"Me, too," Gary replied. "It was my horse. He was a beauty too, a big palomino stud. That's why he went for such a good price. Our neighbor has had his eye on that horse ever since I bought him. He wanted to use him to breed his mares."

Kassidy blushed. She was learning there were things taken for granted on a farm that one didn't normally talk about in polite company.

"But it went for a good cause. Staying out in the mission field was more important than having a beautiful horse."

"What kind of horses do you still have?"

"Dad has always loved Appaloosas. We have two of those. Then there's Mom's little pinto, and a mixed breed that belongs to my younger brother, a cross between my palomino and one of Dad's Appaloosas."

"I'll bet that's an interesting color."

"Yeah. Kind of a pale gold with dark spots on its rump. We call it a *pal-appy.* Or as Dad says, our little *app-pal,* or *apple* for short."

Kassidy smiled. "You're quite the comedian."

"I'm serious, that's what my brother named it—Apple. Ask him tonight."

"I will."

Gary unlatched the barn, then helped Kassidy slip inside. "Watch your step, our majestic animals usually leave treasures in their wake."

Reaching around a corner, he flipped on a switch that illuminated the interior of the wooden building.

"You have lights out here?"

"We backward folk have tried to keep up with latest modern conveniences."

"That's not what I meant," Kassidy said, giving him a playful shove.

"I know. I was giving you a bad time. Come on. Let's meet the horses. If you want, maybe tomorrow we could go for a ride."

"I've always wanted to do that," Kassidy said excitedly. "The only thing I've ever ridden was a pony at a carnival when I was about six. Dad gave in and let me try it. Mom was furious."

"Why?"

"She said it wasn't ladylike to ride horses."

Gary frowned. "Doesn't your mother know that queens ride horses?"

Kassidy shrugged.

"And tomorrow the queen of my heart will join them," he added, leading her down to where the horses were nickering for attention. "Here's Apple."

"He's pretty," Kassidy commented, wondering if Gary meant what he had said about her being the queen of his heart. He kidded around so much, it was hard to know when he was being serious.

"She," Gary gently corrected.

"Oh, she," Kassidy repeated, reaching to pet Apple's nose.

"And be careful, she'll try to nip you."

Kassidy drew her hand away.

"Come meet Mom's pinto. She's a doll—sweetest disposition I've ever seen in a horse."

Kassidy followed him to the next stall. "Do you always keep them cooped up like this?"

"Just during bad weather. Right now we're keeping them close while we finish rounding up our Herefords."

"Your what?"

"Beef cattle. We used to run a dairy, but we lost a lot of money with that. Now we raise cattle for beef. During the summer we take them out into the hills behind our ranch."

"Why?"

"So they can graze on the wild grass. Then in the fall we round them up. We sell some of them and the rest we keep in a large corral through the winter where we feed them hay."

"I see," Kassidy said, patting the pinto's forehead. "Your mom's horse seems nice."

"She is."

"What's her name?"

"Spot."

Kassidy glanced at the brown splotches coloring the mare's cream-colored coat. "Really?"

"No," Gary chuckled. "Actually, her name is Pearl. Mom thinks she's of great price."

Kassidy smiled. "I see where you get your warped sense of humor."

"Guilty as charged. Now, you two get acquainted while I check their water buckets. If you'd like, you can ride Pearl tomorrow. Dad said he needs someone to ride the range and locate some of our missing steers. Interested?"

"Oh, yes," Kassidy said as she stroked Pearl's long nose. To her delight, Pearl leaned closer.

"Hey, she likes you. That's a good sign. She's a great judge of character."

Certain Gary was being a smart aleck again, Kassidy reached to pet Pearl's silky neck.

"I'm serious. She's a nice horse, but she doesn't take to everybody. I think you two will get along fine tomorrow."

Hoping Gary was right, Kassidy smiled. Maybe this weekend wouldn't be so bad after all.

* * *

An hour later when Kassidy and Gary entered the old white farmhouse, the aroma of barbequed meat tantalized their appetites.

"Oh, yeah! Mom loves me," Gary sang out. "This is one of my favorites."

"It's everybody's favorite," Margaret Dawson exclaimed from the kitchen.

Kassidy followed Gary into the large room that was decorated with yellow sunflowers. Everything she could see was covered with the cheery flowers, from the curtains, to the canisters, to the clock that was shaped like a large sunflower. "This room is so cute," she said to Gary's mother, a woman she had met briefly when they had first arrived.

"Thanks," Margaret said, looking up from the metal bowl of mashed potatoes she had whipped together. "I love sunflowers—can you tell?"

Glancing around again, Kassidy politely nodded.

"They're hardy flowers. They grow up bright and beautiful despite what the weather throws their way. They push on past the weeds and rocks—true survivors. I keep them around, hoping their traits will rub off on me," Margaret said, returning Kassidy's smile.

Kassidy had already decided that she liked Gary's mother. Since her arrival at the ranch, Margaret Dawson had done her best to make Kassidy feel welcome. In her mid-forties, Margaret had a warm smile that was infectious. Her short brown hair was naturally curly and framed her heart-shaped face. She was comfortably dressed in a pair of faded jeans and an old, blue, button-down shirt, her attire matching her easygoing disposition.

Margaret's brown eyes twinkled as she gazed at Kassidy, and then at her son. "Did you enjoy your tour of the ranch?"

"Especially the horses," Kassidy beamed.

"She hit it off with Pearl big-time."

Margaret beamed. "I love that horse."

"She's so gentle," Kassidy added.

"Would it be all right with you if Kassidy rode her tomorrow?" Gary asked, sniffing the brown gravy his mother had made from scratch.

"Sure. Hey, stay out of that! We're going to eat in a minute," Margaret chided.

"Okay," Gary said meekly.

"Not only that, if you've been out playing with the horses, you need to wash up."

"We can take a hint," Gary said, motioning for Kassidy to follow him to the bathroom down the hall.

* * *

"Mom, you outdid yourself. This food is fantastic," Gary said before cramming another bite of mashed potatoes and gravy into his mouth.

Kassidy stared down at her plate. Gary and his younger brother, sixteen-year-old Nate, had taken turns dishing up her food. She knew they were trying to be helpful, but there was no way she could possibly eat all that they had given her. As she picked at what was there, she wondered how to get out of this without hurting Margaret's feelings.

"Mom, do you know what Nate did?" nine-year-old Becky inquired.

Twelve-year-old Courtney scowled at her younger sister. "Becky, we've got company."

"Becky, what did your brother do?" Margaret asked.

"Please, no Nate stories; we're eating," Gary joked, laughing with his dad who was sitting at the other end of the table.

"It was nothing, Mom," Nate assured.

"I'll bet," Thomas Dawson replied. Tall with broad shoulders, Thomas was an older version of his son, Gary.

"He had a squirt fight with Courtney when they were milking the goats . . . and he got me right in the face," the indignant nine-year-old related.

Courtney turned a deep shade of red while the rest of the family struggled to keep a straight face.

"Did I miss something?" Kassidy asked. "And why would you have a water fight when you're trying to milk goats?"

Nate nearly choked on a piece of meat as he laughed. "Tell her, Gary," he said when he could breathe again.

"Uh, well . . . you see," Gary struggled as his dad and siblings continued to laughed.

Margaret smiled kindly at the beautiful young woman. "Kassidy, maybe after dinner Gary could take you outside and let you see the goats. We have quite a dairy herd."

"I thought you said you went out of the dairy business," Kassidy replied, still confused.

Gary met her questioning gaze with a smile. "We don't raise dairy cows anymore. We do have a few goats."

"Five big ones and two babies," Becky said, "plus Prometheus."

"Prometheus?"

"He's a boy goat," Becky explained.

"There's quite a market for goat milk these days," Thomas added. "We started raising dairy goats while Gary was on his mission."

Margaret passed the bowl of mashed potatoes back to Gary. "There are a lot of babies who are allergic to infant formula, but they thrive on goat's milk. We've been able to sell most of what we can produce."

"Mom makes cheese out of what's left over," Becky said, stabbing the corn on her plate with her fork.

Kassidy tried to inconspicuously study the slice of cheese sitting on her plate.

Grinning, Gary leaned over. "That's regular cheese from the store, but the kind Mom makes is good stuff too."

Embarrassed, Kassidy took a tiny nibble from the cheese slice.

"Try some of that barbeque. Mom makes the sauce from scratch. It's awesome!" Gary encouraged.

Nodding, Kassidy cut away a small piece of meat with her fork, amazed by how tender it appeared. She poked it into her mouth and was hit with a sudden rush of flavor. "That *is* good."

"Thanks," Margaret said, smiling. "It's a family recipe, one I learned from my mother."

Deciding to give it another try, Kassidy cut a slightly bigger piece. She then sampled the potatoes and gravy and was struck again by how wonderful everything seemed to taste. Although she wasn't able to finish the generous portions on her plate, she did manage to eat until she was full. The problem was, her body wasn't used to handling that much food. As she pushed away from the table, she was plagued by a wave of nausea.

"Should we go out and take a look at the goats?"

Kassidy turned to look at Gary. "Doesn't your mother need some help cleaning up?"

Margaret slipped an arm around Courtney. "My girls have dish detail tonight. I figure, I make the mess; the least they can do is clean it up."

"Yay," Courtney said dryly. "Come on, Becky. There's a TV movie I want to watch tonight."

Leaving his sisters to clean up the mess from dinner, Gary retrieved his jacket and Kassidy's and led her back to the front door. "You okay?"

"Yeah," Kassidy lied. "Let's go see those goats."

Gary opened the door and escorted her through.

* * *

"These baby goats are so adorable," Kassidy said as she reached down to pet the black-haired kids. Their long ears were speckled with white. They blatted at her, bumping their tiny noses against her hand. "What kind did you say they were?"

"Nubians. They're purebreds. Dad said that the only other kind of goat that produces as much milk are the Saanens, but he liked how the Nubians looked."

"What do the Saanens look like?"

"They're white with short ears. Dad thought they'd be too hard to keep clean."

"These two act like they want something."

"They always act hungry. I know Becky fed them both before supper. That's why she was in here getting squirted. If you feed them any more, they'll burst."

Kassidy felt the same way. Trying to keep her mind off the nausea, she glanced at Gary. "That reminds me, what was so funny about the squirt fight?"

Gary laughed. "Oh, that. The best way to explain it is to show you. Come here," he said, leading Kassidy past a series of empty stalls. "This time of year, when the older goats aren't being milked, we keep them together in this large pen. Goats have a bad reputation, but they're fascinating creatures. They're very sociable. We've found that if we keep them together, at least the doe population, they get along better. They're not as likely to escape. It's when they're penned in by themselves that they get into trouble."

"The doe population?"

"The female goats. A lot of people call them nanny goats, but a true goat keeper knows that the girls are called does. And the male goats are called bucks, not billy goats."

"Do they eat tin cans?"

"No, they're very picky. They won't even drink their water if there's straw or hay in it."

"You're kidding. Then why—"

"The bad rep?" Gary finished for her.

Kassidy nodded.

"They're smart, curious animals. They want to know about everything, so they sample stuff. If they pick up a tin can, it's to try out the paper wrapped around it, not the can itself. They prefer green grass and fresh vegetables. You should see what they do to my mom's garden when they get out." He stepped close to the large holding pen and climbed over the wooden panel.

"Gary, will you be all right?"

"They're tame." He selected the nearest doe and pointed underneath. "See this?"

Kassidy nodded.

"It's called a bag or udder."

"That's where the milk comes from?"

"Yep. Now if you look down here, this is the biggest difference between a cow's udder and a goat's. A cow's udder has four . . . uh . . . sections, but a goat has only two."

Kassidy knew her face was as scarlet as the jacket she was wearing.

"And this is how my brother and sister had a squirt fight earlier," he continued, sending a stream of goat's milk toward Kassidy.

"Hey," she complained as the milk splashed on a wooden panel near where she was standing.

"Want to give it a try?"

"I'll pass. Maybe tomorrow."

"How about in the morning? That'll be something you can go home and tell the roommates about. I'll bet none of them have ever milked a goat."

"I'll bet you're right," Kassidy agreed as her queasiness increased. Turning from the holding pen, she took a deep breath. "What is that smell?"

"My new cologne."

"I hope not or I'm never getting near you again."

"You mean like this," Gary said, hopping over the panel to walk up behind her. He wrapped his arms around her and gave her a hug.

Kassidy winced as her stomach continued to gurgle.

Gary sniffed the air. "Phew, I know what you're talking about. Come with me. There's one more goat you have to meet."

"The one that stinks?"

Laughing, Gary took Kassidy's hand and led her to the back of the goat shed. "You have to meet Prometheus."

"Pro-what?"

"Becky named him. She's into Greek mythology right now," he said, pulling her along. "This is Prometheus, the proud buck of the Dawson ranch."

"He smells bad."

"Only during mating season. Right now he's into attracting the ladies, if you know what I mean. The rest of the time he's not too bad."

Unable to control herself any longer, Kassidy turned from the pen and began throwing up. When she finished, she ran from the shed, crying.

* * *

"This should help," Margaret soothed, placing a cool, damp cloth on Kassidy's forehead. "That was a mean trick to get you that close to Prometheus, especially now. He's potent."

"That smell was awful," Kassidy agreed. She was lying on the bed in the guest bedroom, doing her best to ignore the pain in her stomach.

"Gary should've known better," Margaret scolded.

Kassidy forced a weak smile. "He was excited for me to see all of the goats. I've never been on a farm before," she confided. "Unless you count the one I saw briefly on my way to Rexburg the end of August. We stopped at a farm that belonged to my friend's aunt and uncle. I didn't go near the animals then, but I've enjoyed seeing the ones you guys have. You have a nice farm."

"Well, I'll see to it that Gary's a better guide the rest of the weekend." Margaret smiled. "Would you like to try some herbal tea? It might settle things down."

Kassidy gazed up at Gary's mother. She was everything Gary had said—caring, funny, and smart. Why did some kids get all the breaks?

The thought of kids brought back images of the goats and the smell she was sure she would never forget.

"Kassidy, would you like some tea?" Margaret repeated.

"Sorry, I'm not feeling very well tonight."

"I can tell. You're white as a sheet. I'll go make you a cup of camomile tea. It'll work wonders. And don't worry, there's no caffeine in it," she added as she moved to the door.

* * *

"Is she all right?" Gary worriedly asked as he met his mother at the foot of the stairs.

"No thanks to you," Margaret said, poking him in the stomach.

"I didn't think Prometheus would affect her that way."

Margaret motioned for him to follow her down the hall into the kitchen. "Son, she was sick during dinner."

"What?"

"I was watching her. You know what you told me a couple of weeks ago, that you suspect she has a problem with food?"

Gary nodded.

"I think you're right. I haven't been around her as much as you have, but something's wrong." She pulled out a small saucepan and filled it with water. Walking to the stove, she turned on a burner and set the pan on top of it. "And it's sad—she seems like such a sweet girl."

"She is. But she's so skinny. The other day I was tickling her—I could feel her ribs."

Margaret gave him a pointed look. "I see," she said as he blushed.

"The thing is, I'm worried about her."

"Tell me more about her family. You said they're not very close, but give me some details."

Gary frowned as he told his mother everything he knew.

"That explains a few things," she said, pulling a mug down from the cupboard. She found a small box of camomile tea and selected a single-serving bag. Placing it in the mug, she poured the hot water on top of it and set it on the counter. "How serious is your relationship with her?"

"Mom!"

"I'm not saying I object," she said, holding up a hand. "There's an old saying, son. It goes something like this: A bird with a broken wing only needs mending. But once it has healed, it can fly higher than the rest." She sat down on a kitchen chair to wait for the tea to cool. "Your bird has a broken wing."

"How do we heal her?"

"That's the million-dollar question," she replied.

Chapter 20

"So you're rooming with my niece," Kassidy's aunt repeated. The attractive, heavyset woman was dressed in a blue sweatshirt and gray sweat bottoms. The only resemblance she bore to Kassidy was the blonde hair, but Janice Wharton kept hers shorter and swept away from her face.

Bev nodded, relieved that Janice had been home, but nervous over what they had to tell her.

"Come on in," she said cheerfully. "Will you have something to drink? Pop or hot cocoa? It's chilly out there today."

"Pop is fine," Treena replied.

Janice turned to Bev. "Is that okay with you?"

"Sure," Bev agreed.

"Pop it is then. Is creme soda all right?"

"I love creme soda," Bev said.

"I like it too," Treena added.

"Good enough. Three creme sodas coming right up."

Bev hoped she didn't look as nervous as she felt. "Can we help you?"

"I can get it. Have a seat, and I'll be right with you," she said as she bustled from sight.

Bev glanced around the large living room. This part seemed to fit the description of Kassidy's family. It was a beautifully furnished room. A baby grand piano stood in one corner. Opposite it was a white-tiled fireplace. Above the fireplace hung a painting of a cottage in a woodland setting. Bev stepped closer for a better look. She loved the mixture of pastels the artist had used.

"You like it?" Janice queried.

Bev turned to smile at Janice. "I love it."

"Me, too. That's why I'll never sell it," she said as she handed Bev a tall frosted glass filled with ice cubes and chilled creme soda.

Treena stared at the painting, then at Kassidy's aunt. "You're an artist?"

"Some people say that," Janice replied as she handed a glass to Treena.

"Thanks," Treena murmured, glancing again at the painting.

"You painted that?" Bev said. "It's beautiful!"

"Thanks. It was one of the first ones I did after my husband died."

"Oh, sorry. We didn't know," Bev stammered.

Janice sipped from her glass. "It happened about five years ago. After thirty wonderful years together, he keeled over with a heart attack." She walked over to a tan, leather couch and sat down. "Have a seat, girls. You don't need to stand."

Bev followed Treena to a nearby love seat that matched the couch. "This is so soft," she commented as she sat down.

"I believe in being comfortable," Janice responded.

"You have a beautiful home," Treena observed.

"Thank you. My husband built it. It was our dream home. We saved forever. But I'd trade it all in a heartbeat if he could be here with me now. I'd be happy in a little trailer house if he could be there too." She looked pensive for several seconds, then brightened, as if remembering the girls who were with her.

"Do you have any children?" Bev ventured.

"Two, a boy and a girl. They're married now of course. One lives in Salt Lake City with his wife and two daughters. My daughter lives in Washington. Her husband is a computer genius. They have a little boy."

"That's nice," Treena said absently.

"Well, I know you didn't come here to talk about my family. What's going on with Kassidy? I haven't seen her since she was about twelve. You say she's going to Ricks?"

"BYU–Idaho," Bev said before taking a careful sip from her glass. She didn't want to spill it on the expensive sofa.

"That's right. I heard they were changing the name." The telephone rang and Janice frowned. "All I have to do is sit down to enjoy myself and that blasted thing rings. I'll let the answering machine get it." The telephone rang three more times before a machine in the hall picked it up.

"Janice, I know you're there, probably painting away. Listen, I have an idea for Home, Family, and Personal Enrichment meeting next week. Give me a call, and I'll run it past you. Bye. Oh, in case you couldn't tell, this is Evelyn."

Janice laughed. "I knew she'd pull through. Since I started serving as a counselor in the Relief Society presidency, I've tried to let people take some initiative with their callings. I don't think I should be the one to do it all, like our last presidency tried to do. Teach the people correct principles and let them govern themselves. Joseph Smith said that. He's right."

"You're LDS?" Treena asked, relieved.

"Kassidy didn't tell you?"

Treena shook her head. "She doesn't talk much about her family. We had to look inside her address book to find you."

"I see. Is something wrong with Kassidy?" Janice pressed. "Why didn't she come with you?"

"It's a long story, but—"

The telephone rang out again. This time Janice rose from the couch, walked down the hall, and shut off the ringer. "There! Now we can continue uninterrupted. You were saying?" she questioned when she returned to the room.

* * *

"It's so beautiful up here," Kassidy said as she tried to memorize the evergreens and quaking aspens that surrounded them.

"It is," Gary agreed, reaching down to pat his horse's neck. "That trail was pretty steep back there. Are you doing all right?"

"I'm fine, Gary."

"I'm glad your stomach settled down."

"It was probably just a touch of the flu. That tea your mother gave me last night really seemed to help."

"You missed a great breakfast."

"I know, but I didn't dare try it," Kassidy said, as Pearl wandered to a creek to drink.

"I'm just glad you're feeling better."

"Me too," Kassidy replied.

"Well, we shouldn't overdo it. We won't go too much further."

"I'm okay, Gary. I love this!" she said, gesturing around.

"You're going to be sore," he cautioned.

"Probably, but who knows when I'll get another chance like this? You said yourself it'll snow soon. Didn't you say they're predicting light snow showers next week?"

Gary nodded.

"Then we'd better find those missing steers."

Grinning at her spunk, he nudged his horse to follow behind Kassidy.

* * *

"I ought to slap that sister of mine!" Janice fumed. "From the time we were young, she has acted like she was queen of the world— always too good for everyone else. I don't know where that came from, either. Our parents were never that way. Dad was a schoolteacher; Mom stayed at home. We were both raised in the LDS Church. There were just the two of us, but we were complete opposites."

Treena nodded in agreement. She had been around Kassidy's mother several times. Constance Martin was a tall, slender, beautiful woman who strived for elegant perfection. The woman made Treena nervous; she felt like she was under constant scrutiny whenever she was in Kassidy's home. She knew Constance blamed her for Kassidy's decision to attend BYU–Idaho.

"Connie always wanted the fanciest dresses, and would only date the most popular boys. I think she was born with her nose in the air. She's always been a scrawny thing. She must've taken after our grandfather—he was skinny as a rail. The rest of our family has a tendency to put on weight. Mom was a little heavy, I've always been heavy, Dad was very solid. Then there was Connie."

"She goes by Constance," Treena said.

"It figures. The entire time she was growing up we called her Connie. She was a pain-in-the-neck little sister who was always trying to tell me what to do. 'Should you be eating that? Don't speak to me at school, Janice. Someone might think I know you,'" she mimicked.

"You're kidding!" Bev said, outraged. "How could she treat you that way?"

Janice shrugged. "We've never been close. I was feeling bad about that too. The other day I was thinking it was time to settle things between us." Her blue eyes narrowed. "Now I'm not so sure. How old is my niece?"

"Nineteen," Treena answered.

"Pretty much an adult. I say it's high time Connie backed off and let her daughter become who she's meant to be."

"That's why we're here. We feel the same way. But we're not sure how to help," Treena replied.

"I want to spend some time with Kassidy." Janice smiled at Treena. "You mentioned that she loves to draw."

"Yeah."

"That might be a starting point. Maybe I'll give her a call tomorrow night. She'll be back from her weekend date with Romeo, right?"

Treena grinned as she nodded. She absolutely loved Kassidy's aunt and hoped Kassidy would feel the same way.

"I'll tell her that I've been thinking about her, which is true, thanks to you girls. Then I'll offer to come get her next weekend. I am looking for an assistant for my art gallery. She could help me out on weekends. That would give me an excuse to keep touching base with her."

"You run an art gallery too?" Bev asked, surprised.

Janice smiled. "In my spare time. I believe in living life to the fullest. Something I think my niece needs to learn."

Bev agreed, returning her smile.

Chapter 21

Bev waited until after sacrament meeting was over before cornering Ryan. "Hey bud, going to Sunday School?"

"I was thinking about it," he replied. "Why?"

"We need to talk."

"We do?"

Bev nodded. "Wait a minute and we'll chat in here," she said, gesturing around the Manwaring Theater where their student ward held sacrament meeting.

"What's up?"

"Ward activities," she replied as the large room emptied.

Relaxing, Ryan grinned. "You have some ideas about what we can do?"

"No, some ideas about what *you* can do," she said, certain they were alone. "First of all, if you're not interested in Meg, quit rubbing it in her face during activity nights."

Ryan grimaced.

"Don't give me that look. I know what you did last week, and I think it's pretty low. Bringing a date to the ward chess tournament? Honestly, Ryan, what were you thinking?"

"It's not like we're engaged or anything," he retorted.

"No, but you sure had Meg convinced that she meant something to you."

"I had myself convinced too, until I took her out."

Bev glared at him. "What?"

"Look, the dance was okay, but I'm moving on. Meg isn't my type. She's too serious, and like you said—too wound up about her cousin. We spent half of the night following Jesse and her date around."

"Was it that bad?" Bev asked, calming down. This was a side of the story she hadn't heard.

"Oh, yeah. When you set this up, you told me Meg could be a lot of laughs," he accused.

"I said, when she loosened up."

"Guess what? She didn't loosen up all night! And when I took her home, she acted like I was a beast that needed to be locked in my cage. I wanted to give her a quick peck on the cheek to show her there were no hard feelings. She wouldn't even let me get near her."

Bev shook her head apologetically. "Sorry, Ryan."

Ryan began walking out of the theater. "Meg's a nice girl, but it would never work between us. I'm sorry if she got her feelings hurt, but as the Spanish say, '*c'est la vie!*'"

"That's French, you idiot," Bev mumbled under her breath.

* * *

"That was weird," Kassidy said as she hung up the telephone Sunday night.

Bev and Treena looked up from the kitchen table where they had been pretending to study.

"What was weird?" Treena asked, tensing up. This was the phone call they had been anticipating.

"That was my aunt, my mom's sister. I haven't seen her since I was in junior high."

"That's cool she called you," Bev commented.

"Yeah, I guess. How did she know I was here?"

Treena exchanged a concerned look with Bev.

"Maybe your mom told her," Bev offered.

"I doubt it. They hate each other."

Treena drew a smiley face on the paper in front of her. "What did she want?"

"She wants to come pick me up Friday night. She's asked me to spend the weekend with her," Kassidy said as she walked to the kitchen table.

"That sounds like fun," Treena said.

"But I don't know her."

"What did you tell her?" Bev asked.

"I would check my schedule and get back to her. She said she'd call again."

Bev frowned. "You have to check your schedule?"

Kassidy nodded. "I might be going back up to Ashton with Gary."

Treena scribbled through the smiley face she had drawn. "He asked you to go up there again?"

"Yes," Kassidy sighed as she stared off into space.

"I take it you had a good weekend," Bev commented.

"It was awesome. I even milked a goat last night."

"You milked a what?" Treena asked, rising from the table to stare at her friend as Bev began laughing hysterically.

"A goat. Her name is Bianca."

Treena smirked at the mental picture that was forming in her mind.

"Gary said you guys wouldn't believe me. Ask him about it when he comes over for family home evening tomorrow night."

"I will," Treena assured. "I can't see you milking anything," she said, laughing.

"I think there are a lot of things about me that would surprise you," Kassidy said in a hurt voice as she walked out of the kitchen and into the hall.

"Kass, we were kidding," Bev said, sobering. "Come tell us all about Gary's farm."

"Yeah," Treena echoed. "I didn't mean to make fun of you. It just sounds so—"

"Unlike me?" Kassidy said, cutting her off. She entered the bedroom and closed the door.

"That went well," Bev stated.

"My fault," Treena admitted.

"We both laughed," Bev pointed out.

"I should've known better," Treena sighed.

"I've been thinking . . . maybe it's time you and I had a chat with Gary."

"I don't know, Bev. If we mess up what's going on with Gary and Kassidy—"

Bev waved her hand impatiently. "Gary has a right to know. I think he already suspects. If we tell him about Kassidy's aunt—"

"He could talk Kassidy into giving Janice a chance," Treena said, catching Bev's vision. Their voices hushed, they began formulating a plan. Deciding not to wait, they called to see if Gary was home. When he answered the phone, they made arrangements to meet with him in ten minutes.

* * *

"What's this all about?" Gary asked as he escorted Treena and Bev to his old Chevy truck. When they had explained that they wanted some privacy, he had suggested going for a drive.

"Did Kassidy really milk a goat?" Bev asked as she climbed inside Gary's truck.

"That's what you wanted to know?" he countered, pulling himself up onto the worn seat.

"That's our alibi," Treena explained as she slid next to Bev and pulled the door shut.

"What?" Gary asked, looking perplexed.

"Our excuse to talk to you if Kassidy ever finds out that we did," Treena expounded.

"I see. Well, she did milk a goat Saturday night. I should know; I taught her how."

Bev shook her head. "She must like you. That sounds disgusting!"

Gary drove out of the apartment parking lot and onto the street. "I'll have you know she loved it. She also got a big kick out of riding a horse, even if she's still walking funny," he said, remembering how sore Kassidy was after the ride.

"Do you owe ice cream yet?" Bev asked.

Disgusted, Gary glanced at Bev, then back at the road. "This is what you're after?"

Bev glanced at the college campus as they sped past. "Kassidy won't tell us."

"Maybe Kassidy has her reasons," Gary responded.

"Actually, Gary, what we want to talk to you about is pretty serious."

"So, talk."

"First, turn around and pull into that parking lot back there by the football field," Bev directed. "I don't think you should be driving while we talk."

"But you said you wanted to go for a drive," Gary said, confused.

"That was your idea. And we did go for a short drive," Bev said. "Now be a good boy and turn around."

Grumbling under his breath, Gary waited until the oncoming traffic had cleared before flipping a U-turn. "I hope I don't get pulled over for that."

"Bev'll pay the ticket if you do," Treena offered.

"Oh, yeah?" Bev disagreed.

"All right, what's going on?" Gary demanded when he had parked in the campus parking lot.

"Gary, Treena and I talked things over earlier tonight and, well . . . we need to touch base with you about Kassidy," Bev said somberly.

"What about Kassidy?"

Bev glanced at Treena with a pleading look in her eyes.

Giving in, Treena cleared her throat. "Gary, I know you and Kassidy have a great thing going, and we don't want to stand in the way of that. But Kass has a problem. Bev thinks you might already know."

"The eating disorder thing?"

Both girls stared at him in stunned surprise.

"Look, it's not something Kassidy has ever told me, okay. I figured it out on my own. It's not too hard."

"Try living with her," Bev replied. "Food mysteriously disappears and the mess she leaves behind—"

"Don't go there," Treena warned.

"I can imagine," Gary said. "Is she anorexic or bulimic?"

"You have looked into this," Bev commented.

"I talked to my mom about it."

"She knows too?" Treena's eyes widened.

Gary nodded. "I wanted her advice."

"What did she think?"

"She thinks the world of Kassidy. They just met this weekend, but there's like this instant bond between them."

"Did Kassidy talk about the bulimia?" Bev asked.

Gary shook his head. He gazed steadily at Bev. "Kassidy's bulimic?"

Treena nodded.

Gary whistled softly. "I would've guessed anorexic. As my dad would say, there's no meat on her bones."

"I guess you'd know, wouldn't you," Bev teased, laughing as Gary blushed.

"Bev, this is serious," Treena chided.

"I know, I'm sorry. Go ahead, Treena. I won't interrupt."

"Kass doesn't eat a lot, until she binges," Treena explained. "But then she throws it all up, or uses laxatives to get rid of it."

Bev smacked the dusty dashboard, causing them all to cough. "Sorry, but it just clicked. That's where Jesse got the laxative—you know, the one that made me so sick. I wondered why Kassidy would have something like that."

"I'm missing something here," Gary said, confused.

Treena and Bev spent the next twenty minutes filling him in on everything they knew. When they finished, Gary smiled at both girls. "I hope someday Kassidy will realize what awesome friends she has."

Treena frowned. "I hope she'll still speak to us when this is over."

"That makes three of us," Gary replied.

"You'll help us out?" Bev asked.

"You bet," he pledged. "Tell me more about her aunt."

* * *

"Where's Bev?" Karen asked as she wandered into the living room.

Looking guilty, Jesse used the remote to turn off the TV. She knew Meg was opposed to watching television on Sunday and wasn't sure where Karen stood on that issue. She glanced up from the chair she was sitting in. "I don't know. She left with Treena quite a while ago."

"Those two are becoming chummy," Karen observed.

"I'll say. They're always whispering about something. They disappear a lot, too—like on Saturday. I woke up, and they were gone."

"Tyler didn't even know where Bev was on Saturday," Karen mused. "He didn't seem very amused that she was missing. I think he had something planned."

"Probably." Jesse studied Karen's face. "By the way, are things okay between you two?"

Karen shrugged.

"Are you still mad at Bev over the homecoming dance?"

Sighing, Karen sat down on the couch. "It's hard to explain, Jesse. I'd rather not, okay?"

Jesse played with the remote in her hands. "Want to hear something really disgusting?"

Karen glanced up at Jesse.

"My mom has been out with the same guy four times in a row."

"What's he like?"

Jesse hated the sympathetic look on Karen's face. It was one thing for her to feel sorry for herself, but she didn't want anyone else's pity. "How would I know? I've never met him. Meg's mother set them up, bless her interfering heart."

"Maybe your mom likes him."

Jesse frowned. "That's what I'm afraid of."

"Jesse, it's not always bad. Brett, the guy you thought was my dad—he's my stepfather."

Sinking further back into her chair, Jesse stared at Karen.

"My parents got divorced when I was young. Mom married Brett last April."

"No way! I could've sworn he was your real dad."

"He is," Karen said firmly.

"Karen, I didn't mean that the way it sounded," Jesse apologized.

"Brett is the only father I claim, okay? The man who is partially responsible for my appearance in this world is sitting in prison. He's a total loser, and I don't want anything to do with him! I was sealed to my mom and Brett in April."

"My dad's not so hot, either," Jesse admitted. "He stepped out on my mom." The pained look in her eye revealed how hurt she still was by her father's betrayal. "The thing is, he's not a bad guy, but he's made some pretty bad mistakes. I thought maybe someday Mom would forgive him—she claims she has. I keep thinking they'll work things out," she added hopefully.

Karen stared down at the worn carpet. "Sometimes it's best to move on."

"I'll always love my dad."

"And the only dad I'll ever love is Brett," Karen replied.

Jesse met Karen's troubled gaze. "Your other dad must've really hurt you," she guessed.

The telephone rang, providing a welcome interruption. Jesse started to rise but Karen beat her to it.

* * *

Startled by the knocking on her bedroom door, Kassidy shut the bottom drawer of her dresser. The *urge to purge* had been taunting her since her conversation with Treena and Bev. "Yeah?"

"You're wanted on the phone," Karen said, poking her head inside the room.

"Who is it?" Kassidy asked, rising from the floor.

"She said she's your aunt."

"Janice?"

"I think that's her name," Karen answered.

Muttering, Kassidy left the bedroom and headed for the telephone. "Hello?"

"Hi, Kassidy. Long time no chat," Janice quipped. "I was wondering if you'd had a chance to check your schedule yet?"

"I . . . uh . . . need to check with Gary."

"That's the young man you're dating?"

"Yeah," Kassidy hesitantly replied. As she had told Bev and Treena earlier, she didn't know her aunt very well. Most of what she knew had come from uncomplimentary comments supplied by her mother. 'Your aunt Janice is a vulgar excuse for a human being. She's fat, lazy, and a slob,' her mother had assured. Kassidy blinked. If Aunt Janice was so bad, why was she the only one who had cared enough to take her to Sea World? She remembered that day and the fun she had had. In her mind she saw how Janice had burst out laughing when Shamu, the killer whale, had covered them both with water as they had watched the beautiful creature leap into the air and tumble hard into the blue water tank.

" . . . and, I know the seafood's not as good as what you're used to, but I do love the shrimp platter at Red Lobster. After that, I thought we'd go see a movie, provided we can find one that's half-decent."

Drawn back into the conversation with her aunt, Kassidy listened to the plans Janice had made for the upcoming weekend. "Okay. It sounds like fun."

"Are you sure, Kassidy? I don't want to mess up your plans."

"I'm sure. I haven't seen you in years. Let's plan on this weekend," Kassidy replied.

Chapter 22

Meg glanced at her watch and groaned; it was already 10:15 P.M. She had meant to be home an hour ago. Her duties as a resident assistant, or RA, included making rounds of all the apartments in her half of D building at 10:00 P.M. She was to ensure that all of the girls were accounted for and had to kick out any stray young men who happened to be visiting that time of night. The pay wasn't great, but it helped with the rent.

Gathering her books into her backpack, Meg erased the blackboard, shut off the classroom lights, and stepped into the darkened hall. She rested her backpack against the wall and wiggled into the leather jacket she had brought. Then she slipped the backpack onto one shoulder and flew down the hall.

She liked studying in empty classrooms on campus, something she had learned to do last year. Not only could she concentrate better in the isolated silence, but she had discovered it was a good way to memorize terms for her nursing classes. She would spend hours drawing illustrations on empty blackboards and then label the parts of the body, something she had been engrossed in doing tonight for an upcoming test in her neuro-endocrine class. A recent announcement had made it clear that BYU–Idaho frowned on anyone studying in empty classrooms, but Meg had decided to bend the rules in the interest of her grades. She simply couldn't study in her apartment; there was always something going on to provide noisy distraction. The library was readily available, but Meg preferred solitude.

"Man, I'll never hear the end of this," she grumbled to herself as she continued to run down the darkened halls of the Clarke Building. As she started down a long stairway, she heard footsteps behind her.

Trembling, she hurried forward as the footsteps drew closer. Glancing over her shoulder, she stepped out into midair, thinking she was at the bottom of the stairs. Terrified, she shrieked as she fell.

* * *

Jesse gazed at the kitchen clock. "Where is that wayward cousin of mine?"

"What time is it?" Bev yawned as she glanced up from the book she was reading.

"10:30."

"Maybe she's still making her rounds as the efficient RA She might be having a difficult time shooing out the pesky menfolk tonight," Bev replied, confident Meg was fine. She didn't always agree with how Meg handled things, but she had to give the girl credit; Meg could handle herself just fine.

Karen walked into the kitchen wearing a bathrobe. She rubbed a towel over her wet head. "Did I hear someone ask where Meg was?"

Jesse nodded.

"She went up on campus to study around seven."

"And she hasn't returned?" Jesse asked, glancing at the clock again.

"You know how Meg is when she starts studying, the world disappears," Bev said, stretching. "She probably stayed longer than she meant to, then hurried back here to make her rounds, dedicated RA that she is."

"But she always stops here first to drop off her books," Jesse pointed out.

Treena slipped into the apartment. "Hi all, I'm back."

"Treena, have you seen Meg?" Jesse asked.

"No, thank heavens. I'm late getting home."

Karen sat down on a kitchen chair to finish towel-drying her hair. "Where've you been?"

"Guess," Treena said, wiggling her eyebrows.

"Have you been out flirting with our neighbors again?" Bev teased.

"What neighbors?" Jesse asked.

"Those delightful young men of Bunkhouse fame," Bev answered, referring to the men's apartment complex behind Baronnessa. She wondered if Treena had been talking to Gary again.

"Kassidy went to bed early tonight, remember," Treena fired back. "The only time I make visits to The Bunkhouse is as a chaperone for her. Actually I was in building C helping a friend with her lead-sheets. "

"What did you say?" Bev asked, raising a thin black eyebrow.

"Lead-sheets. You know—sheet music."

Karen set the towel on her lap. "Is she taking music theory?"

"Yes," Treena replied. "But this isn't for her class. Debbie has written a song she'd like to perform during one of those unplugged concerts they hold on campus. I was trying to help her figure out how to write it down. It's pretty complicated."

"I remember," Karen mused.

Bev nodded. "That's right, you helped write the music for that musical we were in last year," she said, hoping to evoke a smile from her friend. Lately, Karen had been very distant.

"I wrote the lyrics. Terri wrote the music," Karen corrected. "I just remember how much time it took to get it all put together."

"People, as delightful as this conversation is, we still haven't solved the mystery of the moment," Jesse said, frowning. "Where's Meg?" As if on cue, the telephone rang. Jesse scurried to answer it. "Hello?" There was a slight pause before Jesse exclaimed, "What?"

Bev saw the color drain from Jesse's face and knew that something was very wrong.

* * *

"How in the world did Meg manage to break her leg?" Bev asked the young man who had introduced himself as Karl Bassett. He was the one who had called from Madison Memorial several minutes before. Bev, Jesse, Karen, and Treena were now sitting with him in the Rexburg hospital waiting room. Kassidy was still in their apartment sound asleep. They had left a note on the kitchen table in case she woke up while they were gone.

"I'm not sure. I was in the Clarke Building studying. When I realized how late it was, I was in a hurry to head back to my apartment. I guess Meg was on the same floor. I heard her going down the stairs, then I heard the most awful scream. I ran down and found your roommate lying at the bottom of the stairs. Thank heavens I had my cell phone with me," he said, nervously adjusting his glasses. "I could tell she was hurt pretty bad, so I called the ambulance."

"How did you get our number?" Karen asked.

"It was in her wallet," he admitted. "In fact, here it is," he said, handing the wallet to Bev. "I found it in her backpack. But I didn't take anything, I promise. The money . . . her credit card, everything's there. I was just trying to figure out who she was. And her backpack is still out in my car. I didn't think to bring it in here," he stammered.

Bev gazed appraisingly at the broad-shouldered young man. Curly black hair and honest grey-blue eyes. It was a nice combination. She tried not to be too obvious as she visually searched for a ring on his left hand. Relieved to find nothing there, she smiled. "We'll get her backpack later. Right now the important thing is making sure Meg is okay." She glanced down the hall at Jesse, who was talking to Meg's mother on a pay phone. "So, Karl, while we're waiting, tell us a little bit about yourself," Bev encouraged, ignoring the incredulous look on Karen's face.

* * *

"Meg has a slight concussion and a broken leg?" Jesse said, repeating what the doctor had just shared. She had promised to call Meg's mother with all of the details as soon as possible.

"Yes," the doctor confirmed. "She'll be all right, but I'd like to keep her here overnight for observation."

"Is that normal?" Treena asked.

"With a head injury, yes," the doctor answered. "It's a safety precaution. I'm sure there won't be any complications, but we'll keep a close eye on her tonight." He gazed at the four girls who were sitting in the waiting room. "Meg was pretty vague about how this happened. How did she fall?"

"Karl was the only one there," Bev offered.

"Karl?" the doctor invited, turning to the young man Bev had indicated.

"I'm not sure what happened," Karl stammered. "I found her after she fell. I heard her going down the stairs, then she screamed—and I heard a crash."

"I see. Was it dark on the stairwell?"

Karl nodded at the doctor.

"So maybe she tripped going down the stairs?"

"I guess," Karl replied. "I didn't see her fall, so I don't know."

"And none of you girls were with her?" the doctor pressed.

One by one they shook their heads.

"Meg likes studying by herself," Jesse explained.

"Well, tell Meg that's not always the wisest thing to do," the doctor stressed. "This is a small town, but bad things can still happen. Remember, there's safety in numbers," he added as he turned and walked away.

"Did you see the way that guy was looking at me?" Karl sputtered. "Like this was my fault. I don't even know Meg! And I swear I did not push her down the stairs. I didn't even touch her until after she'd fallen. She was unconscious, so I checked her pulse to see if she was still breathing."

"Easy, Karl," Bev said. "No one's accusing you of anything. I think the good doctor was trying to make a point and he's right. None of us should be out at night alone."

"Last year there was a rape scare on campus," Treena commented. "They finally caught the guy, but it was pretty scary for a while."

Karen slowly nodded. Bev glanced at her friend's somber face and changed the subject. "So, Karl, when did you say you would be putting in your mission papers?"

Jesse hid a smile with her hand. She knew Bev had been disappointed to learn that Karl was a *preemie*—BYI lingo for pre-missionary. There would be no romance between Meg and Karl; he was too young.

* * *

"I can't believe this happened," Meg groaned from her hospital bed. It was one thing to take care of patients, something she enjoyed as a student nurse. She loathed being a patient. When she had regained consciousness in the ER she had been less than a sport about the entire ordeal. Despite her insistence that she was fine, a series of butterfly bandages had been attached to one side of her forehead, suppressing the small gash that had saturated the blue sweater she had been wearing. It could be salvaged; she just hoped the bloodstains could be removed from her black leather jacket.

After enduring a painful session in the x-ray department that confirmed her right leg was broken, the doctor had decided to wait until the swelling went down before putting it in a cast. She was currently wearing a black support brace that would keep the fractured bone in place until it could be cast.

"I'm just glad you're all right," Jesse said, smiling down at her cousin. "You gave us quite a scare."

"Yeah," Karen echoed. "How in the world did you fall down those stairs?"

Refusing to answer, Meg gazed at the IV drip that was hooked into her wrist. "Is this really necessary?"

"Yes," Bev said. "You ought to know that, future nurse. They'll probably take it out tomorrow, if you behave yourself. In fact, I'll bet you'll receive the royal treatment. You've worked with some of these nurses, right?"

Meg gave Bev a disgruntled look, then closed her eyes as a sharp pain raced through her right leg.

"Are you all right?" Jesse asked.

"Oh, yeah," Meg mumbled as she gritted her teeth. "This is great!"

"I called your mom," Jesse began.

"What?" Meg exclaimed, her eyes opening to glare accusingly at Jesse. "What did you do that for?"

"Easy, Meg, we felt your parents had a right to know what happened," Bev stressed.

"That's just what I need!" Meg complained.

"Our parents would want to know if we were hurt," Treena stated.

A nurse entered the room to check Meg's vital signs. The four girls kept very still until the nurse finished checking Meg's blood pressure. "It's a little high," she observed.

"She's in a lot of pain," Bev suggested.

"We hate to give her too much medicine right now, because of the head injury," the nurse explained. "But you shouldn't have to suffer like this either. I'll go call your doctor and see what he wants to do," she said before leaving the room.

Meg closed her eyes as another surge of pain shot through her leg. "I'm going to be sick," she mumbled.

Bev grabbed the plastic emesis basin from a nearby portable table and held it close to Meg's mouth. "It's all right, Meg, let it go, you might feel better," she soothed. "Karen, go tell the nurse Meg's sick."

Karen winced as Meg began losing the contents of her stomach. Turning, she hurried from the room.

* * *

"I really love you guys," Meg purred as the pain medication did its job. "You're the best."

Bev grinned at Jesse. "That's a switch. We'll have to stock up on this stuff. Meg's a totally different person when she's under the influence of drugs."

Jesse nodded. "Maybe we can get some information out of her now."

"Let's go home. She needs to sleep," Karen suggested.

"After we get a few details. Even the doctor wanted to know how this happened," Bev replied.

"And you think she's in good enough shape to tell you?" Karen retorted.

"Just watch." Bev smiled down at Meg. "Meg, we were wondering how you hurt yourself."

"I fell," Meg said, slurring her words.

"We know that," Bev said, ignoring the smug look on Karen's face. "How did you fall?"

"I was being chased."

Bev glanced worriedly at Jesse, then at Karen. "Who was chasing you?"

"A bad man. I know what he wanted. Just like Herman. All men are bad," Meg said, closing her eyes.

A horrified look appeared on Jesse's face. "Meg, are you talking about our cousin, Herman? Handsy Herman?"

Meg slowly nodded.

"Now I think I'm going to be sick," Jesse muttered.

* * *

It was ten minutes after one when the four girls returned to their apartment. From the look of things, Kassidy had slept the entire time they were gone. Too wound up to sleep themselves, the girls sat around the kitchen table, three sets of eyes gazing intently at Jesse.

"What?" Jesse exclaimed.

Bev nudged Jesse's foot with her leather shoe. "You know what— Handsy Herman. What's that all about?"

Jesse lowered her brown eyes, distressed by what she assumed had happened to Meg. For the first time in years, she finally understood Meg's attitude toward men.

"You don't have to tell us," Karen stressed. "Some things are better left unsaid."

Tears formed in Jesse's eyes. "I'll kill him! I swear I'll kill him! If he touched Meg . . ." her voice faltered.

"Handsy Herman?" Bev pressed.

Jesse nodded.

"He's your cousin?" Treena asked.

"Yeah. Herman's dad is a first cousin to my mom and to Meg's mom. The three of them grew up together in Cedar City, Utah. Mom told me that when they were about twelve, Herman's dad tried to kiss her. She leveled him, and he never tried it again."

"Good for your mom," Bev cheered.

"She never liked him after that, though. She never trusted him and that's the same way I feel about Herman."

"I gather he takes after his dad," Bev guessed.

Jesse nodded.

"Did Herman ever try anything with you?" Karen asked.

Jesse shook her head. "I've always been able to outwrestle all of my cousins. Herman was probably scared to try anything with me."

"How did he earn his nickname?" Treena asked.

"He was too friendly with some of my older cousins. Couldn't keep his hands to himself. That sort of thing."

"And you think he tried something with Meg?" Bev asked softly.

"From what she said tonight, I'm afraid so." Jesse slapped the table hard with her hands, causing them both to sting. "Why are some guys such creeps?"

"I don't know," Karen mumbled, looking as sorrowful as Jesse.

"How about that guy tonight—Karl? Do you think he chased Meg down the stairs?" Treena asked.

"I don't think so," Bev said quietly. "He seemed like a nice guy."

"The key word here is *seemed,*" Karen said sharply. "Guys aren't always who they appear to be."

"What is going on out here?" Kassidy asked, yawning as she stepped into the kitchen.

"Pull up a chair. We've got a lot to tell you," Treena said, frowning.

Chapter 23

"I said that?" Meg stammered. "I talked about Herman?" she asked, her green eyes widening with dismay.

Jesse nodded. "That's why I came up to the hospital to talk to you alone this morning." She smiled sheepishly. "In fact, I hope you don't mind, but I borrowed your car. I didn't want to explain to anyone where I was going . . . that's why I left so early," she added, glancing at her watch. It was just past eight o'clock. Meg had always been an early riser, and Jesse hadn't been disappointed that morning. Meg had been wide awake when she had arrived a few minutes ago. "I have to know what happened to you."

"Why?" Meg said, looking away from her cousin.

"Because I care, and I want to help."

"I'd rather not talk about it."

Jesse sat down in the chair beside Meg's hospital bed and folded her arms. "It's high time you learned who the stubborn one in the family really is!"

"Jesse!"

"I mean it, Meg. I couldn't even sleep. I went to bed and did nothing but toss and turn."

"This doesn't concern you."

"It does now! What happened?" Jesse met Meg's glare with one of her own. "I'm not leaving here until you tell me."

"Jesse . . . it's something I'd rather not talk about, okay?"

"Tough! You opened a can of worms last night, and I'm not going to let it go! The thing is, I'm not the only one who's worried about you. Our entire apartment is upset!" Jesse emphasized.

"Great!"

Jesse gazed steadily at Meg. "Yeah, well, they were all standing in this room when you spouted off about Handsy Herman."

"What exactly did I say?"

"Enough for us to guess what probably happened."

Closing her eyes, Meg remained silent for several seconds. "Tell them it's not as bad as you thought."

"I will if you tell me what happened."

"Okay—fine . . . but you don't have to share all of the details with our roommates," Meg stressed, opening her eyes to glare at Jesse.

"I'll be discreet," Jesse promised, sitting back in the padded chair.

"Do you remember the camping reunion our family held a few years ago? I was thirteen, so you would've been twelve."

Jesse nodded. "Wasn't that the year we camped by the lake?"

"That's the one." Meg gazed down at the green hospital bedspread. "Saturday afternoon everyone went hiking but me. You were all so excited to climb to the top of some stupid hill."

"I remember that. You got into a big argument with your mother. She didn't want you to stay behind—she thought you were missing out on all the fun."

Looking miserable, Meg nodded. "I wish I had gone with the rest of you."

Lowering her eyes, Jesse ached for her cousin. She remained silent, letting Meg tell the story at her own pace.

"At first, I stayed in my tent and read. After about thirty minutes, I decided to go for a walk down to the lake. I picked a trail that led through the forest and headed toward the lake." Breathing faster, Meg reached up to grip the plastic bed railing with her left hand. "I had only gone a few steps down the trail when he grabbed me from behind."

"Herman?"

Meg nodded. "At first, I was so scared, I couldn't move. Then he pushed me down into some wild grass and started kissing me."

Alarmed, Jesse saw that her cousin had slipped into a trancelike state as she relived that horrible moment in her life.

"It was like I was paralyzed . . . then his hands started wandering all over my body. That's when I went berserk. I remember scratching

. . . and I kicked him—hard. He lay there whimpering and I kept hitting him. Finally he got up and limped away."

Jesse marveled at her cousin; Meg was a lot tougher than she had ever imagined. "You beat up Handsy Herman? I asked him where he got that black eye. He said he fell down the hill during our hike," she said, shaking her head as she realized he hadn't gone on the hike. "Did you ever tell your mom what happened?"

Meg shook her head. "I couldn't. Would you have told your mother?"

"Yeah," Jesse emphasized. "Mom and I talk about everything. I wouldn't have kept something like that from her."

"Well, there's no way I could tell mine."

"Why not?" Jesse asked, folding her arms again.

"It's too complicated to explain." She closed her eyes. "Besides, my head is really starting to hurt," she added, turning her face away from Jesse.

"Okay," Jesse mumbled, "I can take a hint. Get some rest and I'll come back later to check on you. There's a good chance they'll let you out today, so I'll make some arrangements to get you back to the apartment."

Meg opened one eye. "Thanks."

Nodding, Jesse left the room.

* * *

" . . . and because of what she'd been through, when Meg heard Karl's footsteps behind her, she freaked. She thought she was at the bottom of the stairs, stepped out into midair, and fell," Jesse explained, glancing around the kitchen table at her roommates.

"Ow," Treena winced. "No wonder she looked so banged up last night."

"And Karl was an innocent bystander," Bev pointed out.

"I'm glad her experience with Handsy Herman wasn't as bad as we thought," Treena mused, "but why would it keep haunting her? It happened years ago."

"Some things are hard to understand unless you've been there," Karen said quietly.

Jesse wondered at the agitated look on Karen's face. Shrugging it off, she continued with her analysis of the situation. "Here's what I think: Meg has kept it inside all this time, so she never got over it. She never told anyone. No wonder she never lets anyone get close to her. She's so filled with anger and pain and shame—"

"I need to run. I have a class in thirty minutes," Karen said, cutting Jesse off.

"Is she okay?" Treena asked Bev when Karen disappeared down the hall. "She seems upset."

"She'll be all right," Bev murmured. She turned to Jesse. "So, when do we get to bring Meg home?"

"The doctor was coming in to check things out this morning around ten," Jesse said, glancing at the clock on the wall above the table. It was almost nine-thirty A.M.

"Then we'd better get our acts together and go see if they'll release her this morning. Who wants to come?" Bev asked.

"I'd like to, but I have a class at ten-thirty," Kassidy said, rising from the table.

"I missed my eight o'clock class," Treena sighed. "I probably should hit the one at ten."

"It's Thursday, so I don't have any classes till this afternoon. Jesse?" Bev prompted.

"I have classes all day, but I'll go with you. I won't be able to concentrate much today anyway. Mom called early this morning to let me know that she and Meg's mother are flying in this afternoon. Penny wants to make sure Meg is okay, and my mom decided to come along for the ride."

Bev blinked. "They're coming here?"

"Yep. That should make Meg's day," Jesse frowned.

"Maybe it won't be as bad as you think," Bev said brightly.

"I'm excited to see my mother, but I don't think Meg will share that opinion about hers," Jesse said as she moved to the sink for a glass of water. "Meg's injuries may pale in comparison to what she'll do to me when she finds out Penny Denton is on her way to Rexburg."

* * *

Sally Waterman and Penny Denton drove into Rexburg around 3:30 that afternoon. They had arrived at the Idaho Falls airport shortly before 3:00 o'clock, then had rented a car to drive up to the college town. Jesse had watched for them after they had called from the Idaho Falls airport. When Jesse spotted the car her mother had described, she hurried down to the Baronnessa parking lot.

Tall and slender like her daughter, with short brown hair, Sally Waterman slid out of the blue sedan, as Jesse called to her. "Jesse," Sally said as she swept the young woman into a firm embrace. "It's so good to see you! But I wish it was under different circumstances."

"Me, too," Jesse agreed, as it hit her how much she had missed her mother.

"Where's Meg?" Penny Denton asked. Meg's mother was nearly 5' 6", the same height as her daughter. It was obvious her curvaceous figure had once rivaled Meg's, but time and having children had taken its toll on her slightly plump body. Unlike Meg's hair, Penny's was dark brown, her eyes as dark as her hair.

"In our bedroom up in the apartment," Jesse replied, leading the way. "They haven't cast her leg yet—they're still waiting for the swelling to go down. She's doing pretty good, though."

"I'll be the judge of that," Penny huffed as she followed behind Jesse.

Jesse glanced at her mother, who was doing her best to keep a straight face. Bev was right, this wasn't going to be as bad as she feared—it was going to be worse.

* * *

Jesse poked her head inside the bedroom and saw that Meg was dozing on top of her bed. Earlier they had propped her right leg up on a pile of soft pillows in an attempt to keep it elevated. "She's asleep," Jesse whispered.

"She can sleep later!" Penny exclaimed. "I didn't fly all the way here for nothing."

"What?" Meg mumbled as she opened her eyes.

Jesse frowned as Penny pushed her out of the way to enter the room.

"It's okay, Meg, I'm here now," Penny soothed as she hurried to the bed.

"Mom, what are you doing here?" Meg managed to say as her mother gathered her into fierce hug. Meg peered around her mother to give Jesse a withering look.

"Well, I think that's our cue to leave." Jesse hurried out of the bedroom to where her mother and Bev were waiting in the hall. "I hope Tylenol 4 will continue to be Meg's friend for a while or I'm in real trouble," she quipped, motioning for them to follow her into the living room.

"I'm just glad she'll be all right," Sally Waterman commented.

"She will be," Bev said, flopping down on a chair. "But it might take a while for that leg to heal. They don't even want her putting any weight on it until it's in a cast, and that probably won't happen till Saturday."

"Yeah, it was quite the adventure getting her up the stairs and into this apartment," Jesse shared.

"How did you get her up here?" Sally asked as she sat on the couch next to her daughter.

"At the hospital they used a wheelchair to get her out to Bev's Jeep," Jesse said as she leaned back against the couch. The adrenaline rush she had been experiencing since last night was fading. Suddenly, she felt exhausted. "Then we lifted her up onto the front seat, after we had pushed it back as far as it would go."

"We'd made some arrangements for our family home evening brothers to meet us here at Baronnessa," Bev said, continuing with the story. "They helped carry Meg up the stairs."

"Don't forget Karl," Jesse reminded Bev.

"Karl?" Sally asked.

Bev glanced at Jesse's mother. "He's the guy who found her last night—the one who called the ambulance. He arrived at the hospital as we were leaving this morning," she said with a smile. "So he followed us to Baronnessa to help."

"He gave Meg a beautiful bouquet of roses," Jesse supplied.

Sally smiled. "He did? That is so sweet."

Bev nodded. "Yeah. He's feeling pretty bad about what happened last night. Meg heard him coming behind her, and it scared her. That's why she fell."

"Oh?" Sally prompted. "Why would that scare her? I've known Meg since she was tiny—nothing scares that girl!"

"You might be surprised," Jesse murmured.

"What do you mean?"

"Tell her, Jesse," Bev encouraged. "I think Meg's mother needs to know too."

"I might tell Mom, but I'm not going there with Penny. That one is totally up to Meg. I'm in enough trouble with Meg as it is. Didn't you see that look on her face when her mother walked into the room?"

"Well, you could've warned her we were coming," Sally chided. "Back to my original question, what is it you're supposed to tell me?"

"About Handsy Herman," Bev furnished.

Sally stiffened. "Handsy Herman? What does he have to do with anything?"

"Remember that family reunion a few years ago," Jesse said with a sigh, "the one when we all went camping. We went on a hike—"

"And Meg stayed behind to read," Sally said. "I remember because Meg had a horrible fight with her mother over it. Penny fumed halfway up that hill we climbed."

"I'll bet that's why Meg didn't tell her mom about what happened," Jesse guessed. "She didn't want it rubbed in her face."

"Didn't want what rubbed in her face? What did Herman do?" Sally pressed.

"Not much. It sounds like she beat him up when he tried to take advantage of her," Jesse answered.

"Let me get this straight. Herman got *handsy* with Meg, and she clobbered him?"

Jesse nodded at her mother.

"Good for Meg," Sally chuckled. "That girl has spunk."

"Yes, she does," Bev echoed. "I've learned that one the hard way." She grinned.

* * *

Jesse watched as her mother agilely swam across the small motel pool, her long arms cutting powerfully through the water. Sally surfaced at the end of the pool and pulled herself out, her dark green, one-piece suit dripping with chlorinated water.

"I needed a good swim," Sally exclaimed as she walked to the hot tub and slipped in beside her daughter. "And this feels even better."

"Thanks for inviting me to hang out with you," Jesse said as she reclined in the foaming water. She was wearing the blue flowered swimming suit her mother had helped her pick out before she had left St. George that fall.

"I figured the way Penny was hovering over Meg, you might as well stay here at the motel with me until we head back."

"When do you think you'll leave?"

"On Sunday. Penny and I talked it over earlier tonight."

"Do you think Meg will stay? Penny's trying to talk her into going home with you guys."

Sally smiled at her daughter. "I don't know. I'd hate to see her give up and walk away from everything—she's worked too hard to get where she is."

Jesse nodded.

"Besides, I think she'd suffocate if she moved back to St. George. She's too independent. I think she needs to stay here."

"I think so too," Jesse agreed, surprised that she would miss Meg if she left.

"You mentioned you've been here before." Sally gestured around the large room.

"Karen's parents came up about a month ago. They stayed here and invited us to invade the pool. We had a blast."

"You have some neat roommates," Sally observed.

"We've had some fun." Jesse pulled her hands out of the water to see if her fingers were wrinkled. She studied the prunelike ridges of each finger. "Tell me more about this guy you've been seeing."

"Charlie?"

"That would be the man."

Sally smiled. "You'd like him. He has a fun sense of humor, but he can be very serious, too. He loves most sports, and he lives to mountain bike. In fact, he took your brother and I on a mountain bike adventure last weekend up above St. George."

"He did? What a guy! What does Mitch think of him?" she asked, referring to her twelve-year-old brother. Jesse pulled herself out of the hot tub, sat on the side, and began kicking her foot in the water.

"Mitch hated him at first. Now he thinks he's cool. In fact, that's who Mitch is staying with while I'm up here."

"You trusted Mitch with a complete stranger?" Jesse questioned.

"Charlie is hardly a stranger. I trust him completely."

"Then why is he divorced?"

"Being divorced doesn't make you a bad person," Sally said, frowning. "And stop kicking the water, you're getting me right in the face."

"Sorry," Jesse said as she stuck both feet in the water and kept them still. "Did he tell you why he was divorced?" she persisted.

"His wife left him. He doesn't talk about it much, but I've gathered it had something to do with his activity in the Church."

"She was a nonmember?"

Sally shook her head. "She was a member, but she didn't care for some of the doctrine our Church teaches."

"Like what?"

"I don't know, I didn't quiz him on it."

Jessed scowled. "Maybe you should have. People don't get divorced over nothing. There has to be a reason why his first wife left him."

"Jesse, I'm divorced. Are you saying that I'm not trustworthy because of it?"

"I'm making a point here. You left Mitch with someone you hardly know. What if he's a scumbag?"

"Mitch will be fine. Charlie is a wonderful man," Sally stressed.

"What about Dad?" Jesse persisted.

"Your father was off on one of his infamous sales trips. Mitch couldn't stay with him; I couldn't reach him."

"That's not what I meant," Jesse fumed. "You act like this Charlie person is the best thing that's ever happened to you. Well, what about Dad? You haven't even given him a chance."

"Jess, think about it," Sally exclaimed. "Your father was the one who asked for the divorce. I tried to work things out with him for a very long time. He wasn't willing to change. You *know* all of this."

"But he could change."

Sally shook her head. "Honey, you have to be realistic."

Jesse stood and grabbed a white motel towel, wrapping it around herself.

"Jesse!"

"I need some time, okay?" she said, keeping her back to her mother. "I'll be up in your room." Jesse hurried from the pool area and up the carpeted steps to her mother's motel room. Too late she realized she had forgotten to get the computerized room card from her mother. Sinking down by the door, she leaned against it and thumped her head a couple of times. "Great," she grumbled.

"Need this?" her mother asked a few minutes later, holding out the computer card.

Glaring, Jesse forced herself to stand as her mother used the card to open the door.

"Let's talk, shall we?" Sally invited as she followed her daughter into the room.

* * *

"Meg, I think it's best if you come home," Penny said, sitting on the edge of her daughter's bed.

"I don't," Meg mumbled. She glanced at her alarm clock and groaned. She would have to wait another hour before she could take another Tylenol 4. Not only did it reduce the pain from her leg and head, but it took the sting out of her mother's impromptu visit.

"You're just being stubborn! How are you going to manage with a broken leg? Come home where I can take care of you."

"Mom, I've put too much of myself into this nursing program. I can't give it up."

Penny pursed her lips. "You could transfer to Dixie College in St. George and live at home. They offer a nice nursing program at that college. I don't know why you didn't consider it in the first place."

"We've already had this conversation—it didn't feel right. For some reason, I need to be here at Ricks . . . I mean BYU–Idaho."

"That's what you said when you first applied to come up here. And look what you got for your trouble, a broken leg and a concussion," her mother reasoned.

Meg made another mental note to get even with Jesse.

"Meg, I'm only thinking about what's best for you."

Remaining silent, Meg stared down at her quilted bedspread. It was a dark maroon color, something that matched her current mood.

"What is so special about this school?"

Meg met her mother's searching gaze. "I know I'm supposed to be here. Every time I pray about it, it feels right."

"We're on different wavelengths then, because I don't feel that way at all."

"You're upset because I'm hurt," Meg countered.

"And you aren't?"

Meg looked away again, wishing that her mother wasn't staying until Sunday. It was only Friday morning and already they were driving each other crazy.

"I won't push the issue, but think about it. You don't have to decide overnight." Penny stood. "How many days of school have you missed?"

"Two, counting today."

"That's right. You fell Wednesday night." Penny counted on her fingers. "How many weeks are left in this term?"

"Eight . . . seven. I don't know. I can't think right now," Meg said, flustered.

"My point exactly. You're in no shape to keep up with your studies. Come home and relax for a few weeks. You can start up the next semester at Dixie." Penny lingered by the door. "Meg, you know I love you. I just want you to be happy, and right now, I don't think you are." She walked out of the room and disappeared down the hall.

Turning her aching head, Meg silently screamed into her pillow.

* * *

"I feel so bad about what happened to your roommate," Janice commented to Kassidy as she drove her white Chevy Impala out of Baronnessa's parking lot Friday night. "Is she feeling any better?"

"I think so," Kassidy said as she fastened her seat belt. "Meg's hoping they'll be able to cast her leg tomorrow so she can get around better. But I heard Bev say that they'll make her use crutches for a while. She'll hate that. I wish we could make it easier for her to get around."

Janice smiled. This certainly wasn't Constance Martin, Jr. talking. Unlike her mother, Kassidy obviously possessed a compassionate nature. "Well, are you still up for some seafood and a movie?" she asked brightly.

"Sure," Kassidy replied.

"Chubbuck, here we come," Janice exclaimed, gripping the steering wheel in her hands.

Chapter 24

Karen nervously paced outside of Meg's bedroom Sunday night. Finally knocking, she entered the room.

Startled, Meg looked up from her bed.

"It's just me," Karen said, forcing a smile. She closed the door behind her and stepped closer to Meg's bed. "How are you feeling?"

"Better. The cast helps. And my mother finally left, so maybe things can get back to normal."

"I'm glad you decided to stay," Karen said as she sat down on Jesse's bed. "We would've missed you."

"Really?"

"Really, Meg," Karen stressed. "We're like a family now, aren't we?"

"I guess."

"And families try to help each other, right?" Karen said, hating the suspicious way Meg was staring at her. "Look, there's something I feel like I should tell you. Maybe it will help. I just know it's not leaving me alone."

"What's not leaving you alone?"

"The thing is, it's not leaving you alone either or you wouldn't have fallen Wednesday night," Karen said haltingly as Meg furrowed her eyebrows. "I'm probably not explaining this very well, but I understand why you panicked."

"Oh, really?"

"Yes, really." Forcing herself to remain calm, Karen took a deep breath. "I just want you to know you're not alone in this. I understand exactly how you feel."

"You do?" Meg challenged.

Karen nodded. "You're blaming yourself for what someone else did. What security you ever felt is gone. You don't trust people anymore. The anger makes you want to scream, but this incredible feeling of shame fills you with guilt. The worst part is the fear— always looking over your shoulder, running from noises you can't explain. Jumping when someone touches you from behind. Or in your case, freaking out when you hear someone behind you." She met Meg's wondering gaze with a look of compassion. "Am I right?"

"How do you know that?"

When Karen realized she was gripping Jesse's bedspread, she forced herself to relax and rested her hands on her legs. *I can do this,* she thought, giving herself a silent pep talk. *I can do this.* "I'm going to tell you something, but please keep it to yourself. Bev knows, but I'd rather not share this with everyone."

"Okay," Meg said, looking confused.

"I was attacked during my junior year of high school."

Meg's eyes widened with surprise.

"I was walking across our football field one night, going home from Bev's house. A group of boys had been drinking—they were hiding under the bleachers. I walked right into them. One thing led to another—it was awful," Karen said in a rush.

"Did they hurt you?" Meg asked.

"I was bruised up a little and sprained my wrist . . . but other than that, no."

"You got away?"

Karen shook her head. "I was rescued by a couple of teachers and the guy who started the whole mess."

"What?"

"He had a change of heart when he saw how out of control things were getting."

"He did?"

Karen nodded. "He was the first one to kiss me that night. He thought it was funny. He didn't realize what his friends would try to do."

"I'm glad you were rescued before . . ." Meg's voice faltered.

"And I'm glad you put Herman in his place. The problem is, we're both still carrying around some pretty intense baggage."

Meg nodded.

"Again, I just wanted you to know that I understand, and if you ever need to talk, I'm here." Rising from the bed, Karen offered Meg a shy smile.

"Thanks," Meg murmured. "I'll keep that in mind."

* * *

"You're sure about switching rooms?" Bev asked Monday night.

Karen avoided looking at Bev, uncomfortably aware of how her decision had hurt her friend. "For now. Meg and Jesse aren't getting along. Meg blames Jesse for her mother's visit, and for some reason, Jesse's really been on edge lately."

"I would be too if Meg badgered me round the clock. Boy, that woman holds a grudge! I think she needs some counseling."

"Bev!"

"I'm serious, Karen. She has some issues to settle. I don't think she's ever dealt with what happened during that reunion. You know . . . Handsy Herman?"

Karen nodded.

"I think she needs some help coping with it."

"Maybe I can talk her into getting some counseling," Karen offered.

"Maybe you should go with her," Bev encouraged.

Karen glared at Bev.

"I'm only saying this because of what I've seen since your attack. You probably handled it better than I would've, but you still have all of this anger inside of you. You date, but you never let guys get close to you. You never want to be alone with them, and I've seen that panicked look on your face whenever they put an arm around you. I know Meg's adventure has brought back everything for you. I think some counseling could help."

"I'll pretend we didn't have this conversation." Turning, Karen began pulling her clothes out of the closet.

"I'm concerned about you, okay? If I didn't care, it wouldn't matter. But what I've seen has bothered me for a long time. Sometimes you're like an out-of-control furnace waiting to blow. All this anger over your attack—over your fath . . . over Roger."

"He is *not* my father!" Karen seethed.

"See what I mean? You need to work through some things," Bev persisted.

"And you don't?" Karen snapped, her brown eyes flashing. "As I recall, your track record hasn't been perfect!"

"Karen, you are the sister I never had," Bev exclaimed. "And despite what you may think, I love ya, okay? I would never purposely do or say anything to hurt you, but I'm worried. Please consider what I'm saying. Take some time to cool down and think about it."

Remaining silent, Karen pulled the rest of her clothes out of the closet.

"Oh, nice! The infamous silent treatment. That bugs the heck out of me, and you know it. If you have something to say, say it!"

Karen replied by leaving the room.

* * *

Staring at a page she had read three times, Bev groaned. She had a test in her biology class tomorrow and couldn't retain anything she was reading. "I can't study!"

Jesse glanced at her sympathetically. "You've got too much on your mind."

"I'm beginning to wonder if I even possess a mind!"

"You're still upset over that argument you had with Karen."

Bev looked up from her book to give Jesse a disgruntled look. "What argument? She wouldn't even speak to me! She still won't," she said, sitting up. "It's been three days!"

"Maybe it's a good thing we swapped roommates."

Bev sighed. As much as she enjoyed hanging out with Jesse, she missed Karen. She missed the late night chats and the secret jokes they shared. The gulf between them hurt, an aching pain inside her heart that grew sharper as their bond of friendship withered.

"I'll try not to take that sigh personally," Jesse joked.

"It isn't you, it's this mess with Karen. It's so frustrating."

"I hope you guys can work things out. It's been too quiet around this apartment. I mean, Treena tries to be funny, but she can't hold a candle to you and Karen when you two get going."

"Thanks." Bev set her book on the desk that separated the twin beds. Gazing at the picture she and Tyler had posed for at the homecoming dance, she sighed again.

"Hey, cheer up. Tyler still loves you, and he's a neat guy," Jesse observed.

"He's a sweetheart," Bev beamed.

"You're lucky."

"I know." Bev smiled at Jesse. "And out there is another lucky guy waiting to meet you."

"Yeah, right! I don't think I have the equipment to attract a guy like that," she said, glancing down the front of her shirt. "Instead, I get guys like Patrick—computer nerds who are about as romantic as cold sores."

"I thought you liked Patrick."

"He's all right, but he's no Tyler Erickson or Gary Dawson," Jesse lamented.

"You'll meet Mr. Right someday."

"Yeah, I really believe that one! A few days ago I told you Handsy Herman didn't try anything with me because I could beat him up. That might be true, but I always wondered if it was because I wasn't as pretty as some of my cousins. Or maybe because I'm a toothpick with eyes."

"You're not feeling left out?"

Jesse scowled at Bev. "Hardly! I'm trying to say that guys aren't attracted to me."

"We could change that," Bev offered.

"I'm not wearing frilly dresses!"

"You don't have to. How often do you see me wearing a dress?"

Jessed gazed at Bev. "You have a point."

"It's a combination of things: personality, hair, makeup, and body language."

"Body language?"

Bev grinned. "If you walk around with this attitude like, 'you come near me and I'll break your arm', guys tend to keep their distance."

"I've never broken anybody's arm," Jesse challenged.

"That's good. Now we just have to work on your manners, your attitude, your hair—"

Jesse silenced her with a well-aimed pillow.

"Oh, I see how it is," Bev responded, reaching for her own pillow. "Let the games begin!" she exclaimed as she took a swing at Jesse's head.

* * *

"Girl, you have talent oozing out of every pore of your body," Janice said, complimenting the sketch Kassidy had drawn.

Kassidy smiled at her aunt. This was the second weekend she had spent with Janice. Chubbuck, Idaho, was rapidly becoming a sanctuary from the stress she endured throughout the week.

"When you're ready for some color, help yourself to my supplies. I have oils and acrylics, take your pick," Janice added, nodding around the spacious studio. Located in the back of her home, the studio boasted one wall that was paneled with tall windows. Sunlight filtered into the room, creating tiny rainbows at varied angles, depending on the time of day.

Kassidy adored this room; it symbolized everything she had grown to love about her aunt. Bright and airy, it encouraged freedom of expression. Janice Wharton was not the uncultured slob her mother had indicated. On the contrary, her aunt was a smart, talented woman with a wonderful sense of humor. Hanging out with Janice had given her a strong sense of family that she had never felt at home.

Janice had told Kassidy about the grandparents she couldn't remember; they had passed away in a car accident when she was five. Kassidy had also learned that her mother wasn't flawless as her aunt shared story after story that indicated Constance Martin was very human.

"She got an F on a math test?" Kassidy had repeated last night, stunned. "To hear her talk, she was a straight A honor student."

"I was the straight A honor student," Janice had corrected. "Your mother was too busy focusing on her social life to study. In fact, I bailed her out a time or two with papers she had been struggling to write. If I hadn't proofread her papers, she would've flunked English."

Hearing these stories eased the pressure of being Constance Martin's daughter, although a certain amount of resentment began to flourish. As Kassidy searched through her aunt's photo albums, she relished those pictures that revealed Constance had suffered through numerous bad-hair days while growing up. Torn between a sense of relieved amusement and embittered anger, Kassidy wondered why her mother had been so demanding. "You weren't perfect, why do I have to be?" she had muttered last night. An unsmiling picture of her mother had taunted her until she had closed the album and put it away.

"That horse is kind of skinny," Janice said now, studying Kassidy's sketch.

"You think?"

Janice nodded. "If I were you, I'd flesh him out a bit."

"Her . . . it's a girl. It's the horse I rode a couple of weeks ago."

"That horse doesn't look like it could carry a flea," she said, smiling at Kassidy.

Kassidy pictured Pearl in her mind. Janice was right: the horse's body was too thin. She picked up a special eraser Janice had given her and started to rub out the charcoal pencil.

"Horses need a certain amount of flesh to look right," Janice instructed.

"True," Kassidy agreed as she picked up the charcoal pencil.

"I'd add a bit more there, and maybe there to give it full dimension," Janice suggested.

Concentrating, Kassidy envisioned Pearl, then conveyed that image to the unfinished canvas. When she finished, she glanced up at her aunt.

"Much better. Now that's a horse you can be proud of," Janice praised.

"Thanks for your help."

"Anytime. Just remember, dimensions are important." Janice rested a hand on Kassidy's shoulder.

"I can see that now."

"The way I see it, Kass, all of God's creations were made to be a certain way. Like this project you're working on. You've drawn a horse, a meadow filled with flowers, and a waterfall. This will make a gorgeous painting. But if everything you drew looked the same, those qualities that make each item special would be lost. Because of how you've drawn the horse, it appears regal. The flowing lines of the waterfall give it life. This meadow would seem empty without the flowers. And when you add the finishing touches, you will have created an art form to be admired, something that will touch everyone who sees it."

Kassidy gazed at the canvas, trying to see it as her aunt did.

"I'm convinced that each one of us is a work of art," Janice continued. "We come into this world unfinished canvases, waiting for the touch of our Creator's hand to guide us into our full potential. But if we heed an untrained eye, if we don't accept painful changes that are necessary to give us dimension, something precious is lost." She slipped an arm around Kassidy's slender waist and gave her a squeeze. "You're a masterpiece waiting to happen, Kass."

Wishing that was true, Kassidy stared at the sketch in front of her. What if the canvas contained a flaw, something hidden that would distort the painting when it was finished? Disturbed by the mental imagery, she was relieved when her aunt suggested that they take a break and head down to the art gallery.

* * *

"Karen's still not speaking to you?" Tyler asked Bev Saturday night.

Bev nodded, snuggling next to Tyler as they sat together on the couch in her apartment. It had been an awful week, and she wasn't sure the next one would be much of an improvement.

"I'm sorry," he said sympathetically. "Would it help if I talked to her?"

"I doubt it," Bev replied. "I'm not sure what will help. It was almost a relief to have her mother come get her yesterday afternoon."

"Where did they go?"

"Idaho Falls. Her mother had a doctor appointment yesterday. They spent the night down there somewhere. I guess Edie wanted Karen to go shopping with her today to pick out some furniture for the baby's room. Maybe that will cheer her up."

"I think you're the one who needs cheering up," Tyler stated. Bending down, he kissed Bev, unaware they had an audience.

"Oh, please! Now *I* need therapy," Jesse said as she walked to the fridge. Opening it, she searched for several seconds, then frowned. "I could've sworn there were still a couple of pieces of leftover lasagna in here," she complained as she shut the fridge door.

"They're gone?" Bev asked, glancing toward the kitchen. "I saw them in there yesterday when I made a sandwich for lunch."

"And what happened to all of the chocolate chip cookies? Karen made a double batch Thursday night."

Bev sighed. It had to be Kassidy. Maybe they weren't watching her close enough. Kassidy had quit hiding things in her bottom drawer, but there had been several times in recent weeks when food from their apartment had mysteriously vanished. Bev made a mental note to talk to Treena about it when she came home from work that night.

"I'm starved! Who was supposed to cook dinner tonight?"

"Meg, I think," Bev answered.

"Oh, nice! I doubt she'll be up to fixing anything. She was having a horrible headache earlier and took another pain pill. She's dead to the world."

"Tell you what, why don't we go grab a burger?" Tyler offered.

"We?" Jesse hopefully asked, gesturing to herself.

"Sure. Bev's treat," Tyler joked.

"Okay," Bev replied. "Only we're not going for hamburgers. If I'm buying, it's going to be pizza."

"Pizza it is," Tyler agreed.

"Sounds good," Jesse said as she grabbed her coat from the back of a kitchen chair. "What about Meg and Treena?"

"We'll bring them back something to eat," Bev promised as she grabbed her purse. "Let's go!" she said, leading the way out of the apartment.

Chapter 25

Monday afternoon, Jesse stomped inside the apartment and threw her backpack on the floor. Her mother had sent an e-mail hinting that she might be coming up that way again, only this time with Charlie. That could only mean one thing—their relationship was getting serious. Fuming, Jesse was certain she was going to hate Charlie.

As Jesse sulked around the apartment, Kassidy showed up with Gary. Jesse grimaced when the couple settled on the couch to giggle and watch TV. Disgusted, Jesse retreated to the bedroom she now shared with Bev. Nearly an hour later, the telephone rang. She ignored it, figuring someone else would answer. When it continued to ring, Jesse grumbled under her breath and marched down the hall. As she walked into the living room, she saw that Kassidy and Gary had disappeared. Sullenly she picked up the telephone. "Yeah?"

"Hi, is Kassidy there? This is her aunt Janice."

"She was . . . I guess Gary took her somewhere."

"I see. Could you have her call me back when she returns?"

"Yeah," Jesse replied, grabbing a slip of paper and scrounging a pencil from the kitchen table. After hanging up, she wrote a quick note. Then, picking up her jacket, she headed out of the door, slamming it hard behind her.

* * *

"Man, who shut this door?" Gary asked as he continued to struggle with it. "It's jammed pretty tight."

Kassidy shivered. The wind was blowing, as usual, and she was freezing. "It's not locked?"

"Nope. I already tried your key. I think something's wrong with the doorknob."

"It worked fine when we left."

"Yeah, well, I can't get it to budge now," Gary said as he continued to work with the door. "I'm afraid we'll have to take the doorknob apart to get in."

"What's up?" Bev asked as she approached the couple.

"Gary says our doorknob is broken," Kassidy explained.

Bev slipped her heavy backpack to the cement balcony. "Is anyone inside?"

"No, we knocked several times," Gary said as he continued fiddling with the doorknob. "Is your apartment manager home?"

"I think so," Bev replied. "Let's go see."

* * *

"Somebody slammed this door shut pretty hard," the manager accused as he removed the doorknob.

"I promise it wasn't us," Kassidy said, her teeth chattering. She wondered why no one else seemed to be suffering as much from the cold as she was. Gary put his arm around her, and she leaned close, grateful for his added warmth.

"There, you can go inside. I'll have to see if I can find a knob to replace this one," the manager said as he gathered his tools. "Stuff a pair of socks in that hole until I can get it fixed," he advised. "That should keep the cold out."

"When will you fix it?" Bev asked as she grabbed her backpack.

"As soon as possible," he promised. "Just treat the next one with more respect," he said before heading down the stairs.

"Okay," Bev said as she entered their apartment.

"Well, Kass, I'd better go," Gary said, pulling away from her slender frame.

Kassidy waited expectantly, but once again the anticipated kiss didn't come.

"See you tomorrow," Gary called over his shoulder.

"Yeah," she said, disappointed. Entering the apartment, she did her best to shut the door.

"Here's a pair of socks to wedge in that hole," Bev said as she held out a pair of navy blue socks.

"Are they clean?"

"Yep—I got them out of Karen's drawer."

Kassidy moved aside as Bev stuffed the socks into the hole. "You two are *still* going out of your way to annoy each other?" she observed.

"It alleviates the monotony."

"I think it's terrible," Kassidy chided. "You two used to be so close."

Bev shrugged. She moved to the kitchen and picked up a note. "Hey, this is for you."

Walking across the apartment, Kassidy took the note from Bev's hand. "Jesse was here earlier. She must've taken my aunt's call." She read through the note again:

Kassidy,
When you get back from wherever it is you went, call your aunt Janice. And if you finally owe ice cream, pay up. We could use it around here!

"Dream on," Kassidy muttered, annoyed by the persistent teasing and by the fact that Gary hadn't kissed her yet.

"That looks like Jesse's handwriting," Bev said, peering over Kassidy's shoulder.

"She wasn't in a very good mood earlier," Kassidy mused. "Maybe she's the one who slammed the door."

"I wonder what's eating her," Bev said as she began removing books from her backpack. "She's been moody lately."

"I'll say," Kassidy agreed as she moved to the telephone. She quickly dialed her aunt's number and impatiently waited for Janice to answer. "Hi, Aunt Janice?"

"Kassidy, you're finally home."

"Yeah," Kassidy replied in a tired voice. Right now she wanted to curl up in a warm blanket and take a nap.

"I wanted to check with you about this weekend. Can you help me out in the gallery again?"

"Sorry I can't. I'm going up to Ashton with Gary for the weekend. He asked me about it earlier this afternoon."

"That's okay. Can I plan on you next weekend?"

"Sure."

"All right. Enjoy yourself in Ashton and I'll talk to you later."

"Bye," Kassidy replied.

"Love ya, hon," Janice said.

"I love you too," Kassidy said, missing the triumphant look on Bev's face as she hung up the telephone.

* * *

"Tell me again why we're sitting here?" Meg asked as her fingers continued to drum a silent pattern of panic on the arm of her chair. She was sitting beside Karen in the Counseling Center located on the second floor of the Spencer W. Kimball Building. Glancing at her watch, she wondered if she had time for this. Even with driving to campus, it took forever to get around with her crutches, though she now parked her car on campus. She was in charge of a ward activity later that night—a cake decorating contest. Each apartment was supposed to bring an unfrosted cake and would have a time limit to decorate it with the assortment of candy and frosting that would be furnished.

"We're sitting here because my mother sided with Bev, and I promised her I would come for at least one session of counseling."

Meg frowned at Karen. "I didn't make any promises."

"My bad! Hold up your right hand," Karen ordered.

"Why?"

"Because you're not going to bail on me now," Karen insisted. "Prepare to pledge your life away."

"Look, maybe you're right, maybe I have a problem with anger . . . with men—"

"Which is why we're both here," Karen interjected.

Meg glanced around the waiting room. Only one other person was in sight, a kind, older woman who sat behind the desk where the two girls had signed in. "Do you think this will help?"

Karen shrugged. "My mother and former best friend seem to think so."

Meg's forehead wrinkled with consternation. "About that . . . Bev and I have had our differences—"

"Slightly!"

"But I feel bad that you two aren't even speaking to each other."

"This has nothing to do with you, okay? Don't worry about it. This has been brewing for a long time, ever since school started."

"Why? You've been so close," Meg entreated.

"Maybe too close. Bev knows everything about me, and I know everything about her. What gives her the right to say that I'm not coping with things? I've seen her pull some good ones through the years."

"Oh?" Meg encouraged, eager to hear of Bev's exploits.

Karen began playing with her hair.

"You can't say something like that and not finish the story," Meg chided.

"Bev's been through a lot too—enough said. If she wants to tell you sometime, she can."

Meg offered a small smile. "That's a good sign: you're trying to protect her. You must still care about her."

"I always will. I'm just mad at her right now. I can't believe she thinks I need counseling!"

"And it didn't help when your mother thought Bev was right."

Karen nodded. "I figured I'd get some sympathy. Instead, well, you should've heard the lecture Mom gave me when she took me out to lunch last week after her doctor appointment. She all but threatened me with bodily harm if I didn't straighten things out with Bev."

"Which is why you set up this appointment?"

"I'm not sure how good these campus counselors are," Karen said, changing the subject.

"I've heard positive things about them."

"From?" Karen asked.

Meg took off her glasses and wiped them on the bottom of her shirt.

"Meg?" Karen prompted

"I know a girl who came in for some counseling last year. She was suffering from a severe case of low self-esteem."

"And?"

"She was in my student ward last year. In fact, I was her visiting teacher. She called me one night when she was feeling bad about herself. I had heard about this counseling center in the psychology class I took last year. I encouraged her to talk to one of the counselors."

"And it helped?" Karen asked, her voice softening.

Meg nodded. "Sometimes people just need someone to listen and to say the right things. These people are trained professionals. They know how to help."

"If you're so impressed with this place, why did you balk when I invited you to come?"

Meg's face turned a light shade of pink.

"You're embarrassed," Karen guessed.

"Aren't you?"

Karen nodded. "Yeah. I mean, I don't want people to think I have, you know . . ."

"Problems?"

Karen nodded.

"Same here." Meg lowered her gaze, staring at the carpet.

"I guess we should both take the advice my mother is always giving me and quit worrying about what other people think."

Meg sighed. "The thing is, most people don't really know me. All they see is this person who spends her life studying so she won't end up being a baby factory."

Karen grinned. "I think you'd make a nice baby factory."

"That's not even funny," Meg returned. "Seriously, that is something I hope to avoid. I'll probably want a family someday, but I want my life to count for something."

"I hear you. I would love to write for a big newspaper someday," Karen mused.

"You will. I read your article last week in *The Scroll*."

Karen's eyes widened. "You did?"

Meg nodded. "You have a lot of talent. Don't let it go to waste."

Before Karen could reply, a nearby door opened and Meg's name was called.

"Why am I first?"

Karen smiled. "They always save the best for last."

Meg stood, her green eyes settling on Karen. "I will get even," she said in a hushed voice.

"I'm sure you will," Karen replied as Meg disappeared.

* * *

A week later, Jesse's worst nightmare came true; her mother showed up with Charlie. For several seconds they stood awkwardly inside the apartment, staring at each other. Jesse could see that her mother's description hadn't done Charlie justice. A powerfully built man with blond hair and light blue eyes, he seemed much younger than he was. Jesse knew he was a year older than her mother and that he enjoyed most sports. Her mother had stressed that he was active in the LDS Church, and that he was a construction boss. As Jesse glared at him, she sensed why her mother had fallen for him. It made her hate him all the more.

"So, you're Jesse," he said, flashing a disarming smile as he extended his hand.

"Yeah," she said without enthusiasm, forcing herself to shake his hand.

"Where's Meg?" Sally asked.

"She went up on campus with Karen earlier this afternoon. I haven't seen her since."

Sally nodded. "Is she doing better?"

Jesse shrugged. "She's getting around better."

"Good," Sally replied. "Are you here alone?"

"Nah. Kassidy's in her bedroom sleeping."

"That's it?"

"Yeah," Jessie replied. "Bev's still in class, and Treena went to work about an hour ago. I guess you're stuck with me, or vice versa," she muttered, glaring at Charlie.

Sally's dark eyes flashed with displeasure. "Charlie, why don't you have a seat on the couch. We'll be right back," she said, gesturing to the sofa. She then led Jesse down the hall to the bedroom her daughter shared with Bev.

"Mom, I am not six years old!" Jesse complained as her mother escorted her inside the room and closed the door.

"Then quit acting like it!"

Jesse glowered at her mother. "Why did you bring him here?"

"Because you're not coming home until Christmas, and I wanted him to meet you before then. Is that a crime?"

"You're getting serious about him, right? That's why you're here," Jesse guessed. "You want me to tell you that it's okay if you get together with Charlie. Well, guess what? It's not okay!" she exclaimed, folding her arms.

Sally met her daughter's acerbic look with one of wounded fury. "Jesse, you may think you're all grown up, but you are still my daughter, and I will always demand respect from you!"

"I respect you, but I don't agree with what you're doing," Jesse replied. "Dad called me last week. I guess he's heard that you're dating someone. He wanted to know all about Charlie."

"So?"

"So, he still cares," Jesse pleaded.

Turning from Jesse, Sally teared up.

"Mom, I don't want to fight with you, okay? I'll go have dinner with you guys tonight, but I'm not making any promises. I will always love Dad," she said in a strained voice.

Blinking back tears, Sally turned to Jesse. "Just give Charlie a chance, Jess, that's all I ask."

Certain her mother was asking too much, Jesse nodded.

Chapter 26

Kassidy stroked Pearl's neck. "Hi, girl, did you miss me?" Pearl nickered, nudging against Kassidy's coat. "Yes, I brought you a treat," she laughed, reaching into her pocket for the apple she had cut into slices after dinner. "Want some of this?" she said as she gave Pearl a section of apple.

"I do," Gary said, moving next to Kassidy. "Looks like you're handing out a little sweetness. My turn."

Grinning, Kassidy shoved a large piece of apple inside of Gary's mouth.

Gary nearly gagged on the apple slice, but managed to chew it up and swallow it down. "That wasn't what I had in mind," he said, wiggling his eyebrows.

"It wasn't?"

He shook his head. Stepping closer, he pulled her toward him.

"You want another piece of apple?" Kassidy teased.

Gary answered by kissing her. When he pulled away several seconds later, he smiled. "Now *that's* a treat."

Thrilled that he had finally come through, Kassidy's eyes sparkled with excited joy. "Are you ready for a second helping?"

Nodding, he leaned down for another lengthy kiss.

"Ooooh, gross. Mom, they're kissing!" Becky exclaimed, disgusted.

Laughing at the nine-year-old's reaction, Gary and Kassidy pulled apart.

Gary glanced back at his youngest sister. "Are you spying on us?" he teased.

"No. Mom wanted to show Kassidy that new saddle Dad bought her. It's softer than her other one. She said that way Kassidy won't be so sore tomorrow."

"Maybe she won't even notice how sore she is," Margaret Dawson said, glancing from Gary to Kassidy as she entered the dimly lit barn.

"Mom, why is Kassidy turning red?" Becky asked.

"Never mind, honey," Margaret replied. "Now, would you like to see that saddle?"

Nodding, Kassidy stepped back to allow Gary's mother to pass by. Gary reached for Kassidy's hand and led her toward the back of the barn.

* * *

"How is school going?" Margaret asked as she and Kassidy washed the dishes after a big Sunday dinner.

"Pretty good."

"You seem a lot happier this weekend," Margaret observed.

"Did Gary tell you I've been spending some time with my aunt?"

Margaret washed another dish and handed it to Kassidy to dry. "It seems like he did say something about that. She's your mother's sister?"

"Yeah, only she's nothing like my mother." A fleeting look of sadness shadowed Kassidy's face. How could two sisters be so different? Why couldn't her mother be more like Janice?

"Gary said she's been very good to you," Margaret commented as she scrubbed another plate.

"Janice is great. I love spending time with her, especially in her studio. You should see some of the paintings she's done."

Margaret smiled. "I understand you have quite a bit of talent in that area too."

"Not like my aunt. She has sold several paintings since my uncle died. It used to be a hobby. Now she calls it her catharsis."

"Is it for you?" Margaret inquired.

Kassidy thought about the question before answering. "Maybe. I feel better after I've drawn or painted something."

"I think everybody needs a release like that. For me, it's music. When I've had a bad day I sit down and play the piano."

"You play the piano?"

"A little," Margaret said, smiling. "I took lessons for years when I was growing up. I used to hate it, but now I enjoy playing through the songs I love."

"That's how I feel about art. If I can do something I want, it's fun. It drives me crazy when my mother or an art teacher stands over me, telling me what I'm doing wrong."

"That drives everybody crazy," Margaret replied. "In my opinion, there are too many critics in today's world. We're too quick to tear down—we'd much rather do that than build up. Criticism reigns supreme. If we spent more time praising people for trying to do something, can you imagine how much nicer the world would be?"

"Isn't that how it's supposed to be?" Kassidy asked.

"That's how it could be. It's the agency thing. We're all free to choose what we'll do with our time in this world. Some make very poor choices. And don't forget about Satan. He's out to destroy us any way he can. If he can make us feel bad about ourselves, convince us that we're worthless, then he thinks he's a big success.

"The frustrating part is, he targets people who try to do good in this world. He tries everything he can think of to pound them into the dirt. Whether it's through temptations, sharp barbs from other people, abuse of any kind . . ."

Kassidy flinched, thinking of the arguments she had overheard between her parents. She thought of how they often treated her. It wasn't right. That wasn't how it was supposed to be.

" . . . but in my opinion, we can rise above anything Satan may throw our way."

"We can? How?" Kassidy asked, forcing herself back to the conversation.

"By blocking out the negative messages that bombard us on a daily basis. I think it's important every day to spend some time alone, prayerfully meditating about why we're here. I try to do that every morning. I spend about ten to fifteen minutes studying scriptural passages and then pray about them. It gives me a sense of inner peace to start each day."

"I wish that worked for me," Kassidy said wistfully.

"It can, Kassidy. It works—I promise! It works so well, I do it twice a day: in the morning when I first get up, and then at night before I go to bed."

"I've tried reading the scriptures before. Some of them are so hard to understand."

"I felt the same way when I was younger," Margaret admitted. "Why don't you try an experiment: Try reading one scripture from the Book of Mormon every day. Think about how it might apply to your life, then pray about it. I promise it will become habit-forming."

"Maybe I'll try that." Kassidy reached for a handful of silverware from the sink on her side. She winced as pain radiated from her posterior, reminding her of the ride she and Gary had gone on the day before.

"Did that new saddle make any difference for you?"

"Oh yeah! I'm still sore, but not like last time."

"Life can be like that," Margaret remarked. "After you endure the initial pain of a fiery trial, the rest isn't so bad if you hang in there. And, periodically, our Father in Heaven gives us cushions to ease the bruising we sometimes take."

Pondering Margaret's advice, Kassidy dried the bowl in her hands. Were there enough cushions in the world to block out her pain? Certain she had been blessed with loving relationships in recent weeks, she felt a surge of hope. Setting the bowl on the counter, she reached for another dish, enjoying this time with Gary's mother.

* * *

"What is with the chocolate ice cream in the freezer tonight?" Jesse asked as she glanced around the kitchen table at her roommates. "All right, 'fess up! Who's the guilty party?"

"If Bev had to furnish it every time Tyler kissed her, we'd have ice cream coming out our ears," Treena commented.

"Ha, ha, ha!" Bev retorted, pointing at Karen. "I'm not the only one who lives here."

"Don't look at me," Karen said, scowling at Bev.

Bev looked away, hurt by the unspoken insinuation that they were no longer friends.

"I haven't had a date since homecoming," Jesse announced. She glanced over at her cousin and grinned. "Meg, is there something you haven't been telling us?"

"Don't even go there," Meg warned.

"That leaves one possibility," Treena said, glancing at Kassidy. "Yep, we hit pay dirt," she said, laughing at the embarrassed look on Kassidy's face. "I can't believe you didn't tell me. When did Gary make his move?"

"The important thing is we have dessert," Jesse chuckled.

"Maybe we should save it for family home evening tonight," Treena suggested. "I mean, Gary *did* help earn it for us."

"I knew I shouldn't have bought that," Kassidy said, rising from the table.

"We're happy for you," Treena replied. "As they say, you go girl!"

Shaking her head, Kassidy picked up her plate and set it on the counter. "C'mon, Jesse, let's get these dishes done before Gary and Troy show up."

* * *

Two nights later, Bev found herself driving Jesse all over Rexburg. "Where are we going?"

"You'll see," Jesse grinned. "Turn here. That's it, make a right," she instructed. "Okay, we're almost there."

"Almost where? We've been driving around in circles for thirty minutes."

"It wouldn't be a surprise if I told you, now would it?"

"This had better not have anything to do with my birthday, okay? I'm not in the mood for anything this year," Bev growled.

"Quit being a grump. You'll love this, birthday girl," Jesse teased.

"Right," Bev retorted. "Look, I don't know what you're up to, but I'm done, okay? I'll take you to wherever it is you want to go, but then I'm heading back to our apartment."

Jesse shrugged. "It's your special day. If you want to ruin everything, it's your choice."

Bev groaned. "No more guilt trips," she pleaded. "I can't take it. Every time I see that accusing look on Karen's face, I want to sit down and cry."

"This was probably a bad idea. You're still upset over this thing with Karen. Why don't we go back to our apartment?"

Bev turned to gaze at Jesse. What was she up to?

"I didn't have anything major planned, I just wanted to get you out of the apartment so you'd quit moping. Treena said she'd meet us for a hot-fudge-sundae run when she gets off work."

"She works until seven tonight," Bev pointed out, glancing at the clock on the dashboard. It was a couple of minutes past 6:30. "And I'm not in the mood for a party!"

"Let's go home. I'll call Treena at work and tell her to meet us there. Maybe she can bring home a quart of Ben & Jerry's Blastin' Berry ice cream."

Bev remained silent, certain this was the worst birthday of her life. She had turned nineteen today, but so far the only acknowledgment had been this feeble attempt on Jesse's part to cheer her up. She had thought her father or Gina would at least call, but all of the telephone calls that afternoon had been for Kassidy.

After several minutes of driving in silence, Bev reached over and cranked up the volume on the radio. She glanced at Jesse, but the young woman seemed intent on staring out the window. Sighing, Bev continued to drive and felt relieved when she spotted the Baronnessa Apartment complex.

"Here we are," Bev mumbled as she pulled into the crowded parking lot.

"It's a good thing. All that pop I drank earlier is catching up to me," Jesse said, hurrying out of the Jeep. "Would you mind doing me a favor?"

Bev locked the Jeep before answering. "Now what?"

"Could you go see if my clothes are dry? I stuck a batch of darks in the dryer at the far end of the laundry room. If they're wet, come tell me, and I'll run down and add some more quarters. If they're dry, come on up. I'll get my clothes later, after I finish with some much-needed business," she said before sprinting toward D building.

"I guess I don't have a choice," Bev complained, shoving her wallet into the pocket of her navy blue ski coat. She trudged toward the laundry room that belonged to the Baronnessa complex, shivering despite the thickness of her coat.

As she approached the laundry room, she glanced around, but saw no one. Opening the door, she stepped inside the vacant room.

She shut the door to block the wind and moved to the dryer Jesse had described. Opening the dryer, she scowled at its empty interior. "Wrong one, Jesse," she muttered as she began checking the other dryers. She found a batch of whites that were still warm from being dried but could see no sign of her roommate's clothes. Annoyed, she slammed the dryer shut as someone else entered the laundry room. Bev whirled around to see Karen standing there, glowering at her. "What are you doing here?"

"I came to settle a score."

"Your timing is excellent! I've been having such a good day anyway."

"It serves you right," Karen replied.

Bev frowned. "You know, maybe the silent treatment had its perks."

"Yeah, well, I've decided silence isn't golden, but something else is," Karen said, stepping close to Bev.

"I see. And what would that be?"

"Friendship," Karen replied before drawing Bev into a hug.

* * *

Searching her coat pocket, Karen handed Bev a tissue, then pulled one out for herself.

"I've missed you so much," Bev said, dabbing her eyes with the tissue.

"I've missed me too," Karen replied.

"I'm being serious here."

"So am I," Karen said, her brown eyes glistening with unshed tears. "I haven't been myself for a long time. So, I swallowed some pride and took your advice. I've been meeting with a campus counselor the past couple of weeks."

"You're kidding!"

Karen shook her head.

"You don't know how much I've regretted saying that," Bev sniffed.

"You were trying to help me, something my mother pointed out during her last visit—or should I say *lecture*."

"Go, Mom!" Bev said, her blue eyes twinkling. "I've always loved that woman."

"She sure thinks the world of you. Man, she chewed me out!"

Bev laughed. "I'll have to send her a thank you card."

"Go for it. I think you rate higher on her list right now than I do."

"I doubt that," Bev argued. "I've seen how she spoils you."

"There was none of that last week. Instead, she made me promise to apologize to you and to see a counselor."

"Has it helped—seeing the counselor?"

"A little," Karen answered. "She gave me a few ideas to help me work some things out, but it'll take time. I'm far from ready to forgive Roger Beyer. She did help me realize that I have to start by forgiving myself."

"For what?"

"When I saw Meg go through what she did—like you said—it brought back a lot of things for me. I guess I'm still blaming myself for what happened to me the night I was attacked."

"Karen—"

"It's true. I wouldn't let you drive me home that night, and I ignored everything my grandmother had ever taught me about being safe."

"But you didn't deserve what happened," Bev argued.

"Neither did Meg. But we both feel guilty, ashamed, violated. Bev, unless you've been there, it's hard to understand. You mentioned that I get a panicked look on my face whenever a guy tries to put his arm around me. It's a problem. Ordinary things can trigger feelings of panic and fear in someone who's been through a traumatic incident. Meg said the counselor told her that in the future, if someone grabs her from behind, even if they're a loved one, her first response will be fear—at least for a while."

"That's awful," Bev conceded.

"I know," Karen agreed, nodding. "But we're starting to understand it's a normal reaction, and we're beginning to believe that we can beat this thing. I guess that old saying is right: You have to face your fears to conquer them."

"Don't ever think you have to face them alone," Bev said, reaching for another hug.

"I know," Karen breathed, holding tight to Bev. Several seconds passed before Karen drew back to smile tearfully at her friend. "And speaking of facing fears, I'm here to help you face one of yours."

"Oh?" Bev said, wiping her eyes again with the piece of tissue in her hand.

"You know how you're always afraid people will forget your birthday," Karen teased.

"This chat is the best birthday gift you could've ever given me. I don't want anything else."

Unable to reply, Karen nodded.

"And we need to do something to lighten things up or we'll be reliving our first day here—you know, when we both spouted like saltwater fountains?"

"No more D.I. moments for me," Karen insisted, moving to the door of the laundry room. "I have something else in mind."

"What?" Bev asked, following behind her friend.

"Let's hit the lounge and see if anything is going on." Karen waited until Bev had moved out of the laundry room, then closed the door and walked across the manager's driveway to enter the Baronnessa lounge. She held the door open, waiting for Bev to step through.

Bev walked into the darkened interior of the large room. "There's nothing in here."

"SURPRISE!!!" several people yelled as Karen switched on the lights.

* * *

Bev stood in stunned amazement, blinking as her eyes adjusted to the bright light. She stared at the crepe paper and balloons that decorated the room. A large banner hanging from the ceiling wished her a happy nineteenth birthday. She gazed around at the friends she had made in recent weeks in their student ward and in some of her classes. She smiled at her roommates, then at Tyler Erickson, who wore a silly party hat on top of his head. Turning, she spotted her parents and younger brothers. Squealing her delight as her family rushed forward to greet her, she was caught up in a tangle of arms as everyone tried to hug her at once.

"I told you she needed a party," Jesse whispered to Meg.

Meg nodded, leaning forward on her crutches.

"You're sure we did the right thing moving all of Karen's stuff back into Bev's bedroom?"

"Yes," Meg answered. "It was getting too quiet in my room. I missed having you around, pestering me every five minutes. I was getting way too much studying done."

"She's baaack," Jesse sang out before she ran off to grab a glass of punch.

Chapter 27

The weeks flew by, and Christmas vacation was approaching fast. Bev and Karen made arrangements to travel home to Blaketown with Tyler. Meg and Jesse planned to drive down to St. George together. Treena had received a round-trip airline ticket from her parents as part of a Christmas surprise. Kassidy knew her parents would do something similar if she asked but had decided she would rather spend the time with her aunt Janice and Gary.

The day Treena was to fly out, Gary offered to drive her and Kassidy to the small Idaho Falls Airport. After Treena's flight left, Gary would drive Kassidy down to her aunt's house.

"You're sure you don't want to come home with me?" Treena tempted Kassidy as they waited for her flight to be called.

"I'm sure," Kassidy replied. "I have my reasons for staying."

Treena smiled, glancing over at Gary, who was thumbing through a magazine. "I see."

"It's more than that," Kassidy said, flushing.

"I'm glad," Treena replied as her flight was announced over the public address system.

"Have a safe flight."

"And you take care of yourself," Treena said, gripping Kassidy in a tight hug. She pulled back to wave at Gary. "Thanks for the ride down."

"Anytime. We'll be here waiting to pick you up in January," he promised.

"Good deal," she said, retrieving her carry-on bag. "You two behave while I'm gone."

"Good-bye, Treena," Kassidy stressed.

"I can take a hint. I know when I'm not needed," Treena said, grinning at her friend.

Toting a black bag, she walked toward the scanning device that would allow her access to the plane. The tightened security measures that had been enforced since the terrorist attacks didn't bother her. She knew the delay was well worth the effort it entailed. In her opinion, security was worth any price; she had seen the difference it had made in Kassidy's life. During the past few weeks, Kassidy had been so happy. Humming as she handed her bag to a security officer, Treena caught a final glimpse of Kassidy's smiling face as Gary led her from the airport. Yes, security was a needful thing.

* * *

"Are you sure you won't stay for dinner?" Janice tempted, smiling warmly at Gary.

"I'd love to, but my mom is expecting me home tonight. In fact, she was expecting me about an hour ago," he said, glancing at his watch. "I'd better give her a call and let her know I'm on my way."

"The phone's right there in the hall," Janice said, leading Gary to the telephone stand. She walked back to where her niece was waiting near the entry way. "I'm impressed with your young man," she commented.

"He's awesome," Kassidy agreed.

"And very cute." Janice smiled at the embarrassed look on her niece's face. "I approve."

"Thanks, I think," Kassidy laughed.

Thrilled by the changes she felt certain were taking place with her niece, Janice drew Kassidy into a spontaneous hug. "I'm so glad you're spending Christmas with me." She smiled when she felt Kassidy return the hug. It had taken several weeks to break through the defensive wall the young woman kept between herself and everyone else, something Janice knew was crucial to help her heal. To the best of her knowledge, they were making great strides with her niece. According to her room-mates, there had been no sign of the bulimia for nearly a month. Kassidy had either stopped or had become adept at hiding it. Janice prayed Kassidy had stopped. She loved the girl dearly, and it sliced through her heart to think of how her niece had been hurting herself.

"Thanks for letting me stay here for Christmas," Kassidy breathed when she pulled back a few seconds later.

"Consider this your home away from home," Janice insisted as tears threatened to form.

Kassidy nodded.

"Good thing I called," Gary said as he returned to the front door, "Mom was thinking about sending out the search and rescue unit to look for me."

"The search and rescue?" Kassidy repeated.

"You know Mom," he replied, smiling.

"Yes I do. She's pretty awesome."

"I won't argue with you there," he said. Then, turning to Janice he grinned. "Thanks for lunch."

"It wasn't anything fancy," she protested.

"That's the fanciest sandwich I've had in a long time. What did you call it again?"

"Crab-salad croissant."

"It hit the spot," he said, "but now I'd better hit the road."

"Kassidy, maybe you should escort Gary to his truck," Janice suggested, winking before she moved into the living room.

* * *

"Your aunt's very subtle," Gary grinned.

Kassidy shook her head at him. "So's your mother. All that winking and hinting she does."

"I love both women."

"Me too," Kassidy replied, warmed by that knowledge. For the first time in years she felt content with life. It was a refreshing change. She was starting to achieve an inner peace she had never experienced before.

"And there's a third woman who's right up there with them."

"Oh, really, who?"

"Guess." He pulled her close for a kiss, then gave her a hug. "I'm going to miss you."

"You're coming back down after Christmas," she reminded him as they stepped apart.

"I know," he said, doing his best to look pathetic.

"It's only two days."

"It'll seem like forever."

"We'll survive," Kassidy assured him, warmed by his reluctance to leave. "Give your mom a hug for me when you get there tonight. And call to let me know you made it okay."

"Will do. By the way, no peeking."

"What?"

"That gift I left for you, the one under your aunt's tree. No peeking."

"Same for you. Don't forget to take in that bag of gifts I left in the back of your truck. It's under the camper shell."

"Are all of those gifts for me?" he teased.

"No, most of them are for Pearl."

He lifted an eyebrow.

"Just kidding. I sent something for everyone in your family."

Gary slapped his forehead. "I almost forgot, Mom sent down a package for you that's from everybody up that way. It's still in the truck." He opened the front door, and taking Kassidy's hand, led her down the steps into the driveway. As they approached his truck, he dug the keys out of his pocket. Hurrying around to the back, he unlocked the back of the camper shell and opened it. Reaching down inside, he pulled out a large black garbage bag. "I would have been in big trouble if I'd forgotten to give you this."

"That looks like the bag I set inside your truck."

"It's not, trust me," he said, handing her the bag. "There's a big wrapped box in here. Mom said you can open this on Christmas Eve."

"Christmas Eve?"

"Yeah. She said something about it being a Christmas hug."

Kassidy took the bag from Gary and leaned close for a final kiss.

"Merry Christmas," he said as he walked around to the driver's side of his truck.

"Same to you," she called out. She watched him drive down the street, then carried the bag inside her aunt's house.

* * *

On Christmas Eve, Bev helped Gina fix the traditional snacks her family had enjoyed for years: crackers spread with cheese and topped with mushrooms or olives, chips with dip, fruit pieces with a tasty caramel dipping sauce, steamed shrimp served with cocktail sauce, and sirloin steak cut into cubes for cooking in a fondue pot. Eggnog was mixed together and poured into a fancy glass punch bowl that was reserved for special occasions.

After Bev's father offered a sincere prayer of gratitude, plates were heaped with food, and the entire family gathered in the family room to watch favorite Christmas videos. The selections that year included the animated version of *How the Grinch Stole Christmas*, followed by *It's a Wonderful Life*. At 9:30 the doorbell rang, something Bev sprang up to answer.

"Now, I wonder who that could be?" James Henderson teased his daughter.

"Dad, behave."

"What?"

"You already quizzed Tyler down over Thanksgiving," she replied as she left the room. The doorbell sang out a second time before Bev made it to the door. She swung it open, grinning at Tyler. "Impatient, aren't you?"

"A little," he admitted, stepping inside the large house. "It's freezing out here."

"Come here, and I'll warm you up," she said, leaning close for a quick kiss before taking his coat. "You missed most of our movie-fest, but there's still plenty of food."

Tyler patted his stomach. "I couldn't eat another thing. Mom outdid herself this year. She decided to make everybody's favorite Mexican dishes tonight. I ate so much I'm almost sick."

"What are your plans for tomorrow?"

"That's part of why I came by. Dad had a surprise for us tonight. He's done well this year with his computer store. He announced that for Christmas this year, he's taking us all on a trip."

"A trip?" Bev questioned.

"He's flying us to Nauvoo, Illinois. We'll drive down to Salt Lake tomorrow to spend the night. Then we'll fly out the next day."

"That is so exciting!"

"It is," Tyler agreed. "Mom has wanted to go for years."

"Is everyone going?"

"Yeah. Mom and Dad, Sabrina, me, Kate, her husband, Mike, and that spoiled niece of mine, Colleen."

"You love her, and you know it," Bev said, picturing the tiny girl who was just over a year old. "It sounds fun."

"I know. I asked Dad if he had an extra ticket for you, but he spaced that one," Tyler said.

Bev shrugged. "My parents would throw themselves if I left. They've planned a lot of things to do while I'm here. But it would've been fun," she said wistfully. "Well, if you're heading out, I guess I'd better give you your gift tonight."

"That's the other reason I'm here," Tyler said, retrieving his coat from the couch. He searched through a coat pocket and pulled out a small wrapped package.

Bev stared at the gift. Certain it contained jewelry, her fingers trembled as she removed the bow. She tore the paper and gaped at the small, velvet box.

"Aren't you going to open it?" Tyler asked.

Nodding, Bev flipped the box open.

"What's wrong? Don't you like it?"

"It's . . . gorgeous," Bev said, trying to hide her disappointment as she pulled a necklace from the box. "Thank you."

"I picked it out a few weeks ago," he proudly confessed. "It's your birthstone."

"Yeah, I can see that," Bev replied. "I love it," she said, gazing at the beautiful topaz crystal that hung from a delicate silver chain. "Want to help me put it on?"

"Sure," he said, slipping behind her. She handed him the necklace, and he carefully draped it around her neck, then fastened it. "There you go."

"Thanks," she mumbled, gazing down at the amber-colored gemstone.

"I hate to run off, but I guess I'd better go. I have to get packed tonight."

"Hey, wait. Let me grab your gift; it's under the tree." She moved across the room and sorted through the pile of gifts that were crowded beneath the bushy artificial tree. "There it is," she said, holding up a small, slender box. She walked back and handed it to Tyler.

Tyler smiled. "Do I get a hint?"

"I didn't get a hint," she said, reflecting on the teasing she had endured for weeks about getting a ring for Christmas. The initial letdown was giving way to relief. The pressure was off, at least for now. Maybe her dad was right; things had been moving too fast between them. If this was meant to be an eternal relationship, it wouldn't hurt to delay major decisions.

"Can I shake it?" Tyler asked.

"If you want to."

He shook it lightly. "That didn't help."

"Then I guess you'd better open it," she responded.

Sitting down on the couch, he quickly unwrapped the box. His eyes widened as he pulled out a silver-banded watch.

"I knew you needed a new one," Bev explained.

"It's a tartan watch! It has the tartan design on the face, the MacOwen tartan," he said excitedly, referring to his Scottish ancestry. The watch face contained a blue and green plaid with white and yellow stripes.

Bev nodded. "Your sisters told me which tartan to get."

"This is so cool, but it must've cost you a fortune," he said, glancing up at her.

"It wasn't too bad. I ordered it off the Internet. I got it for a decent price."

"I hope so," he said. Rising, he fastened the watch around his wrist, then stepped close to Bev. "Thank you," he said before kissing her.

Her mood improving, Bev returned the kiss. "You be careful in Nauvoo."

"I will. Enjoy your vacation, and I'll call you when we get back."

Nodding, Bev followed him to the door. He kissed her again before leaving, then hurried out the door. She watched him leave, fingering the necklace around her neck. With a sigh, she closed the door and retreated to the family room.

* * *

Meg was certain she would scream if her parents said one more thing about the advantages of Dixie College over BYU–Idaho. Since her arrival home, she had endured numerous hints and innuendos about what she should do. As Christmas Eve approached, the tension eased, and Meg began to enjoy her vacation from school. The night of Christmas Eve, her family gathered into the living room for the annual reading of the second chapter of Luke. Her father adjusted his reading glasses, cleared his throat, and began to read from the New Testament.

Later that night when Meg had stretched out on the hide-a-bed in the family room, she heard someone creep down the stairs.

"Meg, are you asleep?"

Frowning at the sound of her mother's voice, Meg was tempted to pretend that she was.

"Meg?"

"I'm awake," Meg sighed, watching as her mother walked into the darkened room.

"Would you mind if I turned on a lamp?"

"Go ahead," Meg said, deciding it wouldn't do any good to protest. She blinked rapidly as the light was flipped on. Sitting up, she leaned against the couch. As she stretched out her legs, she was grateful the cast was finally off. The itching had driven her crazy toward the end.

Penny sat down on the edge of the hide-a-bed and gazed at Meg.

"What is it, Mom?" Meg asked, noting how pretty her mother looked in the new pink robe she had unwrapped earlier that evening. It was a tradition in their household to let everyone unwrap one gift on Christmas Eve. The robe had been a gift from Meg's father.

"You have always been one to get right to the point."

"Sometimes," Meg acknowledged.

"So, I'm going to follow your example. On our flight home a few weeks ago, Sally said something that's troubled me ever since."

Meg silently groaned. This was the conversation she had hoped to never have with her mother. But it was something the campus counselor had assured was necessary as part of the healing process; she would have to reveal what had taken place six years ago. Certain that Jesse's mother had already spilled the beans, Meg wondered what was left to say.

"I had mentioned to Sally that it was awfully strange you would panic like that and fall."

"And she told you about Handsy Herman," Meg guessed.

Penny stared at Meg. "No, she said sometimes you aren't as

strong as you want everyone to think. What's this about Handsy Herman?"

"Great!" Meg banged her head against the back of the couch.

"Meg?"

Hesitantly Meg shared what had taken place the summer she had turned thirteen. Convinced her mother would come apart at the seams and then spend the rest of the Christmas vacation lecturing her, Meg was surprised by her mother's reaction.

"I'm sorry, Meg," Penny said quietly as tears began to form. "It was my fault."

"How was it your fault?"

"I should've made you go on that hike. I had a bad feeling about you staying behind, that's why I tried to talk you into going. I was trying to protect you. How do you think it makes me feel to know I failed?" Rising, she paced the room. "That's part of why I stayed at home with you kids. I always wanted to be here for you, to keep you from harm, to teach you everything you need to know about surviving in this world. Being a good mother has always been one of my goals. It's all I ever wanted to be."

Meg thought of several things her mother had done on her behalf through the years and felt ashamed. Why had she been so critical? She had believed her mother had given up her identity to raise a family; she had never understood that being a mother was part of her mother's identity. Slipping from the hide-a-bed, Meg crossed the room. "You are a wonderful mother," she stammered, "and I wasn't exactly the easiest child to raise."

Penny turned to face Meg. "You still aren't," she said with a wry smile. "Meg, you remind me so much of myself—independent, feisty, and we're both too stubborn for our own good."

Meg nodded as she realized what her mother was saying was true. They were alike in many ways—maybe that's why they had driven each other crazy.

"But you also possess so many wonderful traits. You always finish whatever you start. And despite what Sally said, you are strong," Penny stressed. "You're talented, beautiful—"

"A lot of people think I take after my mother," Meg said, reaching for a hug. She smiled when her mother returned the intense squeeze.

* * *

"Treena, I know it isn't much, but that round-trip ticket was most of your Christmas," her mother explained as Treena tried on the new dress she had unwrapped earlier that morning.

"Mom, I love this dress! It's one of my colors—purple."

Treena's mother beamed. "I'm glad you like it. It looks good on you. Your dad and I thought you could use a new dress for college."

"It even hides a few curves," Treena said as she moved in front of the full-length mirror in her parents' bedroom.

"Those curves look good on you," Marcy Graham stressed. "I've always liked them on me," she added, laughing. She stood behind Treena, gazing at her daughter's reflection. "You look beautiful."

"Thanks. I'll never be model material, but that's okay 'cuz I never wanted to be a model."

"Speaking of model material, what did Kassidy's mother want earlier when she called?"

Treena frowned. "Her sister's phone number."

"She doesn't have it?" Marcy asked.

Treena shook her head. "They don't exactly get along."

"I see," Marcy replied pensively. "Is Constance trying to get hold of Kassidy?"

"Probably."

"Did you have the number?"

"Nope. I had a copy of it once, but it's long gone. Kassidy has it in her address book, but that's back in Idaho."

"You mentioned Kassidy is doing better."

"She is," Treena said, relief evident in her voice.

"Maybe Constance wants to wish her a Merry Christmas."

Treena gazed in the mirror at her mother. "I hope that's all it is," she said, praying Janice would run interference if things turned ugly.

* * *

"This is going to be one spoiled kid," Karen said as she gazed at all of the toys her unborn sibling had received for Christmas. Most were still stashed under the huge evergreen tree Brett had found for the holidays. The tree towered proudly from the vaulted ceiling of the living room, blending nicely with the new log home he had finished before marrying Edie.

"I know," Edie sighed. "Every time I went into a store to get some Christmas shopping done, I'd see something cute and have to buy it," she said, retreating to the couch.

"She's about *cuted* us out of house and home," Brett said, winking at Karen. "Good thing she has a job."

"That's why I'm buying stuff now. I'll quit work when the baby is born. I won't be able to afford these things then," Edie defended.

"Ouch!" Brett feigned a grimace. "Did you hear that, Karen? Your mother thinks we'll be living in the poorhouse when she hangs up her nursing shoes."

"Who plays referee for you two when I'm not here?" Karen asked, laughing.

"The dog," Brett said, pointing to the fuzzy Shih Tzu pup he had bought Edie a month after Karen had left for college.

"His name is Barney," Edie retorted, "not 'the dog'."

"He keeps your mother company when she's here by herself."

"He's adorable," Karen said, reaching down to pet the shaggy-looking purebred. White with patches of brown and black, he reminded her of a Muppet character.

"So's your mother," Brett added, patting Edie's bulging stomach.

"Don't wake the baby," Edie cautioned. "She kicks me enough as it is."

Karen grinned. "You think it's a girl too?"

"The ultrasound they did last week told the story," Edie replied. "Ooohh!"

"What's wrong?" Karen asked, moving to her mother's side.

"I'm getting the impression your little sister is a light sleeper," Edie winced.

"She's awake? Can I feel her?"

"Sure. She's an active little toad, as my mother would say," Edie said. "Set your hand right there," she directed, guiding her daughter's hand across her tightly stretched abdomen.

"Whoa, what a kick!"

"That's my line," Edie said, taking a deep breath. "I think I'm going to lie down. Sometimes that settles her."

"Let me move these pillows," Brett offered as he helped his wife assume a comfortable position on the couch. He turned to smile at Karen. "Should we go cook Christmas dinner?"

"I can help. Give me a minute," Edie said.

Brett shook his head. "You didn't sleep well last night, and those ankles of yours are paying for all the walking we did yesterday," he said as he placed a couple of pillows under his wife's feet to elevate them. "There, that's better. You lie there and behave, and we'll take care of things." Leaning down, he kissed her. "Holler if you need anything."

"Thank heavens we put the turkey in to cook last night before we went to bed."

Karen inhaled deeply, loving the smell of cooked turkey and sage. It had been wonderful to wake up to the tempting aroma. "Don't worry about anything, Mom, we'll take care of it."

"I hate this."

"Like you're always telling me, it won't be forever."

"And like you always say, it just feels like that now," Edie retorted with a smile.

* * *

"Charlie, would you like some more pie?" Sally Waterman asked.

Charlie pushed back from the table and patted his toned stomach. "Your cherry pie is the best, but I'll pop if I eat any more. Thanks for dinner." He leaned over to give her a kiss.

Jesse rolled her eyes, hating the way Charlie touched her mother. A part of her wanted to scream; another part wanted to follow Kassidy's example and hurl. Charlie had given her mother an engagement ring for Christmas; he was going to become part of the family despite her efforts to pretend he didn't exist.

"Hey, Jesse, want to come play my new computer game with me?" her twelve-year-old brother asked.

"Sure, Mitch," Jesse said, rising from the table, grateful for the reprieve.

"Jess, why don't you let Charlie go with Mitch? I need you to help me clean up."

Jesse tried very hard to control herself. Her mother had indicated earlier that the best gift she could give this year would be an improvement in her attitude. "Okay," she said. "Next time, Mitch."

"Don't worry about it. Charlie's great at computer games," Mitch enthused. "C'mon, I'll waste your action," he said as he led Charlie out of the small dining room.

"Thanks, Jess," Sally said when they were alone.

"For what?"

"For making today so enjoyable. I was worried about how things would go, but this is the best Christmas we've had in a long time."

Silently disagreeing, Jessed plastered a smile on her face as she began helping her mother clean up the dishes.

Chapter 28

Constance Martin frowned as she waited for someone to pick up the telephone.

"Seasons greetings," a booming male voice sang out.

"Yes, hello. Is Kassidy Martin there?"

"I know she's around here somewhere. She was helping Mom in the kitchen. I'll find her."

Tapping her manicured fingers on the polished oak desk in her husband's study, Constance mentally rehearsed what she planned to say to her daughter. When Kassidy had called last week to announce her plans for Christmas vacation, Constance had been caught off guard. She had sat, dazed, as her only child had increased the distance between them. More hurt than she ever would admit, Constance had fumed ever since, the anger increasing when her husband had blamed her for Kassidy's absence.

"Kassidy was upset when she left here at the end of August. The way you carried on when she lost that pageant, you would have thought it was the end of the world," he had snapped. "One of my top clients wants his son to spend some time with our daughter while he's home for the holidays, and where is Kassidy? Out slopping hogs with some farmer! You know she's doing this out of spite. She can't possibly have feelings for someone like that! Get her back home where she belongs. I don't care how you do it, but make it happen!" Gilbert Martin had thundered at his wife. "As far as I'm concerned, Kassidy is through with that excuse of a college. If she has a shot at getting together with Richard Burke's son, we have to get her back here!"

His words still echoing in her mind, Constance flinched. Gilbert, better known as Gil, had a horrible temper, something she had known before she had married him. Attracted to the handsome, financially set young man, she had convinced herself that she could overlook his character flaws. Despite her parents' protests, she had married outside of the LDS Church, certain Gil's money would cushion her against living from paycheck to paycheck as her parents had done. For years, she had taken comfort in the knowledge that she was surrounded by beautiful things—Gil's abusive language was the price she paid to live as she desired. Keeping busy had always been her solution to the problem: if she wasn't home, he couldn't yell at her. It was an unhappy truce, but liveable to her way of thinking. It also explained why she had put so much effort into making Kassidy a success; she wanted her daughter to excel where she had failed. If Kassidy would use her looks and talents to earn her own way in life, she could attain the independence Constance would never achieve.

"Hello?"

"Kassidy?" Constance prompted.

"Mom! Merry Christmas," Kassidy said happily. "I'm glad you called. I was thinking about you and Dad earlier this morning."

"That's nice." Constance struggled to push aside the unspoken sentiment she felt. Taking a deep breath, she decided to use a no-nonsense approach with her daughter. Unwilling to shoulder her husband's wrath a moment longer, she gripped the phone in her hands. "Kassidy, I've booked a flight for you. You'll fly out from Idaho Falls tomorrow morning to Salt Lake City. Then you'll fly from there to San Diego."

"What? I'm not coming home," Kassidy stammered. "I told you that already. I have plans. Tomorrow Gary is picking me up, and we're—"

"You have no choice in this," Constance interrupted. "You are coming home. It was a mistake to let you leave with Treena this fall. We'll make arrangements to get you into a college around here."

"But Mom!"

"Don't argue Kassidy! Your father said to tell you that he will no longer fund your college expenses if you insist on staying there. You'll be on your own." Constance grimaced, hating her role in this. She should have let Gil call, but he was so angry, he would have made things worse. "Kassidy, this will work out for the best, you'll see," she said, her voice softening. She paused, but when the silence continued, she tried again. "Clay Burke has been asking to see you."

* * *

Closing her eyes, Kassidy slumped against the wall. She hated Clay Burke. He had been chasing her for three years. He was another Jay Michaels, only worse; at least Jay didn't drink.

"Kassidy . . . are you there?"

"Yes," Kassidy heard herself answer.

"Someone will be there to pick you up when you arrive in San Diego tomorrow."

Paling considerably, Kassidy nearly dropped the phone.

"Kassidy—are you listening?"

"I heard you," Kassidy mumbled weakly. Hanging up the telephone, she made her way upstairs to the guest room she had been using. On a chair was the colorful book of classic art that her aunt had given her for Christmas. It had come with a new set of art supplies that had already been placed in the studio for her use as she desired. Next to the art book was the new triple combination from Gary, one he had painstakingly marked and filled with notes. She walked to the bed and stared down at the quilt Gary's mother had made for her. The soft fabric was covered with sunflowers. The note Margaret had pinned to it had stated that it was a reminder that beautiful things could survive in today's crazy world. She had also described it as a Christmas hug. Kassidy sat down on the bed and wrapped herself inside the quilt, certain she would never feel warm again.

* * *

"Kassidy, are you sure you don't want anything to eat?" Janice tried again.

"Yeah," came the feeble response.

Janice peered into the darkened room. She had seen from the caller ID that Kassidy's mother had called and assumed that was the reason her niece was hiding in the upstairs bedroom. Entering the room, Janice walked to the dresser and flipped on a small lamp. "That's better." She closed the bedroom door, then sat on the end of the bed next to Kassidy. "Tell me what's wrong."

"Nothing."

"I don't believe you. One minute you were the life of the party. Now you're up here acting like it's the end of the world. What did your mother say to you?"

Kassidy remained silent.

"I wish I'd known she was on the phone. I would've given her a piece of my mind—not that I have any to spare." Janice frowned when her niece did not react to her joke. "Kass, we've talked about your mother—sometimes she can't help herself."

"I hate her," Kassidy said in a choked voice.

"Oh, now, you don't mean that."

"I do! I hate both of my parents!"

Janice patted Kassidy's leg through the heavy quilt. "Hon, they're not perfect. They make mistakes, like all parents do. If they said something today to upset you, push it behind you. If you dwell on it, it'll make you sick." She waited a few seconds, but Kassidy refused to answer. "Can you tell me what they said to upset you?"

Kassidy shook her head.

"Grandma, where are you?" a small voice ventured, coming from the hall.

Janice smiled, torn between her granddaughter and her niece.

"Grandma, I need you."

"I'll be back later to check on you," Janice promised her niece. "Whatever it is, I'm sure it's not as bad as it seems right now." She stood and planted a firm kiss on Kassidy's forehead before leaving the room.

* * *

"Mom, who was so sick last night?"

Janice turned from the electric frying pan full of sizzling bacon to gaze at her daughter. Daphne was a younger version of herself, only her hair was dark like her father's. "Someone was sick?"

"I thought maybe it was Larry's wife, but I asked about it this morning and she said she's way past that stage of her pregnancy."

A knot formed in the pit of Janice's stomach. "Daphne, can you take over here for me?" she asked, handing her daughter the plastic spatula. "I think I'd better go check on your cousin."

* * *

"I can't believe this! Kassidy is missing and so is my car, plus some high-powered pain pills you last saw in your purse?" Janice questioned Daphne.

Daphne nodded. "I pulled some muscles in my back when I slipped on the ice last week. My doctor prescribed muscle relaxants for me. Kassidy saw me take one last night and asked me what it was. She must've seen me put the bottle back in my purse."

Janice shook her head. This was worse than she had ever imagined. "All right. Let's not panic. First, I'll call Gary. Maybe she went up to see him."

"Without telling you where she was going?" Daphne asked, puzzled.

"I know. This isn't like her." Janice scowled. "After I call Gary, I'm going to call that sister of mine and find out what she said to Kassidy!" Hurrying to the telephone, she scrolled through the numbers recorded on her caller ID, grateful that Gary had called a couple of times each day to talk to Kassidy. She punched in the Dawson phone number and prayed someone would answer.

* * *

"What do you mean my daughter is missing?" Constance exclaimed. "She's supposed to be on her way home."

"What are you talking about?" Janice responded, confused.

"I told Kassidy we had booked a flight for her this morning. She was to fly down from Idaho Falls to Salt Lake, then catch another plane to San Diego."

"What on earth for? She had plans to spend time with Gary's family the next two days."

"Oh, him," Constance replied coolly.

"Yes, him. Your daughter happens to be in love with *him*, if that matters at all to you!" Daphne cleared her throat in a loud fashion. Janice shot a pained look at her daughter but tried to calm down. "Constance, if Kassidy had planned to fly out, I'm sure she would've told me about it. After you called, she was very upset. She stayed in her bedroom, made herself sick last night, then disappeared early this morning."

"She made herself sick?"

"Your daughter has a serious eating disorder. She binges, then makes herself throw up. That's how she has learned to handle stress in her life!"

"Kassidy doesn't do that," Constance protested.

"Oh, yes, Kassidy does! Her roommates told me about it weeks ago. The thing is, she was doing better—till last night. Now start talking! Why were you making her come home?"

* * *

"Slow down, Gary," Margaret advised as she continued to cling to the seat of her son's truck.

"Sorry, Mom, it's a feeling I have. We have to hurry."

"I know," she said, her face lined with worry. Their entire family had searched the ranch after Janice had called but had seen no sign of Kassidy. Earlier Janice had informed them that Kassidy was driving a white Chevy Impala. Janice had also given the information to the police, who had stressed that until Kassidy was missing for twenty-four hours, there wasn't much they could do.

"Do you think Kassidy went back to the apartment?" Margaret asked, gazing out the window of Gary's truck.

Gary nodded. "After we searched the ranch, I went off alone and prayed. I could see this image of her in my mind. She's in trouble, and she's in her apartment—I know she is."

Nodding, Margaret continued to grip the seat as they sped toward Rexburg.

* * *

"Constance, where do you think you're going?" an imperious male voice questioned.

Constance frowned at her husband. "After our daughter."

"They'll find her. She's probably off sulking somewhere. She gets that from you."

Silently disagreeing, she turned her back to Gil and finished packing her suitcase.

"Why are you taking so many clothes?" he demanded.

"Maybe I'm not coming back!" was her terse reply.

"You don't mean that."

Constance picked up her suitcase, then faced him. "I meant every word," she said before leaving the bedroom.

"You'll never get a dime out of me!" he roared.

"All the money in the world won't bring back our daughter if she's dead!" she exclaimed before hurrying down the elegant staircase.

* * *

"I'm glad you were home," Gary puffed as he ran with the apartment manager toward Kassidy's apartment.

"Me too," the young woman replied. "It was the strangest thing: all morning I had planned to go to the store, but one thing after another happened to keep me here. I guess I know why now."

Gary glanced around the vacant parking lot. Most students were gone over Christmas vacation. Janice's white Impala was parked close to building D. He ran up the stairs behind the manager to where his mother was beating on the door that led into Kassidy's apartment.

"We've got a master key, Mom," Gary wheezed as the manager unlocked the door.

As soon as the door was open, Gary rushed inside, followed by his mother and the manager. They found Kassidy on the floor of one the bathrooms, unconscious.

Chapter 29

"Hey, sweetheart," Janice said, her blue eyes tinged with sadness. "Welcome back."

Kassidy stirred around in the hospital bed. "Aunt Janice?" she asked as she forced her eyes open.

"I'm right here," Janice replied, patting Kassidy's covered leg.

"I don't feel so good," Kassidy mumbled, shutting her eyes.

"I don't imagine. We're lucky to still have you," Janice said tenderly.

Kassidy groaned. "I didn't want to die. I was upset . . . but after I took those pills, I tried to throw up. I didn't want to die." A single tear slid down the side of her face.

"It's all right, Kassidy, you did get rid of some of it, or you wouldn't still be here."

Kassidy turned her face to the side as the tears continued to flow. "I'm sorry."

"I know, hon," Janice soothed as she caressed Kassidy's slender shoulder. "You just rest. Everything will be all right."

* * *

"How is she?" Gary asked, the anguish he felt still evident on his face.

"Asleep," Janice replied. "She woke up for a little bit, then dozed back off."

"Can I see her?" a trembling voice asked.

Janice looked past Gary and gazed at her sister. The past twenty-four hours had been hard on everyone, especially Constance, who had aged ten years overnight. Constance looked defeated, her face devoid of color. Her lifeless blue eyes were framed by dark, heavy circles, the result of worry and lack of sleep.

"I need to see Kassidy," Constance meekly repeated.

Janice shook her head. Despite everything that had passed between them, she felt sorry for her sister. "The doctor thinks it's best if we give her a day or two to get her strength back. She's no longer critical, but her condition is still serious."

"You've been able to go in," Constance protested, a pained expression on her face.

"Kassidy was calling for me. They thought it would help if I stayed close when she first came around, so she wouldn't be so scared." Janice glanced down at the polished tile. "Connie, I'm sorry. I know you're worried, but if we're going to get Kassidy through this, we'll have to work together to do what's best for her."

"I never meant to hurt her," Constance stammered.

Nodding, Janice forced a smile. "We have some decisions to make."

"Mrs. Wharton?" Gary broke in.

Janice shifted her focus to Gary. "Call me Janice."

"Janice, the bishop from our student ward is here. He's over there talking to my mom. You might want to talk to him. He found out about a place down in Utah. It's a center that treats eating disorders."

Glancing down the hall of the hospital, Janice spotted Margaret, Gary's mother. "Let's hear what he has to say," she said, motioning for Constance and Gary to follow.

* * *

"Gary?"

"Yeah, it's me," Gary said into the pay phone. Exhausted, he rubbed the back of his neck with one hand.

"How's Kassidy?" Treena asked.

"She's pulling through."

"I should've flown out," Treena said in a broken voice.

"No, like I told you last night, there was nothing anyone could do after we got her here," Gary said, trying to console her. He could hear Treena crying through the phone. "I'm just glad we found her."

"Me too. It must've been awful."

Gary leaned against the telephone booth. "It was rough for a while, but I know we had help—too much to ever say it was a coincidence."

"We've all been praying for her," Treena replied.

"You got hold of your roommates?"

"Yes. They've been calling here to see if I've heard anything else."

"A nurse down the hall said they were getting several phone calls about her. But the hospital can't give out any information," he explained.

"I know. I tried to call a couple of times. They said they'd take a message, but that's as far as I got. That's why I'm so glad you called; I've been going crazy, imagining the worst."

"I promised to keep you informed."

"Promise me this," she said in a strained voice. "Let me know if anything changes, anything at all."

"I will."

"How long will they keep her there?"

Shuffling his feet, Gary glanced down the hall. "I don't know yet. The thing is, we knew she had a problem—long before this happened. It's taken a toll on her body. She's not in very good shape. They have her hooked up to IVs trying to give her body some of the nutrients she needs. Her electrolyte levels are too low. She's a mess."

"I should've done something before."

"Treena, this isn't your fault! You tried everything you could think of. We all did."

"Will she be able to come back to school?"

"I doubt it. They're talking about sending her to a specialized clinic down in Orem, Utah. They think she can get the help she needs down there."

"Oh, Gary, why did this have to happen? She was doing so much better."

"We all thought she was. The thing is, they're not sure she ever stopped binging and purging. Her esophagus is burned, the enamel on some of her teeth has dissolved—"

"She was getting better at hiding it," Treena guessed.

"Maybe. Maybe she did quit for a while."

"She's never tried to kill herself before," Treena said. "I never thought she'd try that."

"She's been killing herself slowly for a very long time," Gary replied. "Hey, my mom's coming up the hall. I'd better go. Will you let your roommates know what's going on?"

"Yes. Keep me posted," Treena urged.

"I will," he promised before hanging up the telephone.

* * *

Kassidy hated being pushed around in a wheelchair, but knew she wasn't strong enough to walk around on her own yet. "Where are you taking me?"

"You'll see," Gary said, grinning down at her.

"More surprises?"

"You'll like this surprise," he insisted.

She leaned back in the wheelchair. "I hope so," she responded anxiously.

"Trust me," he said as he continued to push her down the hall toward a waiting room.

Kassidy's face lit up as she spotted Treena standing beside Gary's mother.

"She came," Kassidy breathed.

"Mom picked her up at the airport this morning."

Brushing tears away, Kassidy smiled appreciatively at Gary's mother, then shifted her gaze back to Treena.

"Hi, Kass," Treena said, leaning down to give Kassidy a light hug.

"I'm not that fragile," Kassidy insisted, clinging to her best friend. "I'm so glad you're here."

Treena held onto Kassidy for several long seconds before pulling away. "I would've come sooner, but it took some doing to exchange my airline ticket," she sniffed.

"School doesn't start for nearly a week," Kassidy noted.

"That's why I came. I want to spend some time with you before it does."

"I'm glad you're here," Kassidy said, smiling. "I just wish I wasn't stuck in this place."

"No problem. I'll hang out here and keep you entertained."

"That'll be good news for Gary. I think he's getting tired of baby-sitting me."

"Never!" Gary said, draping an arm around Kassidy's shoulders. "I can't think of anywhere else I'd rather be."

Kassidy frowned.

"Gary, how would you like to help me run a few errands for your dad?" Margaret asked. "He wanted me to stop by the C-A-L Ranch store and pick up some stuff for the farm."

"Well, I . . ."

"Go ahead, Gary. I'll take good care of her," Treena promised.

"All right," Gary assented. "I won't be gone too long."

"Take all the time you need," Kassidy said, glancing up in time to see Margaret wink at her.

She returned the wink as Gary leaned down to kiss her on the cheek.

* * *

"Where will you be staying?" Kassidy asked as Treena pushed her back to her room.

"With your aunt . . . she insisted."

"Janice is like that," Kassidy said, her throat tightening as she realized how much she loved her aunt.

"She said she would be traveling back and forth on a regular basis until you head to Utah. This way we can both keep an eye on you."

Kassidy gazed down at the sterile tile floor.

"Kass, I'm sorry. What I meant was—"

"It's okay, Treena. I was stupid. I ruined the holidays for everybody, including me."

Treena reached down to squeeze Kassidy's shoulder. "You didn't ruin the holidays. We're like a family—the D-6ers as Bev calls us. We're there for each other, no matter what. When one of us is sick or hurt, we pull together, right?"

"I guess."

"We all love you, Kass. Every one of our roommates wanted me to pass that onto you."

"I don't even know what I'd say to any of them. It's hard enough with you. I want to wake up and find that this has all been a very bad dream."

"More like a nightmare," Treena corrected. "But it's getting better, right?"

Kassidy nodded.

"Is this your room?"

"Home sweet home . . . at least for now. I guess from here they'll ship me to Utah."

"That's what Gary said," Treena replied as she pushed Kassidy into the room. "That quilt is beautiful!"

Kassidy glanced at her hospital bed and the sunflower quilt that lay on top. "Gary's mom made that for me for Christmas. She said it was my Christmas hug. Now she says it will brighten my way to better health." She wondered if that was possible; she had never appreciated good health before. At the moment it seemed like an unattainable goal.

"Wow, look at all these flowers," Treena said brightly. "Someone must love you."

Kassidy smiled. "The arrangement from you guys is on the table." She watched as Treena examined the colorful basket of silk flowers.

"We ordered silk so you could keep it with you no matter where you are."

"Be sure to tell them all thanks," Kassidy said warmly.

"I will," Treena said as she moved to a huge vase filled with pastel-colored daises. "I'll bet those are from Gary."

"They are. The red roses are from my dad." Kassidy's blue eyes were laced with pain.

"Your aunt Janice told me your parents have separated."

Kassidy nodded.

"Have you talked to your mom yet?"

"Not really. She comes in, says how sorry she is; then she cries. I know she feels terrible, but why did she call that day? I was doing so much better."

Treena walked around to face Kassidy. "Were you, Kass?"

Kassidy glanced down at her hands, painfully aware of the distress in her friend's face.

"I thought you were beating this thing, but you were still struggling with it, weren't you?"

"It wasn't happening as much, just once in a while. This pressure would build inside of me. I know it sounds strange, but when I'd make myself throw up, I felt like I was in control," she said tearfully. "It made me feel better," she whispered.

"I feel like I let you down. I should've done something before it got this bad."

"Treena, none of this is your fault. *I* did it! I did this to myself. And now I need help to heal. I want to get better. I want my life back." She offered a weak smile. "You probably thought you'd never hear me say that."

Treena returned Kassidy's smile. "The important thing is that I'm hearing you say it now."

Chapter 30

"How's your mother feeling?" Bev asked as she and Karen waited for Tyler to pick them up for their return trip to Rexburg. Earlier that morning, Brett had driven Karen to Bev's house so Tyler wouldn't have to drive clear out to the canyon where Karen now lived.

Karen leaned against the comfortable couch in the Henderson living room. "Truth?"

Bev nodded, moving from the window to sit beside Karen on the couch.

"I'm worried about her. Even Brett is concerned. You should see how he babies her. That's why he drove me in this morning. Mom wasn't feeling so hot, and he wanted her to stay down."

"What does the doctor say?"

"During Mom's last appointment, he told her to slow down. She's only working two or three days a week now. I'm betting she'll have to quit before this baby is born."

"She's pretty miserable then?"

Karen nodded. "She's always tired, and her ankles look terrible. Whenever she's on her feet for a few hours, they swell like you can't believe."

Several seconds passed in silence, then Karen glanced at Bev. "Have you talked to Tyler since he returned from Nauvoo?"

Bev nodded.

"And?" Karen pursued.

"He had a lot of fun, saw a lot of neat things. He's bringing a video for us to watch in Rexburg, something he shot while they were in Nauvoo."

"Cool. I've always wanted to see Nauvoo." Karen glanced down at her hands. "Bev, you haven't said much about it, but I know you're upset over what he gave you for Christmas."

Bev gripped the arm of the couch. She had known Karen would bring this up eventually.

"We don't have a lot of time to talk about this now, considering Tyler will be here any minute. Just give me a brief rundown. What's going on with you two?"

Bev shrugged. "So I didn't get a ring for Christmas—maybe the timing's not right."

"You're not disappointed?"

Pursing her lips, Bev stared out the large picture window and wished Tyler would hurry.

"I thought you two would get engaged over Christmas."

"So did everyone else."

"I'm sorry."

"I'm not. I was at first, but maybe it's better this way, especially with everything that's going on with Kassidy."

"I know. It's hard to get excited over things after what she's been through."

"I still can't believe she tried to kill herself," Bev said, frowning.

"Treena stressed that Kassidy tried to throw up the pills after she took them."

"Why did she even think suicide was an option?"

"We'll probably never know the answer to that one."

Bev shook her head. "We've both been through some pretty bad stuff, and neither of us thought about doing anything like that, right?" she asked, glancing at Karen.

Karen nodded. "The worst thing we can do is judge her."

"I'm not . . . well, maybe I am. It's just—man, I'm going to miss her this term! She wasn't the easiest person to live with, but I care about her, you know? It hurts."

"I know," Karen agreed.

"At least we won't have to break in a new roommate. The managers must like us after all. Treena will get a bedroom to herself this semester, but I think she's hoping Kassidy will come back soon."

"That's what Treena said when she called me last week. She sounded pretty upbeat, but I worry about her. She's been through a lot. We need to stay close to her."

Bev nodded, grateful that Karen understood. "Karen, I know we talked about this last week, but I want you to know again how sorry I am that I didn't tell you what was going on."

"Water under the bridge," Karen replied. "The way you and Treena were acting, I figured it had something to do with Kassidy's eating disorder."

"Why didn't you say anything?"

Karen forced a smile. "I was hoping you would."

"No more secrets between us, deal?"

"Deal," Karen agreed. A loud honk startled both girls.

"It's Tyler," Bev said, jumping up from the couch to grab her suitcase. "Let's go. Time to head back to BYI."

Nodding, Karen picked up the clothes bag she had brought and followed Bev out of the living room.

* * *

"You have some visitors," a nurse with a kind face said.

Kassidy glanced up from the book she was reading. Her beautiful features were marred by distress—she wasn't ready to talk to her parents. Janice had told her they were undergoing counseling too, but she didn't want to deal with the guilt she feared they would inflict upon her.

"They said to tell you they're the famed D-6ers."

Relaxing somewhat, Kassidy rose from the soft chair in her semi-private room and set the book she had been reading on her bed. "Could you unlock the bathroom so I can fix my hair?"

"Sure," the woman replied, reaching inside her white jacket for a large set of keys. All of the bathrooms in the Center for Change were kept locked as a precautionary measure, including the ones located inside the semiprivate bedrooms. The nurse quickly unlocked the small bathroom, pushing the door open as Kassidy slipped inside to check her reflection.

"Thanks," Kassidy said as she ran a brush through her long blonde hair. "Where are my friends?"

"They're waiting in the family visiting room. Are you ready?"

Nodding, Kassidy followed the nurse down the carpeted hall.

* * *

"I hope this was a good idea," Treena fretted.

Meg smiled. "She needs to know that we still care about her. We've sent letters and called, but in my opinion, a visit like this is much better."

Bev nodded in agreement. She gazed around at the cheery room. Decorated with paintings of flowers, it inspired a feeling of peace. What she had seen of the Center for Change had impressed her. The small facility sported a southwestern motif complete with peach-colored stucco and blue-gray tiled shingles. Located in Orem, Utah, it offered an appealing view of the snow-covered Wasatch Mountain Range. A small basketball and volleyball court were located to the side of the parking lot out front. Earlier, Bev had peered through a window in the large living room near the nurses' station and had noticed two spiral fountains in the backyard. She was certain that during the spring and summer months, the landscaping of this facility was breathtaking.

"She's been here . . . what, almost a month?" Karen asked.

"Yeah," Treena replied.

"Is she doing better?" Jesse asked.

"Her aunt thinks so. She said they're making good progress," Bev answered. "They're teaching Kassidy to find other ways to release the pressure she feels. And she meets every day with other girls who are fighting the same battle. It's like a support group: they understand where she's coming from. They share experiences and help each other try to beat this thing."

"Awesome," Jesse said. "I hope they can help Kassidy."

"Me too," Bev replied.

"How many girls do they treat here?" Meg asked, curious.

"I think around sixteen," Treena said. "I asked Janice about it a couple of weeks ago."

"Sixteen, huh?" Bev said, deep in thought. She wondered how many other girls were dealing with this condition across the nation. Why were so many people caught up in this vicious cycle of self-abuse?

* * *

"Hi," Kassidy said, entering the room. Treena rose from the flowered couch and crossed the room for a hug. Kassidy returned the intense embrace, then faced an onslaught of similar greetings from the rest of her roommates. Her eyes misted as she gazed around at her friends. "You guys will never know how much I appreciate everything you've done for me."

"Now quit," Bev quipped, "or you'll ruin our makeup."

"I can always reapply it for you later," Kassidy bantered. "Now, tell me everything. I want to know what's going on in everybody's lives," she said as she sat on the comfortable sofa.

Bev showed her the necklace Tyler had given her for Christmas. Kassidy noted the disappointed look on her roommate's face and offered a sad smile. "I think it's only a matter of time before Tyler comes through."

"I guess time will tell," Bev replied.

"Meg, do you miss the cast?"

"Not even," Meg chortled.

"It would hamper her dating," Jesse teased.

"Meg's dating?" Kassidy quizzed.

"She's rapidly taking your place as the social queen of D-6," Treena revealed.

"I've been out twice since Christmas," Meg sputtered.

"That's twice as many times as me," Jesse retorted. "But we're still waiting for ice cream."

Kassidy smiled as Meg's face slightly colored. Treena had told her how much better Meg had been doing since Christmas. It gave her hope for her own situation. "So, Karen, what's new with you?"

"Oh, not much. Studying, studying, and oh, yeah, in my spare time, studying."

"And in between all that she tries to keep Bev in line," Meg retorted.

"No special friends on the horizon?" Kassidy asked, hoping Karen would follow Meg's example.

"Not at the moment," Karen answered. "There's barely enough room on the couch for Tyler and Bev, not to mention Meg and her date of the week."

"You guys are not even funny," Meg exclaimed.

"Actually they are," Kassidy replied, "and that's good. I could use a laugh or two."

"Then prepare yourself, I haven't even started," Bev promised, a mischievous gleam in her blue eyes.

* * *

"Your doctor wants to meet with me and Bev?" Treena repeated.

Kassidy nodded. "It's part of my therapy. She explained that I've put you two through quite a bit—especially you, Treena. She said that sometimes she'll bring in family members or friends who have had to deal with a loved one who has an eating disorder. Would you mind talking to her?"

Treena glanced at Bev.

Bev shrugged, then nodded her head.

"Okay, we'll do it," Treena replied.

"I could check to see if she can meet with you later today to save you a trip. I know it's a long way to come, especially in the middle of winter."

"Kassidy, we'll do anything we can to help you," Bev said.

"I appreciate that," Kassidy murmured. "I don't know if she'll want to meet with the others. You two seemed to take the brunt of what I did." She lowered her gaze, ashamed of how her choices had hurt her friends, including Gary and his mother.

"I understand there's a huge mall down the road. I doubt our roomies will lack for entertainment," Bev said in an effort to lighten the mood.

Kassidy nodded. She smiled tearfully at both girls, then said, "I want you to know how sorry I am . . . for everything."

"Kassidy, don't do this to yourself," Treena began.

"Hey, are you guys through yet?" Jesse interrupted. She poked her head inside the visiting room. "We've finished with our tour of the lovely guest rest room down the hall. Can we come back in?"

Bev motioned for Jesse to enter the room. "Is Karen out there?"

Karen took a step inside the room.

Pulling her Jeep keys from her pocket, Bev tossed them to Karen. "How would you guys like to go hit University Mall?"

Karen glanced from Bev to Kassidy. "How long do we have?" she asked.

Bev looked at Kassidy.

"Maybe an hour or so," Kassidy ventured. "If you don't mind."

"Hey, no problem! We could check out BYU in Provo, while we're that close."

Meg slipped in behind Karen. "Do we know where this mall is?"

Kassidy wrinkled her forehead. "I've heard some of the other girls talk about it. I don't think it's very far from here. Let me go check." She hurried from the room.

"Is she okay?" Meg asked.

"Yeah, she seems kind of upset," Karen echoed.

"She's working through some things," Treena attempted to explain. "She wants Bev and me to meet with her doctor, the one who's been helping her with her therapy."

"Why does Kassidy want you to meet with her doctor?" Jesse inquired.

Bev blew a piece of stray black hair away from her blue eyes before answering. "I think it's because Kassidy feels guilty about what she's put Treena through."

"Bev, you've been part of this too," Treena pointed out. She glanced at the other girls. "We all have. How many of you didn't know she had a problem?"

Meg sighed. "While we're in confession mode . . . I've been feeling horrible about this whole thing. I knew—we all knew. How could we live with her and not figure it out? It was just easier to look the other way."

Jesse nodded in agreement.

Bev met Karen's troubled gaze. "Karen knew from the beginning. She's the one who helped me see what was really going on."

Meg smiled warmly at Karen. "I'm not surprised."

Bev turned to Treena. "I think all of us should be in on this counseling session."

"I was going to suggest the same thing," Treena replied. "We've all struggled with what Kassidy has done." She bit her bottom lip to keep it from trembling. "It's been hard on all of us. I know I've never felt so helpless in my entire life."

Bev slipped an arm around Treena's waist. "We're in this together, right?" She smiled when everyone nodded. "We'll meet with that counselor together."

* * *

Treena shifted in the chair she had chosen in the narrow board room. A long wooden table filled most of the room. Soft padded chairs were crowded around it. Tall bookcases lined one wall. In the front, a small television set and VCR sat on a black metal stand. She wondered what kind of movies were watched in this room.

"Treena, are you uncomfortable with the question?"

Treena met the concerned gaze of the psychologist. "Well . . ."

"Be honest. That's what this is all about—sharing what you're feeling." The middle-aged woman smiled warmly, her brown eyes reflecting the concern she felt for the five girls. "Would it be easier if we were alone?" she petitioned.

Treena shook her head. "It's hard to put it into words. You want to know how I feel about Kassidy."

Doctor Jaylene Cameron nodded, her short brown hair bouncing around her head.

"I love her. She's one of my closest friends."

"But has she truly been a friend?" Dr. Cameron gently probed. "Have you been able to confide in her, depend on her, trust in her?"

Tears streaked down Treena's face as she shook her head.

"The past couple of years you've been more of a caretaker than a friend."

Treena slowly nodded.

"You've carried a heavy burden," Dr. Cameron stated, "but you're not alone. I see this quite often with the family members and friends of my patients. The young women I treat are crippled emotionally, and those who love them pay a high price for trying to help."

"But we're supposed to help others," Treena tearfully replied.

"We should never turn away from those who are suffering. But sometimes, without meaning to, we enable them to continue their destructive behavior. The hardest thing is to let them suffer the consequences of what they've done, to avoid helping them cover up what they think they're hiding."

"It's my fault," Treena sobbed, burying her face in her hands.

Bev slid her wheeled chair closer to Treena and pulled her into a hug as she glared at the psychologist.

"No, Treena, it's not your fault," Dr. Cameron soothed. "It's something Kassidy chose to do to herself, and Kassidy isn't entirely to blame. She's hurting, you're hurting," Dr. Cameron smiled at the other girls, "all of you are hurting. That's why I wanted to meet with you. For Kassidy to truly heal, she has to come to terms with what she has done. She's just starting to realize what she has put you girls through."

Treena pulled back from Bev and accepted a tissue from the box the psychologist extended toward her.

"Treena, you did the best you could under very trying circumstances, and I commend you for your efforts to help Kassidy. Contacting her aunt very likely saved your friend's life."

"But she still tried to kill herself," Treena sniffed. "She was staying with Janice when it happened."

"Did Kassidy tell you why she tried to throw up the pills after she took them?"

Treena shook her head at the psychologist.

"For an instant she saw the faces of the people she loves, including all of you."

Treena started to cry again.

"It was the love she felt from all of you that gave her the will to live."

"Why didn't she tell me?" Treena stammered.

"Some things are still very hard for her to share, which is why I wanted to meet with you girls before we invite Kassidy to be a part of this conversation. You need to understand why she did what she did. The bottom line is, she feels very inadequate."

"But she's gorgeous, talented, and smart," Meg countered.

"And filled with self-loathing. Her self-esteem is nonexistent. She has been raised with expectations that are too high for anyone to meet. As a result, she has always felt like a failure. She believes she's unworthy of love."

"Do her parents know? Do they understand what they've done to her?" Treena demanded, angrily clenching the tissue in her hand.

"In my experience, there are no perfect parents. I've spoken with Kassidy's mother. She's a very insecure person herself. She wants her daughter to succeed where she feels she has failed," Jaylene shared, smiling sadly at Treena. "Constance Martin loves her daughter dearly, but she needs to learn to show it in a way that Kassidy can comprehend. The lessons she paid for, the pageants she forced Kassidy to enter—these were Constance's way of demonstrating her love, of showing how proud she was of her daughter's potential."

"But Kassidy saw it as a threat," Meg said, grasping the situation. "Constance thought she was helping her, like my mom when she tries to help me. She means well, but I sometimes I resent what she's trying to do to protect me. Does that make sense?"

"It makes perfect sense. Mothers and daughters have struggled with their relationships from the beginning of time."

"I guess Mom just wanted to create a safe haven for me," Meg mused.

"Unfortunately, there are no safe places in today's world, except for the havens we make for ourselves." Dr. Cameron sighed. "And it's not always an easy thing to find a safe haven here," she said, pointing at her heart, "or here," she added, touching her forehead. "At the Center for Change we've proven that if we can help patients heal spiritually, they can conquer self-destructive habits. We teach each of them that their bodies are gifts, the home for their spirits. We encourage them to meditate and to pray, to get in tune with their emotions. Unfortunately, some patients have learned to block out what they're feeling, and they can't experience spiritual sensations. We try to help them regain that ability. As the numbness fades, they learn to embrace life again. That's when they can start letting go of the pain they carry inside. They face it, work through it, and learn to forgive themselves and others."

The five girls sat in silence, absorbing what they each had felt as the Spirit bore witness of the truthfulness of what they had heard.

"From what Kassidy has told me, I know you've each faced some tremendous battles in your own lives," the doctor continued.

The five girls glanced at each other and nodded.

"And yet you've found ways to continue forward. I want you to know what an extraordinary thing that is. Kassidy has been surrounded by some wonderful examples," Dr. Cameron emphasized. "You are exactly the kind of support system she needs."

"You think we can help her?" she said.

"I think you already have, she just doesn't know it yet. You've given her the strength to make it this far. Your continued influence will have a positive impact on her life. And now, she needs to come to terms with the pain she has caused you. Should we invite her to join us?"

The five girls nodded in unison.

"This won't hurt her?" Treena asked.

"We've already talked about this in great depth. She made the choice to face it today. I'd say that's a big step in the right direction," the psychologist answered.

"But we don't hold anything against her," Bev said worriedly.

"Is that how all of you girls feel?" Dr. Cameron asked.

One by one the five young women nodded.

"That's good. Once she sees that she already has your forgiveness, she may start forgiving herself," the doctor said as she stood to invite Kassidy to enter the room.

Chapter 31

"Bev isn't here?" Tyler asked, disappointed. Lately, he had the impression that Bev was avoiding him. She had seemed distant since Christmas.

Karen shook her head. "She went with Meg; something about helping her get her car tuned up. You're welcome to come in and wait for her. I don't think they'll be too long."

"Thanks," Tyler said as he followed Karen inside the apartment. "It's quiet around here. Where's everyone else?"

"Treena's at work, and Jesse went down to the laundry room," Karen said as she sat down at the kitchen table.

"What are you working on?" Tyler asked, looking over her shoulder.

"Guess."

"Another article for *The Scroll?* What social ill are you fighting now?" Tyler kidded.

Karen stuck her tongue out at him.

"Hey, I'm serious! You do a great job," he said, trying to make amends.

"Thanks," Karen replied. "I'm doing an in-depth report on eating disorders."

Tyler nodded. "It still blows me away when I think about what Kassidy was going through. I never would've guessed she had that problem."

"Unfortunately, she was good at hiding it. A lot of girls are. You'd be amazed by how widespread this problem is. That's why I'm writing this article."

"How's Kassidy doing now?"

"Better, but it'll take time. She'll spend another four to six weeks at the Center for Change, then I'm not sure what the plan will be. From my research I've learned that it can take five to seven years to fully recover from a serious eating disorder."

"Why so long?"

"Most people who are dealing with an eating disorder have unresolved conflicts they have to work through. Until they do that, they're still at risk, and they can slide back into trouble. They often need continued counseling to help them regain good health."

"It doesn't go away overnight," Tyler observed.

"Nope, but I'm impressed with the track record of this clinic down in Orem."

"What is it called again?" Tyler asked.

"The Center for Change. They have a high success rate."

"Do you think Kassidy will beat this thing?"

Karen shrugged. "I hope so. She looked good when we saw her over the weekend. I think she's sorting through a lot of things."

"A lot of us are doing that," Tyler mumbled. Sensing Karen was staring at him, he smiled sheepishly before meeting her questioning gaze.

"As Bev would say, 'Whazzup'?"

"Nothing," Tyler feebly replied.

"Right. I'm a reporter, remember?"

Tyler sank down on a kitchen chair and began playing with one of Karen's pencils.

"What's going on?"

"I don't know."

"Is there a problem with Bev?" Karen questioned.

Tyler shrugged.

"If you expect me to help, you'll have to give me more to go on than that."

A troubled look appeared in his green eyes. "It's hard to explain."

"Try!"

"I'm not sure where this relationship is heading."

"Oh, just that," Karen said. She reached back with one hand, pulled up her medium-length blonde hair, and let it fall back against her neck as she pondered Tyler's last statement.

"Don't get me wrong, it's not Bev, it's me."

"Oh?"

"I think we need to let things cool between us."

Karen frowned. "Why do you feel that way?"

"Maybe I'm not the guy for Bev."

Lifting an eyebrow, Karen stared at Tyler. "Why would you think that?"

"I had it pointed out to me," Tyler confessed.

"What?"

"Bev's dad and I had a long talk during Thanksgiving break."

"You're letting James Henderson scare you?" Karen asked, folding her arms.

Tyler grimaced. "He made sense, Karen. Bev's used to nice things. I'll never be able to provide for her like James expects. I want to teach physics on a high-school level; I want to work with kids. It feels right, but I'll never be a wealthy man."

Looking disgusted, Karen blew out a long breath of air.

"You're not helping."

"Do you love Bev?"

Tyler nodded.

"Then that's all that matters. Do you honestly think Bev cares more about money than she does you?"

Tyler pointed to his wrist. "Look at this watch. Bev told me she didn't pay much for it, but I know it cost her a small fortune. How do you think I felt when I saw this after I gave her a necklace worth half as much?"

"Tyler, you've dated Bev for months. In all that time, has she ever once acted like money is an issue with her?"

Tyler tapped the pencil against the table. "No," he acknowledged.

"Bev doesn't care about money."

"She would if she didn't have it, if she had to struggle and budget like crazy because we couldn't afford things. I don't want that for her. I love her enough I want her to be happy."

"And you think she will be without you in her life?"

"I know she wants to be a doctor. If we got married, it probably wouldn't happen, especially if she ended up pregnant right off the bat," Tyler said, blushing as he continued to beat the pencil against the table.

Karen reached over and grabbed the pencil out of his hand, scowling fiercely at Tyler. "I will ask you this one more time—do you love Bev?"

Tyler nodded.

"Would you ever do anything to purposely hurt her? Because if you did, you would not only answer to James Henderson, you would answer to me and both of your sisters. I happen to know how much they love Bev."

"Tell me about it. Mom, Kate, and Sabrina went with me when I bought Bev's necklace. They thought I was picking out a ring. When I showed them the necklace I had in mind, they walked out of the store. They lectured me about it the whole time we were in Nauvoo."

"Someone else we both know and love thought you were picking out a ring, too."

Tyler flinched. "Bev thought she was getting a ring for Christmas?"

Karen nodded. "We all did."

Shaking his head, Tyler leaned back against the kitchen chair.

"Tyler, you're the only one who can decide what it is you want. Have you talked this over with Bev?"

"No. I don't want to go there until I've made up my mind."

"I think she deserves some say in this; it's only her future we're talking about," Karen chided. "Let me ask you this—have you prayed about it?"

"Yeah, but I must be out of tune. I feel so confused," Tyler admitted.

"What are you praying for?"

"The strength to walk away from Bev before I hurt her."

Karen groaned. "There's your answer! You're praying for the wrong thing. Remember that scripture, Mr. RM, the one that says you'll feel confusion if you ask for something that's not right?"

Tyler straightened in his chair to glare at Karen.

"Have you prayed about whether you should ask Bev to marry you?"

"Yes, I have. I prayed about it before Thanksgiving. Then James asked me what my *intentions* were and made me feel about this high," he said, holding his fingers an inch apart.

"And you gave up," Karen accused.

"I did not. I thought things through," he rebutted.

"Not very well," she countered. "Let me ask you something—how would you feel if Bev started dating someone else?"

Tyler's eyes clouded with angry pain.

"I thought so," Karen said. "Well, I happen to know Bev feels the same way."

"She does?"

Karen nodded. "Gina asked her the same question not long ago. Bev told me about it."

"She tells you everything, eh?"

"Pretty much. Tyler, she's in love with you . . . she has been for months."

"But James—"

"Bev is his only daughter, the only child of his first wife. Do you think he'll go easy on any guy who dares to get serious about her?"

"I don't know," Tyler said miserably.

"He'll put them through their paces, trying to see if they're worthy of his daughter. If you want Bev, you'll have to fight for her," Karen admonished.

Tyler mulled over Karen's advice.

"Are you up to the battle?"

Remaining silent for several seconds, Tyler finally stood and pushed away from the table.

"You're leaving?"

"Yeah. I think I need to go strap on my armor," he replied as he walked toward the door.

* * *

"Aunt Janice?" Kassidy ventured.

Janice turned from studying a floral painting that hung on the wall of the living room in the Center for Change. She glanced first at the nurses' station in the corner, then moved her head until she spotted her niece. "Hi there," she said, crossing the room to give Kassidy an intense squeeze. "How's it going?"

"Good," Kassidy replied. She gestured to a rust-and-green plaid couch. "Should we sit down?"

"Sure," Janice said, sitting beside the young woman. "Dr. Cameron told me you had some special visitors over the weekend."

"Yeah," Kassidy said, smiling. "The D-6ers came to see me."

"That's what I heard. How did it go?"

"Better than I thought it would. They're awesome friends."

"Yes, they are," Janice agreed. "They sure think the world of you." Picking up her purse, she reached inside and pulled out a small sack. "Before I forget, here are the brushes you wanted."

"Thanks," Kassidy replied. "They have some art supplies here, but I need smaller bristles."

"Can I see what you're painting?"

"Are you sure you want to?"

"I wouldn't have asked if I didn't," Janice said, laughing.

Kassidy frowned slightly. "It's part of my therapy."

"Would you rather keep it private?"

Remaining silent, Kassidy stared at the carpeted floor.

"Kass, it's okay. Don't worry about it," Janice said, patting her niece's leg.

"Maybe it would help you understand what I'm feeling. My therapist says you can see the progress I'm making with each painting." Rising, Kassidy smiled at her aunt. "Should we go? The art room is downstairs."

"Lead the way," Janice replied, following Kassidy from the room.

* * *

Despite Kassidy's warning, Janice was unprepared for the strong emotions evident in her niece's artwork. Kassidy began by showing her the mask she had painted when she had first arrived. As part of her therapy, she had been instructed to paint the outside of the mask in a way that would depict how she thought others saw her. The inside was to represent how she truly felt about herself. The outside of Kassidy's mask had been painted white with heavily lashed blue eyes and a bright red smile on the silent lips. One cheek sported a yellow sunflower. The inside of the mask had been painted with dark hues of black and brown. Red tears signified a bleeding heart. It took every ounce of self-control Janice could muster not to burst into tears as she held the fragile mask in her hands.

Kassidy then showed her aunt the paintings she had done. Twice Janice reached into her purse for a tissue, dabbing her eyes as she studied the anguish revealed in the emotional artwork. The first painting showed slivers of mirrors, fractured in jagged pieces, each bearing distorted portions of Kassidy's beautiful features. The second painting showed the aftermath of a violent storm at sea: wooden sections of a boat floated on the calming waves as the darkened clouds receded. A third painting showed a tiny sunflower trying to push its way through weed-infested soil. Unable to speak, Janice drew Kassidy into a fierce hug, tears coursing down her cheeks as she comprehended the depth of her niece's grief.

* * *

Margaret Dawson jumped when she heard someone enter the family room. Turning, she relaxed. "Oh, it's you, Gary."

"I didn't mean to startle you," Gary mumbled.

"That's okay. I wasn't expecting anyone to be home yet. Everyone else is still in school."

Gary flopped down in a recliner. "Where's Dad?"

"In town gassing up the old truck."

Gary glanced at the wall his mother had been studying. "You've been looking at Kassidy's painting again."

"Yes. That girl has a lot of talent," Margaret said, glancing again at the painting Kassidy had given her for Christmas. It was a beautiful rendition of Pearl in a forest setting, grazing in a flower-filled meadow with a waterfall in the distance.

Nodding, Gary stared at the painting, then down at the floor.

Margaret sat down on the forest-green couch under the painting. "How are you doing?"

"Okay."

"I know better than that," she declared.

Gary interlocked his fingers and pressed them against his stomach. "I need to see Kassidy."

"Give her time, Gary. She's not ready yet. She needs some space while she works through some things."

"That's just it, Mom, what if she's never ready?"

Frowning, Margaret gazed at her son. She had known this would be tough on Gary but hated what Kassidy's condition was doing to him. He had lost weight since Christmas, and his grades had dropped. He frequently skipped class to come home, where he moped around the ranch like a lost calf. One afternoon she had made the mistake of suggesting that he date other girls. Erupting in a flurry of angry words that he later regretted, he had made it clear that Kassidy was the only girl he would ever be interested in.

"Would it help to call her?"

Gary shrugged. "Like you said, I need to give her some space. Kassidy's doctor said I was crowding her while she was in the Idaho Falls hospital. She felt smothered."

"You did come on a little strong," Margaret reminded him. "But Kassidy knows it's because you love her so much."

"But does she love me?" he asked, his eyes dark with pain. "What if she gets better and decides a country farmer from Idaho isn't good enough for her?"

Margaret sighed. They were finally getting at the heart of the matter. "Kassidy isn't that way, and you know it."

"I don't know anything anymore. Her roommates went down to see her last weekend. I asked Treena if Kassidy had mentioned me at all . . . she never even said my name."

"I'm sure she had so many other things on her mind—"

"Do I even exist in her world anymore?"

"Gary, there's an old saying—quit pulling a face—that I think applies to your situation. It goes something like this: If you keep a beautiful bird in a cage, it remains because it's a prisoner. If you set it free and it flies away, it was never yours to begin with. If you set it free and it returns, it's yours forever."

Gary leaned back in the chair, frowning at his mother.

"Remember the first time you brought Kassidy home and we talked about your bird with the broken wing?"

He slowly nodded.

"Her wing is healing. She'll relearn to fly. After that, it's up to her to determine the direction of her flight."

"This isn't helping."

Margaret glanced up at Kassidy's painting. "I suspect Kassidy will always be a part of our lives. Give her time to heal."

"I hate this!"

"Things of worth exact a high price." She stood when she heard the front door open. "But that doesn't mean you have to suffer in silence. Let's go upstairs and have your dad give you a blessing . . . I think you need it." She began climbing the carpeted stairs, relieved when she heard Gary climb up behind her.

Chapter 32

Constance studied her nails as she waited for her daughter to enter the small room. She was still sitting on the couch in Dr. Jaylene Cameron's office, where she had been sitting most of the morning. She sighed; if only Gil had been more willingly to come to this session. He was here, but only because she had threatened an ugly divorce if he didn't try to make this work. He was out pacing in the hall, too upset to sit in one place for very long.

Earlier they had met with Dr. Cameron, together and separately, as the psychologist tried to explain what was going on with their daughter. Gil had hated the entire thing.

"Where does that excuse of a doctor get off telling me I'm to blame for Kassidy's nervous breakdown?" he had roared earlier.

"Gil, no one's blaming you for what happened. And Kassidy didn't have a nervous breakdown; she has an eating disorder," Constance had corrected.

"Right!" he had snorted. "She's doing this for attention!"

Constance shook her head. Why had she ever married Gil? She had made so many mistakes through the years. Several of those mistakes, she suspected, were responsible for what had happened to Kassidy. Even though the doctor had stressed there was no single cause for an eating disorder, Constance had read enough to know that a dysfunctional family life rated high on the list of probable causes. Things had been bad between her and Gil for years. During that time Kassidy had witnessed the fighting and the icy silences that had followed. She had endured emotional abuse from both parents. A solitary tear escaped from Constance's eye as she realized how unhappy they had all been for far too long. She longed to make things right, to pull this family together before it dissolved permanently, but she wasn't sure it was possible. For now, they had to concentrate on getting Kassidy through this illness, a disease that would require all of the love and support that she and Gil could muster to save their daughter.

* * *

Kassidy forced herself to walk down the hall, dreading this encounter. Here in the clinic she felt safe, sheltered from screaming words that tore through her heart. She doubted even Dr. Cameron could shield her from the anger she was certain her father would disperse, or from the cold disapproval she had seen so many times in her mother's face.

"Kassidy, are you okay?" a gentle voice asked.

Glancing up, Kassidy was relieved to see Dr. Cameron standing by the nurses' station. At least she wouldn't have to face her parents alone.

"It won't be as bad as you think," the doctor assured. "Your mother seems very willing to do whatever it takes to help you through this."

"She does?" Kassidy responded, surprised.

Dr. Cameron nodded. "I am concerned about your father. He's a very angry individual. That reminds me, have you had much to do with his parents or other members of his family?"

Kassidy shook her head. "My grandparents live somewhere around Chicago—I don't think Dad's had anything to do with them for years. Mom said once that Dad hated his family. Something about his dad being kind of mean. The funny thing is, I think my dad grew up to be just like him."

Nodding, Dr. Cameron made a note in Kassidy's chart. "Well, let's go have a visit," she encouraged, reaching into her sweater pocket for a set of keys. Turning from the nurses' station, she unlocked the door that led out into the hallway where her office was located. She smiled reassuringly at Kassidy before stepping through the door.

Feeling extremely nauseated, Kassidy followed the doctor and prayed silently for strength.

* * *

"Could I have a few minutes alone with Kassidy?" Constance pleaded with the doctor.

Dr. Cameron glanced from Constance to Kassidy. When Kassidy nodded, the psychologist smiled her approval. "That should be fine. Kassidy, I do want to talk to you later this afternoon, after lunch, okay?"

"Okay," Kassidy said as the psychologist stepped out of the office. She sat back down in the soft leather chair she had occupied during their session and waited for what her mother had to say. Her father had left a few minutes earlier, claiming he needed to use the rest room. Everyone knew it was a ruse to escape the therapy session.

Constance looked up from where she was still sitting on the couch. "I want you to know again how sorry I am about all of this," she said, her voice wavering.

Kassidy gazed at her mother. She had never seen her look this vulnerable before. Something inside of her softened. "Mom, we can't change what's happened."

"I know," Constance said, reaching into the pocket of her dress for a handful of tissue. She wiped the tears from her reddened eyes. "That doesn't mean I won't regret it the rest of my life."

"We can start fresh," Kassidy offered.

"I'd like that," Constance smiled. She stuffed the tissue back inside of her dress pocket. "I know I don't usually say what you need to hear. I've never been very good at that," she stammered. "But . . . I do love you," she said in a strained voice, "and I want to help."

Bursting into tears, Kassidy sobbed, shaken by the words she never thought her mother would ever say.

* * *

Dismayed, Constance stared at her daughter. "Kassidy," she finally said, rising from the couch, "please don't cry." When the tears increased, Constance glanced around for help, though she knew they were alone in the room. Moving close to Kassidy, she placed a trembling hand on her daughter's head and stroked the soft blonde hair. She gasped when Kassidy clung to her waist. Besieged with emotions she wasn't sure of, she pulled her daughter into an overdue embrace.

Out in the hall, Dr. Cameron grinned with relief. Kassidy and her mother had taken an important first step on the road to recovery.

Chapter 33

"Karen, sit down." Bev motioned to the chair beside her in the hospital waiting room.

"I can't relax. I've never had a baby before."

Meg laughed at Karen's nervous pacing. "Your mother is the one having the baby."

"I know, but it's too early. It's only February fourteenth. She wasn't due until the end of this month."

"I've learned that babies don't always wait for their predicted debut," Meg responded.

"You're sure you don't want to go back into delivery with your mom and Brett?" Bev tempted.

"I'm sure," Karen replied. "That's a little too much education for me."

"But if *you* went, they might let Meg and me in to watch," Bev hinted.

"Bev, I'm not going there, okay?" Karen said firmly. "Talk Gina into having another baby; then you can go watch her. Or, better yet, marry Tyler and have one of your own. Then you can observe up close and real personal like."

"Not funny!" Bev responded. She turned to see who was entering the large room. "Tyler! What are you doing here?"

"My date for the evening fled town. I'm here checking out the Idaho Falls chicks," he grinned.

"Excuse me while I go pound some sense into this confused young man," Bev said, stepping out into the hall with Tyler. "Did Treena tell you where we were?"

Tyler nodded. "I caught her at Albertson's. She said you were all here but Jesse."

"Yeah, get this, Jesse is baby-sitting tonight for our managers. They went somewhere for Valentine's Day."

"It'll be good for her."

"It's not Jesse I'm worried about."

"She'll be fine with the kids. She's a kid at heart."

"That's true," Bev agreed.

"Speaking of Valentine plans," Tyler said, his green eyes bright with excitement. "Can you spare a minute?"

"As long as we don't go too far. I have a bet riding on the outcome of this delivery."

"Oh?"

"Karen thinks she's getting a little sister. I'm betting it's a boy."

"You think it's a boy?"

Bev shook her head. "I just like to be different."

"I'll say," Tyler replied, grinning when she smacked him on the arm. "Come on, this won't take too long," he said, leading her down the tiled hallway toward the hospital nursery.

Bev glanced inside at the sleeping infants. "They're so cute."

"I'm glad you think so. What would you think about creating some of those?"

Choking, Bev turned beet red. "What?" she managed to say.

Tyler laughed, then knelt down on one knee and presented her with a velvet-covered box.

Bev's eyes widened. "Tyler—"

"Ah, ah, ah! I get to go first: Miss Beverly Dawn Henderson, will you do me the honor of becoming my wife?" he asked, opening the box to reveal a small diamond ring.

Bev stood in shock, unable to reply.

"I'm getting a complex here," he said nervously. "I know it's not a huge diamond, but—"

"It's the most beautiful diamond in the world," Bev tearfully exclaimed.

Grinning, Tyler stood and removed the ring from the box to slide it onto the ring finger of Bev's left hand. "Happy Valentine's Day," he said before kissing her.

* * *

Meg poked Karen in the ribs as Tyler and Bev walked into the waiting room. "Uh-oh. Something's up; look at those grins."

Tyler enjoyed the shocked expressions on the girls' faces when Bev held out her hand to show off the ring.

Squealing, Karen jumped up to hug them both. "It's about time!"

"Congratulations," Meg added, settling for a handshake from Tyler and a quick squeeze from Bev.

"When's the big day?" Karen asked.

"I'm thinking June sometime," Bev answered. "That way we can finish this semester."

"Finish what this semester?" Gina Henderson asked as she appeared in the doorway behind her stepdaughter.

"Mom, Dad—what are *you* doing here?" Bev asked, stunned.

"Do you think I would miss being here for Edie?" Gina retorted, an amused look in her dark eyes. "Where's my hug?"

"Well . . . uh . . . first, there's something we need to tell you and Dad."

Gina smiled back at James. "More news? This is an exciting day."

Bev held out her hand as Tyler flinched, certain James Henderson would scoff at the small ring.

"Oh, Bev!" Gina exclaimed before drawing her into an emotional embrace. "Congratulations!" she added, giving Bev an extra squeeze before her father took over.

Tyler accepted Gina's embrace, looking over her shoulder at James who was gazing with interest at Tyler.

After untangling himself from his daughter, James moved across the room toward Tyler, a scowl on his face. Gulping, Tyler stood his ground. "Tyler Erickson," James boomed out, "I have something to say to you!"

"Dad!" Bev warned.

"James!" Gina echoed.

James broke into a wide grin. "Anyone who can endure my lectures and still want to marry my daughter is all right with me," he said, extending a hand toward Tyler.

Tyler shook the man's hand, wincing at his viselike grip.

"Welcome to the family!" James said as he continued to shake Tyler's hand. "I trust you remember everything I stressed over Thanksgiving?"

Tyler nodded, relieved when James released his hand.

James leaned close to Tyler. "Take it with a grain of salt," he said quietly. "I wanted to see what you were made of. I figured if you were man enough to stand up to me, you'd be man enough to handle Bev—and that will take some doing."

"I heard that," Bev objected.

"See what I mean," James said, slapping Tyler on the back. "Good luck! You'll need it."

A nurse stepped inside the room. "I'm looking for a Karen Randall," she announced.

Karen moved forward. "Is everything all right?"

The nurse smiled. "Yes, but your mother thinks you might want to come get acquainted with your new baby sister."

* * *

Karen beamed as she followed the nurse from the room. She barely heard the excited exclamations that echoed behind her as she hurried down the hall. Stopping outside the wooden door of the delivery room, she glanced at the nurse.

"It's okay, go on in. Your family is waiting."

Taking a deep breath, Karen slipped inside the beautifully decorated birthing room. "Mom?"

Edie tearfully beckoned for Karen to approach the hospital bed. "Come say hello to Sharon Adele Randall."

Karen sniffed, grateful that her sister would carry their grandmother's name. She leaned down to kiss her mother's cheek, then gazed with wondering love at the dark-haired face in her mother's arms. "Can I hold her?" she pleaded.

Nodding, Edie carefully handed the tiny infant to Karen. "Support her head . . . like that."

"She's so little," Karen said.

"And she has my looks," Brett said, grinning.

Karen laughed at her stepfather who was wearing a sterile gown over his clothes. Her sister made a small mewing sound. Karen watched as Sharon struggled to open her eyes. "Hey, little sis, it's me, the one who's going to teach you everything you need to know about life."

"That's a scary thought," Brett teased.

"Lesson number one: ignore Brett and always listen to me," Karen returned, enjoying the outraged look on Brett's face. "Oh, and another thing, never live in fear," she said, touching Sharon's tiny hand, "even if this world seems like a scary place. Heavenly Father made it just for us, and He'll never let us down." She planted a kiss on Sharon's forehead before handing her back to their mother.

Epilogue

June 14th

"Bev looks beautiful," Meg enthused as she helped Jesse unwrap another gift.

"She does," Jesse said, glancing across the Blaketown stake center gym. Bev had chosen a long-sleeved white gown that was covered with a myriad of white beads and artificial pearls. Instead of a veil, she had elected to wear an elegant white hat that matched the dress. "And look at Tyler in that charcoal tux. Man he looks sharp! I never thought Bev would talk him into wearing a lavender bow tie and cummerbund, but it looks good on him."

"It does," Meg agreed.

"Where did Treena go?" Jesse asked, glancing around at the gift table.

"She said she had a special surprise," Meg replied.

"Isn't that Treena standing in line with Gary and some girl?" Jesse asked, gazing across the room. Her mouth fell open. "That's Kassidy—she came!"

Meg stared across the gym. "She looks good."

"Gary must think so; look at the grin on his face," Jesse commented. "Isn't that Kassidy's aunt standing behind them?"

"Yep, that's Janice. She must've come with Kassidy. That's who she's staying with now that she's out of the clinic," Meg related. "And it looks like Gary's mother is with them."

Drake and Jake, Bev's five-year-old brothers, came running to the table with more gifts. "Careful guys." Jesse smiled at the two little boys who were dressed to match Tyler.

"Jake," Drake hollered over his shoulder as he raced his brother across the room.

"I'll bet those two are a handful," Jesse commented.

Meg nodded. "I'm sure they learned their best tricks from Bev." She gazed at the reception line. "Why didn't Treena tell us Kassidy was coming?"

"She told you it was surprise," Jesse said, reaching to unwrap another gift. "I wish I could see the look on Bev's face when she comes through the line."

"We'll see it," Meg promised. "When Kass gets to Tyler's parents, we'll head over and watch the fun."

* * *

Treena smiled as she introduced Kassidy, Gary, Janice, and Margaret to Tyler's parents.

Sue Erickson smiled politely at each one. "It's so nice to meet you," she said.

"It's nice to meet you, too," Kassidy said, returning Sue's smile. "Tyler's a great guy."

"We think so, but don't tell him—it'll go to his head," Greg Erickson joked. He turned to greet the next person in line.

"Kass, you remember Bev's parents?" Treena asked, starting over with the introductions as they continued to make their way through the line.

Gina hugged Treena, then reached for Kassidy. "I'm so glad you could come. Bev will be thrilled to see you."

"I wouldn't have missed it," Kassidy said. "She looks incredible."

Gina glowed with delight. "She does, doesn't she?"

"Did you make her dress?" Treena asked.

"I'm not that talented," Gina laughed.

"Who's the best man?" Kassidy inquired.

"That's Tyler's brother-in-law, Mike Jeffries," Gina explained. "He's married to Tyler's older sister, Kate."

"And those two girls on the other side of Karen are Tyler's sisters?" Kassidy asked.

"Yes, Karen is the maid of honor; then it's Sabrina, Kate, and that tiny girl is Kate's daughter, Colleen."

"She's a doll," Kassidy said as she gazed at the toddler who was wearing a lavender dress.

"She is. She looks a lot like her mother, auburn hair, green eyes—the works," Gina said.

Treena pressed forward as the line moved. She could hardly wait to see Bev's reaction to Kassidy's surprise appearance. She shook hands with Mike Jeffries and introduced everyone to him, then grinned at Tyler. "Hey guy, congrats again!" She groaned when he gave her a big squeeze.

"Thanks," Tyler said. "Long time no see," he added, glancing at his watch. "It's been at least an hour since you came through the first time."

"I'm escorting someone very special this time around," Treena explained. She stepped back to reveal who was standing beside her.

"Kassidy!" Tyler exclaimed.

"Kassidy?" Bev echoed, turning from the older couple who had been offering their congratulations. Stepping away from the flowered arch, Bev gripped Kassidy in an intense embrace. "You came!"

"I told you I'd try," Kassidy said when Bev released her. "Congratulations!"

"I've thought about you today. When everyone else showed up at the temple to take pictures—something was missing," Bev said, her blue eyes misting. "In fact, when this line slows down, I want a picture of all of us before we go our separate ways."

"Can I have a copy?" Kassidy asked.

"You bet!" Bev promised. "Are you heading back to Chubbuck tonight?"

Kassidy shook her head. "We reserved rooms in that new motel outside of town."

"Good! That'll give you a chance to visit with everyone—except me."

"Come see me when you and Tyler get back from your honeymoon," Kassidy invited.

"Count on it," Bev promised.

* * *

"What a wild party that was!" Jesse said tiredly. "They won't have to buy a thing for their apartment. I've never seen so many wedding gifts in my life." She sank into a plastic chair at a large round table that was covered with a lavender tablecloth. The centerpiece was a delicate white vase filled with fresh lilacs.

"They're both from the same town, and they come from large families," Karen noted.

"They have tons of friends," Treena added, sitting beside Karen.

Meg smiled at Kassidy. "And so I'm glad you were able to come."

"Me, too," Kassidy added warmly.

"How are you feeling?" Treena asked.

"Tired, like the rest of you," Kassidy acknowledged. "It's a good feeling."

"Where did Gary go?" Meg asked.

"To get my aunt a bottle of caffeine-free diet Coke," Kassidy said, laughing. "I swear my aunt Janice is hooked on that stuff."

"She's an awesome lady," Treena said.

"She is," Kassidy agreed. "I'm glad she asked me to stay with her. I think my parents need some time and space to work things out."

"It's getting better between them?" Jesse asked wistfully.

"I never thought it would, but now that Dad's giving in to the counseling, he's doing a lot better," Kassidy replied. "There's no guarantee they'll get back together, but it's a start." She gazed with discernment at Jesse. "Are you okay with your mom's new marriage?"

Jesse yawned, covering her mouth with her hand. "I wasn't given a lot of choice. Charlie's okay—I know he'll treat my mom right, but it's not the same," she said, a hurt look in her eyes.

Meg smiled at her cousin. "Welcome to life."

"Speaking of change, while we're waiting for Romeo and Juliet to change their apparel, why don't we discuss our plans for this fall," Treena suggested.

"I'm coming back to good old BYI," Jesse said, stretching. "I'm excited about this new program they're developing for computer science majors. We even get a new building!"

"I'm coming back too," Treena echoed. "I have two more years to finish my teaching degree."

"I have three more years ahead of me," Karen shared.

"Kassidy," Treena prompted, smiling.

Kassidy straightened in her chair. "Want another roommate?"

"You're coming back?" Karen asked excitedly.

"Yep. I'm majoring in art."

"Good deal!" Jesse exclaimed. "Meg, what about you?"

"Well, I graduated from the RN program in May—"

"Hey, I just thought of something, Meg graduated from the RN program, Bev graduated from the RM program," Jesse giggled, unable to resist the bad joke. She ducked as a handful of wadded-up napkins were thrown her direction.

"As you were saying, Meg," Karen prompted.

"Somebody needs to keep Jesse in line," Meg said. "I've been offered a job at Madison Memorial Hospital in Rexburg. I figure I'll work part-time and take a few more classes. I'd still like to become a physician's assistant. So, if everyone's okay about it, I'd like to room with the infamous D-6ers at least for another year."

"It's more than okay." Karen smiled, grateful that Meg would be returning.

"Okay, that's five. Who's going to take Bev's spot?" Jesse asked.

Karen grinned. "I have a suggestion," she said. "See that girl over there by Tyler's younger sister? They're standing by what's left of the wedding cake."

Everyone turned to look at the cake. Earlier, Bev and Tyler had gleefully smeared each other with handfuls of the white-frosted, chocolate cake.

"That's Terri Jeppson," Karen explained as everyone glanced at the brown-eyed brunette. "She graduated from high school the end of last month and was accepted into Ri . . . BYI."

"Isn't she the girl who sat at the guest book all night?" Treena asked.

Karen nodded. "She's a lot of fun. You would love rooming with her. Think about it."

Meg smiled. "What's to think about? I say any friend of yours is a friend of ours."

"Thanks. I'll go tell her," Karen said, rising from the table to cross the room.

"Today's been hard on Karen," Kassidy observed.

Meg nodded. "She feels like she's losing her best friend."

"I know how she feels," Kassidy replied, glancing at Treena. "But I've learned that you never lose a true friend. The relationship might change, but some friendships are eternal, no matter how much distance might lie between you."

* * *

Bev walked out of the women's rest room with Gina, who had helped her change out of the cake-smeared wedding dress. "Well, I guess I'd better go say good-bye."

Gina tearfully nodded, making a final adjustment to the new dress Bev was wearing. It was a pink flowered design, something they had found in Pocatello several weeks ago.

"Remember, Mom, you're gaining a son, not losing a daughter," Bev reminded, hugging her stepmother before walking into the gym. She waved at the cheering table where her roommates were sitting and crossed to where Terri, Sabrina, and Karen were standing.

"I thought my mother was going to choke when Tyler smeared your face with that cake," Sabrina joked. "Looks like you got most of it off."

Bev laughed. "You'll note who cleaned up faster. I got Tyler worse than he got me."

"I think so too," Terri agreed. "Hey, guess what? I'll be filling in for you this fall."

"Serious?" Bev asked, glancing at Karen.

"We'll have to call the manager to seal the deal, but I think it'll work out."

"Hey, sis, it looks like my brother has recovered," Sabrina said as Tyler walked into the room wearing a blue, short-sleeved, dress shirt and black dress pants.

"We are sisters now, aren't we?" Bev replied, smiling at Sabrina.

"I think we have been for a long time," Sabrina answered, reaching for a hug. She stepped aside for Terri to take over; then both girls discreetly walked away to give Karen and Bev a few moments alone.

"Don't you cry!" Bev tearfully threatened. "This has been the happiest day of my life."

Karen reached for a final embrace. "I'm going to miss you."

"Don't go there, okay?" Bev begged. "Remember, Tyler and I will be returning to BYI this fall, too. We'll expect you over for dinner—or should I say to cook dinner every so often," she invited, pulling back. "Deal?"

Karen nodded.

Gina walked up to Bev with the bridal bouquet. "With all of the excitement that went with cutting the cake, look what you forgot to throw."

"Oh, no. Is that bad luck?" Bev asked.

"Not if you throw it now," Gina said, smiling. "I think there are enough single girls still floating around this room—it'll work."

"Okay, but first I want to get a picture of everyone, now that I'm wearing real clothes."

Gina nodded and went to find someone with a camera.

"Hey, D-6ers—past, present, and future—come over here for one more Kodak moment," Bev hollered to her roommates, Sabrina, and Terri.

"Does that include me?" Tyler asked as he wrapped his arms around her waist.

"It had better not, Mr. 'You're-Going-to-Pick-Up-Your-Own-Dirty-Socks' Erickson!"

"That's quite a title," Karen laughed.

"That's what I was thinking," Tyler agreed. He moved out of the way as Bev assembled all of her friends for the final picture. Amused, he waited until a couple of shots had been snapped by his father-in-law, then maneuvered his way into the center of the group next to Bev. "Okay, now a shot of me with all of my girls."

"Excuse me," Gary Dawson objected as he walked across the gym floor. "I believe one of those girls has better taste than that," he said, squeezing in beside Kassidy. "Now take the picture," he directed.

James Henderson complied with the request and took another shot with his expensive camera.

"Okay, girls, stay together. Bev has one more thing to do before she leaves tonight," Gina called out, handing the bouquet of white daisies and lavender lilacs to Bev.

"I forgot to throw this thing earlier," Bev said as she moved away from the group of girls. "Sabrina, you can pretend to be a part of this, but as your new big sister, I'm not going to let you get married yet. You're too young," she informed the future high school senior, laughing at the outraged look on the younger girl's face.

"I was wondering when you'd get around to this. That's the reason I came," Jesse quipped.

"Well, good luck; here goes," Bev said as she turned her back to her friends. Taking a deep breath, she threw the bouquet over her shoulder, then whirled around to see who would catch it.

Meg's eyes widened when it nearly landed on top of her head. She grabbed it to keep from being hit.

"I knew it!" Jesse crowed.

"Chill, okay? I don't even have a boyfriend," Meg replied as the traditional teasing began.

"Yet," Jesse added triumphantly. "As you pointed out to me, life is full of change." She ducked before Meg could hit her with the bouquet.

Afterword

Written by **Dr. Julie B. Clark PhD**
Psychologist/Therapist
Corporate Vice President/Co-Clinical Director/Co-Founder of
the Center For Change

When I started doing therapy, back in the early '80s, it was rare to have a client who was struggling with an eating disorder. In fact, it was such an anomaly that most therapists didn't even know what to do or how to help. Of course, the alarming rise of eating disorders in recent years has changed that. We now recognize eating disorders as addictive disorders that people develop to cope with pain and often trauma. Much like alcoholism, eating disorders are used to numb the pain and distract individuals from issues that seem too difficult or too hopeless to change. Sadly, our society has aided in the rise of this approach to coping. The media has plastered us with images of women and men who appear perfect and successful; whether those images are emaciated, computer-enhanced, or steroid-induced, the idea that image and external beauty are all that matters is impressed upon the world.

What a tragedy to have a beautiful young woman sit in front of you intent on destroying herself because she is experiencing self-hatred. I often grieve over the plight of these young women and I recognize my limitations in effecting change. The reality is simple: we are the only ones who can change ourselves.

I have spent many hours with tearful parents and families who feel so helpless in the face of this all-consuming scourge. I say scourge because the rise in eating disorders over the past ten years is stunning. Where before maybe 1 in 25 struggled at the college level, it is now estimated that 1 in every 3 women are struggling with some form of an eating disorder. People die from eating disorders. The mortality from an eating disorder is higher than any other mental health issue. It's astounding and frightening, especially when women keep returning to this addictive disorder for comfort. Like a shroud of seeming security, the eating disorder blankets them and lulls them into thinking that they will be happier, more loved, admired, and successful. Sometimes they use eating disorders to punish themselves or to numb themselves from painful emotions.

The impact of eating disorders is extremely devastating in all aspects of a person's life. They will give up relationships, health, spirituality, and mental strength for the illusion of what they think the eating disorder can do. They don't realize how difficult it is to let go once they start down that self-destructive path. Like every bad habit, it has become a part of them.

At the Center for Change, we work to help change those habits and replace the dysfunction with hope and truth. A person struggling with an eating disorder cannot change without help and support, even though that will often be the last thing they want. Embarrassed and ashamed, they feel undeserving and worthless. Self-hatred and deprecation are rituals of their everyday experience. It takes effort, constancy, time, and support to patiently push through destructive thoughts and behaviors.

I have had the opportunity to work with some of the most amazing women. The journey to recovery is so like the chrysalis and the caterpillar emerging out of the darkness of the cocoon into the beauty of the butterfly. It is inspiring to see the changes that people create in their lives as they reach inside to find what they really want and humble themselves enough to know that they can't make the journey alone. No one can. We all need encouragement and support to find the courage to face ourselves and whatever issues feed the eating disorder, without starving and killing the individual. This can only be done with the help of our Father in Heaven. The spiritual component to recovery is essential. It provides perspective, hope, and the understanding of individual worth and the personal journey of growth. Isn't it amazing how Satan has gone after one thing that he can never have—a body.

The most important message is that there is hope and change is possible. The change process is unique to every person, just like a work of art or a stanza of poetry. Change is alive and dynamic and requires nourishment and nurturing to survive. The time to confront and change the destructive patterns is now. Don't wait until your life has been drained and the consequences of the eating disorder take an irreversible toll. If any of you are struggling or know someone who is struggling with an eating disorder, I send my love and encouragement. Recovery is possible!

About the Author

Cheri J. Crane is a former resident of Ashton, Idaho. She attended Ricks College where she graduated with an Associate degree in English. Shortly after that, she met and married a cute returned missionary named Kennon Crane. They made their home in Bennington and began the task of raising three sons.

Cheri enjoys numerous hobbies, including cooking, gardening, and music; she also loves spending time with family and friends. She heads a local chapter of the ADA (American Diabetes Association). Cheri has spent most of her married life serving in the Young Women and Primary organizations, and currently serves as the ward teacher improvement coordinator and the ward girls' camp director.

Cheri is the author of six other novels: *Kate's Turn, The Fine Print, Kate's Return, Forever Kate, Following Kate, and Sabrina & Kate.* She can be reached by contacting Covenant at: www.covenant-lds.com